C000295184

BLOOD RUNNER

SHAINE SMITH

Copyright © 2022 Aurmilia Publishing

Cover Design by Fanderclai Design

Edited by Nicholas Lawrence Carter

All rights reserved.

No part of this book may be reproduced in any form or by any electronic or mechanical means, including information storage and retrieval systems, without written permission from the author, except for the use of brief quotations in a book review.

 Created with Vellum

For my Family

CHAPTER ONE

The outfitted C-130 that flew over the major metropolitan Temporal Space about three times a day listed in the air smoothly and calmly. On board were 100 people squeezed together. A normal C-130 would hold around 90 to 93 people, but these were specially manufactured for one purpose and one purpose only: to drop its cargo to the ever-changing world below. The cargo being the people on board.

Chess Harlow was one of the cargo. Strapped in and bouncing his leg quickly, trying to stave off the nerves bubbling up in the back of his head, he could feel the zip of adrenaline shooting up his back and into his hands. He was itching to get his hands on a gun, a knife, or any type of weapon and work through the stress that he was having. It was about ten minutes to drop off, and he just couldn't wait any longer.

He looked to the people on his right. Many of the people that were strapped in, just like him, were chatting with each other, smiling and laughing. This was all just a game to them. Something that rich kids did after work or on days they just had nothing to do. A ticket to a Temporal Space Arena was easily over $1,000 or more, depending on where the arena even was. Living in Los Angeles, all of Santa Catalina

Island was enveloped in a Temporal Space when The Event happened. A massive invasion of rock and energy from space that no one saw coming. The casualties were minimal, but it left behind pocket dimensions that human beings could not dissipate. They called them Temporal Spaces.

After some rigorous study and years of black box funding for some more extreme testing on humans, it was found out that one couldn't actually die in a Temporal Space. They were simply respawned, so to speak, in the same place that they died. When humans began harnessing the pockets of energy left behind from the event, they feasibly made it so that the "respawn point" was outside Temporal Space. So that you stepped into it before you entered the space itself, you would respawn outside of the bubble.

This was used for War more often than not. Many Temporal Spaces were bombarded with soldiers who fought for their countries and died, only to return to the other side as if nothing had happened. When major government officials and some of the richest people in the world realized what they truly had on their hands other than a machine for war, it quickly turned into a sport.

A Battle Royale. One winner to take it all.

Overnight, people were becoming weapons experts, training and honing their skills. When the first Battle Royale game happened all those years ago, it was a mess of a show, and no one even won. The final two contestants shot each other, and it ended in a tie. Fearing that they would lose the grand idea they had on their hands, billionaires and officials banded together to establish academies, training fields, and tournaments. Something more official and something that would be taken seriously. That's how the term "Blood Runner" came about.

People weren't contestants or players; they weren't even subjects. They were crowned as something that was to be revered and respected. Those who finished Battle Royale Academy and earned their Royale License could be designated as a Blood Runner.

That's where Chess sat now. After paying his $1,500 for a ticket to just blow off some steam, he sized up his competition. Everyone in this plane had done the same thing he had to, sat in the same classes he did to learn the ins and outs of Temporal Spaces and Royale rules. Every single person on this bus was a Blood Runner, be it casually or not. He could see a couple of people sitting up like him. Eyes forward, legs bouncing, veins popping out of their skull, ready to kill. That's what some people saw this as, a free license to kill people. While others treated it as glorified airsoft, something to do on a Saturday afternoon when there was nothing left to do, Chess and a handful of others saw this as training. Practice. Practice for something more, something grander.

Usually, when one entered a Royale Academy, the goal every single one of them strived for was to compete in the Point Nemo Tournament. The final and all-out tourney to be declared the best Blood Runner in the world. This was something that Chess wanted. Wanted for himself, wanted for his father. He had a long time until he got to where he wanted to go, though. The Point Nemo Tournament wasn't for another year, and he had to rise the ranks to get there. What was he doing right now? Playing in a misnomer match that had no bearing on his future.

His father wouldn't want him to waste his time like this, but Chess felt he had to do this. Had to fight and compete to get some of the honor back that his family had lost. So what if these matches didn't mean shit in the long run? He was doing something that he knew he was better than everyone else at. Every one of these people would be staring down the barrel of his guns by the end of the match. He was almost bored thinking about it.

Would anyone be watching a match like this? It was LA, and all of the scouts for the tourneys were holed up here or in New York City, looking for new blood to play on their teams. Chess didn't play for any team, he played for himself, and if he were to accept anything, it would be for the Official American Team for the World Cup at Point Nemo. If that were to ever happen and if anyone were to be watching him, wanting him to join the crew. Like that was ever going to happen.

The C-130 rumbled a little bit, turbulence. A couple of girls at the back of the plane hollered out and giggled at the bump, tracing this as just another night out, something to do. As per their right to do so. Chess couldn't help but feel a little annoyed the majority of the people on board weren't taking it seriously as he was. Not that it was going to matter in a matter of hours. They would drop out, land on the grass, and fight to the death until only one was left standing. Then he would leave the space, pay for another ticket, and more than likely do it all over again.

When his father died, he left behind all the money he had won over the years as a Blood Runner. He was a millionaire and owned a lot of good assets. A nice house, multiple cars, jewelry, and goods worth a lot of money. Chess ended up selling most of it besides the house to fund his Blood Runner habit. He was almost out of money and would have to start looking for a job soon if he wanted to keep going. His leg shook a little bit more, thinking about how he would have to go without Temporal Spaces in lieu of working. It wasn't something he wanted to think about. He wanted to take his mind off of everything in the world. He just wanted to compete.

"Hey."

Chess looked up to see someone looking at him, holding his own arm as if it were hurting. Why would someone be on the plane if they were in pain? Chess's eyebrows furrowed, and he looked at the man with a confused demeanor, waiting for him to continue whatever he was going to say.

"First time? It's okay to be nervous."

Chess tried his best not to let loose a huff of a laugh and looked away from the guy. While his leg was still bouncing, he dropped his head, letting it hang loose at the neck and his shoulders shook. To the guy, it looked like Chess was having a fit, but in reality, he was laughing to himself. First time? He wished. He would never feel the moment of jumping out of the plane for the first time ever again. The feel of holding a double-barreled shotgun and unloading the shells into someone's face for the first time ever again. He would never see the wall of clouds that closed in around them as the Temporal Space reset its surroundings, disposing of those that would get lost within it for the first time ever again.

So many things he would like to experience for the first time, so many moments in time that were taken away from him by the storm. He was about to do it all again and *again*, and he loved it. No, it wasn't his first time, and he suspected that this wasn't the guy's first time either, but none of that mattered. None of it was going to matter when they landed on the grass. This was Solos, and every single one of these people was his enemy. Including this well-meaning stranger. That's all he was to Chess, a stranger.

Chess pushed a hand over his buzzed haircut, almost close to bald but still a bit of fuzz to signify he had hair. One could tell he had black hair. He was well built, having trained almost every day since he entered Battle Royale Academy and graduated. The outfit he picked was a white wife beater and brown jacket paired with his tried and true pair of jeans. Something simple, his uniform of choice. He thought of what he would wear if he were part of the Point Nemo tournament. The uniform for the Americans, representing his country. He grimaced. He didn't care about patriotism; he just wanted to be the best. Become the best.

The back of the plane started to open slowly. The sunshine of the midday sun bled into the cargo pit of the C-130. Chess's face lit up in the light, his slitted eyes and high cheekbones seemingly glittering in the sunlight. He pushed the sleeves of his jacket up to show his biceps and readied the jump pack provided to him on the back of his chair. In one fluid motion, he buckled the straps to himself and fastened the rest of the straps to his legs. It would take no more than a couple of seconds to wiggle out of the jumpsuit and get to work. He just wanted to be on the ground already. Right when he was thinking of jumping out, the loudspeaker from the cockpit flared on, drowning the sound of the wind with the pilot's voice.

"Welcome aboard to the midday Santa Catalina Royale. This is your pilot for this evening, reminding everyone to please wait the full sixty seconds before departing the cargo pit. We will be entering the Temporal Space in no less than thirty seconds, and from there, we wish you and the rest of the group a happy Royale."

After the male pilot was finished speaking, he seemingly passed the radio to a woman that was speaking now.

"It's a wonderful 78 degrees Fahrenheit in Santa Catalina, and the projected duration of the storm is about six hours. As always, at the sound of the buzzer, you are free to leave the cabin and begin the Royale. Good luck, Blood Runners!"

Chess busied himself by looking at the screens above everyone's seats showing the map of the island. There were plenty of places to drop, but he wanted something closer to the water. The buildings there were always loaded with good guns and supplies. Something to get his mana up to charge his magic while he was in the space.

That was another aspect that many liked about Temporal Spaces. One could harness fire, ice, earth, or aero to help them win the game. Plenty of people wanted to jump at the chance to use magic in a place where magic wasn't truly real. Inside Temporal Spaces, magic was very real, and many people were magic-only users. The problem was mana, and the only way to replenish the ever-depleting source was by using Temporal Crystals found around the map. They weren't easy to come by, and by the time the storm was halfway across the map, most of the crystals were already gone. Magic was used as a support rather than an outright attack structure, but that didn't stop most magic enthusiasts from playing it heavily. Chess wasn't one of these people, but he was fond of aero magic to blow back an opponent, which was the extent of his magic use.

Other than that, it was your normal fare. Guns, blunt weapons, vehicles, and fists. Chess knew exactly how he would handle himself once he jumped out of the plane and got onto the ground. How he would eliminate everyone who decided to waste their money trying to go up against him. He knew exactly what he was about to do.

The buzzer sounded, and one by one, as if they were being lit on fire, people started to run out of the cargo pit. Some looked back and did a little pose as they flew out the back, their parachutes flaring open once they reached the halfway point to the ground. Chess did the same, as did the well-meaning stranger talking to him before. They both jumped out at the same time, the stranger giving a loud victory holler on his way down. Chess focused on the task at hand: getting his feet on the ground.

The drop was long, the wind hitting his face and eyes almost too much to bear. He should've put on the protective goggles, but the sting was well worth it. It reminded him that he was alive, breathing, his heart pumping, and his hands working. He took a big gulp of cold, crisp air as he fell and eyed up his locations. The water was near, and he could see a couple of buildings already ready to be looted. No one was around. Looking to his left, he could see the stranger had decided to stick with him, the well-meaning words of his first time starting to sour more than they did initially. He was looking to get a cheap first kill, thinking Chess was a newbie. Chess knew his game pretty well.

He fell closer to the ground than he would've liked before deploying his parachute. It was a calm fall until his feet hit the rock-hard dirt below him, and he tumbled, rolling a couple of times and then stopping, his hands on the ground and knees bent. He wasted no time after that, shedding his parachute and breaking off into a full-blown run; he pumped his arms as he ran into the first house, busting his shoulder against the door.

There was no one home; no one lived on the island anymore since the Temporal Space took over. It belonged to The Storm and Blood Runners now. Since the storm wasn't going to come for another hour, Chess took some of his time looking thoroughly for weapons before exiting the building, a handful of ammo in his hand, to search the next house. That's when he saw the stranger slowly lowering onto his position. Chess ran into the next house over and shut the door. Maybe it was luck, but a pistol was laying on the coffee table across the room. The ammo he had picked up beforehand would work with it as well. He took the pistol and made his way to the back of the house. That's when he heard the door busting open from the front.

The stranger didn't waste any time. He ran from one room to the next, his fists up and barely looking for anything that could help him win his fight better. He was bloodthirsty and looking to end Chess's life right then and there. First time? All the better for him to take advantage of it. When he couldn't find Chess in any of the rooms, he went to the back of the house to see an open door. Without thinking too much, he ran out the back, only to be greeted with an empty space. He looked left and then right, hoping to see the back of Chess's head as he was running away. That's when he heard the whistle coming from above him.

The stranger turned, and before he could register what he was looking at, he was shot in the shoulder. Within Temporal Spaces, you couldn't feel pain; your body parts would still not work as intended if they got shot. Hitting a major artery, the stranger went down like a box of rocks, landing on his back before he tried to crawl away from Chess. Chess, however, was standing on the roof of the house, looking down on the stranger for a couple of seconds before he jumped down, walking casually toward him. When they were face to face, man to man, Chess rose the pistol and aimed it at his head.

"What's wrong?" Chess asked—his voice nothing more than a whisper. "First time?"

CHAPTER TWO

Instead of hitting the bigger part of the port town city where Chess was certain the majority of the people landed, he dredged along the outskirts of the forests. The island was massively mountainous, and it would take a while to even get over a couple of the smaller hills. He would have to take his time and follow the roads until he reached another outpost.

Thanks to the influence of Temporal Crystals and a bit of engineering, the whole island was retrofitted to become a Royale Haven. The port town was kept the same way since the storm had arrived. With it staying the same way, it had become popular with the LA Royale scene. Pulling his phone out of his pocket, he opened the Royale App on his phone that was synced to the round he was playing right now. A map of the island and his biometrics synced from his smart watch were displayed on the screen. A number at the top left was also displayed; after a couple of seconds, the number depleted by one until it stopped at 56. So, there were 56 people left in the game and dropping.

Crouching behind a bush, he turned his phone to landscape mode, the app tilting along with it, and he pinched to zoom into the port town area. A heavy red circle was floating over the area, signifying a massive influx of activity. He was usually never wrong about the port town and stayed as far away as possible from the cities. He's played on this island way too long to know where and where not to go. Pinching into his location, he noticed a yellow circle nearby between the hills he was next to. It would take no more than a couple of hours to get there, and by that time, he was sure whoever was there would be long gone or dead. Not that he would find any bodies, but what was left behind might prove useful.

One of these days, he would have to stop playing so defensively. Scavenging the war zone and moving in the shadows to win his games. Only coming out on the aggressive at the end of the game when he knew he had nowhere else to hide. Whatever won him the game, that was how he was going to play it.

He pocketed his phone and made a mental note to move East before hopping out of the bush and running up the road. As far as he saw on the map, there was no activity where he was running around. He knew he would come across a hamlet of houses soon enough if he kept going down this path, and if he were lucky, he would find something a little bit better than his current pistol. Something like an AR-15 or pump action shotgun. Something with a little more kick to it. Even though the app said there wasn't activity around him, that didn't mean there weren't people around.

One of his biggest fears was someone getting the jump on him from the shadows, even though that was his main fighting style. Maybe because he knew how effective it was to an unassuming victim, all he had to do was get his hands on a better weapon before the sun went down. Right now, it was high in the sky, somewhere around 3:00 in the afternoon. In six hours from now, the sun would set, and the storm would be eating everything on the island, ready to reset it to the point before they all jumped out of the plane. He had to move fast.

Chess ran for a few minutes before scaling up a small hill. Looking over it, there was a group of houses built and placed for the sake of Blood Runners. He was salivating at the thought of the weapons that could be found inside and decided to hold back for a moment. He had a bad feeling about the area, but after waiting for over ten minutes, looking in all directions, he decided to go for it. Anything would be better than the pistol that was running out of ammo.

He ran into the nearest house and was met with a couple of boxes that hadn't been opened yet. Wrenching them open, he found AR bullets and more pistol ammo, which he pocketed. Moving to the next box, which was long and made of wood, he kicked it until it broke open to show lots of hay and one battle rifle. It had a magazine in the chamber, and the bolt was drawn back, ready to fire. Chess's eyes dilated at the sight of it.

Picking it up and checking the weight of the weapon and the sights, he moved to the last box and hit it with the butt of his new gun, breaking it open quickly. A stack of Temporal Crystals fell out of the box. Putting his rifle on safety, he slung it over his back and picked up two handfuls of the crystals, squeezing them in his hands. After a couple of seconds, the crystals burst, and the energy swelled around his fingertips and palms, traveling up his arms. He didn't have to pull out his phone out to know that his mana was half full already, and he wasn't going to rely on magic to get him through the game anyways. He had to keep moving; the storm was going to land soon.

Pulling the battle rifle back out and running to the next house, he busted through the door but stopped in his tracks when he saw what was waiting for him. Four opened boxes, already looted. Spare ammunition and shell casings were spent around the floor, and clear signs of a struggle could be seen throughout the house. Knocked over chairs and broken glass everywhere. All of the stuff like this would be fixed and reset when the storm blew through, ready for the next round. For now, however, this was telling Chess that someone was nearby, possibly right on top of him, if he wasn't paying attention.

He crouched-walked toward the back of the house where a door was waiting for him. It was slightly ajar, meaning someone had used it to make a quick getaway. Would this person still be around, or were they smart enough to go further into the island to escape the oncoming storm? Chess didn't know and really didn't want to find out either. He would rather play this safe and keep out of harm's way until the very end if he could help it. Nevertheless, he persisted carefully.

The sounds of the grass swaying in the wind, followed by the songs of birds in the trees, flying away from the oncoming storm only to be reset once again in a never-ending cycle, had never sounded so loud in

Chess's life. He could almost feel the pressure of someone else around him, something stalking in the bushes and shadows. It was overwhelming.

Taking it step by step, stalking himself around the other side of the house he had just come out of, he turned around quickly and readied his rifle. There was no one there.

He allowed himself to breathe for a moment before he heard the snap of what seemed to be a twig coming from his right. He banked left and pushed his body to slide out of the way before a barrage of bullets came raining down through the window of the adjacent building. The building he had not yet been looted or searched through. Someone was in there, waiting for him, but it seemed they didn't want to wait any longer.

Chess landed on his side, quickly rolled onto his belly, and rolled left into some bushes. The bullets were still coming from the window and they only stopped after Chess had righted himself upwards and aimed down the sights toward the house. It would've been so easy to light up the house and blind fire anyone waiting inside. It wasn't like they could see him, and he would've had an advantage for knowing where his opponent was first. It was clear that whoever was inside was frazzled, blind firing out of a window and more than likely reloading with shaky fingers. All Chess could do was wait. Wait for this person to come out and face him like a human being rather than a curtain of bullets behind a window. He was fortunate that none of the bullets had hit him, to begin with.

He found himself breathing hard through his nose, trying to control the oxygen in his lungs from coming out of his mouth and making more noise than he had to. A bead of sweat traveled down from the top of his forehead and down the valley of his cheekbones, and he pursed his lips and waited, his finger switching the safety from on to off. Either way, one of them would be walking away from this village alive. Only one of them, and he was going to make sure it was him.

Movement came from inside the cabin. The sounds of feet moving from one end of the room to the other before the sounds stopped. More than likely looking to see if they had hit Chess and if he dropped anything good. No such luck for this person, but it told Chess where they were in relation to himself. He readied his finger, his forefinger straight and waiting on the trigger, not yet ready to fire.

He swallowed once, twice. Another bead of sweat fell down his forehead, and then the sounds of the door opening broke him from his continued concentration. It was a girl, one of the giggling girls he saw with her friends in the C-130. She was likely playing a casual Battle Royale round with her girls to pass some of the time. It was in the middle of summer, and most people were off from school and college. Even Battle Royale Academies took off for the summer as well. She was more than likely peppy, rich, and bored. Soon, she was about to be dead.

Chess waited for the girl to go down the stairs and round the house before he would emerge from the bushes. It was a long wait as the girl looked left, right, and left again with her AR in her hands. She was shaking like a leaf and wearing the latest tech wear gear that was popular with Blood Runners, Chess included. A crop top with a pistol vest paired with a skirt and leggings combo with lots of belts and pockets. Her hair was done up in a ponytail with a black bow on top. She would've looked much cooler if her knees weren't knocking together and she wasn't shaking like a Polaroid.

Eventually, the girl made her way over to the other side of the house, her front still to Chess as she surveyed her surroundings. How she didn't see Chess clearly in the bushes waiting for her, he would never know or care for that matter because all it took was for her to turn her back for a couple of seconds.

And then she did.

Chess stood up and aimed down the sights, moving forward slowly as he pulled the trigger. The first couple of bullets whizzed by her, but as she realized what was happening and turned around, the third and fourth bullets hit their mark right in the chest and the right leg. She hobbled a little bit and tried to bring her gun up to her hip just to fire off a couple of rounds, but Chess foresaw that. Aiming precisely, he hit the girl's hand, and she dropped the weapon before he went back to aim for her head. It took two pops, and her body fell to the ground and dissipated into purple crystals. She would be teleported outside the arena, back to the station where they registered for the game in the first place. She would have to sit there and wait for her friends until the game was over, more than likely watching everything happening on live feeds strewn about the island.

He wondered if anyone saw the kill he had just landed, and it was two kills in a matter of an hour too. He had a couple of hours to go until the storm would catch up with him; he had to move—and move fast. Like it or not, he would have to go into the port town and fight through the onslaught there.

Taking out his phone and checking the count, the number had gone from 57 to 43. More than likely, an onslaught was happening at the port town. It would be an easy place to rack up some kills; he had to admit. Shouldering his gun, he bent down to take the girl's ammo and pocketed it. She had nothing else of note to take. Some Temporal Crystals and a knife. Nothing worth taking.

He pocketed his phone and began to run to the port town. Behind him, the rumblings of the storm closing in on his position were fast approaching. Looking over his shoulder, he could see the ring of black and gray lightning webbing from the clouds as the storm started to hit the mainland. He didn't have much time left; if he wanted to win, he had to make it into the town.

CHAPTER THREE

When the light had gone out from behind the girl's eyes, she was already standing in a pod-like casket, waiting to walk out. Plenty of people were already standing outside but not watching her. They were sitting on benches, drinking water, talking on phones, what have you. Many of them were crying or throwing a fit in a corner somewhere. She knew where she was, the Respawn Room.

Pushing the door out let the next person that 'died' on the Royale battlefield have a turn to respawn; she stretched her arms over her head and made a show as if what just happened didn't really bother her. It bothered her immensely. The rest of her friends—who ditched her when it was time to jump—were more than likely having the time of their lives out there, shooting people up while she couldn't even get through a couple of houses before getting gunned down. Pathetic.

She pulled out her phone and checked her messages before taking an empty spot on a bench. It was a locker room type of floor where people who just got back from the island could take a breather before returning to the real world. It was better to take your anger out on the free punching bags the company had set up in the corners of the room or walk the short distance to the gym on the other side of the floor and workout than take it out on someone else. The girl thought about going for a brief walk on the treadmill just to clear her head; it might do her some good. That's when the phone buzzed in her hands—an SMS message coming in through the Royale app.

"Hey, where are you guys?! I'm by the Palm Tree grove!"

The girl snorted and typed out her reply.

"Nowhere near you; I got whacked by some tryhard in a jacket."

"Annabelle, we are never bringing you with us again if you can't keep up."

This made Annabelle feel a little hurt. These were her friends, and it was their idea to go Blood Running. She didn't even want to go. Because of them, she attended the academy and got her license just so she could go out and get absolutely dominated every time she dropped into a Temporal Space. She was never good at this type of game and vowed to give it up for good. However, her only friends loved to be Blood Runners, and she felt she had no choice but to tag along. She was learning all too harshly that her 'friends' were starting to get sick of her.

"Well, excuse me for trying to have fun. I thought that's what this was."

"I'm coming up to Palm Point soon. Someone meet me there. We can team up."

"I'm on my way."

They had completely ignored her. Not that it was any type of big deal. They would likely die and respawn sooner than later, and she would see them from her treadmill smiling and laughing that it was all just a game. They didn't have to take it so seriously. Then they could go back to boba and burgers and hang out by the pool for the summer. Things normal people did. That's all she wanted to do. As far as she was concerned, Blood Running was for losers with no job.

What hurt the most was that she was spending her hard-earned money on Royale Games and wasn't even winning anything back. Looking up to one of the massive flat screens showing some of the live feeds of the island, the prize pool was listed at the bottom. Everyone paid their $1,500, and it was pooled into a lottery. Whoever got a Battle

Royale got to walk away with all of it. There were only 15 people left, and she was sure that the jacket-wearing fuck that shot her the hell up was one of them. She scoured the feeds looking for him but never got a chance to catch him on camera. He must've liked taking the stealth route of playing, which she thought of as a bitch move. What's the point of Royale if you don't run and gun everything? What's the fun in hiding?

After she had her fill of sitting on a bench and texting her friends, who ignored her, Annabelle got up from her spot and moved over to the gym. It was separated from the Respawn Room by a large pane of thick glass Wirth the words 'Santa Catalina Royale Gym" plastered all along the side of it. While her clothes were not really gym accessible, she was wearing sneakers that were good enough for walking. She wasn't going to be doing any high-intensity training, just going for a walk.

She found an empty treadmill beside a man running his absolute heart out. He must've died super early on and was blowing off steam. She didn't blame him. She was still happy she lasted as long as she did before she got clapped. Starting up the treadmill and setting the speed to 2.5, a brisk walk, she looked up to the absolutely massive OLED screen hung at the front of the gym. She walked and watched the rest of the game, trying to find her friends on the stream or if they would pop up anywhere. As she was walking, an attendant that was walking around placed a plastic bottle of water on her treadmill and walked away. Annabelle didn't give her the time of day, just grabbing the water and cracking it open, taking a couple of big gulps before putting it back.

She was used to this kind of life. Being waited on and wanting for nothing. While she hated being a certified Blood Runner, she was one of the privileged fortunate that could even pay to get their license. The academies were not too kind to those who didn't have the money to compete in Blood Running, and it was seen more as a luxury sport for those with enough to play. Annabelle thought of herself as somewhat humble, but she knew where she came from. She would brush this whole thing off, go back to her mansion in the hills, and never speak of Blood Running again. Not if she could help it. She just wasn't good at it and could admit that to herself.

As she opened the bottle of water and took a sip, she almost choked when she saw the man who killed her pop up on one of the hidden feeds. He was skulking around a house and looking into the interior of the city, about to make his way in. Her eyes squinted, and she walked faster, her heart pumping—not with adoration but hate. She hated this man, whoever he was.

Not able to take another second of watching him on the screen, she stopped the treadmill, walking only a few minutes on it, and made her way out of the Respawn Room. The arena building was anchored to a massive convention center, and a slew of people milled about almost aimlessly. Some were dressed up in their best Designer, knowing win or lose, they would just be teleported back unscathed and as they were dressed. Others were wearing something out of a military movie, filled to the nines with tactical gear, helmets with pads, and the like. There was a little bit of everybody in the arena, and she was just on her way out of the venue.

When a massive scream erupted from the middle of the presidio, Annabelle turned to look at what everyone else was watching. A massive display, stretching the length of the venue wall, was showing the game. A drone must've been deployed to catch the last moments of the action right before it ended. Flying high in the sky and trained on a street corner, the number at the top of the screen read '2'. It was the fuckface that killed her, and some other guy left.

'Come on; I know you can kill fuckface.'

She whispered a silent prayer to the other opponent, hoping it would be enough to win him the game and not give the guy that killed her the satisfaction of a Battle Royale. Bullets were flying through the air, and the guy that killed her was taking cover behind a building. Annabelle's heart dropped when he broke off from his position and moved to flank his opponent. He was going to do it; he was actually going to get the Royale in front of her.

She looked down at her phone and saw she had a couple of texts from her friends, most of them rage texts from losing the game so late into the match. She knew they were likely waiting in the Respawn Room or working off their anger just as she had not moments ago, and she just walked by them, not noticing. To be honest, she didn't want to talk to them after how they treated her over the phone. If she was so trash at the game—she knew she was—then what was the point of hanging out with more tryhards? Her mind was so muddied with anger and false hope that her assailant would lose that she turned around and meant to storm out of the venue but ended up bumping into a person on her way out. Her gaze was locked to the floor, her mind so full of thoughts that she didn't see who was standing in front of her.

"Oh, sorry, I—"

When she finally looked up to see who she had bumped into, she saw that the man wasn't even looking at her. He had no interest in her as if she never bumped into him at all. His arms were crossed, he was wearing all black techwear and designer shoes, and his hair was curtained over his eyes, parted in the middle. He had a slight tease of a tan but was more or less white. His eyes were locked to the screen as if his life depended on it, and he had a light smile on his plump lips. He was beautiful, and Annabelle found herself staring at him for more than a couple of seconds before she blushed and averted her gaze.

Almost compelled by the man, she turned back around and looked at the screen, watching and waiting for the moment that the winner would be declared. They were in the middle of the street, her killer advancing on a limping and hip-firing opponent. He had his AR rifle on his shoulder and aimed down the sights, placing carefully aimed bullets into the man's chest cavity. In a matter of moments, the man went down and dissipated into a flurry of crystals.

On cue, after the last man was standing, a flurry of drones deployed from multiple spots on the map closest to him and deployed confetti. All of which would be cleared and reset after the storm blew through. After turning to one of the drones and then turning away from it didn't look at all like he was enjoying winning. He almost looked bored, apathetic about the whole thing. After a couple of seconds, his body also dissipated into crystals, and he was warped back to the Respawn Room. On the screen, Annabelle learned her killer's name.

[#1 BATTLE ROYALE!!: CHESS HARLOW! WINNER!!]

"Huh..."

Annabelle partly turned back to look at the guy she had bumped into. He had made a noise in his throat that sounded more like a question but ended up silently laughing.

"Guess he's not giving it up after all."

Annabelle wondered what he meant by that—his voice a thick British accent—but before she could ask any questions, he turned and left. All that was left for her now were strangers in a venue.

CHAPTER **FOUR**

Chess was looking as he did before he boarded the plane. His clothes pristine and no longer covered in debris and dirt, no more cuts on his lips and cheeks, and his clothes weren't torn up all to hell. Coming back to the Respawn Room—some people congratulated him while others gave him the angry cold shoulder—all was the same as before. His designer clothes perfectly intact, and looking pissed off.

It wasn't like he had anything really to be mad at. Okay, that was kind of a lie. He had people he owed money to, others he promised stuff for. Bills to pay. While Blood Running was an escape mostly for him to get away from it all, he also needed the money to live. The money that was left to him was running out and fast.

Standing in front of the teller's office after getting out of the Respawn Room, he kept up his pissed-off demeanor. Not speaking to anyone as they passed by him. Some tried to pat his shoulder and tell him good game, but he was just standing there, letting it happen. He just wanted to get his money and go.

"Ok, Mr. Harlow; here is your prize money. $150,000. We want to congratulate you on another Royale well earned! Congratulations!"

Chess took the money from the teller woman and thumbed through the cash before putting it back in the small manilla envelope they provided. It wasn't like a mail envelope where it was some cheap yellow paper material. This envelope was shiny, made of aluminum, with embossed logos. It glittered in the light, and as far as Chess was concerned, it was a big red flag saying, 'hey, come rob me! I have a shit-ton of money in my hands for the taking!'.

"Thanks," Chess said as he turned away from the teller and made his way down the venue stairs.

While people were still mulling about, waiting for their turn to get scanned in for the next games and pay for their tickets, some looked up and even pointed at Chess. He wasn't some kind of unknown figure in the LA Royale scene; he was almost pretty infamous for his careful tactics and aggressive late game. How it hasn't gotten him killed, many of them would never know. While some were smiling at him and waving, trying to get his attention, many were whispering amongst themselves and even jeering at him. Haters weren't uncommon. It was a lot of money to win, and not everyone was supportive of one man walking away with all of it.

There were events across the world and even within the US where the top three winners got a cut of the whole prize, but when it came to the LA rules, it was pretty cut and dry. Winner takes all; the number one in the Battle Royale earned it whether people liked it or not. Chess took the glittering manilla folder filled with bills and made his way out of the building.

The first step was to make it to the bank without any issues. Usually, he would just order an Uber and make his way over there, but checking his bank account on a widget on his phone, he grimaced at the number. He would make it for sure, and he had wads of cash in his hand to cover it, but he knew more than half of what he was holding would be gone by the end of the day. He might as well get the hard part out of the way and, even though he shouldn't have done so, ordered an Uber to someone's house. The someone he owed money to. Luckily, when the car showed up, he didn't notice a band of people following behind him. He was still out in the open, not in an alleyway or building where he could've been mugged easily. Still, when he entered the back of the car, he couldn't help but notice the looks on some of the venue goers' faces as he drove away. Full of envy.

THE UBER STOPPED A COUPLE OF BLOCKS FROM THE HOUSE where he was supposed to be showing up. Away from the hustle and bustle of city life, away from the skyscrapers and office buildings, he now found himself in a bungalow-type area with lots of nice-looking houses. The type of housing you would expect valedictorians and straight-A students to come from. Not the home of a kingpin that's been keeping him afloat all these years.

He's been paying the $1,500 tickets to get into Royales and play his matches, but what he didn't tell anyone was that the money was coming from someone else. His house was paid off; all he paid for was property tax every year. His cars were spoken for. He was on a steady diet of ramen noodles, peanut butter sandwiches, and scrambled eggs just to save money despite living in a lavish home. He blew all his earnings and inheritance on Blood Running. He didn't have any explanation for any of it. At this point, he needed it. Needed to be a Blood Runner. When he sat at home, away from the venue, all he did was sit on his bed and stare at the wall waiting for time to pass by. Waiting for the next opening to get back on the plane. The storm reset everything on the island every 10 hours. The window to get in and the competitive nature of the ticket system made it hard to consistently keep coming back.

He had to deliver this money before he did anything else. This was the guy that was paying for his tickets this whole time, and this was the first time in a long time Chess had finally landed a Battle Royale. Every time he came back from the venue and walked out into real air and sun, he would get a call from his 'sponsor' who had more than likely watched the match on the BRTV Livestream. The call was always short, to the point, and authoritative.

"So you didn't win."

Chess didn't get the call this day, which meant that his sponsor was definitely watching him. That he knew it was only going to be a matter of time until Chess was at his doorstep with the money he owed him. This is why Chess stopped the Uber a few blocks away; he didn't want to give the man the satisfaction of watching him bound up the stairs straight to his house in a hurry. He didn't even want to see him. What would he do if he didn't show up with the money? If he just pocketed it all? Would he send hitmen to his house? Unlikely, but he knew the outcome of just running off with it would not be pleasant. More of a nuisance that Chess was willing to put up with rather than hand over the money.

Some of it was a pride thing. He didn't want to hand over his hard-earned money to someone that had been paying his way this whole time and didn't even lift a finger to help him train or anything like that. This was a toxic pull of give and take by the thousands. Better to get it over with than spend more time at this house than he had to.

As Chess rounded the corner to make it into the neighborhood, he saw the man he was about to meet sitting outside his house in a lavish chair, smoking a cigarette. Leave it to this guy to just be waiting for the money when he knew it would come. Chess found it so annoying, knowing that he would be walking away with nothing but scraps. All of the games he played, all of the losses that were so close. All of the begging he did to get another ticket. Now he had to pay up, and he and his sponsor knew he would be back. Whatever was left to Chess after he gave up his cut would be gone within weeks. Be it bills, be it food, or more than likely be it Blood Runner tickets. It would all be gone within days, and he would come crawling back.

As Chess walked up the driveway to this home, he grimaced as he saw the man take the cigarette out of his mouth and give a wide grin. The tease of peach fuzz on his face and his shaved head glistened in the sun, threatening to set anytime between now and a couple of minutes. He wore casual designer clothes and had one earring in his ear with mirrored sunglasses. Just the absolute definition of a douchebag, in Chess's opinion, but he had no one else to turn to.

"There's my favorite Blood Runner! Finally got yourself a Royale, I see. Took you long enough, was starting to think I was just wasting all my money on nothin," he said, his voice a sickening tang of jovial.

"Cut the shit, Miller. You know why I'm here." Chess cut sharply.

"Woah, woah now, hold on. We don't have to do business right here in the open where people could see. Nice Neighborhood, but you never know when snakes are watching. Come inside for a spell."

Miller, first name Niko, was a middle-aged man that could pass as Chess's uncle if they were ever seen in public together. Luckily, Chess never had the chance to be around Miller any longer than to ask for money and beg for tickets. He was a long-time family friend of the Harlow family, was there way before his dad even started Blood Running, and was a kingpin for many other Blood Runners. Chess wasn't the only person crawling to him asking for money, but because of the connection between Chess's late dad and Miller, Chess was given 'special treatment'. Be that first to get tickets, first to get the money, first to be let in on any information that Chess would eventually blow off anyways.

Chess knew this was going to be a talk about upcoming tournaments. Events that would net him a shit-ton of cash if he were to pull his head out of his ass and apply himself in the fight. At least that's what Miller would say to Chess and was more than likely going to say it, seeing as he had control over all of his money at the moment. Chess hated the position he was in, but all he cared about in the long run was the ability to compete ins Royales. He didn't care about anything else. So, he would take the humiliation and, with a scowl, walk into the lavish home with Miller leading the way.

"Little birdie told me there were a couple of big events on the horizon. People coming down from the East to watch a couple of games for scouting," Miller said, finding a recliner chair and pulling up a small table.

"Scouting for what?"

Chess asked the question but wasted no time pulling the manilla envelope out and slamming it down on the table that Miller had pulled up. Equally, Miller wasted no time pulling the money out and started thumbing through the bills with a content look. Asshole.

"You tell me. You're going into the next match, and you're going to perform the same exact way you did tonight. And you're going to get another Royale and come back to pay off the rest of what you owe me."

"I need to be able to live too. I get that I'm bleeding you dry or whatever—"

"It's not whatever, you little shit!"

Miller sat back in his chair but issued the authoritative tone straight to Chess's face. Chess just stood there, his shoes still on Miller's nice carpet, digging into the shag. He alternated his weight from one foot to the next as he waited for him to finish yelling. He knew what this was going to boil down to. If Miller wanted, he could take the entire cut and leave Chess with nothing, and he would *still* owe him money. He reckoned he would have to win at least three more Battle Royales to pay back everything he owed and then a couple more just to get his life back in order. This wasn't easy. He was good, but sometimes it came down to pure luck if you got the Royale or not, and Chess wasn't all that lucky.

"Listen to me. People are coming from all over the fucking globe to watch the next couple of games for what I am to believe is to be for the World Royale. They're scouting, and you're going to get into the fucking American Team," Miller said, going back to counting out his cut of the bills.

"And what if I underperform on purpose? I'm not looking to end up like my father. The World Royale killed him, and now you want me to end up the same way?" Chess asked, venom in his voice and his arms crossed.

"Your dad didn't die because of the Blood Running. He didn't die because of a Royale league. He died because of a little shitstain called Lucas Kennedy."

Chess's ears perked up at the mention of this man's last name. He knew it.

"Lucas and your dad were inseparable, almost like brothers. Until the World Royale came for both of them. Your dad was a lot like you, just wanted to play, but Lucas convinced them to compete against one another. Lucas for the British and your dad for the Americans. Somewhere in the middle, Lucas changed, and not for the better."

Chess knew some of this story. When he went to his father's funeral and saw the Kennedy family there, way in the back as if they didn't want to attend. There was an air of animosity between the two families, but Chess was too young at the time to compartmentalize it, to even understand it. All he knew was that Blood Running killed his dad, drove him to madness, and ended his own life over it.

"You're saying because of this one man, my dad killed himself what, because he started to be mean to him or whatever?" Chess asked.

"Lucas wasn't always the bloodthirsty Blood Runner you see on TV these days. I know you've seen him work. He's part of the World Royale Board now and oversees everything that happens between the world teams, but I caught wind that he resigned and is going to be competing again. One for the road type deal."

"And where did you hear that?" Chess asked.

Miller continued to thumb through the last of the bills before he spread Chess's cut out and pushed it forward. Chess wasted no time snapping it up and pocketing it. Just under $3,000. Bill money.

"You remember a man by the name of Damon Kennedy? His son?"

The color drained from Chess's face, and his hand was still in his pocket, fisting the wad of cash that was allowed to him. He was starting to shake and tried his best to look calm. He swallowed and looked Miller dead in the eye. The man was smiling, but Chess was not.

"I... I know of him."

"He's in town, and he knows everything. Told me he's about to compete with his dear old dad for the cup. You're going to beat them."

"So what, a revenge mission? I'm not interested."

"I'll forgive all debt and let you keep the winnings."

Chess stopped in his track, almost turning to leave but was kept hold at the promise. He didn't want to believe it, but he knew Miller was an honest man. Never lied, never stretched the truth. Was straight and narrow as it came, and he knew that he was being serious. He would drop all his debt? Let him finally walk free from it all and keep the money? All he had to do...

"All I have to do is win, right?" Chess asked.

"All you have to do is win," Miller confirmed.

Chess stood there for a couple more seconds before he turned his back to Miller and started storming out of the house.

"I'll think about it." Chess finally said, his hand on the door.

"Chess Harlow, this isn't about revenge! It's about justice! Lucas can not get his hands on that Royale Cup! Everything your dad fought for would be for nothing!"

Chess didn't respond, but he turned his head slightly to look at Miller. He huffed a sigh out of his nose and then exited the house. The sound of the door shutting on Miller's face was something akin to finality.

CHAPTER FIVE

It took him another Uber to get back to downtown, where his bank was located, but by the time he walked into the doors, he was already checked out for the day. He wanted to get back to his house and crash on his bed, forget about the world, and what for the next Battle Royale. This time, with the money left to him, he would be able to pay off a couple of bills and save the rest to buy the next ticket himself. The feeling of not having to beg Miller for another ticket gave him a feeling of elation in his chest, even if he wouldn't let it show. A feeling of being able to take care of himself even if it was only for one game. That was one game he didn't have to feel like he was working himself out for it.

The tellers at the front desk smiled as Chess walked up to the front and pulled out the now much less inflated manila folder filled with only $3,000. He pulled out the bills, his driver's license, and ID and placed them on the desk, his face devoid of emotion.

"I'd like to repost this sum into my bank account, please," Chess said, his tone a million octaves lower than normal due to exhaustion.

He had been running himself ragged all day, from running all over an island and killing scores of people in a game to driving all over the city to deliver the money that he won but wasn't even his to keep. He was running on fumes by this point and wanted to lay down. Just lay down forever if he could help it. Forget the world, forget his responsibilities, forget about his dad. He couldn't if he tried.

After what Miller said about Lucas Kennedy, Chess had a lump in his throat thinking about the other Kennedy he hadn't spoken to since Blood Runner Academy. A man with curtained hair and a wicked smile. A man that could cut you down a million meters and stand above you while not even blinking. He was cold. Malicious. More than likely the only person on Earth that Chess actually feared. The only person on this Earth that Chess had ever opened up to. That type of familiarity and vulnerability made him feel weak. He wanted nothing to do with Lucas or his spawn of Satan's son ever again.

Yes, it was tragic how his dad died. He was too young at the time to really compartmentalize any of it, but he understood that it was the game that pushed him too far. Not bad blood between friends, between rivals even. All his father thought about was the game of Blood Running. The memories he has of his dad all come up with him carrying a gun. Getting ready for the next war. It wasn't fair. Now, Chess was doing the same thing, as if a phantom of that curse were coming back to haunt him. His turn on the gurney of Battle Royale.

He wasn't trying to think about Lucas, his son, or even his dad right now. He was thinking about cashing in his money. The teller woman in front of him smiled and took the envelope. She pulled out the sum and thumbed through the bills in quick succession. $3000 exactly, no more, no less.

She looked up for a split second and then back down to the bills before she placed them in another envelope. She tapped it several times on the counter and then took his identification cards.

"You're a Blood Runner. I can tell," she said, trying to make small talk.

Chess didn't answer, his eyes looking straight forward and his breathing even. He didn't emote; he didn't look annoyed. It was like he was just existing. This didn't deter the woman.

"There's supposed to be this big tournament coming to the west coast soon. Did you read about it in the news?" she continued.

"Do you mean the World Royale?" Chess said back deadpan.

"Oh, so you know it! If you try out for it, I wish you the best of luck!"

The teller woman clicked a couple of keys on her computer and finalized the transfer to Chess's bank. Pulling out his phone, he felt the buzz of a notification. A banner notification was displayed at the top stating that money had been deposited into his account. He was just shy of $3000 richer, but he knew it would all be gone within the week. Three days at best.

He thought about the nights he would be eating peanut butter sandwiches and ramen noodles just to satisfy his itch for Battle Royales. Eat just enough to function so he could crawl back into the fight. How many more fights did he truly had in him. Missing a Royale felt like death to him; every minute he wasn't in the field, he felt like a failure. This wasn't a healthy way of living, and he knew it, but he couldn't stop.

Chess waited for the woman to give his IDs back before he simply pocketed them and turned on his heel, not bothering to say goodbye or good day. His manners had taken a dive somewhere between his father's death and his inheriting the house. He just lost all will to be happy. All will to emote at all. He felt he could only smile when he was about to gun someone down. He knew it was unhealthy. Again, he didn't know what to do about it other than compete over and over again.

He didn't want to call an Uber again to get home, but at this point, he really didn't have a choice. He was in the middle of the city and dropped off by the bus that wasn't running this way at this time of day. If he really wanted to, he could walk to the other side of the city and wait for the bus there that would take him all the way home, but he was too lazy to do even that. He pulled out his phone again and opened the app.

He was idly walking while doing this, going from one block to another where people weren't really walking. This wasn't a busy part of the city; most people were in their cars or buses going elsewhere. He would be able to stop in front of the Mcdonald's and ask for an Uber there, no problem. Just as he was in the middle of that thought, the pressure of hands gripping his collar and jacket forced him out of the cloudy haze in his brain.

Someone was pulling him, pulling him into somewhere. Was he about to get mugged? Killed? Before he could see who it was, he was spun around forcefully, and his arm held behind his back. The person holding him up put all their pressure on his body, pushing him into the brick of the building he was holding him up on. Chess's breathing had elevated, his eyes bugging out of his head. If this were Royale, he'd have no problem doing whatever he had to whip around and push a knife into his assailant's neck. But, this wasn't a Temporal Space. This was real life where time kept ticking, and there were real consequences for killing someone. They didn't come back.

Was that going to happen to him? Was this person going to kill him right here in the middle of the city? Anyone could look into this alley and see that he was being held up, but as the seconds marched on, no one had come to help him. No one called out or alerted police to his position. In a city of millions, he truly felt alone.

"Slow as always. Thought you'd learn to speed up," came the voice right in his ear.

He knew this voice and his blood went cold. Suddenly, he froze up, physically going stiff in Damon Kennedy's hands. The demon himself back to haunt him. He didn't have to see him to know he was smirking.

"Fuck you!" Chess seethed through his teeth and finally started to struggle. He knew Damon wouldn't kill him.

"We had enough of that at Academy, don't you think? I came to ask you something."

Damon said the last sentence with a bit more push, pushing Chess a little more to subdue him. When Chess calmed down enough, Damon continued.

"How does fifty thousand and a year's worth of Blood Running sound for you to stay out of my way and not show up to the Battle Royale scouting event?"

After he had asked him, he let go of Chess and smartly backed up because the second Chess was free; he whipped around and made a hard swing. There were repercussions for killing someone, but others deserved a black eye. If Chess had his way, he would tear Damon limb from limb if he saw him in the arena and prayed for that day to come.

"Calm down now; it's just a question," Damon said, backing up more into the alleyway.

He was wearing designer clothing from top to bottom, and his chestnut hair was curtained over his eyes, parted down the middle. His eyes were striking, slit, almost black they were so brown. A stark contrast to Chess's striking blues.

"What makes you think I want your fucking money? What do you get out of me staying the hell out of your way? You never thought of me as your equal!" Chess finally stopped swinging and was panting hard.

The memories of Academy, when they were barely adults, just turned 19, the both of them were figuring out each other, their lives. Chess had put his whole faith into a boy once upon a time ago that saw him as nothing more than competition, and Damon ate it up. Ate it all up.

Now here he was, both of them aged 27 and about to fight to the death in a city back alley. If he knew he could get away with it, Chess would've stabbed him right here and there and be done with it. He dealt with enough humiliation for one day, for one lifetime.

"I've been watching you play for the past couple of weeks. My dad and I are in town for the upcoming scouting event. If you had known about it, I knew you would show your ugly mug and try to get the Royale, impressing whoever was going to watch. I want you to stay home for it," Damon said.

"Why? Feeling threatened? I've improved since Academy. I'd wipe the floor with you." Chess stood at his full height but was still panting. He was furious.

"There's nothing to feel threatened by. I just don't want to have to kill an old flame on the battlefield, is all." Damon lied.

"Keep your fucking money. I want nothing to do with you, and you want nothing to do with me. Let's keep it that way and stay the hell away from me. Whatever we had back then was the past."

"So you *will* do it? You'll compete?" Damon asked as Chess turned to walk away.

Chess stopped just shy of the alleyway entrance but didn't turn around. He didn't have to. Damon was an asshole, was able to make you feel like bacteria on a worm, but other than when he was in a Temporal

Space, he was mostly harmless. He was fast, skilled, rich, and cunning. All things Chess really was not.

It had been a long time, a long time since they had held each other in a way that wasn't through hate. Whether Damon meant the things he said to him back then when they were alone was left to mystery, Chess didn't care about it now. He didn't care about Damon anymore, but he didn't want to let him get the upper hand over him, either.

"I'll think about it," Chess said over his shoulder before walking out of the alleyway for good.

Damon stood there, waiting for Chess to be completely out of sight before he took out his cell phone and hit a speed dial number. It rang a couple of times before someone picked up.

"He's gonna do it," Damon said in a deadpan voice.

"Good," a voice said on the other end. "I look forward to seeing him again."

CHAPTER SIX

Chess never ended up calling the Uber. He was too heated to stand in one place to wait for a car. He had to walk off the anger he felt burning within the bottom of his core. Seeing Damon again after everything that had happened, everything they went through together, to see him again in the middle of nowhere. It was asinine. Felt like a horrible fairytale.

Walking to the other end of town, Chess prayed he wasn't late on missing the bus that would take him to the other end of the city where he lived. He tried to think about what he would do when he got home. He had a plan already, but after what had happened, he felt like he was stuck in this horrible limbo. A cacophony of excuses he could come up with spun around in his head that would make him not compete in the next Royale. He shouldn't. He shouldn't take Damon up on his word. The money that his ex was going to offer him just to stay away. That thought alone made him want to do it.

It wasn't like he was scared of the man. He was downright terrified. He didn't want to be near Damon Kennedy and didn't trust him as far as he could throw him. Knowing that Damon would compete in the next Royale made his stomach turn. He was supposed to be in the

United Kingdom, doing whatever the hell British people did all day. Not in Chess's hometown of Los Angeles.

It was all for the stupid tournament that Miller also talked about. That little birdie talking to him could've been anyone, but he had a sneaking suspicion that it was Damon himself. Anything to get a one-up on Chess. It had always been this way between them. Now he was here and bribing him not to compete. Just for the hell of it, he should've said he would do it. Just to see the look on Damon's face. Would he even emote at all even? History would tell him that he wouldn't; Chess learned from the best not to emote at all.

Once he got to the other side of the street and made his way down the blocks to get to the other side of the city, he pulled his phone out and navigated down his text messages until he reached the person he was looking for. He hit the contacts page and the phone button, putting the phone to his ear. It rang twice before the person on the other end picked up.

"Go for Bijou," a cheerful voice said on the other end of the line.

"Bijou, Damon is back in LA. Did you know about this?" Chess seethed into the receiver.

"What?! No! I didn't even know you two were even still talking," Bijou admitted.

There was noise around Bijou; she must've been inside the mall or still at work. Either way, she wasn't at home.

"We're not. I want him dead," Chess said, looking both ways before crossing the street.

"Well, that's nice. He came back to LA just to see the one person who hates his guts. You think he'd avoid you like the plague."

"Who wouldn't avoid me."

"Self-deprecating humor isn't funny, Chess."

Bijou Williams was one of those motherly types of people who sometimes cared a little too much. Right now, her current project was getting Chess to kick his Blood Running habit and get a real job so that he wouldn't have to rely on others all of the time. She knew about Chess's run in's with Miller and others to whom he owed money. The last thing Bijou wanted to see was her best friend end up in a ditch for crossing the wrong person, no matter how hard Chess says he is. There was always a bigger fish in the sea to eat you, and Bijou didn't want to see him get eaten.

"He didn't call you at all? Didn't try to get in touch with you this entire time?" Chess asked.

"I already told you I didn't know he was in LA. I didn't even know he was still alive. He's kind of like you, always Blood Running."

"Yeah, well, he has a bit more assets than I do. He just offered me fifty thousand dollars to stay out of the upcoming scouting games next week," Chess said, stopping at a crosswalk.

"Chess, that's great! You can keep that money and start your life back up. You can work for me if you want to; we have positions open at the boba shop!"

"I'm not working at the fucking boba shop," Chess deadpanned.

"Well, did you take the money?"

"No, I didn't take the money!"

Chess looked both ways even though the light indicated he could walk before he crossed the street proper. He looked like he had murder on his mind and walked as if someone had slapped his mother. People passing by him moved out of the way as he made his way over to the bus rotunda, trying to get home. Luckily, the bus he had to catch was still in taxi, waiting for everyone to get on board. He hopped on as quickly as possible and made his way to the back of the bus to sit down.

"I think it would've been a better deal. You get money, you don't have to deal with Damon, and you can take a break with all that Blood Runner nonsense," Bijou said, her voice sounding a little downcast and sad.

"You're just mad you're bad at the game," Chess rebutted, looking out the window.

"I'm not bad at the game! It's just not my thing."

"That's why you followed me into Blood Runner Academy right? Because you suck at the game?"

"You're changing the subject."

The bus started to move, and Chess was on his way home. He would have to get in and think about what he wanted to do next. Think about the threat of money looming over his head, money that could seriously help him out around this time. However, there was the pride factor. Chess didn't want to just give the game to his ex and rival. It wasn't that he still cared about him or anything like that or wanted to see him one last time on the battlefield; it was more for himself than anything to do with Damon.

"I'm not changing anything; I don't want to think about this. Or even talk about it, for that matter," Chess said, sitting back in his seat. He lowered his voice now that he was around other people and focused on his breathing.

"And yet, here you are calling me. This is bugging you big time, and you have no one else left to call other than your benefactor, maybe," Bijou said.

Chess could just imagine her checking her nails as she said that. Mostly because she was right; there was no one Chess could really call and talk to about any of this other than her or Miller, and Miller didn't really give a shit about his past love affairs. That's all Miller was going to see this as anyways.

"Don't call him my benefactor. I hate that term," Chess complained.

"So what's the consensus? You're going to do it? You didn't take the money that could've really helped you out of this sticky situation, but now you really have nothing to do but to do it," Bijou said.

"I don't know yet. I don't like how Damon just threw money in my face to get me to stay away, but..."

"But..." Bijou beckoned.

"But... I don't want to just give it to him. I know that if he competes, he's going to be number one. He always has been; things like that never change."

"And you think you won't be able to beat him then? If we're thinking like that, you must think he's got one over you. You think you haven't improved? Chess, I *saw* you on the Livestream today!"

Chess didn't say anything, opting to look out the bus window and watch the city go by. He didn't want to think of himself as 'improving' or anything like that. The stability of his life—or lack thereof—after he got out of Blood Runner Academy has been the same for years, and he wanted to keep it that way. Including his skills. He didn't see himself as improving; he saw himself as always one step under Damon like he always did. When he snapped out of the fog that was what he thought was love back then and realized he was being used, he completely shut down. He had no interest in himself, training himself, bettering himself. He just wanted to exist at this point. It was no way to live, but it was what was comfortable to Chess, even if he constantly owed someone money or time. It was what he was used to now.

"It's been a while since I saw you even get *close* to a Victory Royale, and you got it today! And you go Blood Running every day! You're getting better. You think you can't go toe to toe with Damon anymore? Really?" Bijou continued over the phone.

"It's not just that, but if I win and make it into this competition, I'll be carted all over the world to compete in something I have no interest in."

"Then don't do it," Bijou simply said. Chess made a noise that sounded like a grunt, and Bijou laughed in response.

"But you don't want to let Damon off the hook. I can read you like an open book even on the other side of the city, dummy. You have to do it."

"I don't have to do anything."

Chess was starting to shut down, and Bijou could feel it coming a mile away. She gave a short sigh and then turned the phone to the other side of her head, propping it up on her shoulder. She was still at work and in the middle of orders while she was taking to the time to talk to him, but because this had to deal with Damon, she let it slide.

"I think it would be really nice for all of us to meet up again for dinner or something, like old times at the Academy. You can't let a grudge like this control your life," Bijou said.

"Watch me. He used me," Chess retorted.

An old lady sitting next to him turned her head slightly to look at Chess but ultimately minded her own business. It was obvious that she was eavesdropping on his conversation, though. Chess made it a point to look at her but then quickly back out the window, lowering his own voice.

"I want nothing to do with him, but I don't want him getting an edge over me anymore. That's it," Chess finished.

"That's why you're gonna do it?" Bijou asked.

"That's why I'm gonna do it."

It was quiet over the phone for a little bit before Bijou gave her second sigh of the conversation.

"Okay, I'll do it with you guys. What's the worst that could happen?" Bijou said abruptly.

Chess rolled his eyes and sat deeper into his seat.

"Bijou, this isn't a regular Royale match; if you place in a top score, you're going to have to quit your job and tour the world for this shit. Are you sure it's worth that? I know how much you saved up to buy that Boba place."

"I can have my managers run the business while I was away, and besides, that's *if* I make it. I just want to see you guys again; I don't hold a grudge like you," Bijou said.

"If you cared about me, you'd stab him the next time you see him for me; I'm not going anywhere near him," Chess complained.

"Suit yourself, but I'm joining the Royale next time! Tomorrow right? I'll buy my tickets now. You should too."

Chess grumbled at Bijou's words. He didn't really want to do it; he didn't want to be near Damon. However, as he hung up the phone on Bijou and moved to the mobile app to buy his tickets, he noticed they were selling fast. Only twenty left, and they would be gone. He purchased a ticket without even thinking about it and sat back in his seat, feeling deflated.

Tomorrow would be a long day, and his bones were already aching thinking about it. He would have to face off against his ex, hopefully for the last time.

CHAPTER SEVEN

Whether Chess figured he was going to go home and craft some master plan as to how he was going to tackle the Damon problem, that never happened. Instead, he went home and stared at a wall for hours on end until he eventually succumbed to sleep. For dinner, he went to sleep. It was routine like this for a while now since he barely had any money to his name anymore.

Maybe it would've been better if he did take the money and ran off with it, he could at least order something to eat for the first time in months instead of having sad noodles again for the fourth week in a row. How his body was continuing to function, Chess didn't know. At this point, it was through sheer willpower and rage.

The rage within him was building, knowing he would have to board a plane in the next couple of hours with Damon on board with him. Bijou showing up was a bit of a buffer, but it didn't conjure fond memories and whimsical fancy knowing that the old gang was getting back together. After Academy had ended, they all pretty much went their separate ways.

Bijou opened a boba shop and stopped Blood Running altogether, Damon went back to England after he and Chess broke up, and Chess, well, he never stopped. He had been doing the same thing every day for the past couple of years without fail and without a dollar to his name. Now he was going to compete in something that, one, he didn't care for, two, was going to make him filthy rich if he won, three, his ex-boyfriend was going to wipe the floor with him in, and four, killed his dad. He wasn't going in this looking for vengeance.

It wasn't like he could care less about what happened to his dad; he missed him dearly. What happened, happened. Unfortunately, he couldn't stop the cycle from continuing, and if he were going to keep going like this, he would likely end up the same way. Dead on arrival from an excess of Battle Royales. Becoming so obsessed with the game and to best the best of the best that it would eventually kill him off as it did his dad. He didn't want to go out that way, but he really had no other way of life. It wasn't like he hadn't tried to get out. To get another job somewhere else. He has been fired, quit, and straight up walked out of jobs to go Blood Running. He couldn't stay away to save his life.

Thinking of his dad as he walked to the bus stop bound for the event arena, he had to remind himself that he wasn't going to stress himself out to the point of death over a boy. He wasn't going to let Damon get his way and have his way with him anymore, but he would have to force himself to cut him off when things got too extreme. He would compete in this one round; if he bested him, then fine; if he lost, then fine. He wasn't going to follow Damon all over God's green acres just to prove a point. Damon wanted to insult him by throwing money in his face, and thinking he was just going to roll over and take it was just too much to handle. He would do this and then cut him off completely.

The bus was packed, and Chess picked a few people out that were definitely going to compete in the tourney. By the way, they dressed in designer clothes and wore combat vestibules, hats, and face masks with sponsors plastered all over them. They were likely hoping to get on the Livestream in a bid for fame and fortune. Someone other than the World Royale people would pick them up, and they would be professional Blood Runners. It wasn't something that Chess was after. He didn't care what these people hoped for; he was just trying to settle a score.

What did he really think was going to happen? In his wildest dreams, he would shoot Damon in the face and refuse the title from the

World Royale people, go home with his money and disappear off the face of the planet. Just one win was all it would take for Chess to feel better about the predicament he found himself in. All of the time, Damon had gotten one over on him, used him for wins, as bait, and anything else Damon could get over him; he just needed one win, and that would be it. He wasn't going to be like Damon and look for a comeuppance over and over again. One and done.

A buzz in his pocket pulled him from his thoughts, and he pulled it out to read the text. It was from Bijou.

"Hey, I'm at the arena. Waiting for you. When are you getting here?"

Chess took the time to actually reply to her. Usually, he would just leave her on read and meet her when he was going to meet her, but because today was going to be high stress for everyone involved, he replied to her.

"About 5 minutes away. Bus."

"Okay, cool. Damon is here."

The pit in Chess's stomach dropped to the bottom of the ocean. He didn't know if that meant Damon was standing next to her or if he was just loitering around. As if karma and life were to answer his question, a second text came in, but it was a picture. Bijou had snapped a quick selfie of herself and Damon next to her, holding up a peace sign and smiling with no teeth. Bijou was all teeth and holding up a peace sign as well.

Well, that was just great. His only best friend and his main rival were together in the same space, and he would have to be forced to meet with them. Hopefully, Damon won't pin him up against a wall this time, as if he would let him get away with doing that a second time.

A part of him wanted to be mad a Bijou, but honestly, Damon never did wrong by her. Why would she be mad at him just because Chess had pledged the rest of his life to the downfall of his ex? It wasn't fair to Bijou, and she had the right to be friends with whomever she wanted. He would have to be cordial, at least up until the Battle Royale, then all bets were off. It was sad because he would be hunting for Bijou as well—if she lasted long enough for him to find her. When it came to her, it was all in good fun. In fact, he would've looked forward to this if he wasn't being watched by World Royale officials and competing against Damon. This whole thing sucked, and he wasn't even off the bus yet.

Looking at the picture for a couple more seconds, he almost couldn't stomach the look on Damon's face. He must've known that this picture would go to him, yet he still smiled as if they were best buddies, as if nothing ever happened between them. He squinted his eyes and stared into Damon's. They looked dead, truly uncaring. As if, just like him, he was living day to day. His life was just passing him by. He didn't care how Damon felt, and he wasn't going to ask.

Eventually, the bus stopped a couple of blocks outside the arena, and Chess had to get off. The pit in his stomach didn't get any smaller; he was dreading walking into the space, knowing what was waiting for him. He would play it off nice for Bijou's sake, but he wasn't going to like it. If Bijou were smart, she wouldn't drag this out for any longer than it had to be, but something was telling him that wasn't going to happen.

The scent in the air was sweet; food trucks had come for the people standing outside watching the upcoming game on the massive TV screen outside the stadium. Soon, the C-130 would take off, and the people inside would give these people a show they wouldn't forget. After all, this was going to be the match that started the World Championship for Blood Runners. As Chess rounded the corner and made it to the crosswalk toward the massive stadium and auxiliary airport. The streets were filled with Uber drivers and food trucks. It was a regular fanfare.

Plenty of people were standing outside, filming content on their phones for Tik Tok and YouTube. People danced and posed outside of the venue to post on their social media; all these people were like Chess. Come from money or were filthy rich. Chess—technically—was rich; he just always owed someone money and could never hold on to it for long. That being said, he didn't want to associate himself with these kinds of people.

Bijou was a little bit the same, but she had one foot in reality. While she also came from a little bit of money, the money she had, she reinvested into her own business. If anything, she was more middle class now, probably the poorest person at the arena and competing. Not that any of that shit mattered, it didn't to Chess.

He climbed the long path of stairs up to the arena, knowing what was waiting for him when he got to the top. Would they be somewhere inside the venue, or would they come out and meet him? He made it a point to change his clothes before he came to do this event. Not for Damon's sake, but because he's been Blood Running in the same clothes for about a week now. Call it depression or laziness; he decided if he was going to show his whole ass to the people recruiting for the World Royale, he should be wearing fresh clothes and not smell like shit. He had been wearing the same type of clothes and using the same shampoo and conditioner since he was fifteen. He never used cologne. He knew that Damon was going to say something to him about it.

The familiar scent of his body care products and his clean-shaven, well-dressed persona would turn at least Bijou's head. She knew that Chess was more of a homebody that didn't change much. She accepted him for who he was even if he went days without showering or changing; that's just how he was. Damon, however, was going to be a problem. The nights when they slept together in the same bed, the scent of his hair nudged into his nose and vice versa. He didn't want to hear it if Damon had anything to say. Any memories he had, he could keep to himself.

The answer to his question was waiting for him inside the venue. He could see Bijou standing next to the man who held him up and almost robbed him in an alleyway yesterday. Okay, maybe not all that, but it sure felt like it.

Bijou was a healthy girl with long, curly blonde hair and big blue eyes. She looked like a storybook princess and always kept her appearance up to the best of her ability every day. She was holding her phone in her hands, and Damon was standing right next to her, leaning over to look at what she was trying to show him. They were more than likely catching up. After all, it had been years since they all had been together like this again. Bijou was more than likely eating it all up. When Chess had come into view, both looked up, and both sported a smile. Damon's a little more sinister than Bijou's pure smile.

"You made it!" Bijou exclaimed, bounding over to Chess and

pulling him by the arm toward Damon. "The gang's back together again! Let's take a picture!"

"Bijou, no, I—"

Chess tried to interject, but right as Bijou lifted her phone to take another selfie, Damon snaked around her and pulled Chess into an embrace with his arm. Bijou was in the middle up front and flashed her best smile. It was a snapshot of a very surprised-looking Chess and some genuine smiles from the other two friends.

CHAPTER EIGHT

Chess couldn't help but mope the entire time. The entire venue was packed to the brim with Blood Runners and event watchers; it would've been so easy to slip away and forget about the both of them. While this plan would've been fine if it was just Damon, it didn't seem fair to Bijou. She had been nothing but patient and kind to him since Blood Runner Academy; he shouldn't just dip on her. If anything, he should use the money—or whatever money he would have left after this—to visit her boba shop and give her his business. That would've been the right thing to do.

Damon was a whole other conundrum that Chess didn't want to deal with. He would have to scan in and board a plane soon with him on it; even worse, they might drop in the same area. He wanted to be as far from Damon's drop point as possible if he could help it. Something in his gut told him he wasn't going to get his wish. Chess stared at the back of Damon's head with disdain before the boy looked back over, and Chess adverted his gaze. He hated seeing the smirk blossom on Damon's mouth from his peripheral view. He knew he was looking at him.

"Take a picture," Damon said, his deep voice jeering and meant to get on Chess's nerves.

Chess got up from leaning on the wall and made a couple of

purposeful steps toward Damon, cracking his knuckles as if he was going to put him out before the match even began. Damon just stood there, his smug smirk still prominent on his face. Bijou was the one to get in between them, with a strong hand on Chess's chest. Chess just looked at her with fire in his eyes and then scoffed, turning away from both of them.

He wanted to punch Damon's lights out so bad, so *fucking bad* it didn't feel fair. That he could stand there and act that way after everything that had happened. He was acting like nothing had happened like he was just supposed to forget about it and move on. Chess should've moved on, but he never did. He just couldn't.

Something within him was stuck, wanting to come out and express itself but just couldn't. He truly felt stuck. He didn't want to give Damon the satisfaction of a response, but he didn't want him to just get his way, either. Some part of him didn't want him to stop. He shook his head as he put his hands on his hips and paced around idly. He looked more like he was trying to cool his head, not hoping that Damon would give him more attention. He hated himself that he was low-key craving it, but his pride wouldn't let him take any of it in. As if it was in his blood to fight back. He shook his head again, running a hand over his buzzed hair.

"I really want to enjoy my last time Blood Running with you both without ya'll killin' each other! Can we get through today, and then, whatever happens, happens?" Bijou said, her hands on her hips.

She looked to Chess and then to Damon, who only shrugged his shoulders and looked at the ground.

"I'm not doing anything wrong," Damon said, half laughing.

"Yeah, you never do anything wrong, right? Always the overachiever, the perfect fucking student—"

"Enough!"

A couple of people passing by gave side glances and started laughing amongst one another. They were making a scene, and Bijou wasn't about it. Chess didn't want to put himself in the middle of a scene either, but Damon just brought the worst out of him. The past was the past, but he couldn't let it go. How he wished he could just forget and move on with his life, he felt tormented by these memories.

Chess stopped yelling and turned his angry eyes to Bijou without meaning to. Bijou only crossed her arms and raised her eyebrow at his anger, not phased by it in the slightest. Chess calmed down and adjusted his jacket, looking away from both of them again. Before Bijou could say anything else, a notification came on over the speaker in the venue.

"All Blood Runners for the 12:30 Event, please make your way to the Scanning Processor for Respawn. Those waiting for the 7:30 Event times, please have your tickets ready when it's time for Screening. Thank you. Again, those here for the—"

"We better go line up then," Bijou said, pulling her ticket out of her back pocket.

Chess was fingering his ticket in his jacket pocket, and Damon was holding his in his hand, his arms crossed.

"First come, first serve then, is it? Not by ticket number?" Damon asked.

"Yeah, we just go up and line up, and who gets there first gets in first," Bijou said.

"Hmph," was all Damon could say, pulling an eye roll from Chess.

"What, England still uses ticket numbers? What is this, first year of academy?" Bijou joked.

"You make fun of it, but it's a system that works," Damon rebutted.

"A system for rich people, maybe. Here, people can get the first ticket and still be last in line; everything is fair here," Chess said, throwing a look at Damon.

As he looked over, he saw that Damon also matched his gaze, his curtained hair swaying as he walked and a tease of his younger peaking out from his white teeth from a crack of a smile. Chess begged himself not to get wound up. Not now, not in line. It wasn't worth it. He wasn't worth it. Not anymore. Chess scoffed for the millionth time that day and fixed his eyes forward.

People were already lining up and droves, and there was going to be a full house on the plane this time, all one hundred players fighting for their lives for a spot at the Royale and a spot at fame. Every single one of these people knew that the World Royale Scouts were watching. Whether it be Livestream, TV, or personal drones—if they had the money for it—they were all going to be watching. Even if some lost, there was still a good chance that one could get picked up for another team.

Either way, all of them were on the spot, and it was down to this game that would rule a life-changing Victory Royale for the sole survivor. It could've been any one of them. All three of them could walk out with no sponsorships and no money in their hands, and at the end of the day, that didn't bother Chess so much. He wanted to slug a bullet into Damon's face so very badly, but if Chess walked away from this with his pride, then he would take that too. To see the smile on Bijou's face, a friend he deeply cared for, laugh like they were back in classes again.

"Little bit of culture shock, love," Damon suddenly said, his gaze also toward the front. It wasn't hard to figure out who he was talking to.

Bijou rolled her eyes as Chess popped the knuckles on his left hand and clenched his jaw. He didn't want to hear that word ever again. Not out of his mouth anyways.

"We're going to enjoy this game, right? We're both going to enjoy ourselves?" Bijou tried to ask, looking between both guys and looping her arms around their arms.

"I'm going to enjoy putting a slug between Damon's eyes," Chess said.

It was the first time in a long time that Chess had even uttered his name in the open like that. He wanted so so badly to forget.

"I'm going to enjoy staying away from Chess," Damon said in tow.

Chess flinched, and Bijou felt him stiffening up in her arm. Damon saying his name like he did, as if it were just another Saturday afternoon and they were going to get lunch. Maybe do a quick Royale before taking a nap together. Disgusting. Chess looked down and away from Damon's eyesight, so he didn't see the sneer spreading across his face.

"The three of you? Tickets, please," the attendant said, holding her hand out.

They each produced their torn tickets and placed them in a shredder bucket, clearing them for entry. The door opened for them to enter the Royale Lobby, and in a single file, Chess first, they entered.

Chess knew these grounds like the back of his hand. Being here almost every day helped him to know the layout pretty well. When he looked back to see Bijou and Damon looking around for the Respawn Scanner, he took Bijou by the hand and walked down the hall to where it was. Damon smiled but followed at a safe distance behind them.

"This place is nice. Not run down and dingy like the academy," Bijou said, looking around. "They have pictures hung up on the wall; there's carpet. Is that a gym?"

Bijou quickly looked at the Respawn Gym before being led to an occupied Respawn Scanner. Once the person inside was finished and walked out on the other side, Chess lined up behind Bijou and let her go first inside.

It was a massive egg-looking capsule with glass surrounding it. Once Bijou stepped inside, she stood in the middle, to which a blue emitting light scanned over her whole body. Once that was done, the outline of her body glowed white, and the machine made a noise. She was registered into the Respawn Scanner. If and when she won or died, she would be sent back here from the Temporal Rift.

As Bijou was finishing up her final checks in the machine, Chess made the mistake of looking over to Damon. Damon was looking right into his eyes. They stared at each other for a good couple of seconds before the sound of Bijou on the other side of the Respawn Scanner pulled him from his stupor.

"Chess! Your turn!"

Chess's mouth made a hard line as he walked into the machine, going through the motions to get ready for the game. The scanner came, there was a light, and then a noise. He walked out right when Damon also walked out of his machine, but this time his gaze did not linger. Pushing past Bijou and Damon, Chess made his way to his usual seat in the lobby to await the plane. Bijou shrugged at Damon and then followed Chess out to the lobby.

Plenty of people were talking, laughing, and taking pictures within the space, getting ready for the event. Chess picked the normal chair he usually sat in, right by the terminal gate, crossed his foot over his knee, and sat back, waiting. Bijou and Damon picked the seats that were in front of him. It felt like an airport, but it had a gym that Bijou kept looking back at.

"I still can't get over the gym. What, you die and blow off steam in there?" Bijou asked.

"Yeah, actually. That's what it's for. Plenty of people run in there right after Respawn to watch the rest of the game and walk on the treadmill," Chess mumbled, throwing his head back and sighing.

"Better than sitting around and sulking about losing. I might give it a try," Damon said.

This made Chess bring his head back down and look at Damon with a judging eye. Bijou looked at both of them with wide, waiting eyes, knowing something was about to go down.

"So you're admitting you're gonna take the L then? You're gonna lose?" Chess asked.

Damon didn't say anything; he sat back in his chair, crossing his legs and looking at Chess with an all-knowing smirk. While Chess' smile was full of malice and hatred, Damon was smiling at Chess as if he didn't know what he was talking about. As if this was nothing more than innocent banter.

"Because, as I recall, the great Damon Kennedy didn't lose. He just used whoever he could to stay at the top," Chess finished, chewing on his bottom lip, trying to keep himself from saying anything else.

"I never said I was going to use the gym after losing. Maybe I'll hit the treadmill before picking up my prize money," Damon said, bubbling a laugh that matched Chess's hard gaze.

"You fucking wish. You're not gonna win. Not this time," Chess said.

"What makes this time any different? You're still the same Chess I remember."

Chess stilled, stiffening, and stared at Damon with wide eyes. Damon uncrossed his legs and leaned forward, his arms on his knees as his innocent smile was replaced with a hard stare of his own. The true side of Damon. The cruel and callous side.

"You wear the same clothes, use the same shampoo, live in the same house, and from what I've been seeing, use the same tactics in Blood Running. What makes you think this time is going to be any different, love?"

It was a beat of a second, but it was all it took. Chess swung, and his fist landed square into Damon's jaw.

CHAPTER NINE

While the punch didn't knock Damon out completely, the brunette stumbled out of his chair and countered with an attack of his own. Wrapping his arms around Chess and pushing up from the balls of his feet, he slammed his ex into the chair behind him; Chess tried to scratch and pull him off, but Damon's jacket was too thick to do any damage.

People were starting to notice and were pulling out their phones to record and watch the fight. Someone in the back yelled, "World star!" And the hooting and hollering commenced. Chess didn't care; he was too busy trying to murder who was once the love of his life turned into his greatest enemy.

"Dumb bitch!" Chess hollered as he brought his foot up enough to kick Damon away.

They both got up from their chairs that they were tackled into and started throwing swings. Bijou had ran out of the scene as fast as she could. Normally she could diffuse the situation before it got to this point, but this was more than she was equipped to deal with. With a disappointed look, she watched as the two men beat the ever-loving shit out of each other in the middle of the Royale Lobby.

"Fucking stop!" Damon screamed as he swung another punch.

"Should've kept"—Chess threw a punch, landing on Damon's ribs—"your fucking mouth shut!"

"Police!"

Both men froze mid-swing, Chess having a handful of Damon's shirt in his fist and Damon holding a heavy hand on Chess's shoulder. Chess was sporting a fat lip and a bloody nose, while Damon would have one hell of a shiner come the morning. None of them looked innocent, and they were more or less caught in the act. When the policemen came barging in and followed the pointing fingers toward them, they separated and took steps away, glaring at one another. They had to end the fight to compete, but this fight was far from over.

"What seems to be the problem?" one of the larger officers asked as he approached the roughed-up boys.

This is when Bijou stepped in and tried to play everything off as one big joke. She laughed nervously and gestured to the two boys with her hands as she spoke.

"These two, you know, always at it! They used to date, but, you know..." Bijou tried to joke, doing her best to get on the cop's good side.

"Y'all gonna be fine to compete, or are you fixin' to kill each other right here and now? Cuz we got a cell, y'all can do that in down at the station if you're gonna keep causing a ruckus," the cop said, his hand on his belt.

Chess looked down to see the handcuffs dangling from his waist and swallowed. He didn't have time to go to the station and wait out his holding period there. He had a Royale to win and Damon to kill on the battlefield. He was sure that Damon was feeling the same way, but Damon was wrong about so many things. So many things that, at face value, seemed like he was doing everything the same way. The same clothes, the same shampoo, the same style of fighting. Damon didn't know what he was truly capable of. He would prove him wrong.

"We'll behave," Damon said first.

"Yeah, we'll stop," Chess followed up.

"Right. Whatever domestic y'all are havin', do it on your own time in your own house. Not in public, ya hear?"

Both the boys nodded, and the cop and his body turned tail and made a move to leave. Chess watched them go and then looked into the eyes of the people who, more than likely, wanted to see them get taken away in handcuffs. The disappointed looks on their faces, some of them still recording on their phones or taking selfies in front of them. Chess was ashamed; he didn't care how Damon felt. On the other hand, Bijou turned around to face the boys and let out the biggest sigh of her career.

"Really?" It was directed at Chess.

"You're lucky I didn't press charges," Damon followed up, sitting back down in his chair and putting a hand to his jaw.

"Suck it up; I didn't even hit you that hard. Didn't take you for such a softie," Chess complained, dropping into his chair and tilting his head back to stop the bleeding.

Both of the men were quiet for the longest time. On the clock by the terminal gates, it showed that there were still twenty minutes until departure. The plane would be showing up any minute to take them to the island. For no, however, they were in each other company, and it was already turning violent. Bijou didn't want to know what they would do to each other if they crossed paths in the storm. Something told her they wouldn't be using guns, but the slow, painful kill of a knife or their hands. She shuddered.

She truly loved these boys. They were her friends. After everything that happened, she was sure she would lose Chess for good. That breakup was the stuff of legends, throwing furniture, screaming, hitting, threats and accusations. When Chess stormed out of the dorm room that night, his bag of overnight clothes and his laptop with him, and came to Bijou's dorm—forbidden by gender, but Chess didn't care—she remembered holding him all night as he cried.

"*Why?*"

"*Why couldn't he just love me for me?!*"

Bijou didn't know.

She looked over at Damon while he was preoccupied with his jaw. The man saw Chess as a pawn to play on the battlefield. A human shield, almost. Chess never got an edge on the battlefield because he was always in Damon's pocket. Chess was obsessed with him and would've done anything for him. However, when that day came when Chess came to his senses and realized what was going on, Damon didn't deny it. In fact, he bolstered the claim and took pride in it, knowing he would graduate as the top Blood Runner of the Academy, thanks to him. He used him.

Now they were sitting across from each other, exchanging blood and spit from fighting, knuckles dusty from the contact of skin, and neither of them was satisfied. Bijou was surprised that Chess held in that much for as long as he did. She knew it was coming, but she would've hoped it would've happened on the battlefield. Not in front of her face.

"It's gonna be reeeeeal satisfying to pistol whip you in the back of the head come this match," Chess said, lowering his head. A bead of blood seeped out and curved over his lip, and he licked it clean. "Real satisfying."

"You won't find me," Damon said, sitting back and crossing his arms. "You never knew where to go without me."

"I run this island. You have no idea how many times I've run this island. You're at a disadvantage here, not me," Chess angrily said, sitting forward.

"We'll see," was all Damon said to that. He sat back and sighed through his nose, looking away from Chess. "We shall see."

It was quiet for a long time after. None of the boys talked, looked at each other, or even checked their phones. Bijou was keeping up with work emails on her phone, but when she looked up, she always found the boys in the same position. Chess is looking left, and Damon looking right. Then Chess looked right, and Damon looked down. Sometimes they were looking at the floor, but never at each other. They were simply waiting. Waiting to squash the beef on the battlefield and be done with it. Whatever plans Damon had for the rest of the World Royale were left to him; Bijou didn't want any of that mess. However, she didn't know what Chess truly wanted. Did he want to compete in the World Royale too? Something told her that he didn't, that he was only here to settle the score with Damon. Anything was possible, though. She never really knew.

Eventually, the plane did taxi into the dock, awaiting passengers. It was another C-130, and all one hundred of them were going to cram in there with parachutes strapped to their backs. Bijou swallowed out of fear; she never did like this part. In fact, this is why she stopped Blood Running altogether. She was never good with heights and falling just made the phobia worse. She was always scared she would never pull the pin fast enough and plummet to the ground, wasting a good run. She would respawn, of course, but it's just the fear of it that got to her.

Chess looked behind him and saw the plane, then he looked back and caught Damon's eye for a fraction of a second before looking away. He could just hit him again if he really wanted to. And he *really* wanted to. That thought was scrubbed from his mind as the intercom within the lobby flared to life, and a woman began speaking.

"Please make your way to line up. Boarding will begin in ten minutes. Again, please begin to line up; boarding will begin in ten minutes."

Chess wasted no time. He was usually the first on the plane and almost the last off. It was kind of his lucky strategy that won him some games, not all but some. Bijou and Damon followed right behind him when they saw him move.

"You want to stand in line for ten minutes straight? Don't you want to sit?" Bijou asked, getting kind of annoyed and thinking of the drop again. She nervously bit her nails.

"All the good seats in the back get taken, and I want to be right next to the drop point," Chess simply said, stuffing his hands in his pockets and sniffling hard, trying to get the blood back in his head.

"I guess," Bijou said, looking around.

Plenty of other people lined up as well and were more than likely wanting to get a back seat along with Chess. The first one out led the others, and you had a better view beforehand of where the storm was starting. Staying inside the circle was key, and if you knew where lightning was going to strike, you would move out of the way, wouldn't you? Chess knew it all too well, same with Damon and Bijou.

"What's the main rules of this island? Anything goes, or are there stipulations?" Damon asked.

"Didn't you read the brochure for this place, or do you have another boy toy reading for you now?"

Damon squinted his eyes and looked away, this time actually pissed off. He wasn't going to get his answer straight away without a smart quip from Chess, and he would have to get used to it. As long as Chess had the freedom to air out all his grievances, he would do it and didn't care who heard him.

"Anything goes. Just stay inside the circle. Classic Royale, solos," Chess said, turning away.

"Solos. Man, I was hoping to partner up with you, Bijou," Damon said, his smile coming back.

Bijou suffered a laugh herself, but she knew better than to really trust Damon on the battlefield. He was an irreplaceable friend. She didn't like what he did to Chess, but she didn't want to lose both of them and be forced to choose. That being said, she would stay far away from Damon if she could help it during the match.

"Maybe they'll do teams at 7:30?" Bijou said, turning away from Damon.

"They do Teams on Wednesdays and Fridays. Sometimes Mondays and Sundays." Chess turned to Bijou. "It'll be solos at 7:30 too. What, were you gonna come back for round two?"

Bijou smiled at him. She didn't agree with the vindictive side of Chess, how obsessive he was at getting revenge, but again, he was irreplaceable. She loved these boys like family and didn't want to lose them. It was a shame that they ended the way that they did. If only she could turn back time.

CHAPTER TEN

In the back of the C-130, Chess and Bijou sat shoulder to shoulder with Damon sitting across from them, Bijou's side. Someone else was sitting at the very back end of the plane, Damon letting them have it. Chess guessed it was because he didn't want to start another fight almost 10,000 feet in the air, but he put the fighting out of his mind and prepared himself for combat.

He always had the same ritual coming on and off the plane and into the ground. He sat with his head in his hands and breathed. To some, he looked like he was nervous about the whole thing and didn't want to come on board in the first place. That couldn't be farther from the truth. He did his breathing exercises and cleared his mind of anything pertaining to the outside world. Eventually, even the plane stopped existing in the back of his mind. It was only him and the clarity of his mind.

He wasn't going to let Damon take this away from him either. It was so vital to his performance on the battlefield that he decided to start clearing his head before the plane even took off. Things like Damon and the added stress of having him on the battlefield with him made him breathe in and out in slow bursts, then he inhaled for ten seconds and exhaled for five. Rinse, repeat. He pushed a hand through his buzz-cut hair and then back down again. Feeling his body breathing and living, he was alive. He would stay alive.

Chess looked up, folded his hands into a prayer position, held his hands in front of his mouth, his elbows on his knees, and looked straight ahead. He was looking into the eyes of a stranger, someone he didn't know, but to the right of this stranger was Damon. He looked at him, dead on. Damon looked back. Brown met blue, and this time, there was nothing swimming within Chess. Not hate, no rage, no anger. Just focus. He focused on Damon's shoulders, his broad torso; he looked at his legs and then back at his head. Almost sizing him up before they got on land, and they haven't even taken off yet.

"You okay, man?" the stranger asked.

"Fine," Chess said, his hands still pressed against his mouth. "Worry about yourself."

The stranger didn't say anything after that but glanced at the man next to him, at Damon. Damon only looked at this man and smiled. No teeth or anything like that, just a smug smirk as if he knew what was going on. In truth, he had never seen Chess do this. This was something new. He watched his ex go through his ritualistic motions slowly, over and over again. Rubbing his head, letting his head hang by the neck and his breathing. Something told him that Chess wouldn't care if he watched; he was so preoccupied with himself that he didn't care who watched him. It was mesmerizing.

If it weren't for the past, he would've unbuckled and swapped places with Bijou by now, breathing with him. It seemed to be working on calming him down, and a part of him wanted to try it. However, this wasn't the past, this was the present, and if he tried anything funny like that, he would more than likely start another fight. Contrary to popular belief, he didn't really want to fight. He wanted to make up for past mistakes and move on with his life, but Chess was making that hard.

If Chess wanted so badly to have a vendetta against him to the point of murder, then so be it. He wouldn't stoop so low to that level, but he wouldn't give up on Chess either. A part of him still loved him, somewhere deep down. As he watched the boy breathe in and out again, his eyes closed and brows furrowed, Damon bit his lip and looked away, in inner turmoil. Things could've been so different between them. What he did wasn't right; how he defended it was even more wrong, but what was done was done.

The plane was nearing 10,000 feet. The cabin rocked with turbulence, and Bijou had a hand to her mouth, trying to keep the puke inside her body. She didn't want to jump; she would do anything not to jump, but this was going to be the last time she was going to Blood Run with her boys, and she willed herself to get over it.

Putting her hand down and stifling a sickening burp of fear, Chess looked over to her and offered a rare smirk. Bijou met it was a queasy smile of her own and a thumbs up. She looked at Damon and showed her thumbs up to him as well. Damon met it with a thumbs up of his own and a smile. The smirk that was once on Chess's face dwindled, and he looked on at Damon with passive eyes. His head was clear, and he didn't have any animosity at this moment. It was now only the hunt, the game. There would be no fuck ups this time. It had to be a perfect game.

"Welcome aboard to the midday Santa Catalina Royale. This is your pilot for this evening, reminding everyone to please wait the full sixty seconds before departing the cargo pit. We will be entering the Temporal Space in no less than thirty seconds, and from there, we wish you and the rest of the group a happy Royale."

Chess tightened the straps on his parachute and looked dead ahead. He wasn't looking at the stranger, more so through him and focused. He was going to jump first and get a head start in the abandoned shopping district. Usually, that was an endgame area when the storm was on your ass, and only five people were left. This time, he would scope it out for the best weapons and make his way into the forests, hunting Damon down. It was practically his only goal. The only reason he was truly here. He didn't really care about the money, fame, or the chance at the World Royale. As he turned his head to look at Damon, the back of the C-130 opened, showing the island below.

He didn't have to look down to see the purplish storm that was beginning to roll through, that would eat everything in its wake and reset the buildings, guns, and equipment in random places. Those caught within it would wither away, die, and Respawn back in the lobby with a chance to try again another day. There was virtually no threat as you would always be ported back to safe harbor upon death. It all came down to your guts and willingness to take a bullet or knife to the chest.

Sixty seconds passed, and people from the back started to unbuckle and race toward the exit. A couple of people turned around and jumped backward, saluting or throwing the bird at the rest of the players. Some of them jumped with their phones in their hands, live-streaming the descent. Chess wasted no time himself.

Unbuckling and sprinting to the exit, he jumped, did a slow back-flip, and plummeted to the surface. He saw he was a good bit ahead of the storm and fell head first to land. Plenty of people were ahead of him, falling at rapid speeds toward the ground, and after a couple more seconds, the first parachutes started to deploy.

Chess always waited until the final seconds to deploy his chute. He wanted to fall fast and hard, hit the ground running, and not look back. He didn't know if Damon would be falling with him or if he ever got off the plane at the same time as he did. He hoped he didn't. A part of Chess wanted the chase. To hunt him down and finish it. It was almost in his blood to do so, a bloodlust that couldn't be sedated.

The terrain was approaching fast, and he would have to pull his chute anytime now. As he looked up to see if anyone was falling near him, he was the familiar locks of blonde hair, now in a ponytail, falling just as quickly as him and tugging erratically at her chute pin. It was Bijou.

"Fuck."

Chess pulled his chute right when Bijou finally pulled her and started to fall slowly to the earth. Not exactly where he would've liked; there was a lot of activity ahead of them in the small town that Chess wouldn't touch until the late game. However, he couldn't just leave Bijou to fend for herself after years of not Blood Running. She would've been eaten alive out there.

Outside the town was a lush forest that had been overgrown since the Temporal Rifts had shown up. It would likely take over the whole town in a hundred years' time, and no one was coming in to chop the trees down; it was too dangerous with the storms rolling through. Plus, the storm would just put the trees back. Humans had to get in Blood Running and Royales while they still had time. Bijou landed in the brush of this forest.

Her parachute was tangled in the bushes and low-hanging branches. While wrestling her parachute off her back, she frantically looked around for a weapon, anything that she could use against an assailant. There was nothing in her vicinity, nothing that she could see anyways. She was stranded and without a gun or a knife to save herself. She would have to start moving.

Once the parachute was finally off, Bijou kept low and moved around the bushes, trying to stay out of the clearings and inch her way to a building. There must've been something left in the town that was up ahead, and most people likely moved on anyways. Nevertheless, she couldn't stay there, the storm was closing in, and she was more or less on the outskirts of the island. No matter which way she looked, however, she only saw trees and bushes. Not one building in sight. She must've fallen farther from it than she realized.

Bijou sat still for a couple of seconds, It wouldn't be long until the storm hit the mainland, but she had a couple of hours until then. So until then, she just felt her arms and torso to make sure she lived, that she made the landing alright, and she was alive. It was quiet. Off in the distance, the familiar staccato of a light machine gun flew through the air. It wouldn't be long until someone came across her and shot her down too. She had to remember the basics of Blood Running in the back of her head and reviewing inwardly before she got up and made her move. Think laterally, move quickly, shoot first.

"Think laterally, move quickly, shoot first.... Think laterally, move—
"

There was a crack of a twig near her that spooked Bijou out of her mantras. She jumped and pulled her hands to her chest in fear, knowing she didn't have anything to defend herself with. This was it. Her last and final Blood Run, and she didn't even get to see her boys on the battlefield for it. Whoever was about to come around the trees was going gun her down for points and move on, and that would've been it. The end of Blood Running for her.

When the rustling became louder, the steps turned into a run, and the leaves crunching was ever prominent in her ears. Bijou closed her eyes; she didn't want to look in the face of her killer. However, the running stopped, the footfalls stopped, and the parting of leaves was heard. The victor was staring right at her, but she wasn't going to look. When a couple of seconds passed, and she wasn't shot down, she opened her eyes and pulled her head out of her hands, looking up. Chess was standing there, hands parting a bush and showing another rare shit-eating grin.

"Fancy meeting you here," Chess goaded.

"Ohh! Chess!" Bijou pretended to be mad, but she couldn't help but get up and run into his arms, grateful that Chess returned the hug.

"I'll buddy up with you until the end, and then you're going to have to fight me, kay?" Chess said, throwing her a pistol—a Beretta M9.

"Kay. Can't promise I'll be any good," Bijou said, holding the gun in her hands and looking to the ground.

"Don't have to be," Chess said, looking over his shoulder at her. "Just stick with me, but not too close. We'll spread out and flank who we need to. Be on the lookout for that jackass too."

"That jackass happens to be my friend too, you know." Bijou huffed, walking next to Chess.

Chess was carrying a Kalashnikov slung over his shoulder, holstering another M9 on his hip. On his leg, he had a massive hunting knife that had blood on it. Chess had killed to get it. Bijou looked at the knife and then at Chess, keeping her mouth shut.

Chess didn't say anything, not wanting to start a fight about who Bijou chose to be friends with. He just wanted to play the round. Now that he found Bijou, the games could truly begin.

CHAPTER **ELEVEN**

It had been over twenty minutes since the C-130 had entered the lower atmosphere when a sleek, black Range Rover pulled up to the venue. People moved out of the way once the valet and driver had come to assess the passenger, helping her get out of the car with ease. Most people watching the massive TV above them for the start of the game watched as an ethereal being emerged from the backseat.

Wearing a matching pencil skirt/suit combo and high heels as tall as the building she was about to walk into, a woman with dark skin and a curly afro paired with red-rimmed glasses walked onto the sidewalk and away from the car. The valet quickly whisked it away, letting the woman go about her business and make her way inside the venue.

The match had already started, but it would be another couple of hours until the meat of the action would happen anyways. She had plenty of time to get into the venue pilot house that oversaw the island from afar, the storm in clear view and multiple monitors tracking Blood Runners.

A man who looked like his eyes were going to bug out of his head pushed past a couple of people standing near the door and hurried down the stairs trying to get to her. He took the stairs two at a time, inwardly praying that he didn't trip and fall on his face in front of his boss. He stopped in front of her, his hands on his knees and heaving air into his lungs. The woman took her sunglasses off and handed them to him, him taking them while still breathing heavily.

"Ma'am, they're on the ground. 86 left in the match and counting." The man heaved. He fell in line with her as she started walking up the stairs; he killed himself trying to descend.

"MVP for the match speculation?" she asked.

"Uhh, Damon Kennedy, ma'am. Came from the UK to compete in today's match. He knows this is for recruitment and has over six kills so far," the man said.

They made their way into the venue, people moving out of the way from the strong presence she was giving off as she walked to the elevators. She was a force. Looked strong, projected strength and class, and didn't look like you could touch her even if you coulda for it. The man with her was shaking like a leaf the entire time he was standing next to her.

"Coffee waiting for me up there?" she asked, putting her sunglasses in her bag and handing the bag off to her lackey.

"Yes, ma'am. Lunch provided as well."

"I already ate."

"Of course," the man said, adverting his gaze from her.

After a long elevator ride to the pilot house, the doors opened to a room full of uniformed moderators and some well-to-do dressed people standing around holding champagne. She looked dressed for the occasion, her dress clearly looking like money and heels with red bottoms. She walked in, refusing the alcoholic drink and taking the Starbucks cup another lackey had on standby. More than likely having Uber Eats'd it over before she showed up. She never drank alcohol; it was bad for the skin.

"Ohh! Another one! Man, I was counting on him too!" one of the men shouted out as he looked at a large screen to the right of the room.

A young man had his head blown off with a shotgun blast, and the winner continued, picking from the drops after he turned into nothing more than purple Temporal Shards.

"Must be hard to use magic; no one is using it," a woman said, looking around.

"It's not that it's hard; it takes skill. You have to watch to see who has the skill to use it and use it correctly," the man said, pulling the woman closer to him around his arm.

He turned a bit and caught sight of her from across the room, drinking her coffee and looking at the leaderboard score screen. Damon Kennedy's profile at the top spot of the scorecard, his picture on full display at the top. He wasn't smiling, his hair getting into his face and his lips full. He looked like a model, not a Blood Runner. Under Damon's picture were four more runner-ups. All four of them looked the part. Mean mugging the camera and chopped hair or shaved heads. One of them was Chess Harlow. With his head faced forward, neck bent back a bit as if he didn't care; he was getting his picture taken, eyes dead behind the lids. There was a ghost of a smirk on his face, it was barely there, but one could see it.

"Farren Connor! You actually showed up!" the man said, letting the other woman go and making a beeline toward her in one swift motion.

Farren, sipping her coffee and pushing her hand against her afro to adjust the strands, turned to the man with an unamused look on her face. She preened her hair a couple of seconds more before putting her hand on her hip and pulling the coffee from her lips. Her plum lipstick left a mark on the plastic lid.

"Levi. To what do I owe the pleasure?" Farren sauntered, trying not to click her heels on the floor out of annoyance.

"Was wondering if you already had your eye on the top Runners for your upcoming team. Wouldn't expect nothing but the best coming from you," Levi said, putting his hands in his pockets.

Levi Jones was a man of middle age and thinning hair that he kept dying to keep it looking as natural as possible. A well to do man that found his luck in the betting and management of Blood Runners and Blood Running. He is very adamant about the 'make your own luck' thought process, no days off kind of mentality.

Farren answered the question with a sip of her coffee and a rather blazing look. She wasn't interested in getting into betting matches with Levi and was far from showing any interest in what was going on on the screen path this time. The match had just started, and anything could change, she wasn't going to be sticking around in these heels long enough to wait out the finale, but she had an obligation to show up when it started anyways. She would stick around for the first hour, then leave for lunch. By the sixth hour, she would return for the results; whoever won, she would get her hands on.

It wasn't going to be hard. Almost everyone competing in this event today knew what it meant. The chance at the World Royale and unfathomable wealth, fame, and notoriety. Not many would give up a chance at that, and there was always the second runner-up if the first one dropped out. Then again, that would pique her interest more. If the winner wanted nothing to do with it, she would rather that happen and go for the chase than deal with yes men that did everything she said. That wasn't going to happen, though. Not for something as big as this.

"Just came in to see how it was going," Farren said, sipping her coffee again.

"And what are you seeing?" Levi asked, turning back toward the massive monitors. "Game's just begun, but I'm already out a couple thousand because some fuckwit decided to play hero and got himself killed."

"Betting at the beginning, your luck's not that good, darling," Farren said, a hint of a smile on her face.

"Good enough to get me this far."

They watched the monitors for a good couple of seconds before the sight of a girl getting blown to smithereens by a fire spell blast rippled across the airwaves. Farren simply took another sip of her coffee and watched as the girl with golden hair that obtained the kill crouch walked over to the remaining supplies and picked up a better gun, leaving the one she had behind. A shotgun with a sawed-off barrel. A man came up behind her, and Farren watched as they both talked, the man with a shaved head talking mostly with his hands in a very animated way.

"That's gonna suck if it comes down to just them, and they have to kill each other," Farren said, pointing to the couple on the screen.

"It never ends up being the duos. One of them always dies off right before the ending hour." Levi snickered, looking at the couple as well.

Something about looking in the boy's eyes intrigued Farren, and she watched him a little more closely as the camera continued to focus on them. They were sitting still for a moment, the boy offering bandage wraps to the girl and covering her six as she healed. A wash of green light rippled over the girl as her heat regenerated, and the scratches and scuff on her body suddenly evaporated into thin air. The boy looked over to her, nodded, and then they both ran out of frame. After a couple of seconds, the camera feed went to another point on the island.

"Who were they? Does anyone know?" Farren asked, looking around at the maintenance people running around.

A boy that looked fresh-faced came over a couple of seconds later with a clipboard with one single piece of paper clipped onto it. The boy image was at the top, almost in a mugshot-like homage—his profile and the front view of his face. He looked mean and tired at the same time, his hard eyes and barely there eyebrows making him look more animated than intended.

"Not sure who the girl is yet, but the man is definitely Chess Harlow. Santa Catalina Island veteran."

"Chess..." Farren repeated as she looked down at the paper sheet.

"Yes, Chess Harlow. The bane of my existence. He either slaughters any bet I place or squanders the win when I *do* bet on him," Levi said, nothing but contempt in his voice.

"How do you still have money if this man is single-handedly killing your bets?" Farren asked, handing the clipboard back to the maintenance worker.

"He's a force of nature, and honestly, I thought about betting on him if there wasn't another contender in the ring that could for sure best him," Levi said, pointing to another monitor on the other side of the room.

Farren followed his finger to the other side of the room, where a black-haired man with a face full of thunder was running at full speeds down a grassland. In his hand was an AK-47, pointed to the sky as he booked it to his destination. The camera trained on him panned out to show him hunting down another man running for his life.

"Bold," Farren said, sipping her coffee again.

"Damon Kennedy is the son of one of the greatest Blood Runners of all time, and he's showing great promise himself. He's fast, tactile, and a genius on the battlefield. He and Chess Harlow are rivals."

"Hmm."

Farren kept the lid of the coffee to her painted lips as she watched Damon hunt his prey down. With a quick fan of his hand, a whirlwind of a gust shot from Damon toward the running assailant. The man running for his life was picked up from the ground, spun around a couple of times in the air, and hovered there while Damon slowed down to aim. It was a couple of pops from the assault rifle, and the hovering man was reduced to nothing more than crystals. Damon picked up a couple, crushed them in his hands, replenished his mana, and moved on, not even bothering to look at the man's other dropped equipment.

As Farren lowered her coffee from her mouth, she noticed the area Damon was about to enter. A place that she knew Chess and the mystery woman were going to be coming out of soon.

"This is about to get very interesting. I can tell. Call me if either of them dies."

With that, Farren pushed her half-finished coffee into Levi's hands and turned on her heel. As fast as she arrived, she left just as quickly, intent on discovering everything she could about these three. Perhaps—she thought—over an early lunch.

CHAPTER TWELVE

"I still got it!" Bijou hollered over the grasslands as she picked up a couple of Temporal Crystals and took them into herself.

Squeezing her hands tighter around the crystals until they burst around her, Bijou couldn't help but smile as she turned back to Chess to see if he was congratulating her. Chess was not. He was covering down her six, his eye through a scope as he looked over the rolling hills and rippling grass. The wind was picking up, and the lines of white rolled over the hills as the gusts whipped by moved Bijou's ponytail, her hair caressing her cheek. She wasn't mad at Chess; this was just how he operated.

Wanting to get a rise out of Chess a little bit for taking this so seriously, Bijou spun her fingers around a couple of times and summoned a small gust of wind using Temporal Magic that brushed past him. He wobbled a bit and then fell over on his hip, grunting. Looking up at Bijou with a raised eyebrow and a grimace, Bijou was nothing but all smiles and laughs as she put her hands on her hips and gave him a knowing look.

"Can't you have just a little fun while we're here? It's my last Blood Run, after all," Bijou said.

Chess picked himself up off the ground and dusted the dirt off his pants before he covered their six yet again, looking at the hills through his scope. He grunted once.

"It's not about having fun if the person that takes this the most serious in the world is after your ass. At that point, it's pure sport," Chess replied.

Bijou kneeled next to Chess and looked over the plains he was patrolling. It was rolling grass as far as her eyes could see, but some trees could've provided cover to those trying to get across the field unscathed. Chess was adamant about nabbing someone here, anyone. In the back of his mind, he wanted to get a strike on Damon. The thought of nabbing him from across the map with a rifle made the hairs on the back of his neck stand up. Just the look of pure surprise before the end. It's what Chess deserved.

Bijou had since looked over to their right, nothing more than trees and forests that they had just come out of and didn't feel like going back in. Other than the last guy they ran into, it didn't look like there was much life left on this side of the island. They were going to have to move if they wanted to make any headway in this match. No one was coming out this way anymore, where the storm was coming from.

"We shouldn't stay here for any longer than we have to," Chess said, slinging the gun over his shoulder and getting up from his spot.

Bijou stood with him. Looking out to where Chess was looking, an open plain with sparse trees and not much else. It was a deathtrap unless they could get through it quickly and without getting spotted. She swallowed, she knew this wasn't good, but they didn't have any other choice but to cross it.

"Should we stick close together for this?" Bijou asked.

"That would be the smartest thing to do. I won't use you as a shield, though," Chess said, reloading his glock and aiming down the sights for a couple of seconds before holstering it.

"Can't promise I wouldn't do the same, though." Bijou giggled.

Chess just looked at her with a passive gaze, and Bijou stopped laughing. She bit her lip and looked away, knowing it was a touchy subject with him and she shouldn't exacerbate that. What Damon did to Chess all the way up to graduation wasn't right, but even Bijou had to admit that it was a little bit blown out of proportion. Damon had moved on; he had become a better man and lived his own life. They were all dumb kids trying to figure themselves out in Academy, and life went on.

Somewhere within her, she wished that Chess would move on from this too. The grudge he harbored for Damon was nothing less than a curse. Something that just stuck to Chess's soul until he was expunged from life. Short from death, there seemed to be no other way for him to get over it. Would winning this match really help with how he was feeling? Somehow Bijou doubted it. Even if Chess did win, he was still going to harbor this curse of a grudge with him for the rest of his life.

The wind whipped by, blowing Bijou's ponytail toward their destination. Out into the open plains with no cover whatsoever. The pit in her stomach grew a little wider once she realized Chess was truly going to go through with it and brave the plains, knowing anyone could come over those hills and kill them outright. She held onto her gun a little tighter, keeping her finger off the trigger so that she didn't shoot herself in the foot inadvertently. It would be stupid if she got this far only to off herself in the middle of the match.

"What hour are we on?" Bijou asked.

They both took out their phones as they stopped by a thick tree, taking some cover. The app used for Royale was open on both of their screens, and the circle signifying the storm coming had already materialized. It had been two hours since they dropped down now, barely anywhere near mid-game. Sixty-two players were left, and Chess knew Damon was one of them.

A couple of red circles indicating activity weren't too far off from where they both were standing, meaning they were likely to run into somebody crossing the plains. A showdown in the grass wasn't something Chess wanted to do, but if he had to do it, he would. Bijou grimaced at the circle, not really wanting to get into any more fights. She wanted to drop one last time with her friends before she gave Blood Running up for good, but the stress and anticipation that came with battle was something she was ready to give up.

"Second hour, about to turn over to the third. We have to keep moving if we want to reach the middle by midday," Chess said, pocketing his phone and huffing a sigh through his nose.

"It's going to be a shitshow when we get there, isn't it?"

"It's a shitshow everywhere, Bijou. Come on."

It wasn't for another couple of minutes until Chess and Bijou came across some more houses. They were built before the storm had taken over the island and were likely filled with weapons and ammo they could use. All the guns brought to the island were randomly strewn about the island after every reset, making no two runs the same. The last time Chess was at these houses, he got lucky to cash out with a sniper rifle, but it could be very different this time.

"I'll take this house over here," Bijou said, pointing to a house across the street.

"Keep your ears open for any movement. Once you're done, we'll meet at the stop sign," Chess said, pointing to the road sign at the end of the street.

Bijou flashed him a thumbs up and booked it toward the house across the way. Chess watched her go for a couple of seconds, scoping out the sides of the house before turning around and entering the house he chose. Again, there could very well be nothing inside of them, but it didn't hurt to look and try to get better gear.

Once he was through the door and shut it behind him, the silence rang in his ears. Without Bijou around and her own footfalls and commentary along the way, Chess almost forgot how *quiet* the game could be at times. Sometimes it was so loud he thought his eardrums would rupture and not recover back at respawn. The sounds of gunfire and screaming, the yelling and taunts thrown every which way. It was a culture Chess loved deep down, he wouldn't want it any other way, but in moments like these, the science was unnerving.

He couldn't even hear Bijou from across the street, which should've been a given, but with how quiet everything was, he figured he would be able to hear her open doors at least. No dice, however. With that, he began to search the house. Starting with the living room and working his way into the kitchen, he found almost next to nothing in the way of gear and supplies. There was a granola bar and a couple of eggs in the still working fridge. If he had enough time, he could make himself a meal and eat up; lord knows he needed to eat, but the storm was hot on their heels already, and they couldn't afford to stop and cook. He took the granola bar, unwrapped it, and took a bite. It was bland, the big-name brand type that didn't boast a lot of flavors. Every other week, they airdrop packaged foods and shut down the island to restock perishables for the storm to redistribute throughout the island as the land resets. How the storm knew to put food in the fridges, Chess would never figure that one out. Munching on the granola bar, he didn't bother his mind too much with the details he couldn't control and looked out of a window toward the street. There was a man standing outside looking in.

Chess dropped the rest of his food and dove behind the couch for some sort of cover before he peeked his head over the top to look at the man again. He was standing outside, looking around like he was looking for someone or something, and looked like he hadn't seen Chess yet. When the man turned his back to Chess, Chess got up slowly and got ready to unload his gun into this guy's back. It was a dirty move, but if it worked, he wasn't going to complain about it. Just as he was about to unload through the window, Bijou walked across a window of her own on the other side of the street, and the man clearly saw her. Hunching his shoulders up and taking a couple of steps back, gripping his gun tighter, the man watched Bijou stop in front of the window, pick something up and toss it away before she looked back out. They met eyes, and Bijou dropped to the floor. That's when the man broke out into a full sprint toward the house she was in.

"Shit!" Chess hissed and tried to round the couch as fast as he could to get out the front door.

By the time Chess was out in the street, the man hunting Bijou was already at the door of the adjacent house. It was against time now that Chess would make it in time to help Bijou. Technically, they weren't supposed to be helping each other, it was a free for all match, but Chess couldn't just leave her to die. Not if he could do something about it. Before he knew it, he was barging into the front door, hot on the heels of the man that went in after Bijou. He had to find her before this guy did, and time was running out.

Forcing his shoulder onto the door to bust it open almost off its hinges, Chess wasted no time crossing the street and running into the adjacent house. Switching to his pistol, he slug the rifle over his shoulder and made a mad dash for the stairs. He was hoping that his hunch was right, that this guy immediately went upstairs to snuff out Bijou. Once he heard footsteps that were not his own above him, he made his way fully to the stairs. That's when the guy busted out from the closet, intercepting him.

Chess made a grunt as the guy ran into him and shoved him against the couch across the room. He was armed with a rifle, but Chess didn't know if it was truly loaded or not. If the guy really wanted to, this close range, a fire blast would be more than enough to take him out, but they were just wrestling.

Bijou came down the stairs at the noise of the commotion, thinking that Chess had gotten him, but she slunk back to the top of the stairs when she realized they were wrestling for dominance over the couch. Chess was pushing back on the rifle that the guy was pushing onto him with, and there was no clear winner yet.

When Chess was able to get a free hand, he reached down and pulled the hunter's knife from his hip, snapping the cord that was holding it to his pants. He made two quick jabs to his assailant's side, hitting his mark on the second swing and driving the knife deep into the man's gut. The assailant clearly felt his health draining and backed away with a gasp. While no one could feel life-threatening pain, the feeling of your life draining away was something you could feel. You could kiss, hug, pat down, and sleep all you wanted in a Temporal Space before the storm got you, but you couldn't feel pain.

The man backed away and readied his gun. Despite bleeding out and slowly losing his health over time, he was going to try and gun down Chess and Bijou one way or another. Chess reached for his pistol, but it looked like he was going to be a little late on the draw. When Chess was just coming to terms that he might have lost, a large gust of wind blew through the house, rocking the furniture and putting out the fire in the crackling fireplace. Bijou had spent all her crystals on a major wind spell that blew them off their feet. Since this wasn't a Duos game, Bijou could still hurt Chess, so she had to be careful. It was very obvious that she could kill Chess if she weren't paying attention.

Chess's back hit the wall, and he quickly sprung back to his feet with a grunt. The man was writhing on the floor, trying to reach for his gun that was blown from his hands, but his wrist met the business end of Chess's boot. Stomping hard on the man's wrist, the last thing he saw was Chess's wry smile as he pointed the barrel of his pistol in his face. It took two shots in the chest, and the face before the man turned into nothing more than a pile of purple crystals on the ground. It wasn't until the man dissipated that everything in the house finally calmed down, and the wind stopped howling.

"Is it over?" Bijou weakly asked from behind the banister.

Looking around and then running a hand over his shaved head, Chess nodded to Bijou.

"Yeah, all clear."

"That was scary! He was coming right for me!" Bijou half laughed, coming down the stairs.

"He was actually hiding in the closet, hoping you'd come down to him. Got the fuckin' jump on me and everything. Shit."

Chess shook some dust and ash off of himself before stuffing his pistol in his pocket and looking toward Bijou. She had come downstairs and taken a good look at her handiwork. Chairs and tables were strewn everywhere; curtains ripped off their frames and windows blown in. It was a mess, to say the least, and a mess that the storm would fix when it blew through. Bijou wasted no time picking up the crystals and popping them in her hands, taking in the energy.

"I spent all of my mana summoning that gust. Almost took you out with him." Bijou giggled.

Chess spared a small smile and pulled out his phone. While Bijou was busy gathering crystals, Chess checked the position and direction of the storm. Looked like it was going to center on the upper west side of the island this time. They would have to haul serious ass if they wanted to make it to the middle in time. In the middle of that thought, a distant sound rang out in the distance.

Before Chess could even compartmentalize what it was, Bijou's head separated from her shoulders, and she dissipated into a flurry of crystals she had just picked up and weapons she had on her person. Chess dropped his phone and pulled his rifle from behind his back, cussing up a storm. Bijou was gone, a sharpshooter sniper having taken her out, but who? Who else was around here and not making their way to the center like they were trying to do? All Chess knew was that Bijou was out of the game, and he tried to control his breathing before he scanned the window.

He put some curtain on a broken chair stick and stuck it up out of the window. The sound of another crack rang out along the hills. The bullet hit the decoy sheet and splintered it.

He was being hunted.

CHAPTER THIRTEEN

The splintered wood and smoking fabric of what was once a curtain lay on the floor as Chess scrambled to gather his bearings. He looked over to the pile of crystals and weapons on the ground where Bijou was once standing. Was she watching him from the respawn room right now? He hoped so because she was about to witness Chess lose his ever-loving shit on live TV.

Dropping the decoy on the ground, Chess took his weapons and a couple of Bijou's crystals, popping them in his hands as he made his way to the stairs. He didn't know what else to do but to get to the high ground and recon for his assailant. While he was on the move, the other person could also be on the move. That, or they were lying in wait, just searching and waiting for the moment Chess popped his head out of the window. He knew he only had one shot to look down his scope and pinpoint the aggressor. If he messed this up, there would be no second chances. He would lose the game and his chance to get one up on Damon. He couldn't let that happen.

As Chess's back hit the wall in one of the upstairs rooms, he tried not to think about the storm that was about to roll through his area soon. Did his assailant know that as well, just trying to keep them both there to see which one would chicken out and run first? Chess wasn't going to give this person the satisfaction of that. He was going to deliver a bullet straight through to their head for what they did to Bijou. He was really looking forward to their final battle at the end of the round; now, it was looking like that would never happen. This was supposed to be her last game ever, and she was going to go back to work for good.

Honestly, good for her, Chess thought to himself as he pulled his rifle out from behind his back and loaded a bullet into the chamber. She had a career and future ahead of her. Money saved and relationships to foster. She had all these things that Chess didn't have, and he was happy for her. Now Chess was going to try and avenge her blind. He didn't know where this guy was, and he was going to risk his head the second he popped it out of the window.

Taking a deep breath, Chess rose his gun and inhaled deeply before whipping around and aiming it out of the window toward the hills. He saw him.

Black clothes, dark hair parted down the middle, and eyes that held nothing but internal rage and concentration. Chess pulled the hammer back on the rifle and aimed down the sights. He had one chance to get this shot off before he was seen, and the man was already looking up. He had to shoot first.

Squeezing the trigger and letting the bullet fly from his gun to his target, Chess couldn't stick around long to see if the bullet landed or not. He thought he got a good look at it hitting its mark before ducking away from the window. There was a pause, and then a shot rang out behind him. A bullet entered the window and hit the adjacent wall on the other side of Chess.

He had to leave now, or it was going to be over for both of them. While he would love to stay and watch his assailant get caught in the storm and die, he wasn't going to have much luck escaping it either. His best bet was leaving through the back door and running linear to the house. Keep out of the sniper's line of sight.

He hated that he would have to cut and run, but if he wanted to face Damon, he was going to have to do it. The storm was cutting a little too close to him for comfort. If he could just stay perpendicular to the house, he should've been fine to run, but who was to say that the sniper wouldn't just follow him? He had to make a decision and make it fast.

Slinging his rifle over his shoulder again and ducking past the window, another bullet whizzed by him as he made his way to the stairs and then the back door. There were other houses around that he could duck and weave between on his way out, but he would have to cut through another house if he wanted to not be seen by the sniper. So be it.

Busting through the door of the house he originally started in, he ran as fast as he could to the back door and slammed it open. In front of him was nothing more but grass and trees =; he would have to Hoff it as fast as he could to the center of the map before either the storm got to him or the sniper did. He didn't like the odds, but it was his only option. Make it to the middle and bunker down until the finalists showed up. Then it would be all or nothing. No regrets because he knew he would see Damon there. There was no denying that.

Running away like that, though, he prayed it wasn't caught on a drone camera and showed off to millions. He could hear Miller in his head now.

"You ran away? Your dad would've stayed and fought."

Yeah, well, he wasn't his dad. His dad was dead. It was only him out here on the battlefield, and the ghosts of relatives past weren't coming to save him. He had to look out for himself the best that he could.

Running as fast as his legs would take him, Chess pulled out his phone and checked the map. The storm was fast approaching and would engulf the houses he was previously at in a matter of minutes. Wherever the sniper was, he didn't know. If he fucked off to another part of the map or followed him, Chess tried not to let it cloud his mind. He was only a good thirty-minute jog from the center, and he could make it. He had to make it; he had no other choice.

BIJOU'S BODY MATERIALIZES AND FORMS IN A RESPAWN POD A hundred miles from the island center. She let out a sharp gasp and held her hand to her neck as she remembered what had happened to her before she was ejected from the game. Stuff like this, missing body parts, and losing your head, literally, was why she didn't like Blood Running, to begin with.

It seemed like such a fun game; everyone was doing it when she entered academy to get her license, but when she got into her first couple of games, she realized it wasn't everything that it was cracked up to be. If anything, it was worse. She didn't want to hold a heavy gun and feel the recoil and knock back of bullets flying from her fingertips. She didn't like to see the bodies of people she shot disintegrate into nothingness. She knew they weren't really dead, but what if one time it was true? What if she killed someone someday, and they didn't respawn? Questions like that were what filled her mind as she stepped out of the pod and rubbed her neck as if it was sore. Behind her, another person materialized and, muffled by the clear door shut around him, started yelling out expletives at the top of his lungs and beating on the walls.

While she was having an internal crisis, people around her were carrying on as if this was just a normal day. Just another day of killing and being killed. People were walking on the treadmills and lifting weights in the gym next to her, blowing off steam from their losses until the next match, whenever that was going to be.

She didn't feel like working out. She wanted to get out of here, to be honest, and go back to her boba shop, where she felt happy. She liked working there and owning her own restaurant. It was leagues better than hiding in a house and waiting to get shot up by a tryhard stranger that only cared about body count. She wanted to go, but she couldn't. Not yet.

Quickly exiting the respawn locker and waiting room, she hunted down the first sitting area with a large TV mounted on the wall and picked a seat. An attendant came around almost instantly and set a bottle of water next to her on the table. It was more than likely a basic brand of water, but the label on the plastic was that of the venue they were playing at. She nodded and thanked the attendant cracking it open and taking long gulps of mineral water. She watched and waited for the drones in the field to center in on the last remaining players on the field, and she knew that Chess or Damon would show up; they had to. They were the most talked about players in the game; she was surprised the feed wasn't showing one of them already. It was playing a replay of a random guy knife throwing his way into a victory and moving on to the center of the map.

Pulling out her phone, she navigated the Blood Runner app, found Chess in her friends list, and started composing a message. Whether Chess was too busy to read it and even reply was up to him, but she felt it was the right thing to do.

"*Sorry for that; it was a fun game, though.*"

After checking her email, Bijou pocketed her phone and looked back at the screen. The sight that greeted her was one she was waiting for but one she wasn't ready for. Damon was running at full speeds through trees and tall grass, his sniper rifle held in one hand and the barrel pointed to the sky as he booked it past the foliage. She wondered where Chess was and if Damon was already hunting him down. When Damon suddenly stopped and dropped to one knee, readying his rifle, he took a couple of deep breaths and moved his finger to the trigger. Whoever he had scoped was about to get ejected; Bijou knew it. That's when a bullet hit the tree next to Damon's head, and Damon started to back off, taking cover behind another tree.

Bijou sat forward. So the hunter was being hunted all the same as well. Whoever Damon was tracking was also tracking him, and Bijou had a good idea of who it was. She watched as the drone took a close-up shot of Damon, his back against the tree, as he took a couple of deep breaths and held his rifle to his chest, trying to make himself small and not get hit. His hair was sticking to his forehead from sweat, and his breathing was erratic. If he really wanted to make a break for it, he could. The trees were dense enough to run through and still had some cover. Bijou watched with bated breath as she saw the scene unfold in front of her. That's when the drone lifted into the air and away from Damon to the other assailant on the other end of the field. It was Chess.

They had finally met up in the middle, and the storm was hot on their asses. If they didn't get out of this area in a couple of minutes, both of them would've lost the game. She didn't realize it, but she was holding her own breath, only regaining her breathing, when she heard the door behind her open, and the sound of people talking invaded her concentration.

She turned to see a tall black woman with a beautiful head of curly hair in an afro style walking to the elevators. She was wearing impossibly high pumps and dressed like money. She looked like the type of person to bet on games like this and was lucky. When she took off her sunglasses and handed them to the first man her hand bumped into, she turned to look at Bijou and stopped. Both women just stared at each other.

"You, girl. You were with Chess Harlow?" the woman called out.

"Uh, uhm... yes, ma'am," Bijou stammered.

She was intimidated by this woman's strong stature and even more intimidated when she started to walk toward her, the click of her pumps hitting the marble floor ringing in her ears. What could a rich woman like this possibly want from her? Before Bijou's mind could get the better of her, the woman thrust a hand out for her to shake, holding it there until Bijou would take it.

"Farren Conner. USA Blood Runner Team Captain. May we talk for a bit?"

Bijou just stared up at her and then at her hand. Taking it and shaking her hand a couple of times, she got up, taking her water with her.

"Sure. Anything you'd like," Bijou said a little timidly.

"Great. Follow me," Farren said and quickly turned on her heel to the elevators.

Bijou followed, and before she knew it, she was heading up to the pilot house.

CHAPTER FOURTEEN

Chess's back was against a slab of raised concrete; somewhere along the way, a grenade had listed it from its foundations. Chess could use it for cover while he was quickly reloading. Someone was on him and on him hard. It was a sniper vs. rifle battle, and the assailant was winning by a landslide. Chess just had to push in more and flank this guy so that it would be a fair fight. Man to man.

It wasn't like he hadn't sniped a couple of people in his days before this game. Plenty of times, he had picked the sniper rifle and hunted down player after player on his way to a win. Having one of his own tactics used on him was a disgusting irony he didn't want to laugh at but couldn't help but do so. Done in by his own dirty tricks.

Above him, he could hear the buzzing of a media drone flying above him. He wondered what he looked like on the TVs now. If Damon was already out of the game and watching him. There was no way. If anything, he knew he was going to run into him after he was done taking care of this sniper. He had no other choice but to pull through this and challenge Damon face to face.

Chess broke from the concrete slab, now fully reloaded, and sprinted to the other side of a dilapidated building. They were in the center now, and the storm was rolling in. This would be when people were going to get picked off one by one by the winds and lightning found in the clouds closing in on the center. The eye of the storm would float for a good thirty minutes and then close, resetting the island completely. Chess figured he had about an hour left before he was going to be eaten by the storm rather than by the hands of Damon. Or rather, his hands around Damon's neck.

As Chess was running through the streets of the small town found in the center, he saw a couple of bodies running around, entering businesses, and jumping from windows. Chess dove under a car and watched the fight play out. It was between a girl and a boy, and the girl was advancing slowly while firing an AR-15. She was looking to win this scrimmage, and Chess slowly came out from under the car just as she landed a couple of good hits. The boy went down in a flurry of crystals, and the girl didn't even stop to pick anything up. This was it; the final moments of the battle and stopping meant death.

Chess didn't know where his sniper assailant was, but he knew he had to deal with this girl before he could deal with him. He rounded the car and lobbed a grenade in her direction, pulling her attention to him. Just before it went off, both of them dived behind cars, and the explosion went off, making the car she was hiding behind raise off the ground for a moment before falling back down with an ugly wail of a screech. The metal waning and bending under pressure. He knew she was still alive.

Rounding the car and trusting his instincts, Chess fired a couple of bullets in her direction, billowing smoke hiding them from each other. He didn't hear the sounds of someone crying out in surprise, and even through the smoke, he would've been able to see the sparkle of the Temporal Crystals falling to the ground. He was either missing something, or she wasn't there anymore.

Not wanting to chance fighting in the smoke and breathing that in along with fighting, Chess backed away and made a break for a car across the street for cover. That's when a bullet hit the wall in front of him. Chess whipped around and pulled his pistol out of his jeans and aimed it true, watching as the girl moved out of the smoke, her gun raised and aimed as well. Chess kept backing up, hoping to dive behind the car and give himself a fighting chance. He pulled the pistol because it was automatic and faster, knowing he would get quicker hits than her.

The girl was reloading while walking toward him, a bold move since Chess thumbed the hammer back quickly and put his finger on the trigger, ready to blow her away. A shot rang out in the distance, and the girl was blown to the side by an immense force. She hurled air from her lunge as if she had just been punched and then expired, her body melting into crystals. The sniper was here, and he went fro the girl first.

Knowing this was more than likely his death, but he couldn't fight the hunch that was itching in the back of his mind, Chess walked out tot he middle of the road, still holding his pistol in his hand, hammer cocked. A man was walking down the opposite way toward him. His rifle was not raised, and he was just sauntering toward him as if he had all the time in the world. Behind him, Chess could see the ugly purple clouds swirling in the distance, closing in on both of them. He didn't have to look at his phone to know they were the last ones alive.

He didn't care about the competition; he didn't care who was watching anymore; he didn't care about the money. As Damon Kennedy walked slowly toward Chess, he only cared about payback. Payback for the embarrassment and the shame. Payback for the lies and the deceit. He never cared for Chess, and Chess couldn't let it go; he just couldn't let it go anymore.

"Howdy!" Damon called out.

He threw the rifle to the ground as if it was nothing more than trash. Chess watched it fall, and his gaze was back on Damon's hand, pulling out a revolver from his side holster. A Showdown? It was looking like it, and Chess was game. Whoever was quicker was the winner.

Chess said nothing to Damon's greeting; however, his eyes slit from the sunlight and anger alone. He dropped his rifle to the ground just like Damon, getting ready for the made-up showdown they had silently agreed upon.

"I knew you were quick on your feet, but I didn't know you were a marathon runner as well," Damon said, standing still in the road.

"So it was you that blew Bijou's head off? Your friend that stuck up for you?" Chess hollered out.

"She was in my way."

They were silent for a couple of moments before Chess adjusted on his feet, nerves getting the better of him. He didn't want to admit it, but he was intimidated by Damon. As they stood there facing each other, Damon's hair whipped in the oncoming wind, and Chess's jacket billowed around his frame; it was a matter of time until one of them made a move.

"Oh god, I can't watch!"

Bijou covered her eyes and turned away from the screen as the two boys were facing each other down. She knew they weren't going to die, they would simply respawn back in the Respawn Room, and one of them would have a bad attitude about it later, but it just seemed so final. Seeing them face off against each other in a desolate land like that with potholes from grenades and bullet holes in buildings surrounding them. The smoke and dust flying through the air. It was down to whichever was the first to move. In the bottom corner of the screen, the number 2 was visible; it was just the two of them left on the map. The technicians and maintenance teams were stock still, watching the screen.

Farren had her arms crossed; her stance relaxed as she watched the large flat screen with the two boys staring each other down. They were quiet for so long that it seemed neither of them was going to make a move. The storm was closing in, and in the middle of the silence, a maintenance worker called out, "Ten minutes until storm consumption!"

"What are they doing?" Farren asked herself.

She bumped Bijou on the shoulder with her elbow and gathered her attention. Bijou looked up from her hands and made the mistake of looking at the screen for a split second before looking at Farren. Her shoulders were bunched up, and she was obviously waiting for the gunshot to fire.

"They have a history, correct?" Farren asked, her eyes still on the TV screen.

"Uhm, yeah. They dated in Academy," Bijou said, looking at the TV again.

"Interesting."

The shot rang out, and Bijou jumped, surprised by the sound. Her mind didn't process the action until the body hit the ground. When it was all said and done, Chess's body dissipated into a flurry of crystals and weapons as the media drone lowered on Damon. He spun his pistol around on his finger and holstered it, the look of complete voidness on his face. He showed no emotion over what he had just done and didn't look into the camera when it came around to show him off for victory. The screen panned out to show his whole body, and then a couple of seconds later, he, too, was fizzled out of the map to the Respawn Room.

"Well, that settles that." Farren turned to Levi, standing near the window, and made a circular motion with her hand. He quickly came over, taking his phone out, ready to jot down any notes she might have had or requests.

"I want them both on my team. You too," Farren said, bumping Bijou again on the shoulder.

"Me?! I died pretty early on! I'm not good at Blood Running!" Bijou tried to deflect.

"No, but you're a good mediator between them. If you fail, then you fail, but I'd like to have you on regardless," Farren said.

Levi was busy tapping names into his notes and starting to make the necessary calls. As he put the cell phone to his ear, he turned to Farren with a look in his eye that Farren couldn't really place.

"And the money?"

Farren smiled. "It goes to the winner, of course."

By the time Damon had materialized out of the Respawn Pod, there was already a flurry of people—reporters, journalists, fans, and eliminated players alike—come to congratulate him and ask him questions. He exited to a flurry of noise and pushing, trying his best to get past them all to get to the waiting room. If his hunch was correct, then Chess was already out of the building by now, on his way to anywhere. More than likely a bar or his house to wallow. Damon wasn't going to let him do that without saying goodbye to him, at least, whether Chess wanted to or not. He still wanted to see him.

"Damon Kennedy, how did it feel getting the winning shot?!"

"Mr. Kennedy! You just won the 100,000 cash pool and the chance to compete in the World Royale! How do you feel?!"

"Damon, what's next for you? You're going to give up the UK team to play for the United States?"

Damon did his best to push past the reporters and criers before he found an opening in the room. He pulled his coat off and tied it around his waist, trying to get out of the building. Just as he figured, Chess was nowhere in sight. Farren and Bijou were just coming down the elevator as he bolted from the Respawn Room to the main lobby. It would be quite a walk from the hallways back out to the main atrium, but if Damon was quick enough, he could catch Chess before he hopped on a bus.

The hallways were void of people except for one. Chess was five steps from the door when Damon called out to him. He couldn't believe it, but Chess actually stopped. He didn't turn around, but he stopped. Damon knew better than to walk up to him, knowing it was going to result in another fistfight between them, but he kept his distance and watched. Watched what Chess was going to do, seeing if he was going to turn and talk or leave. He did neither, so Damon started talking.

"I was taking you seriously."

Chess said nothing to that, but his fists balled, and his shoulder shook. Damon took another step forward, closing the gap between them.

"This wasn't like back at Academy. You're different now than before. I wasn't playing with you like you think I was."

Chess turned around. "That's why you were hunting me and shot Bijou in the head right in front of me just to say 'I still got you, bitch!', that's right?"

"I already said she was in my way," Damon said through clenched teeth.

"In your way for what? I was in the window too."

They stood at a stalemate, and Damon didn't say anything. Chess had a wild look in his eye, knowing he was being played with. He wasn't going to allow himself to be made the fool again. When Bijou appeared at the end of the hallway, Chess looked over at her and then back to Damon. He huffed a sigh and turned back around, walking out of the venue.

"Whatever."

Chess pushed the doors open with significant force, walking out of the stadium and scaring the ticket lady standing near. When Bijou caught up with Damon, she gave him a sympathetic smile, but he didn't return it.

"Sorry for shooting you," Damon said.

"It's all good," Bijou answered. "But what's going to happen between you and Chess now?"

"What do you mean? The match is over, I won, and I'm going back home," Damon said, turning back around to walk back to the Respawn Room. Might as well soak up some fame before he bounced out of America.

"You won't even compete in the World Royale?" Bijou asked, walking with him.

"What's the point if he's not going to be there," Damon muttered.

"Well, I was just talking to the captain of the USA team, and she wants both of you for the team. Me too," Bijou said.

Damon stopped and looked at Bijou with wide eyes. "No, she didn't."

"She did. Chess is probably going to get a call any moment now to come back to the venue. That is if he decided to do it too."

Damon pulled out his phone and quickly moved to Chess's number, having gotten it from bijou before the match started. He was going to get to him before anyone else did about this, and he was going to make sure he competed. A pat of him wanted to see what Chess was like when he got his revenge, but as he put the cell phone to his ear, he had already made up his mind that he wasn't going to make it easy on him.

CHAPTER **FIFTEEN**

Chess was halfway out of the venue when he felt his cell phone buzz in his pocket. He didn't want to pick it up; it was either one of three things. Miller wondering what the fuck happened, Bijou trying to calm the situation down, or tax collectors. None of these things were what he wanted to deal with, m but when he pulled his phone up and saw it was a random number, he couldn't help but scratch his itch to know. At the least, he would answer, and if he didn't like what he heard, he would just hang up.

"Hello?"

"Chess, don't hang up; it's Damon. I—"

Chess hung up almost immediately. First, he was pissed that he somehow got his number; second, there was no way he would be able to stomach listening to his voice after what happened. Not toying with him, his ass. They were both in the window at the same time, and if Damon really wanted to go for him, then he had all the room in the world to do so. He was trying to send a message to Chess by taking Bijou out first.

"Could've been you."

Chess shook his head, trying to get the thought out of his mind. If Damon really wanted to kill him, he could've. He was convinced of that.

The image of Bijou's head separating from her body replayed over and over in his head. How he wasn't messed up from all of the gore and death that was around him so far, he wouldn't know. However, seeing Bijou get laid out like that was a different type of hurt, especially since it came from the hands of the person she trusted.

She was likely saying good game and smiling about the whole thing, but Chess couldn't handle the thought of Damon cherry-picking when he wanted to be loyal to his friends or when he didn't want to be. When they 'got in the way' or anything else that Damon could come up with, Chess was already over it. Damon could do whatever he wanted now; he didn't care. He was going to go home and, god willing, take a long break from Blood Running. He wanted another showdown with Damon, and he lost. That was all that had to happen. Now he could go home a more hollow man than he was before.

Before, he was filled with rage and regret. Regret that he didn't say all the things he wanted to before, regret that he didn't throw that punch the right way to knock his ass out. Rage at the mere thought of seeing him again. Now he just felt empty. Nothing.

Now he had to deal with the thought that Damon had his number and could call him whenever he wanted. The thought of changing his phone number flittered through his mind before he crossed the street to get to the bus station. He didn't want to deal with that right now, though. He didn't want to deal with anything. He was even dreading getting home and staring at the wall because he was going to be alone with his thoughts. He knew all of the memories of the past and the present were going to read their ugly heads back up in his mind, and he was going to have to deal with them. He didn't want to.

His cell phone shook a second time, and this time, he really tried to ignore it. It could've been bijou or someone else, but he didn't want to talk to anybody. Boarding the bus, he made his way to the comfortable spot in the back before taking his phone out and checking the missed call. It was from another number, but it was different than Damon's. He wasn't going to save Damon's number in his phone, but this number was different. As he checked it, his phone started to buzz again, the same number on the screen greeting him.

It could've been Damon on a second cell phone; lord knows, he was rich enough to have more than one. It could be someone else. Whatever it was, he answered and put the phone to his ear, not saying anything. He didn't have to; the voice on the other end started talking the second they figured out he had picked up.

"Chess Harlow, this is Farren Conner, USA Blood Runner Captain. I want to extend an invitation your way to compete in the World Royale and have a cache at being the world's best Blood Runner."

"Not interested," Chess said, his voice deep and controlled.

He didn't want to give any inkling that he was in anyways wanting to compete in anything like this. He was content doing Santa Catalina until he died.

"Your friend, Bijou Williams, is here saying she is also willing to compete if you join in," Farren said, her voice smooth and suave. Almost like she knew she would hook Chess one way or another.

"I said I wasn't interested. Get someone else."

"Someone like Damon Kennedy?"

Chess didn't say anything. He simply listened for a couple of seconds, both of them only breathing into the receivers of their phones before one of them started to speak again.

"He won anyways; wouldn't he compete regardless? Or is he going back to the UK Division?" Chess asked.

"He is willing to fight for the USA title under one condition; he wants you on the team. I want him; he's good."

Chess grimaced at that sentence.

"But, I've also seen your records here at Santa Catalina. You're no pushover, either. I think you have a good shot of taking home the gold in this one. I'm offering you a spot on the team if you'll take it."

"I'll think about it," Chess dismissed.

"There is no thinking about it; I need an answer by tonight. You have my number; call me when you figure your life out. If you don't do it, I lose all three of you for the team, and petty differences aside, I think you guys have a genuine shot at the title. Talk to you soon."

With that, Farren was the one to hang up on the phone, Chess getting the busy signal on the other end. He looked at his phone with disgust on his face and then pocketed it. Damon was more than likely calling to tell him about this venture as well. He wasn't going to let them talk him into submission. He was going to go home and think on it like he said he would and more than likely never call this Farren lady back. Lying low and not showing his face for a few days seemed like the best course of action.

He knew he was going to get a call soon from Miller, too, asking about the match and matching up against a Kennedy and all that. The rules of revenge and the story he truly didn't care about. His dad was dead; Blood Running killed him—the same as it was going to kill Chess one of these days. He didn't have a mom, and he was an adult on his own. What happened, happened, and he wasn't looking to seek revenge from someone that didn't affect his life.

He wasn't even close with his dad all that much. The memories he had of him were of competing and moving around from place to place to Blood Run, and that was it. He didn't have any childhood friends, and when he went to Academy, that's when it happened. It was hard for that first year, but what he assumed was affection from Damon turned into nothing more than deceit and vulnerability. Back-to-back, blows to his life like that had made Chess into the man howe was today. Cold, detached, not really for or about anything or anyone outside of Bijou.

The scenery passed by slowly as these thoughts filtered through his head. The fact that his life had gone so downhill after his dad's death, the fact that his relationships just wouldn't work out. Now he was wanted for the World Royale just so Damon could have a shot at it; just because this Farren woman wanted Damon more than him, he was just the stipulation. He shouldn't even give her the satisfaction. He should just lie low.

The bus stopped at a terminal a few minutes from his house, and Chess walked home the rest of the way. It was a long ride, each stop longer than the last, but he finally made it home just as the sun was starting to lower into the sky. It had been a long day, and the last thing he needed to see was the car in his driveway that was not his. It wasn't Miller's either, and it would've had to have been something pretty big for Miller to show up. It couldn't have been bijou; the car was too nice. Sighing, he readied himself to meet with whoever was going to pop out of that car and either tell them to fuck off or kill them, depending on who it was.

"You wouldn't have come if I told you I wanted to meet up," Damon said as he got out of the car and shut the door.

Chess was about to catch a murder charge.

"What are you doing here? You proved your fucking point; you can go back home now," Chess said, walking past Damon and to his door. Damon followed, pushing a hand through his hair.

The look on his face was different from the calm and collected Damon or the detached and cruel Damon that Chess knew. This was a worried and hurried Damon, a side of him he rarely ever saw. Usually, Damon was on top of everything, always in control of his environment, but something else was at play here that worried him. Chess stopped at the door, his hand on the door handle, and turned to Damon. They were no more than mere feet away from each other, and if Damon tried hard enough, Chess was pretty sure that Damon could feel the pure hate emanating from his body like a waterfall.

"I know it seems like a stupid contest to you, but this is bigger than that," Damon started.

"If you're going to bring up my dad, then save it. I don't want to hear it," Chess fired back.

"My dad isn't the reason your dad is dead!"

Chess stopped, his gaze to his door as he had turned around to leave Damon in the dust right then and there. Lucas Kennedy, Damon's father, World Runner Champion, and the complete bane of Rhett Harlow's existence. They used to be best friends, but the competition got to them both. In the end, though, only one truly came out on top, and now Chess was suffering for it every day. There wasn't anyone else. No one else he knew that got in the way.

He let go of the door handle and slowly turned to Damon. The hard look on his face was back along with Damon's. They were just staring at each other, almost looking for answers in each other's eyes, but none came. Everything that Chess knew was being contradicted to his own face at his own house. He should've clocked Damon for it alone, but he stood his ground. Almost getting arrested at the venue was enough real-world excitement for one day, and he didn't want to go in for an assault charge.

"What?" was all Chess could say.

"My dad and your dad were the best of friends, but my dad wasn't the reason your dad killed himself. The answer lies in the World Royale, but I can't do it without you," Damon said.

He held his hand out to shake, and Chess just looked at it, then back to Damon's face. He was out of his mind. Damon, however, took another step forward to try and solidify it. He wanted him on just as badly as Farren but for a different purpose.

"I'm looking for the answers too, but I need you. I won't do it without you," Damon said.

"If I do this and you lose, I never want to see you again. Do you understand me?" Chess said.

It was almost like Damon couldn't help himself when he asked, "What if I win?" A smirk on his face the whole time.

Chess wanted to kill him so badly but instead took Damon's hand in his and squeezed. Damon squeezed back with an equal amount of vigor.

"Then you'll never see *me* again either."

"Is that a threat?" Damon asked, almost in a whisper. He knew what Chess meant.

"A promise."

CHAPTER SIXTEEN

"So he'll do it?"

Levi was standing around with Farren as he held his phone to his ear. Damon was on the other end of the line. It was obvious that Levi was on his toes, nervous about the whole thing. He was with Farren on the team building. While it was off-season, he made his living and pleasure with betting on Royales, but now it was the big time. The World Royale was coming, and he had to get serious. In order to do that, he needed both Damon *and* Chess. He knew they would carry them through to the end game onto Point Nemo Final Royale, but he needed them, to begin with.

It was sounding promising on the other end of the phone, and Farren stood and waited with her arms crossed, watching Levi as he just stood there. Damon was saying words, Farren could hear it, and she rapped her fingers over her arm a couple of times in impatience. Levi looked up into her hair-covered eyes and then back down to the floor, saying affirmations and quips here and there as he tried to wrap up the call.

"Okay, Okay, got it. We'll talk soon. Bye."

Levi hung up the call, and while pocketing his phone, Farren stepped forward, her heels clicking on the floor loudly.

"Well?" she started. "Are they joining or not? We don't stand a chance without those boys. No offense." Farren looked over at Bijou, who shrugged her shoulders and shook her head.

"I'm sure you're good too, but those two are going to make a significant dent in the tourneys, and I want to beat the rest to the punch for once," Farren finished.

"It has been a while since the USA had made headway in the World Royale. Ironic, isn't it? We kill in the Olympics, but in Blood Running, we're getting killed," Levi said, putting a hand on his hip.

"I thought we were doing well in the last World Royale I was watching a couple of years back," Bijou said, holding her jacket.

She didn't know what to do with herself, stuck in-between two very important people in the Blood Running scene, and then it was just her standing there. She fiddled with the zipper of the jacket a couple of times, trying to calm herself down as Farren looked her way and then Levi. While Farren didn't say anything, Levi at least huffed a bit of a laugh. It did nothing to calm her down.

"Dear girl, that placement in the last World Royale was nothing more than a joke, and I knew we could've gone all the way if we had tried."

The last bit of the sentence was directed toward Farren, who didn't rise to the bait. Still looking at Bijou, but not really looking at her, just in her direction, Farren looked lost in thought. She didn't say anything for a long time before she huffed her own sigh and turned back to Levi.

"You got this then? We can move forward with training and recruiting?" she asked.

"Leave it to me. I'll make sure the boys show up at the site as requested. Miss Williams here as well," Levi said.

"Good, I have some calls to make, and then we'll be ready to go. More than likely first thing next week." She turned to Bijou. "If that works for you."

"I have managers at my store that can run my business while I'm away, but I'll do my best not to choke it early," Bijou said, smiling.

Farren did not reciprocate the smile, instead turning on her heel and walking back toward the elevators.

"Now would be a good time to get your lives in order because this time next week, we'll be training nonstop. Call who you need to call and get it done. You'll receive an email from me within the day."

Bijou nodded to Farren's words and watched as she got on the elevator, her heels clicking on the metal of the bus. As quick as she came, she was gone just as fast, and now it was only her and Levi left in the pilot house. The rest of the maintenance crew and workers were cleaning up for the next game, resetting stations, and logging data from the previous match. It was a well-oiled machine, and Bijou watched it with a passive eye. In the back of her mind, she was spiraling. She had so many calls to make, schedules to redo, and managers she promised she wouldn't place first to apologize to. She didn't place first, but she *was* picked to play for the USA team, and for that, she still had to say sorry.

She knew it would blow over well, but it was still a lot of work to do. She couldn't help but spiral a bit, but she would get through it. On top of that, she had to call Chess and see how he was doing. Since Damon agreed to play for the USA team, that meant Chess also agreed to it, and she had to know how that went down. If she really wanted to, she could go to his house, but that was a little far out of her comfort zone; plus, if he had just seen Damon, he wasn't going to want to see anyone else. He was more than likely wanting to cool down after that.

"Another busy year ahead of us."

Levi sighed to the side of Bijou, and she turned her attention to him. He was wearing a sleek suit, and his hair was slicked back, but he had a look on his face that was more so of exhaustion than anything else. The wheels were in motion now, and the competition was going to get underway soon. Even Bijou was feeling the crunch, Levi's exhaustion rubbing off on her.

"It's not going to be easy; these World Royales take a lot out of me," Levi finished, pulling his phone out again and thumbing his way through a couple of menus.

"When is the first competition date?" Bijou asked.

"It won't be for another year. We're going to be training and getting our game plans ready for when you go up against the other countries," Levi said, tapping on the screen several times. He put the phone to his ear and moved away from her. "You have time to get your life in order, but training isn't going to be easy. I look forward to seeing you on the field."

Levi gave her a wink and moved away, answering the call he made when the other person on the other end picked up. Bijou was left there with her own thoughts for a couple of moments. She wanted to talk to Chess; she wanted to talk to Damon. She had things she had to do. It was all becoming too overwhelming, too fast.

"HE SAID HE'LL DO IT."

Levi was in the elevator going down to the venue atrium on his way to his car. The valet was likely waiting for him, the engine warm and ready to go. Lucas Kennedy was on the other end of the line, the sound of liquid being poured into a glass sounding on the other end of the line.

"And the other boy?" Lucas asked.

"Harlow?"

"Who else would I be talking about?"

"It's assumed he agreed to the games as well. Damon wouldn't agree to do it unless Chess was going to compete."

"Good."

There was a pause on each end of the phone as the elevator doors opened, and Levi made long strides to the exit, trying to get to his car as quickly as possible. There were ears everywhere; even though this was for the USA team, people from all over the world were watching and waiting for news and information that could be used against them. Levi didn't want to say anything that was going to compromise the team prematurely.

Looking left and right, the phone still in his ear, Levi met the eyes of a couple of people, people that knew him, others that knew of him. He didn't get to where he was by being quiet about his betting and wasn't let out of the limelight for his luck. He was famous, and he knew it; now, he had to switch from the playboy gambler to the reliable side coach at the drop of a hat. The media would be hounding him soon enough, and he had to finish all his loose ends before he could divulge any information freely.

He knew what he was going to say to the cameras; he knew what he was going say to Farren in secret. It was one thing to keep information from her, but nothing got past the champion, and with Lucas Kennedy on the line, he wasn't allowed to keep anything secret from him. Levi knew that at a snap of his fingers, Lucas could end his whole career at the drop of a hat. He was walking on eggshells and didn't like it, but this was what had to happen.

"What happens next?" Levi asked as he exited the venue, keeping his eyes forward. He didn't want to give off any indication that he was talking about anything important but failed miserably.

"Next, we play the game normally. I expect my boy to come out on top in all of this. He's a Kennedy, after all. I expect nothing less from him," Lucas said, his voice syrupy thick over the phone.

"Of course. You know the process best. It would be better to have you along as a member of the staff this year since your son is competing. Makes sense," Levi said.

"Conflict of interest. People would assume and assume right that I would only do it to make my son stronger. I don't care about the rest of the USA team."

That was obvious. As Levi entered his car and switched his phone over to Bluetooth, he buckled in and started to drive away, quickly getting stuck in city traffic. Now within the confines of his own care, he felt he could speak freely and without restriction.

"I know you want your son to prosper in all of this, but that Harlow boy is no pushover either. He's a force to be reckoned with, and by the time the World Royale comes around, he and Damon are going to go head to head," Levi said.

"Did I ask about any of that? I don't care what the Harlows do; that chapter of my life is finished."

Levi swallowed and made a slight turn onto the highway, moving toward his estate. It was going to be a long week of planning ahead of him alongside promoting the growth of Lucas's only son. It wasn't fair to the rest of the team, but he wasn't being paid to be fair. He was being paid to make sure Damon won the World Royale.

"Anything else I need to be aware of?" Lucas asked.

"Not right now, no. Training starts next week, and we're going to be going through the paces of basics by next month. Your son should already know his basics, but I'm telling you with no disrespect, you have to watch out for Chess Harlow. He's not going to go down without a fight."

There was a significant pause over the other end of the line, and for a moment, Levi was wondering if he had actually gotten through to the man on the other end of the call. There was a deep sigh and then the sound of the phone being shifted from one ear to the other.

"I'll be there by next season to pick up the slack. I don't want any hangups, no *distractions*," Lucas said, emphasizing the last word heavily.

He knew of their relationship; it wasn't a secret, and Lucas didn't care. However, now that it was going to affect the World Royale and their family's status as champions, it was beginning to become a problem. A problem that he would stamp out early if he had to.

"Understood. See you then," Levi said and hung up.

It was going to be a long couple of months ahead of them.

CHAPTER SEVENTEEN

"The main objective of Blood Running is what?"

Farren was walking from one end of the bleachers to the other as Bijou, Damon, Chess, and 47 others were sitting and standing by, listening to her. These were their chosen few to lead the USA Blood Running team to victory, or Farren would die trying to get them there. If they could at least make it to the semi-finals, they would've been doing a lot better than they did last World Royale, and even then, she felt like that was a little more than enough to hope for.

"To survive until you win," a student said from the back of the room.

Farren pointed to them and smiled. "Correct. The goal is self-preservation until it's the right time to strike. You can't take care of the opposition if you can't take care of yourself," Farren said.

She walked over to a laptop hooked up to a massive screen and clicked a few buttons. On the screen, a PowerPoint slide came up with graphs, lists, and information about the games they would be attending and playing coming up in the World Royale.. Chess took the time to look over the information before he adverted his attention to Farren, who had moved to the front of the screen and pulled a pointing stick out from her pocket, extending it. She pointed to the first picture that was present at the top of the screen. It was of a desert and vast plains of dead grass and rock.

"Our first game is being held in Nevada in the Mojave Desert. It will be between the USA and Spain."

There was a collective murmur amongst the players, and Chess looked over at Bijou, who was looking over at him. After a couple of seconds, she looked the other way, where Damon was sitting. Chess and Damon made sure to sit on opposite sides of the bleachers for the college gym they were renting out. They made eye contact, and then Chess looked forward, chewing the skin off his bottom lip to keep himself from saying something stupid.

"This match will be a free for all 50 versus 50. You're encouraged to attack the opposition, but friendly fire is also activated. The final 30 from the initial 50 will be passed on to the next game."

The murmur got louder as people looked left and right at one another. They might not see them later after these games, eliminated right off the bat and sent home. At the end of the day, it was going to be only one of them that could make it anyways, and it might not even be an American player.

Chess didn't even bother to look over to Bijou again, knowing that he would be looking into Damon's eyes again for no reason. There was no reason he had to look at him. He agreed to do this, but he wasn't about to be best buds with the man he agreed to do this for.

Farren walked to the other side of the projector screen and pointed at a wall of text, beginning to read from it. It was the rules of the game, the meaning of free for all, and the stipulations every team has to adhere to to ensure a fair game for the World Royale. A player raised their hand, and Farren pointed at them.

"So friendly fire is activated, does that mean we should go for our own players too?"

"There will be one winner or a tie at the end of the match, and the 30 on each side will go on to the next stage. You *can* kill your teammates to make it go faster, but it's not recommended."

Still, the murmur persisted, and Chess could tell that there were going to be some that would prioritize themselves over the whole team. He knew because he was one of those people. He wasn't here for team building and camaraderie but to win or get even. Either one would give him—hopefully—the satisfaction he had been looking for. Something in his gut told him it wouldn't be as he thought it would be. He still felt empty inside, but nevertheless, he was here and had to compete. Win for himself, win for his dad and bring a trophy into an empty home, or get one shot off on Damon Kennedy and quit the whole team once he got what he wanted.

Sure, it was selfish, but no one else had to know his true intentions. Maybe Bijou, and he had a feeling Damon knew what he was truly doing here, but everyone else could be damned. He wasn't here for them, he wasn't here for Farren, and he wasn't here for the United States. Patriotism could choke for all he cared.

"I would like to assume that you would all play fair and nice to your teammates and not kill one another trying to get ahead. This is to test your skill against the next team, and it was completely random how it was picked," Farren said. "You all will be working together in a couple of games from now, and if you last long enough to play them, now would not be the time to make enemies."

People looked at one another, and Chess chanced, looking over again at Bijou to see her reaction. Taking out your own, making enemies. Chess would call it something more of tying up loose ends. He knew he was completely consumed by revenge and couldn't stop it. In a way, it didn't seem fair; this was no way to live a life, but it was the only life Chess had left in him.

What else other than Blood Running did he have to live for? Revenge seemed all that was left to him now.

"What if we already have an arch enemy on the team?" Damon called out in a smug tone.

After he said his piece, he looked over and matched eyes with Chess. They stopped and stared at each other for a couple of seconds, Farren looking between them. After a few moments, Farren sighed and stepped forward, slapping the pointing stick in her hand.

"I don't care what the beef is; I don't care what the history is. We're here for the future of Blood Running, not to settle old debts. Do I make myself clear?"

Chess was still looking at Damon when he settled his jaw and nodded. He brushed a quick hand over his shaved head and looked down at the bleacher floor, his arms on his knees, shaking his head.

"Understood, ma'am," Chess muttered.

"I understand," Damon also said.

Bijou looked over just in time to see Chess look in the opposite direction of them and shaking his head, muttering expletives under his breath. He was pissed and really wasn't afraid to show it. The future of Blood Running could fuck off for all he cared. He wasn't here for that, and if he could get a lucky shot off on Damon, he was going to take it.

"Okay, now for the drills. We have a year until this first match. We're going to be traveling, staying, and training at the Temporal Arena in Missouri," Farren announced.

There was a buzz with the players and an excited buzz at that. First off, it was going to be a full year of training, no breaks, and they were more than likely going to stay in a dorm again while this was going on. Seconds the Temporal Arena is one of the largest contained Temporal Spaces ever manufactured by man. A good ten miles wide and in an oblong shape, the Temporal Arena was perfect for contained matches, competitive Blood Running, and practice. On the off seasons, it makes a killing in sales from casuals looking to play a couple of rounds. It was like Santa Catalina, but they didn't have to drop in by plane. A massive trolly spanning the entire arena took players up and dropped them off, leaving the player to pop their parachutes in time.

Chess felt excited, but he was also feeling a pang of anxiety. He had never seen the Temporal Arena in Missouri and hadn't competed in any other Temporal Space other than Santa Catalina. In one way, this was going to be good practice; on the other, he had no advantages in the way of vantage points or hiding spots. He was going to be as naked as the rest of the group.

"Traveling? We're going to be staying there?" a person asked.

"Yes. The Winterstay Lodge that is right next to the venue, like five steps away, is hosting us for the year. Your rooms are all paid for, and as long as no one throws their TV out the window, we should be fine to stay there for as long as our training takes. When the World Royale starts, we'll be on the road, and those eliminated go home."

Everyone understood this. Then someone else raised a hand.

"Will we be bunking with people, or do we all get our own rooms?"

"You will be in groups of four to a room. I hope that is acceptable. The rooms are very nice with a kitchenette, microwave, one burner stove, and small fridge. There are flat-screen smart TVs in every room, and we'll be in the heart of truck stop America, meaning you'll have access to all the Uber Eats you want or can walk to fast food.

"While you're in the team up until either you are eliminated or win, you will be given a per diem allowance every day. A sum of $30 for food and necessities. If you spend it all, you have to wait until the next day to get paid again. This comes out of people's taxes, so don't waste it."

"Thirty bucks isn't even enough for one Uber Eats run these days," someone complained.

"Not if you get the Eats Pass," someone else said.

"Who had money for that?!"

"Enough."

Farren again walked to the middle of the floor and collapsed the pointer stick, pocketing it.

"You were all chosen for your skill, wisdom, and tenacity. You are the best of the best. I'm hoping to shape you into something better by the time the World Royale comes around. You're going to train, and you're going to hate it. You're going to hate me, but I don't care. I want to bring home that trophy, and I know you all do as well."

Farren looked into the determined eyes of the players before her, men and women and non-binary people who wanted nothing more than to win and bring home the glory to the United States once and for all. When she looked over to Chess for nothing more than a split second, she noticed he wasn't looking at her; his gaze was still toward a door on the other side of the gym. Looking at Damon, he was looking at Chess. When Damon and Farren's eyes met, Damon huffed a sigh and then looked away.

"This is going be a long year." Farren huffed. "Let's try to keep it cordial and make some friends while the year is good. You never know; anything can happen."

Farren said it mostly for the boys avoiding her gaze, but the other players nodded along with her words and then started to converse with each other. People meeting up and shaking hands, promising to bunk with one another. When someone asked if it was co-ed, Farren said yes, and girls started pairing up with boys. Bijou watched it all happen, hoping someone didn't get pregnant in the middle of training, but with 4 people to a room, it would be pretty awkward to do it with two other people listening and watching.

Nevertheless, she got up from her seat and moved over to Chess. Taking him by the arm, Chess got up and shot her a look before he realized she was taking him over to Damon. He tugged and tried to pull away, but Bijou's grip was airtight. Damon sat in his seat, elbows on knees and fingers intertwined as he watched Chess and Bijou pull up to him. Chess looked away, hands in his coat pockets and shuffling where he stood.

"Bunk with us," Bijou said to Damon.

"Yeah, sure. I don't see how that's not going to get me murdered in the middle of the night by mister tall, dark, and revenge drunk over there," Damon said, motioning to Chess.

"Cut the shit, Damon. I'm not going to touch you in the outside world. You think I want to go to jail over you?" Chess fired back. He hated seeing the smirk on Damon's face, looking away again after he said his piece.

"It's four to a room, though; who's going to be our fourth?" Damon asked.

"Me."

Farren walked up and put her hands on her hips. All three looked at her, mostly surprised, but that emotion died out quickly.

"I guess the captain needs a place to bunk too. What, you don't get your own headquarters room to yourself?" Chess asked.

"Believe it or not, I'm under the same stipulations you all are. Same per diem and same lodging. I know under my supervision, there won't be any discord"—Farren looked over at Damon—"or fights."

Damon looked away, putting his hands up in mock surrender.

"Don't look at me; I'm nothing but cordial," Damon said, smiling

"Yeah, right," Chess said, sniffling.

He could still feel the nosebleed Damon gave him not a day ago. Could still taste the blood on his tongue. He peered over at Damon, who was looking at him. While they stared at each other, only one thing was going through both of their minds.

It was time to get even.

CHAPTER EIGHTEEN

The plane and bus ride to Missouri was a smooth trek. Everyone moved in a single file line and acted like adults about the whole thing. All in all, it only took a day to get to where they needed to go.

The Temporal Arena was located in Kansas City near the major metropolitan area. There was no shortage of restraints and even convenience stores where the team could load up on food or supplies. Needless to say, when Chess and the rest of the group got into the elevator to go to their assigned room, he looked out at the city at night, taking in the fact that he wasn't in California anymore. Out of the frying pan and into the fire.

"The cell reception here sucks," Bijou said, trying to compose a text message. "Managing my business all the way out here is going to test my patience."

"I thought you said you had managers that could take care of your business while you were away?" Farren asked, putting a hand on her hip.

"Well, I do. It's just I like to know what's going on with stuff," Bijou said.

"Are you a Virgo?"

Instead of giving Farren a confused look, she gave her a knowing one. An almost annoyed one. She might be her coach, but at the end of the day, they were just two people trying to make out here in this rat race called life.

"I'm a Capricorn, thank you, and I'm not a workaholic before you go off on that. I just like to stay on top of things," Bijou said, finishing her text.

"If you say so."

The elevator stopped right after Farren said her piece, and they all got out. Their room was at the end of the hall, and Chess couldn't wait to put his bags down. He only brought what he needed, a duffle bag with a week's worth of clothes, a toothbrush, extra pair of shoes, and his wallet. It was a far cry from the bags upon bags Bijou and Damon took with them to bunk with. More or less, there were things from home they wanted to keep, like laptops and tablets, books, and stuff like that. Chess didn't need all of that; he had his phone if he really wanted to read or look something up. He just hoped he didn't forget his charger; he'd hate to have to bum off Bijou.

"Alright, room 440, this is us. Get in and pick a bed; they're all twin size, four to a room, so don't fight over them. I'm going to put my stuff down and head to the lobby to do some work." Farren turned to Bijou and shook her own phone with a smile on her face. "You're right, the service here sucks, but it's best in the lobby if you want to get some work done with me?"

Bijou smiled and heaved her bags onto the bed nearest the window on the left side. She pulled out her MacBook and its charger before smiling at the boys. She knew this was not going to end well, but she had business to take care of first. She could only hope and pray they didn't get into a knock-down, drag-out fight while she was away with Farren.

"Going to do some work. You guys can have the room until we get back for dinner," Bijou said, moving to the door.

"And what are we supposed to do?" Damon asked, his accent thick on his tongue. He looked over to Chess, who looked at him back and then back to Bijou.

They could all feel it, the tension in the air. Bijou didn't want to leave them, but she had calls to make and people to talk to. Text to compose and emails to sign off on. She didn't have time to babysit two boys that may or may not kill each other when they were left alone.

"You two are grown, men. I'm sure you'll figure it out," Farren said, answering for Bijou.

As quick as they had come into the room, they left just as quickly, laptops in arms, and toward the front lobby. It was a nice lobby, with meeting tables and soft chairs; one could get a lot of work done in an environment like that. Chess figured she would take all night getting back up to the room and only to sleep. She wouldn't be back until midnight at the earliest.

The door shut, and the silence that followed was deafening. As if waiting for its cue, the room AC unit turned on, and Chess could feel a slight breeze hit the back of his legs. He shed his jacket, wearing nothing more than a white t-shirt and jeans, and dropped his duffle bag on the bed.

"That's all you brought with you?" Damon asked.

"Damon, don't talk to me. Not right now; I don't what to get into it with you right now." Chess complained and sat on the bed, his back toward Damon.

"I'm not even fighting with you; I just asked a question," Damon retorted.

"Yeah, and I was going to answer like a dumb fuck, and you were going to snap back with some smart jackass thing to say like you always do. I'm not falling for it."

Chess looked over just a little bit to say his piece and then looked out the window. They had a pretty privileged view of the buildings, skyscrapers, and lit-up roads from car taillights on the highway. It was almost like TV, and Chess could feel himself spacing out. Looking over to the TV in the room, Chess was happy to see the remote right next to it but thought about having to log into his youtube account once he had it turned on. There were games he wanted to watch and music he wanted to listen to.

He had ways to kill time in here without letting Damon get to him, but for now, he took out his Bluetooth earphones and connected them to his phone, laying back on his bed and kicking his shoes off. He would listen to music until he passed out or until Damon stabbed him in his sleep, whichever one came first. With the way things were going, he would almost welcome death. It would be better than being stuck in the same room as his ex.

After a couple of minutes, Chess opened his eyes to see what Damon was doing, if he decided to leave the room as well or still staring at him. Damon's back was to Chess, who had turned the TV on. He was flipping through the channels that the hotel cable came with and not finding anything good, deciding to stop the channel on some trashy 'you are the father' type show.

While he couldn't hear it over his own music, Chess found himself watching the TV just to see people moving and talking. He couldn't hear their words but could see their mouths move, which was enough for him. The reality of living people is that he wasn't alone in his hotel room. When he got into bouts of spacing out like this, it was easy for him to convince himself that he was the only one left on Earth, that other people were a thing of the past. Only when he was killing them in Temporal Spaces was he cured of those thoughts, only to gain them right back once he went back home.

It felt like a curse. He didn't watch TV or listen to music. He just stared at a wall as if he were going into sleep mode and only activated when the next Royale was to happen. That was no way to live, and he knew it, but he didn't know what else to do with himself. This was the first time in a long time that he had to share his space with other people, and it was his fucking ex-boyfriend, of all people. He could've handled anyone else, but if he just kept his mouth shut and focused on his music, he would get through the night.

But this was going to go on for a whole year.

Chess signed through his nose and closed his eyes again, trying to slink back into his music. The vocals and guitars weren't doing it for him. He was too distracted by... everything. Getting up from the bed and throwing his earbuds back in his bag, he pocketed his phone and took one of the cards that let them back in the room, pocketing it as well. Damon looked over to see Chess packing up to go somewhere and cocked an eyebrow.

"Going somewhere?"

"Don't worry about it."

It was a quick back and forth, and Chess was already heading for the door.

"Getting something to eat?!" Damon hollered after Chess, but the door was already shut in his face.

Chess made his way to the elevator cars and briskly sauntered out of the lobby, catching a look from Bijou as he walked past her. She looked disappointed as if she knew this was going to happen but didn't wish to see it. They didn't fight, but she didn't know that. For all she knew, they could've gotten into a screaming match, and he stormed out. While that wasn't the case, Chess wasn't sticking around to clear up the details.

It was pitch black outside as he stepped onto the sidewalk and presidio of the hotel they were staying in. After a whole year of that same room, he thought he would go insane. Even then, he was stuck in a huge house with rooms he hadn't been in in years staring at the same walls for years on end as well. It was change, but that didn't mean he had to like it.

Stuffing his hands in his pockets, still only wearing a t-shirt and jeans, he picked up the pace toward a fast food chain to get something in his stomach. A chicken sandwich maybe and some fries. The thought of soda hitting the back of his gullet made his skin prickle. How long has it been since he had a meal like this like at all? He had been living off of cup noodles and spaghetti this whole time. This was going to be his first fast food venture in years.

He had to chalk much of it up to the fact that he just didn't have the money. Always owing somebody something, Miller waiting for his cut. He could only imagine the look on Miller's face now, knowing he was all the way over here training for the World Royale. He would say something along the lines of 'I knew you could do it' or 'avenge your father'.

He had no desire to do so. What happened happened. Was he a little fucked up from it, more than likely. However, whatever was going on with his dad, he didn't know. He didn't know the half of it, and when he took his own life, leaving him technically an orphan at the age of 18, Chess wondered for years what was it about Blood Running that was so damn serious. What was it that Lucas Kennedy said that tipped him over the edge? What was it all about that made him be in the middle of all of it?

"Fuck it."

Chess walked into the fast food restaurant, ordered his chicken sandwich, French fries, and soda, paid with his per diem allowance, and sat his happy ass down in the back of the place. Right next to some gaudy artwork and a poster asking for hires. Maybe to get out of the hotel room, he would take up a job here when he wasn't training. He knew Farren wouldn't allow it, but even out of the room, he was going crazy just thinking about being back inside it.

He ate in silence. There was no one else in the restaurant except the workers and himself. The soft 80's playlist that was playing through the speakers set the vibe of Chess floating through time as if anything he had ever done and everything he had ever felt had not been real.

CHAPTER NINETEEN

"Pick up the pace! You're going to be running long distances, and there's not always gonna be a car to bail you out!"

Farren was working the crew of 50 to the bone. While the main Temporal Arena could be used for training, they opted for the nearby gym and pool to do their training. The city that the Temporal Storm had engulfed was leveled and turned into a rural utopia with a lake and sparse neighborhoods. The managers of the area didn't want skyscrapers people could camp in or get stuck in, so the rest of the buildings were transformed into simple houses and buildings, like schools and police stations. Of course, no one worked there, and no one lived there; it was all for show.

Now, they were at the local gym and pool, working their asses off to train for the upcoming spar that was less than a year away now. It had been a couple of months since they all had been staying at the hotel, and no one had bowed out yet. All 50 had stayed and trained for the shot at the top. Some for America, some for themselves. Others for other reasons. As Chess jogged on the track in the inside field, he cleared his mind of all other stressors. Running on the field and the track affected his mind, calming and focused.

They were all wearing the same style of tracksuit, a red and white with blue accents outfit made just for the team by some big company. Adidas or Nike, Chess didn't really know or care. It was soft, though, and breathable. The only thing he worried about was if he was going to be forced to wear it during the games. They weren't exactly stealthy, with the blinding white material and red accents jumping out to the eyes. Chess held the hope in the back of his mind that they would be able to pick their outfits for the Royale and not have to wear the tracksuit.

"Hustle! Two more laps and then break time! Come on; you can do it!"

Farren was clapping her hands and urging the rest of the team members to push it to the limit before the bell sounded. Levi was standing right next to her, looking rather out of place and weird in his own tracksuit. It was weird to see him without a suit on; that's what most of them were used to seeing him in. Now, he wore the same thing everyone else was wearing and cheering on the rest of the team as well.

"Just a few more laps to go! Come on, team; we can do it!" Levi hollered.

You're not the one running, old man. Chess thought to himself.

As Chess pushed himself to finish the rest of the laps, Bijou came up to his side and jogged alongside him. Chess looked over at her and spared a smirk, slowing down a little bit to jog with her.

"Training again, huh?" Bijou huffed.

"It's been a while since we hit the arena. Maybe we'll get another go at it next week," Chess said.

"You almost had Damon that last time, but he got blindsided. I think he's still mad about it," Bijou said, trying not to laugh.

The last time they were all training in the Temporal Arena, Chess was on a blood hunt for Damon the entire time, even opting to drop when he did to get a head start on his location. However, an hour into the game, Damon was shot and eliminated by a lucky shot someone got off on him. It was a complete blindside, and the 'other' side of Damon came out on that player when the match was over. It was the final ten players, and he finished 8th.

Chess was almost impressed when he watched Damon lose his mind to the player that blindsided him. Talking about the ethics and good sportsmanship of not camping a spot to get a shot off. When the player argued that he would do anything to bring home the gold, Damon looked like he would rip his head off his shoulders. Needless to say, those two don't really talk or see eye to eye, just like he and Chess.

"Yeah, well, he can get over it. Everything's fair in Blood Running when you have a gun," Chess said, making a turn on the track. Only a couple more feet to go.

The sound of feet coming up behind them made Chess groan. He knew who it was; he had been passing him, this making it twice now on the track. Damon rounded around Chess, pumping his arms and breathing through his mouth as he focused on the end goal. Chess rolled his eyes and kept his pace with Bijou.

"He's serious." Bijou half laughed.

"He can be whatever he wants as long as he stays out of my way," Chess said.

"It's been months; you guys haven't found common ground to settle on yet? What about the games we play and stuff in the room? Nothing?" Bijou inquired.

"You forced us to play those," Chess said.

This earned him a hearty elbow in the ribs, and he laughed. It was rare to see Chess laugh about anything, but it was easy with Bijou. She was easy to bully, and Chess was comfortable with her. She was one of his only true best friends.

"Really? Jenga? Ludo? Nothing helped?" Bijou asked, half whining.

"I think Ludo made me hate him more if we're being totally honest," Chess said.

"Yeah, that was a bad choice of a game, but I love it. I think you loved it too," Bijou said.

They rounded the corner and made their way to the home stretch. Damon was up ahead, already finished, placing his hands on his knees, huffing air into his lungs. Other players congregated around him, catching their breath and taking a short break. Chess and Bijou weren't the last people to finish, but by the time they crossed the finish line, they weren't in as bad shape as Damon and the others were.

"The trick is the jog at a steady pace, not gung-ho it until your heart gives out, Damon!" Bijou said, catching her breath and patting Damon on the back.

Damon coughed a couple of times and then stood back up to full height. His hair was sticking to his forehead, and he wasn't wearing a sweatband today. His parted bangs clumped together with sweat, and he flashed Bijou a smile, his canine extra sharp in the sunlight. Chess looked away.

"Nothing wrong with giving it my all." Damon sniffled, rubbing his arm over his nose and shaking his limbs free of tension.

"Nothing wrong with it, but"—Farren walked up and tapped Damon on the head with her clipboard softly to get his attention—"you blow all your steam in the mid-game and don't have enough energy to run the rest of the way, you're going to be fucked. Especially in the third game."

"First game is with Spain; who are we going up against in the third game?" Bijou asked.

"I don't know yet. The first and second finalists still have to be decided, and then we're off to Serbia," Farren said, crossing her arms.

"The Great Royale. The Serbian Storm," Damon said mostly to himself.

It was the largest Temporal Storm in the world, spanning miles and miles of land, and the storm took a whole week to finish resetting everything. It was going to be a test of endurance and will, to brave the cold and wilderness, the vast nothingness and snow to get to the middle or wherever the storm decided to end. Sometimes it wasn't in the middle, it was in the east or west of the storm, but it was usually always the middle zone. If he were to play it smart, Chess would drop on the outskirts of the map and pick up all the rare guns and ammo that would go forgotten by those that would drop in somewhere more near the middle.

"What's the plan for that? Trios?" Damon asked, still trying to get air into his lungs.

"You'll have to find out when I do. We don't know yet. Let's get through the first game and then worry about the rest of the matches," Farren said.

"Good hustle out there, team!" Levi said, walking up to the group and patting Bijou on the back.

Bijou looked from Levi to Chess with a confused look before she crossed her arms and placated the situation. It was awkward, but she allowed it to happen. After all, it must've been exciting for him to be a part of the World Royale at his age, even as just an advisor.

"Next is swimming. We'll get changed for that soon. Get up to the building when you're ready," Farren said, patting Levi on the shoulder several times and making him come with her.

"Swimming. Bane of my existence." Chess huffed, popping his back of any cricks.

"On top of the lake in the arena, where else are we going to be swimming? You're not going to catch my happy ass in any ponds in Serbia," Damon said, crossing his arms.

"I think it's for another game. More than likely the second game. That, and—" Bijou started.

"And the Final Royale is at Point Nemo. In the middle of the ocean," Chess finished.

"Exactly," Bijou said.

"How are we supposed to fight in the middle of the ocean?" Damon asked.

"An artificial island was built at Point Nemo years ago, no bigger than the arena here in Kansas City, but it's filled with water and not many places to hide. We're going to be swimming more than we're going to be running," Chess said, not looking Damon in the eye as he answered.

"The training is going to pay off in due time. We just have to do it," Bijou said.

She had been sitting on the ground, catching her breath for the past couple of minutes but got up off the floor and dusted herself off, making her way to the stairs. "See you guys in there then."

Chess nodded toward her and finished stretching his arms to try and release the tension wound up in there. He expected Damon to walk off as well, making his way to the pool, but he stayed. Both of them silently stretching amongst other players and ignoring each other.

"What are you thinking about or dinner?" Damon said in a careful tone.

"Don't know, don't care," Chess answered dismissively.

"Because I was thinking we could all go out tonight, you know, pool our money together and get something nice other than fried chicken for the fifth night in a row," Damon offered.

Chess thought about it for a moment and looked up to the sky. As much as he was never going to admit it, Damon was right. All this training and they were ruining it by eating fried foods and junk. There was more than enough in their per diem a day to eat healthy if they wanted to, but who could say no to fried chicken? Chess couldn't. The second the gang says bucket, he comes running, and he hated it.

"Why did you have in mind?" Chess asked, still not looking in Damon's direction.

"I don't know, something big. The year is almost over; we've got a couple of months of training left before the match with Spain. I wanted to treat everyone to a meal."

"It's not really treating everyone if we're pooling our money together," Chess said, finally looking in Damon's direction.

He wish he hadn't.

Damon was giving Chess his signature smile, more of a smirk than anything, and his sweaty face and arms in his tank top were proudly showing as he had tied his track jacket around his waist. Chess looked down at it and scoffed.

"What is this, the 90s?" Chess said, pointing to the jacket.

Damon looked down and then back up at Chess with the same smile. It was the first time they smiled at each other in a long time, and when Chess realized it, he turned away from Damon, his smile falling back to a scowl.

"If you want to go somewhere tonight, I won't stop you. I'll pool my money for it," Chess said.

"Sweet! You won't regret it!"

Damon slapped Chess on the back with a flat palm and booked it to the stairs before Chess could retort. Chess watched him go, climbing the stairs two at a time as he caught up with Bijou. They were more than likely talking about the dinner date he had cooked up in his head, and Bijou was enthusiastically agreeing to whatever he was saying.

Looked like tonight was going to be a date.

CHAPTER TWENTY

Farren decided to stay behind as the three pooled their money together to get an Uber to a hibachi restaurant. Something simple, but it was different from the fried chicken and french fries they had been eating for the past months. The fact that they were able to keep the weight off was a miracle in itself, but tonight was for something different.

Damon sat up front while Chess and Bijou sat in the back, watching the city pass them by on the way to the restaurant. Chess wasn't going to go unless Damon told them beforehand where they were going and when Damon said hibachi, Chess couldn't say no. Food was a big weakness to him, and he would overcome even the worst of situations if he got a meal out of it. So, even though he didn't want to be going out with Damon like this in the middle of the night, he agreed to go to hibachi.

"Might be a while before we can all do this again," Bijou said as the car was eerily quiet.

Damon must've clicked the 'no talking' option for the ride, knowing no one but Bijou was going to want to say anything. Damon smiled and looked over, however, humoring her.

"Which is why I wanted to treat you all."

"Again, it's not treating if we're *all* paying for it," Chess said.

"It's the thought that counts. You would've been eating the same cup of noodles or fried chicken tonight if I didn't offer this up. Right?" Damon asked, his eyes toward Chess.

Chess didn't say anything; he simply sighed through his nose and looked out the window. The man driving the car looked in the rearview mirror at Chess and then at Damon. He could feel the tension in the air and moved to turn up the radio, trying to drown out the fighting that might come. Damon sat back in his seat and looked at the driver, and the driver was doing a good job avoiding his eyesight. It wasn't like he was scared of the man, but this drive needed to be over as soon as possible.

"After we eat, then what? Back to the lodge and pass out? Because that's what I want to do," Chess said.

"I was thinking we could all play Ludo again and settle the score once and for all," Bijou said, rubbing her hands together with a mock smile.

Chess simply rolled his eyes and groaned while Damon equally complained from the front seat.

"Bijou, no. We almost threw the damn game board out the window last time," Damon said.

"Jenga then. Checkers, Chess, something. The year is almost over, and I have to go back to work after all of this. I won't be able to take time off." Bijou looked toward Damon, who had his eyes forward toward the windshield. "And you're going back to the UK; who knows when we'll ever see *you* again."

"God willing," Chess added.

"Yeah, yeah, okay. I get it; you want memories. I'll give you memories," Damon said, turning back to look at Bijou.

Bijou didn't say anything. The look on Damon's face was hard to read. Was he mad or agitated? Perhaps this was just him playing again, and Bijou just hadn't caught on yet. Damon was so hard to read sometimes outside of his smile, and even then, that was a hit or miss that it actually meant he was happy. Before Bijou could get another word out, Damon looked over to Chess, who was looking at him, then he turned back around in his seat and sat down.

"You want memories. I can come up with memories," Damon said under his breath.

"You lot with the Blood Running team?" the driver asked, trying to break the tension.

"Yeah, we're going to compete in a couple of months," Bijou answered, not reading the room.

"That's interesting. Good luck to y'all. I'll be watching on the TV back home. I'll root for ya."

Bijou nodded, and the boys didn't say anything. Eventually, the car turned into the hibachi restaurant parking lot and stopped. Damon was the first to get out, taking his phone out and adding a tip. He knew better than to be causing a scene in someone else's car, so he tipped extra. When Chess and Bijou came around from the other side of the car, Bijou waved goodbye to the driver, and they walked inside.

Damon had set up a reservation ahead of time. Within moments, they were seated with another party, Damon, and Bijou sitting on one side of the table and Chess taking the empty chair on the other side. The chef preparing their food started to chop vegetables and add oil to the grilling pan. Stacking onions and flipping meat and shrimp around while Bijou and Damon talked. So much for a perfect night out, he didn't even get to talk with his one friend.

Taking his phone out, Chess decided to take a few photos of the hibachi to make a memory. He would text them to Bijou later to put in an album or something. He snapped a couple of photos before the flame on the hibachi grill lit up into a large flame, the light around them dimming and the show taking over at the forefront. Chess even looked up from his phone to watch the fire swirl in the air as the chef added more il and flipped the vegetables. He looked forward and saw that Damon was looking right at him. They stared at each other for a good couple of moments before Damon looked away, smiling at Bijou and engaging in conversation.

Chess thought nothing of it before he reviewed his photos. In every single one, Damon was looking right into the camera. Not his eyes forward as if he were looking at Chess; he was looking into the camera, into Chess's eyes through the photo. Chess whipped his head up again, a scowl on his face before he noticed that Damon, once again, was looking at him. With a chopstick, he popped a shrimp into his mouth and chewed, looking Chess in the eyes the entire time.

FARREN AND BIJOU WERE ALREADY ASLEEP. DAMON HAD PUT his headphones in and laid down, but the light of his phone was still alight. He was awake, but Chess was minding his own business. The hibachi grill date was over; it was a memory now. Damon promised a memory, and, well, he made one. Chess wasn't going to forget the look in Damon's eyes in those photos, even after he deleted them. He couldn't send those to Bijou. It felt too... intimate.

Sighing and getting up out of bed, Chess quietly walked from his bed to the door, grabbing his wallet from the key bowl. He just wanted a soda, something to calm his nerves down before he went to bed for good. The sight of Damon's eyes boring back at him like that was giving him the shivers, and not in a good way. It almost felt foreboding, as if he knew what was about to come. What was in store for them?

Cold revenge? The need to get even? The past coming back to haunt them? Chess wanted to end it. He didn't want to feel this way all the time; he didn't want to feel hate like this anymore, but he couldn't help it. He couldn't help but feel this way, this cold, callous feeling of revenge he had to enact. For what? His own pride? It felt a little shallow to admit that he wasn't doing it for anyone other than himself.

Chess didn't look back as he exited the room and walked down the carpeted hallway toward the elevators. He exited from the first floor out a back door that led to a patio with vending machines and helped himself to a soda. It was highway robbery, the prices for it, but he needed it. If he was going to get any sleep after tonight, he needed it.

He sat in the dark, looking up to the night sky. Thanks to the skyscrapers and the general city light, there were barely any stars to be seen in the sky except for Venus and the North Star. It was calming, the sounds of crickets and the distant noise of cars and trucks in the background accompanying him. He was left alone with his thoughts, not bothering to bring his phone with him. Sipping on the soda, he didn't bother to keep an eye on the door either. It was just him and time to kill until he decided to go back inside to go to sleep.

When the sound of a door opening behind him pulled him from his thoughts, he didn't even bother to look over to see who it was. He shut his eyes and calmly breathed through his nose, focusing on being calm. He couldn't start yelling in the middle of the night; he had to be calm. With his eyes still closed, Chess listened to the sounds of someone dispensing a dollar bill into the vending machine, making a choice, and then taking their prize out of the bottom of the dispenser. When Chess opened his eyes, he was surprised to see not Damon but a random player he had been training with grab a water and gulp it down. They made eye contact, and Chess just stared at him for a few moments before the man pointed at his soda.

"Those can't be good for you this late at night," he said.

Chess looked down at his soda and then to the ground. He downed the rest of it and pitched it in the trash can.

"You get to bed too." Chess pointed and walked toward the door.

Using the hotel key card, he let himself back in and walked back to the elevator. It was going to be a long ride up; it was a good twenty-second ride with nothing but him, the quiet, and his thoughts again. When the car door opened up, Damon was standing inside.

Too shocked to react, Chess was forcefully pulled by the collar and pulled into the elevator car by Damon. Quickly pressing the button for the highest floor—an easy thirty seconds, but that's all he would need—the car doors shut behind them.

"What the fuck?!" Chess hollered out, but he was blindsided by Damon grabbing him by the collar again and slamming him up against the car wall.

"What about you? Want to make some memories? All year you've been avoiding me, and the year's almost over." Damon slammed him against the car wall again, ignoring Chess's tight hands on his forearms, pushing him away.

"Year's almost over, and it's gonna be you against me, and I don't really think you want that." Damon seethed. There were no more smiles, no more grinning. The cold stare of his dead eyes was drilling into Chess.

"I want that!" Chess gritted back between his teeth. "I want it for me!"

"It's ALWAYS about you."

Damon slammed him against the car door, shaking the elevator before dropping Chess's shirt. Chess backed away but not by much; they were, needless to say, face to face in a stuffy car filled with their breath and sweat. The elevator climbed higher; the floor was almost here.

"It's always about you," Damon repeated. "Always been about you. Just wish you'd see me in there too without having to go through yourself first."

"What?"

The elevator chimed, and the doors opened. Neither of them got off, and without looking, Damon clicked the correct button for their floor. After a couple of awkward seconds, the doors closed again, and Damon made his move. The car was lowering, and Chess stood his ground, ready to fight back. Damon took three long steps forward and stopped right in front of Chess's face. Their breath mingled, both of them breathing out of their mouths. Chess could taste him just from this, their chests bumping just barely. Chess's fists balled and tightened, and he finally closed his mouth and swallowed, looking away.

"It's always been about you. I don't think you ever asked me how I felt about it. You work about yourself."

The car door opened.

"Let's see how far that will get you in the games. Good night."

Damon stepped out but held the door open for Chess to follow. When they were both on carpet, Chess watched Damon walk back down the hallway toward their room and keycard himself in. Chess, on the other hand, walked to the window and slunk down to the floor, not ready to face his demons in the room just yet. With his back to the wall and his arms on his knees, Chess looked at the floor in despair. Then, he licked his lips.

The taste of Damon was still as he remembered it being. Even if it was just a breath.

CHAPTER TWENTY-ONE

The year came and went. There were no more incidents in the elevator anymore or at all for that matter. For as much as Chess ignored and avoided Damon, Damon was starting to do the same. They were making distance between each other, only getting ready for the inevitable disappointment that was revenge to come in the games.

The only good thing to come out of this was that Chess got his wish, kind of. They all wore a uniform for the USA team, but it was a darker, more mutable color. Something he could use to his advantage for sneaking and hiding in darker places. He didn't wear black for the fashion in Blood Running; it had its uses, too, and he was happy to see the darker uniforms. In a sense, they were still the same as the tracksuits, the only color on them being the American Flag on the shoulder.

Chess slipped the jacket over his shoulders and zipped up the zipper to his chin, looking himself in the locker mirror. This was it. The spar with Spain. Only 30 people were going to make it out of this moving forward, and he had to make sure he was one of them. He knew that the Mojave heat was going to kill him with material like this covering his body, but it was better to be hot than get sunburns all over his arms and legs. Behind him, Damon was also getting ready.

It was going to be a shitshow. Too many people have made relationships and enemies in the year of training up to this point. Chess wouldn't be surprised if it weren't just him looking out for themselves and others to gun down on the same team. He turned around a bit to glance at Damon, who was also putting on his jacket. Taking a rubber band, he pulled what little of his hair back into the smallest ponytail imaginable, some of his bangs still falling into his eyes, but not many strands. Just enough to split the iris. He turned and met eyes with Chess.

"You sure?" Damon asked.

"Sure about what?" Chess answered.

"You know what. You're going to hut me down and secure your spot at the top."

"Is that what you think I'm going to do?" Chess asked, crossing his arms.

Damon didn't say anything, his arms at his sides and his eyes cold. Chess snorted and uncrossed his arms, looking away from Damon.

"You don't know shit. Stop talking out of your ass and play the game," Chess said, moving to walk out of the locker room.

The venue at the Mojave Desert in Arizona wasn't massive. A respectable mile wide, one of the shortest storms too, with a playtime of 30 minutes before reset. It was all contained by a mile-wide circle acting as the base, pilot house, and respawn venue. The Spanish team was in the North, while the USA team was getting ready in the South. This was going to be a test of wit, a test of quick thinking, and the ultimate test of time management. Too slow, and the storm will be right on your ass; too fast, and you might get killed early. Chess swallowed, thinking about his route and plan.

The whole team had been given the aerial map of the arena a week before the game was set to begin. Chess, Bijou, and Damon sat up all night, almost studying it and formulating their plans. Bijou was going to go West, while Damon and Chess opted to go North and hide in between some buildings set up there. Chess wasn't afraid to go in guns blazing, but he was a little more muted than Damon was about things. Damon was happy to run straight forward and that the opposition head-on. Good enough for Chess if it got him out of the competition early. Something within him told him otherwise. Damon wasn't going to go down that easily.

Most of the team was going to opt for a flanking position and go around the sides, skirting the storm as it swept through the arena. It was going to be a close shave, which was why Damon and Chess decided to just go forward and find cover. There were going to be a lot of cheap shots and close calls, but Chess wouldn't have it any other way. It was going to be hard; it was going to be fast.

Damon followed Chess out, and they met up with Bijou, who was already on her way to the exit. She smiled at them even though they both looked like they would rather be anywhere else right about now.

"Gangs back together. Again. Didn't think it would work out this way, you know, World Royale and stuff," Bijou said with a half smile on her face.

"Feels like fate we would all cross paths like this again. One big blowout for all time," Damon replied, trying his best to crack a smile.

"Won't be for as long as Academy was, but I'm here. We'll see what you can do," Chess said.

Bijou nodded and walked with them to the venue respawn pods. One by one, they lined up and got scanned and recorded, Levi and Farren standing by watching them to make sure there were no accidents or mishaps. One by one, they each got scanned in and waited in the atrium, ready to run out into the arena. There wasn't any drop ship and no cart system. The arena was so small you just had to run out and book it. If you found a gun first, then you were lucky. The rest might just have to deal with knives or, at worst, their fists.

When they were processed, Chess and Bijou stood by the east door while Damon was standing in the middle door. Ahead of them, they could see the vast desert and Joshua trees littering the land. Some buildings that were erected for the arena stood proudly in the distance. Chess would hit one of them first and try to get any weapon he could get his hands on. A pistol, at least. Anything else would be a bonus.

Chess got ready, lowering his body to get heady to dash out of the door when they opened. When the speakers above him came on and started shaking, he didn't flinch; he just waited.

"Welcome to the first preliminary game to the World Royale! We have a full house today in the Mojave Arena to witness the USA team and the Spain Team battle it out for the chance to compete in the Final Royale! Only 30 people from each team will continue to the next round, and we can't wait to see who will be lucky enough to survive! This is The Mojave Arena Showdown!"

Chess looked to his right; Bijou was swallowing and rocking back and forth on her feet, crouched down like Chess and ready to run. She was nervous, and it was obvious on her face, but this time Chess couldn't protect her. She would have to take all the training she got this past year and apply it. He wished her the best.

Looking to his left, Damon wasn't giving Chess the time of day. Chess didn't dwell on his either, giving him a passing glance and then focusing his attention on the glass doors. They would open any second now, and Chess could hear his heart pounding in his ears.

"Remember. Lateral, quick, shoot first, and run!" Farren called out to the back of the group of 50. "You keep your head about you, and you can keep it on your shoulders! This is it!"

Time stood still for a couple of moments. Chess inhaled and exhaled through his mouth once in a long breath, and then a buzzer sounded above him. Before he even processed what it was, the glass doors opened, and he booked it into the sand. It wasn't like beach sand where it was soft and hard to run on, this was hard dirt and coarse sand packed into the earth. Chess was running at full capacity toward the nearest building in the distance.

Even though it was a whole mile, the land was flat, and, in the distance, he could see the dots of other humans on the other side of the venue coming to him. He kept that in his mind as he slammed into the door of the building he made it to and looked around quickly. Nothing on the first floor. He moved to the second floor, where a sniper rifle and a box of ammo was waiting for him.

"Better than nothing."

Chess picked it up and immediately set up a vantage point in the window facing the North side exit. Through the scope, he saw plenty of people booking it the same way he had been toward the buildings on their side. Chess scoped out the top windows of these faraway buildings and saw the glint of glass in the reflection. Someone was aiming at him.

Chess dived down just in time for a bullet to slam through the room and hit the wall behind him. Luckily, he didn't catch any of the shrapnel from the hollow point bullet as it shattered into a million pieces. Chess quickly got back up and pulled the bolt on the rifle, knowing his assailant was reloading and likely still in the window. Chess was right.

With a well-timed shot, Chess saw the assailant fall to the ground, and he waited a good ten seconds before he realized he wasn't getting back up. A faint purple glow could be seen within the room. He got him.

Backing out of the window and moving to the bottom floor, Chess made his way into the kitchen, which he hadn't checked before he went upstairs, to find an M9 Beretta sitting on the stove. Slinging the rifle on his back, he quickly took the gun and loaded it with the ammo sitting on the table, exiting the house soon after. All around him, people were still running forward and yelling war cries. It was a tense arena, closed off and cramped by Chess's standards. He felt if he were to turn around now, a member of the other team would be right behind him.

However, when he did turn around for a moment, he saw the purple lighting storm already forming and moving its way into the desert sand. The mixture of wind, sand, and clouds made the purple storm look more brown than purple, but the color still remained. It was like one big sandstorm rather than a Temporal Cloud.

Chess wasted no time, booking it from where he was and running to the next house. He already had ammo and weapons; he would be using them for cover now more than anything. Since gunfire could be heard closely, he had to assume members of the Spanish team had already cut through the middle and were meeting the USA team halfway. People were being eliminated; how many so far, he didn't know. All he knew was that there was to be one winner at the end of this match, and the last 30 to stand would go on to the next round. He had to be among those 30.

Chess holstered the gun and drew his rifle back out, peering from the side of the building into the desert before him. There were more buildings and cars strewn about. He saw a couple of heads pop up in the distance, but they moved on too quickly before he could get a shot off. Chess decided his best bet was to get closer, stick to the middle, and not get caught in the storm. With one hand holding the rifle, he unholstered his pistol and broke away from the house, running at full speed down the middle, aiming the gun center mass at anyone that got in his way. If it was his own team members, then so be it.

He got two shots off on a couple of people before he reached the next house, but he didn't stay long. Before the bodies erupted into Temporal Crystals, he noticed one of the patches bore a USA emblem. He had killed one of his own, but other than grimacing at the fact of it, he didn't have time to dwell on it. The storm was coming and was practically on his tail by now. He wasn't moving fast enough. Not as fast as he would've liked to be moving, at least.

He broke away from the next house and made it to an abandoned car with broken doors. Enough cover for a couple of seconds, but what stopped him was Bijou. She had somehow gotten ahold of a submachine gun and was breathing hard and fast, her back to the car as she hid. Chess stopped by her and aimed the rifle over the hood, scanning for anyone else.

"I think..." Bijou started. "I think we're to the last 30 already. I saw so many of our team fall. They're good."

"Not good enough," Chess said and fired. Hit.

"Where's Damon?" Bijou hollered over the noise.

"Do I look like I know? I'm not his keeper! Look, you need to make it to that house if you want to stand any chance! I'm breaking off over here." Chess put a heavy hand on Bijou's shoulder. "Good luck!"

Bijou nodded and then tore from the car. As fast as she could, she ran for the house and hid behind it, gunfire and pullets following her in her wake. She barely missed being shot by millimeters but made it to safety. When Chess watched her dive behind the house, he turned to move to his destination but was stopped by a player from the Spanish team. Chess quickly raised his rifle, but the man kicked him in the chest, making Chess fall flat on his ass. In the distance, Chess could hear Bijou calling his name.

This was it. He was going to die. At least he got a couple of them before he went out, and he hoped he was at least the 30th person to get eliminated. He had to go on; he had to keep fighting.

Despite falling hard on the ground, Chess pulled his M9 from his holster and pointed it upwards before the other player could aim his weapon straight at him. The Spaniard waited for a beat too long as a shot rang out, and he fell to the ground, shattering into purple crystals right in front of Chess's eyes. Looking back, not only was the storm on his ass, but Damon could be seen running toward him with a semi-auto rifle in his hands.

"Get up! Get..." Damon hooked his hands around Chess's arms and pulled him to his feet.

When Chess was back to kneeling, he pushed Damon off of him and looked him in the eye. Damon had dirt and sweat covering his whole body, no doubt having gotten into a tussle with someone else before saving Chess.

"Why?!" Chess hollered out.

"Because I'm not going to let anyone kill you if I can't kill you first! If we can't kill each other first! Seemed like a waste of playtime," Damon hollered back, his eyes forward to the battlefield. When he looked back at Chess, he was surprised not to see a scowl or a grimace. Chess was gobsmacked.

However, that didn't last long as Chess finally snapped out of his stupor and settled his sniper rifle on the hood of the car again, ready to pick off stragglers. Damon and Chess picked off players one by one until they were too close for comfort. Chess ditched the sniper rifle and started aiming the pistol, knowing he would have better luck with it at this point.

Looking around, Chess noticed significantly fewer people on the playing field than before. They must've made it into the next round now, no matter what happened to them. That didn't mean that Chess wasn't going to go down fighting. He rounded Damon and broke away from the car, trying to get to the house Bijou was holing up at. When he reached the door and went inside, he saw a Spanish player standing over a mountain of crystals, popping one into his hand to absorb the mana. Bijou was eliminated.

Thinking quickly, Chess held a hand out, summoned a ball of fire about the size of a large beach ball, and hurled it at the assailant. The player barely dodged it in time, but his suit was burned slightly, showing charred skin. It wouldn't take much now to settle the score.

Chess aimed and fired off a couple of rounds, none of them making their mark, and watched as the player bolted out the front door into the open. Stupidly, Chess followed.

Hurling another fireball in the player's direction, the player dodged it just in time and blindly shot off rounds from his own gun back toward Chess. Feeling the pressure of a bullet in his shoulder, Chess stopped and aimed his gun straight and true, slamming the trigger and hitting the player square in the back of the head. Chess was shot in the process and bleeding out, but he had to get even for Bijou.

Looking over to where the car was, Chess couldn't see Damon anymore. He couldn't see anyone anymore. The desert was devoid of people, and only he and the storm were left. He knew people were hiding in homes, behind cars and trees, but they wouldn't come out now. This was the last stand; wherever Damon was, he was watching and waiting for his time to strike.

When a heavy hand landed on his shoulder, Chess whipped around, aiming his weapon only to see it was Damon standing right behind him. Chess dropped the weapon at his sides and sighed.

"Couple more left? The bell didn't sound for the other team to be eliminated yet," Damon said, looking around.

"Wouldn't know where they were," Chess answered, turning back and looking out to the desert.

"Let's walk. Be careful," Damon said, briskly walking off toward a colony of houses, more than likely hiding the rest of the players.

For all Chess knew, they could've been the final USA members alive on the field. They had to play it smart. Putting a hand on his wounded shoulder, Chess grimaced at the thought of bleeding out and dying before the game was over. What a waste that would've been.

Chess and Damon put their back to a house and made their way inside quickly. They were quiet, not shutting the door behind them and tiptoeing around, trying not to make a sound. Then, the wood above them creaked. Someone was in the house with them.

Damon looked to Chess and then to Chess's wound. Looking Chess in the eyes, he didn't say anything, but he nodded and took the lead, moving up the stairs, gun raised. Step by step, they took the stairs until

Damon his an awkward step, and the wood below his foot creaked as well. The gunfire came shortly after that.

Damon and Chess ran downstairs to avoid getting shot, and the sounds of heavy feet bounding down the steps would be forever burned into the back of Chess's mind. He was either going to be the victor or the loser here. Move on or lose. With one hand on his wound and the other raised toward the stairs, both of them hiding behind a couch, they watched as a portly man on the USA team came downstairs with a shotgun. They all stopped and stared at each other, knowing each other's faces. The portly man laughed and dropped his weapon.

"Did you guys check the app? I think it's just us now," the player said.

"Is it?" Damon asked, pulling his phone out and checking.

Sure enough, only 3 players were left, and they were all standing in the house. Chess heard the rotor sounds of a media drone outside the window and turned to look at it. Something horrible dropped to the bottom of his gut, and time slowed as he looked back at Damon. Damon's hand was raised, rifle at the ready. In cold blood, he gunned down the player with the shotgun in three short bursts, his body nothing more than crystals when it hit the floor.

Before Chess could even react and he had his gun halfway up in the air, Damon punched it out of Chess's hand and tackled him to the ground. Straddling him, Chess's body was becoming too weak from the blood loss to fight back. He looked down the barrel of the gun and weakly at Damon.

"Why?"

"Can't let it be too easy for you."

Then Damon fired.

CHAPTER TWENTY-TWO

"Yo, that was a dick move, man!"

Damon walked out of the Respawn Pod with a neutral look. Whether he knew that he was going to be met with opposition when he got back or not was a mystery, but the man he shot was right outside his Respawn Pod, yelling up a storm. Next to his Respawn Pow was another, one that Chess was still inside, and he was giving him a look from Hell itself.

"I know there can only be one winner, but did you really have to do me like that?!" the player continued to yell.

Damon walked out of the pod, and the player stepped back a couple of steps, letting him have his space. He was pissed, but he wasn't about to get into a fistfight, and not with Damon, of all people. The man was a walking enigma, this whole year, no one other than Bijou and Chess—and that was being generous—could figure him out.

Damon gave his teammate a hard look, his eyes cold, and the player backed away, his face down in defeat. No, Damon didn't have to do it like that, but what else was there? Go outside and have a rock, paper, scissors match to see who would shoot who first? He could hear his father in his eardrums now if he were to comply with something like that. He could feel the hand on his cheek burning if he allowed that to happen. If he didn't immediately take action and strike.

He didn't care what this player thought of him; he could be as mad as he wanted on his own time. When the pod opened to let Chess out, Damon looked over but not completely at Chess, just in his general direction. With this player, it was one thing; he could handle people that could tap but not walk. Chess, however, didn't fear god or man and would've thrown down with him in the middle of the venue if he really wanted to. When seconds passed without so much as a breath between them, Damon looked over at Chess.

The rest of the team looked on as Damon and Chess had this standoff; everyone saw what Damon did on the drone cam. Most were appalled, others angry that he could do such a thing to his own teammates. Nevertheless, there were some that wouldn't trust Damon as far as they could throw him now.

"Chess..."

"Save it," Chess snapped back at Damon.

Right before Chess walked off, Farren came around the corner with Levi and tried to holler out to him, but Chess was long gone, back to the locker room to change into his regular clothes. This tournament didn't mean shit to him, he just lost one of his opportunities to get even, and Damon knew that's what he wanted most. Wasn't going to make it easy on him; he knew that, but he didn't realize the lengths and drastic measures that Damon would go through to make sure Chess never saw peace again.

"Let's reconvene at the lobby, and we'll go through the paces. Some of you are going home today, but I want you to keep training to come back for the next World Royale, okay?" Farren said.

The lot of 50 nodded and agreed, moving toward the locker rooms to change and make it to the lobby in the East Wing of the circle. The ones that definitely knew that they were leaving were crying into the arms of the friends they made this past year and walking off. It seemed like such a cruel way to send it off, getting people invested in each other's lives for a whole year just to rip it away.

It wasn't like they couldn't swap phone numbers and text, but realistically, how many of these relationships were going to last outside of the World Royale? They were going to be working to the bone to finish and bring the trophy home; there wasn't going to be any time to keep up with stuff like that. Damon thought of this as he watched people pass him toward the locker rooms. Bijou caught up with him, but she wasn't smiling.

"Good luck getting on his good side after *that*. What were you thinking?" Bijou asked.

"I wasn't. I just acted," Damon said, walking off. Bijou followed.

"That acting is going to get you sent to the hospital if Chess retaliates," Bijou said.

Damon didn't say anything. Again, it was all about Chess. How Chess felt. How Chess took it. Damon shook his head and willed the thoughts out of his mind.

"At least it makes a memory," Damon said, smirking at Bijou.

Bijou did not return the favor.

"That's not funny."

"WILLIAMS, FAULKNER, KENNEDY, HARLOW, AND... THAT'S IT. You all will be continuing to the next round of games. Congratulations."

It didn't feel like a win. Out of the 30 that passed, Bijou, Chess, and Damon made it, though. It was going to only get harder from here as the next games were trios, and Chess had a feeling he wasn't going to be paired up with anyone that liked or respected him. He was usually a go-it-alone type of person; trios and duos weren't really his style. He could do duos, but trios made his blood pressure rise just thinking about it. Micromanaging people and telling them what to do, he wasn't that kind of a leader.

Despite the reality of the games continuing and Chess having to see Damon once again for them, he just had to buck up and continue. What was he going to do if Damon was even eliminated from the first round of games? Leave? Forfeit? He knew what he was there for and failed his first attempt at pulling it off. Three more games to go.

Chess sighed and put his arms on his legs, head hanging low, just thinking about what more he had to go through. At least Bijou made it through. That was something he could look forward to, but things were only going to get harder from here. It wasn't like he didn't believe in Bijou, but he still couldn't understand what she was doing here in the first place. She didn't even want to come.

As Chess thought of this, he looked toward Bijou, who was sitting and facing forward, then he looked at Farren and Levi. They were talking quietly behind a clipboard about something before Farren broke away and walked toward the group.

"Again, congratulations to those of you who passed. We'll be flying back to Kansas City tonight and going over the game plan for the next round first thing in the morning. I expect you to get your sleep on the plane and the second we get back to the hotel. The games are coming hard and fast now. There's no stopping," Farren said.

While most of them got up to walk to the exit and toward the busses taking them back to the airport, Chess caught a glimpse of Bijou talking with Farren and Levi before turning around and was face to face with Damon. It was almost like he was begging to have his face kicked in the way he was looking at him.

"So, how was it?" Damon asked.

"How was what?" Chess responded through clenched teeth.

"Dying to me again. How was it?"

Chess threw a punch, to which Damon took a step back. People stopped and watched Chess have his mini blowout, and when Chess realized what he had done, he looked toward Farren to find her staring at him with her arms crossed. He tried to calm down and popped the crick in his neck several times before facing Damon again.

"Nothing I wasn't used to already," Chess replied.

"Now you have to ask me."

Chess just stared at him like he was stupid. Damon made a 'come hither type move with his hands and patted his own chest a couple of times, a smile threatening to break free from his lips. Chess wanted to kick his teeth in so goddamn bad.

"Ask me how I feel," Damon continued.

"Why in the hell would I do that? I don't care how you feel." Chess spat.

Damon nodded and took a couple of steps backward toward the doors. He looked disappointed and satisfied all at the same time. As if he knew that answer was going to come and was disappointed that it had come. He knew, and he didn't know all at the same time, and it made him look conflicted. Without saying another word, Damon turned around and walked out the door toward the busses.

"What was that about?" Farren asked as she walked up to Chess. "You're not fighting again under my supervision. We've been through a whole year without incident."

"I'm not fighting!" Chess snapped back. "He asked me how I felt and then tried to make me ask him how he felt."

Bijou looked at the ground and fiddled with her hands as Chess talked. It was awkward because she knew what Damon was feeling, how he wanted Chess to see him, not see through him. To tell him that he's sorry, but he can't get through. Chess just didn't care enough yet, or perhaps at all. Maybe he would never care.

"And how does he feel?" Farren asked.

"Don't know and don't care, that answer good enough for you? Let's just get the fuck out of here."

Farren put her hands in the air in mock defeat and walked off toward the busses. "You're the boss, I guess."

As Farren and chess made their way to the busses, Levi caught Bijou's arm for a split second, keeping her from following Chess. She looked back at him, confused, but then looked away, knowing what he was about to say.

CHESS STUPIDLY PICKED THE SAME BUS THAT DAMON WAS ON and didn't realize it until he was sitting across from him in the hallway. They both had window seats, so they were a good ways away from each other, but since the bus hadn't moved yet, Chess had to sit there and seethe at the fact that Damon was trying o swap seats with the guy sitting next to him.

"I don't think that's a good idea," the teammate said.

"I didn't ask what you think. Swap seats with me," Damon said over the bus's forceful air conditioning.

Chess willed himself not to look Damon's way the whole ride back to the airport. It was only thirty minutes on the road, so it shouldn't be too hard. Be on his phone or watching cars go by, he could pass the time without having to talk to him. Why Damon wanted to sit next to him in the first place, he didn't even know.

Eventually, the feeling of something vibrating buzzed both Damon and Chess. Chess, thinking it was his phone, sat up and reached for it, only for him to realize that it was Damon's phone. He checked the caller ID, grimaced, and gave Chess a slight smile before he answered.

"Dad."

What followed was a flurry of screaming over the receiver that Chess heard loud and clear. He tried to pretend he didn't hear anything, his face toward the window and his hands in his lap. Eventually, he began to fiddle with his hands, clearly uncomfortable from hearing the reprimanding Damon was getting over the phone. They were grown men, but Chess knew. Chess remembered the stories. The back of his dad's hand on his face, the disappointment, the never being good enough.

Damon did everything he felt he had to do on the battlefield so that his dad would be happy or at least satisfied with his fast acting of taking both players out. Even if one of them, he would've liked to drag it out more. His dad didn't like slow, gradual games. That wasn't how a Kennedy acted.

Damon hummed affirmations and agreed with everything his father was yelling at him about. A lot of 'yes dad' and 'no sir'. After five long and painful minutes, the phone call was over, and Damon pocketed his phone. The bus began to move.

Chess sat straight in his seat and fumbled with his thumbs for a good minute before turning his head slightly toward Damon. He made a move to say something, but Damon cut him off.

"I don't want to talk about it."

"I was going to ask if you were alright."

Damon froze, his eyes locked to the seat in front of him. His breathing was normal, but his eyes looked like they were going to bug out of his head. Eventually, he looked back at Chess, both looking into each other's eyes.

"Do you mean it?" Damon asked.

Chess nodded after a couple of seconds. "I remember."

Damon shook his head and looked back down into his hands.

"You don't know the half of it."

CHAPTER TWENTY-THREE

The calls didn't stop coming in until late into the night. Chess and Bijou did their best to stay out of the hotel room every time the phone so much as buzzed on Damon's side of the room. Bijou spent time with a friend she made during the year, and Chess was killing time in the lobby, messing around on his phone until the battery was past time to charge. He never liked to have his phone below 10 percent, and it was teetering on five.

Pursing his lips and rolling his eyes, Chess decided to head back upstairs and at least charge his phone. If he were that desperate to get out of the situation, he would just head to a fast food restaurant and kill time there eating or something. At the very least, he could hoof it over to the Temporal Arena and walk around. There weren't any games going on, and the storm was halfway to reset in the middle of the night anyways, but it wouldn't hurt to walk around. There were pamphlets and plaques he could read, halls he could walk down. It wasn't like he was going to rob the place; he just didn't want to be around to watch Damon get yelled at by his dad at the age of 27. Some things just didn't change.

Even when they were back at the academy, Damon's dad would routinely check in, coming into the school to 'speak' with his son for hours. The red cheeks and puffy eyes from crying paired with long nights in each other's arms afterward was something Chess didn't want to see again. He didn't want to hear it again, either. The fact that Damon's dad had this power over him all this time, even into his adulthood, was baffling.

It had to be because of money or a manor or something. Something in his dad's name that he was lording over him with. Chess didn't know what to even think of first; it could've been anything, even just the loyalty to his own life. He would say or think something along the lines of *'at least you have parents,'* but even Chess wouldn't put up with this. He would've cut his dad off years ago if he was like this. That led him to believe that Damon's dad had something over him.

Getting into the elevator, Chess hoped that everything was calm in the room by the time he got up there. He walked into the hallway and made the long stride to the door, stopping just outside and pressing his ear to the wood. Damon was still talking on the phone; Chess could hear him talking a couple of octaves above normal, his accent thick with rage. Chess stood there, his eyes focused on the doorknob as he tried to focus on the conversation.

"No, dad, YOU listen... no, it's like I said... You don't understand; it's not like that... Dad, I love him!"

Chess's eyes went wide, and he pressed his ear harder to the door, trying to hear more. Was he talking about him? Talking about how he loves him to his father? It had to be about someone else; they hated each other's guts.

"It's always about you."

That phrase pulsed in his head several times before he tried to snap out of it. Right before he came to his senses, he heard the heavy footfalls of someone coming to the door. Right as Chess pulled away, pulling his phone out of his pocket, Damon whipped the door open and stood there, looking Chess in the face.

While his cheek wasn't red from a slap, and his eyes weren't as puffy as they used to be in Academy, he was visibly upset and pissed. His eyebrows were furrowed, and his breathing was labored. They stood there for a few seconds before Chess pulled his phone up and shook it several times.

"Phones dead, I—"

"Yeah, whatever."

Damon pushed past Chess, Chess letting him bump into him as he walked to the elevators. More than likely going to the vending machines or fast food. Something to calm him down after another vocal fight with his father. Things just weren't going the way his dad wanted them to; even though he was the one to win the first game, something was still wrong. In that way, Chess felt for Damon. They had history, but nobody deserved this.

Chess walked into the room and plugged his phone in on his side of the bed. From his window, he could see the vending machines clear as day on the bottom floor. The tell-tale signs of his brown hair didn't show up. Wherever Damon was, he was more than likely going to stay out all night. After a couple of minutes, Chess pulled his phone up and texted Bijou that the coast was clear and that she could come back to the room. Within minutes, Bijou was back in the hotel room, kicking off her shoes and slamming down on the bed.

"Dude, I'm wiped. I'm gonna pass out. Tell Damon if he comes back that if he gets a call, take it outside," Bijou said.

"Can't promise he'll listen to me, but sure," Chess mumbled.

Hours went by. Eventually, Farren returned to the room at midnight to find a snoring Bijou and a wide awake Chess sitting on his bed, flipping through his phone. She placed her MacBook on the bedspread and pulled some clothes out of her bag, getting ready to change for bed.

"Still not asleep?" Farren looked over to Damon's bed to find it empty. "And he's still not back yet? He's gonna hate me tomorrow; we got drills."

"Yeah. Not sure where he is," Chess said, his voice tired and deep.

"You seem tired. Why not go to bed."

Chess looked at Farren with a quizzical eye and dropped his phone into his lap. He didn't answer her, but they had a good staredown for a couple of seconds. After Farren scoffed and shook her head, she made her move to the shower, where she shut the door behind her.

"You both are gonna hate me then!" Farren hollered from behind the door.

Chess didn't care. He would do drills dead tired if he had to, not that he wanted to, but he would do them. Tapping his finger on his wrist several times, he searched his brain for anywhere Damon would go for hours at a time. Not bothering to let anyone know where he was or was going to be. Not coming up with anything logical, he went with the second-best option. Intuition.

When Farren came out of the bathroom about thirty minutes later, dressed for bed and hair pulled into a bonnet, she found that the only person left in the room was her and Bijou, who had just rolled over in bed snoring. She looked over to Chess's bed and saw the phone was unplugged and gone along with the boy. She huffed a sigh and shook her head for the third time that night. These boys were going to be the death of her and her team.

THE HALLWAYS OF THE TEMPORAL ARENA WERE DARK AS dusk. The lights were turned off for after-hours, but the doors were still open. The Arena was a 24-hour facility, but some areas were shut down to the public during the night. Chess was walking down one such hallway.

To his right, a massive window about three stories high and as wide as a football field showed the purple storm at its beginning raging through the arena as it consumed and reset everything within its borders. A purple and blue haze of color were awash on Chess's face as he walked, his hands in his hoodie and looking straight ahead. He used his guts to find Damon, and other than trashy food for three hours straight, there was really only one other place Damon could be. When Chess walked down the curve of the arena plaza, he found that which he was looking for.

Damon sat on the linoleum floor, looking into the window as the storm ebbed and flowed together and within itself. The lightning crawling over the puffs of clouds danced around one another, and the colors changed from purple to blue to purple again. It was a constant reminder of trier reality, the flux between worlds that just happened to show up on the planet one day. They didn't understand it fully, but what they did know was affecting their lives directly. Chess silently walked up to Damon and sat beside him, only a couple of feet of floor between them.

Time passed, and none of them said anything. Chess didn't even know what he could say. Back in the day, there was nothing more than holding him and letting the moment pass. Damon was very strong about it, barely crying in his arms and pretending that nothing was wrong the very next day, the facade in high effect. Chess didn't know if that was going to happen again this time. If Damon was even going to seek comfort and if Chess could even give it. Chess felt conflicted, but he stayed. Stayed and watched the clouds fold over one another and the lightning crawl.

"I wasn't fast enough."

Chess sat still, not moving his head as Damon spoke. He simply listened.

"I killed you in cold blood, and I wasn't fast enough. I didn't want to do it," Damon said.

"What do you mean?" Chess asked.

"I wanted a fair fight; I was going to offer us to run to different houses and... it doesn't matter in the end. What happened happened. I saw the media drone, and I knew he was watching."

"Your dad?"

Damon nodded to Chess's question. He sighed, brought his knees up to his chin, and hugged his legs. He was really upset; Chess never saw him do this. Damon was the kind of person that was sure of himself, reserved, and confident. This Damon was somebody that he didn't know. He didn't know this Damon, and Chess found himself looking. Then staring.

"He saw everything," Damon said.

"What's he got over you that you can't just say fuck him? I get he's your dad, but—"

"But nothing!"

Damon put his legs back down and turned to Chess. They were both looking at each other, Damon's breathing labored and his eyes red. He was distraught, and Chess didn't know what to do.

"What my dad is to me, what he's done for me. Everything I have is because of him, and I can't lose this because if I lose this Royale, I lose everything!" Damon finally said. "Everything."

"What like your house and your cars? Does he own those?" Chess asked.

"They're all in his name, yes. He can kick me out if he wants to."

"You don't have any money of your own?"

"You don't either."

Chess couldn't even be mad at that. He inherited the house, lost the cars gambling on Blood Running, and always owed someone some sum of cash. Damon was right, but it still didn't answer his question.

"So, you're owning him money too?"

Damon nodded at Chess's question.

"So by 'everything', he really means everything?" Chess asked.

"Everything."

Damon placed a hand over Chess's, and Chess looked down at it. Every drop of blood in his veins was telling him to pull away, act like it burned him, and be disgusted with Damon. Remember all the things he did to him and what he used him for. The past.

Now, Chess couldn't even move. The finality of everything swimming in his mind. The words of Damon ringing in his ears.

"*It's always about you.*"

"Damon."

Damon looked up and into Chess's eyes. His hair was parted perfectly down the middle, his bangs fluttering over his eyes, mahogany brown in the purple light. They sparkled, then swam as tears threatened to overflow from his tear ducts.

"How do you feel?"

It was such a simple question, but Damon sat there, stunned for a few moments. His father never asked how he felt after getting yelled at or reprimanded. Chess had gone all these years since Academy brooding over himself and lusting after a revenge so cold that it might kill him. The people he cared about most were too busy or within themselves to see him.

However, Chess was looking at him. Wasn't looking through him, he was looking at him, and he asked again.

"How do you feel?"

Damon smirked and then chuckled for a moment. Then the chuckle turned into a roaring belly laugh as the tears finally fell from his eyes.

"Like shit! " Damon laughed, rubbing a tear away and looking Chess in the eyes again. He was happy to see Chess actually smiling.

"Probably because you stayed up past midnight. Want to head back to bed?" Chess offered, taking his hand back and getting up off the floor.

He offered a hand for Damon to take to help him off the floor, and Damon took it. One strong hand in another, Chess pulled him up off the floor. They stayed that way for a couple of seconds, their breath mingling once more, but then the clouds cleared. The storm had ended, and the whole arena was reset. The next storm wouldn't materialize for another couple of hours, so now it was green hills and houses as far as the eye could see. Chess looked away from Damon long enough for Damon to look down at their hands still held together. Chess was so warm.

Eventually, they let go and walked back to the hotel where a sleeping Farren and Bijou were waiting for them. Chess crawled into bed, plugging his phone in but sat back up to say something else.

"Next time you run off like that, text me, okay?"

"Figured you wouldn't want me around you, let alone texting you," Damon said, pulling the covers over himself.

Chess shrugged and laid back down. "I'll lift the ban for emergencies. But emergencies only!"

Damon laughed as Chess pointed at him from his bed.

"I got it. I'll text you."

CHAPTER TWENTY-FOUR

When Damon woke the next morning, he assumed to see Chess sleeping in the bed ahead of him. Instead, the beds were empty, even Bijou's. They could've gone down for breakfast early, but with how he and Chess went to bed at the witching hour last night, he didn't see Chess waking up that early just to eat.

There was a great deal about Chess he just didn't know anymore. Things he's missed out on, things he's just ignored and let go of. Chess was a completely different person than the Chess he knew at university. This cold and callous Chess that didn't even want to look his way. This Chess that held his hand last night, out of what? Pity? Damon hoped it wasn't because of that. There was a lot Damon could put up with and harbor, but pity wasn't one of them. He'd rather die.

That said, Damon got out of bed, showered and brushed his teeth, and then got dressed to go downstairs. He played it safe and put on his tracksuit for training since it would likely be a full day of drills and running. He hoped he would be able to get out of it, but something within him told him he wasn't going to be able to.

In the lobby and cafeteria of the inn, he was used to seeing a couple of people coming down and eating the cereal or muffin they put out for breakfast every morning, but there was no sign of Chess or Bijou. He could've looked for Farren, but there was a good chance she was busy planning today's events and speaking with important people. He was on his own in a sense. No matter, really. He would just eat and go back to the room unit the got the email calling for training.

After taking a couple of muffins and an orange juice, Damon returned to the elevator, where he caught Bijou getting into a car. When she spotted him, she held the door open and motioned him to come in, which he did. He gave her a soft smile and offered a muffin, which she took with a smile herself.

"Early start to your morning?" Damon asked.

"Could ask you the same thing. You were out all night last night. You and Chess." Bijou giggled, taking a bite out of the muffin.

"Yeah, well, we came back and fell asleep at the same time. I expected him to be with you or something."

"Huh? He wasn't in the room with you?"

Damon looked at Bijou with a confused look in his eye.

"What do you mean he wasn't in the room with me? Of course, he wasn't in the room with me; he's gone," Damon said.

"That's weird. He was in the room when I got up and got around for the day. He must've gotten up right after me," Bijou said, looking away from Damon.

Damon looked away from Bijou after giving her a confused side eye and focused his eyes on the elevator car doors. They would be opening soon, and he would have to sit in his room and wait for training or for Chess to come back.

Why would he wait for Chess, though? So they could fight some more? Chess might've regretted doing what he did last night, asking Damon that question and holding his hand. He didn't want to chance that Chess might hold a grudge doing that and take it out on him. There was just too much going on for him to have to fight with Chess put on top of it. His mind was spiraling, and he knew it, but he tried to focus. The second game would be coming up soon, and he had to get ready for it. There wasn't any time to get lost over a boy.

But this wasn't just any boy, now was it? And Damon knew it.

Bijou opened the door for both of them, and when Damon sat his food down on his bedside table, which was becoming overrun with papers and items, he sat back on his bed and pulled out his phone. He promised Chess he would text if it was an emergency, but he didn't promise it was only if he was the one that was gone. Now Chess was missing, and he wanted to know where he was. He composed a text, a short one. Sweet and to the point.

"Where are you?"

It was all he had to ask; if he got any type of answer, then fine; if he didn't, then fine. Again, he really shouldn't be devoting all of his brainpower to one boy. Again.

He thought back to Academy. How he used Chess to appease the people in his life. To get ahead in studies and Blood Running and earn his license with flying colors. He used Chess; he had to admit it. He used him so that he didn't show any weakness to his father. That he was capable of turning on anyone that got in the way of victory. In the process, he lost Chess. He not only lost him but killed his spirit.

This new Chess, this mean and cold Chess that yells and cusses, throws punches and never smiles. He didn't want to know this Chess. He wanted the old Chess back but feared there wasn't a way to get him back. What happened last night at the Arena was one thing; Chess overheard the yelling and the fighting. However much he heard, Damon didn't know. Something because of that brought his old Chess back, even just for a moment. Should he have to go through the humiliation and shame that his father brings him just to get a hint of Chess back in his life?

Was it really that worth it?

"Damon."

Damon looked up at Bijou. He didn't realize he had been staring at his phone for the last minute, waiting for a response.

"Your muffin?"

He looked at his hand and, sure enough, was squeezing his breakfast in his fist tightly until it was nothing more than crumbles in his hand and on his bed. That was going to be annoying to sleep on later. He was so focused on reaching Chess, *his* Chess again, that he was obsessed with it. He wanted his Chess back.

The problem was, as the minutes drowned on and the muffin was still squished in his hand, Chess wasn't coming back., He wasn't responding, and he wasn't going to let him know where he was. He regretted everything he did last night; Damon just knew it. Was it all truly out of pity, and he was regretting it now? Damon didn't want to believe it.

A banner notification came down from the top of his phone screen from Farren, CC'ing everyone in the team that was left to meet up at the gym for drills and training. It was going to be another long week of this until the next game, and while Damon was wanting to reach Chess, he had other people to please as well. When would he get to live for himself? When he earned enough money that wasn't taken away from him for the family estate? To the house he 'owned' but really didn't own, it wasn't in his name.

In a way, Damon felt trapped. He felt free training but still felt trapped by the expectations his father had set on him, and he was scared of what lengths he would have to go this time to maintain them. What he might have to do to Chess this time. He didn't want anything to happen to Chess this time, but he was afraid he wouldn't have a choice.

Fight for a man who might not even want him or appease the people that were in his life no matter what? It was a choice he was going to have to make and soon.

He didn't know how he was going to feel when he saw Chess again, Chess didn't ever reply to his text, but he was at training, sitting on the other side of the field away from Bijou and Damon. He had an unreadable look on his face, something was bugging him, but he wasn't really letting it show. He sat on the grass and picked at it, throwing the reeds of the plants away once he plucked them from the ground. He looked to the ground and ahead but never toward Damon and Bijou.

"What eating him?" Bijou asked, bumping Damon on the arm lightly.

Damon was looking at Chess passively, but when Bijou got his attention, he pulled his eyes away from the man.

"Not sure. He wasn't answering my texts," Damon answered.

"What texts? Since when did you two text again?" Bijou asked, sounding a little bit impressed.

"Last night, we... it's not important. We just talked last night about stuff. Everything," Damon said, crossing his arms.

"Well, if you guys talked without fighting, I call that a win. I want to sit down with you guys again and have another dinner like we did a couple of months ago," Bijou said, rocking back and forth.

"Yeah, that would be nice."

Farren walked out from the doors, followed by Levi, as they walked to the thirty players left in the squad. This next game would cut them by half yet again, and more would be going home defeated. Damon wasn't going to let that be him; looking at Bijou, he hoped it wouldn't be her either. Looking over at Chess, he met his eyes for a moment before Chess slowly moved his head away from his gaze. He still couldn't know what his emotion was, but he didn't look happy. He just looked like Chess, the Chess he had been presenting this whole time. Not the Chess who came out last night and seemed to be caring and asked him how he was feeling.

The one question he wanted to hear, why did it feel so fake now?

"Good morning. Today we're going to do basic drills, and then we're going to hit the Arena for a mock battle. You'll be doing a free for all basic Royale where every man is for themselves," Farren said, pulling her clipboard up and looking through the papers.

"We're hoping to get through the week with flying colors and little mishaps. We have some people coming to visit the team soon to talk to you all, and as the team gets smaller and smaller, we'll be getting more sponsorships and visitors. That being said, we're still going to train as hard as we can to bring home the gold," Levi said.

Bijou looked to the ground but nodded along with what he said, and Damon was staring at Chess. Chess was just looking off into the distance, not really looking at anything. Damon would think the mention of the Arena and using it today would light a fire under him, but he just looked lost, if anything. When Farren clapped her hands several times, people sprung into action and made their way to different parts of the field for stretching. Damon followed Bijou over to Chess, who had just gotten up from the ground himself. He looked into

Damon's eyes for a split second before sighing and turning his attention to Bijou.

"Where were you this morning?" Bijou asked, her arms crossed.

"Couldn't really sleep. Got up early," Chess responded.

"Really? Because you were knocked the fuck out when I got up this morning. Damon too," Bijou said, motioning to Damon.

Damon tensed up and looked away, crossing his arms, wanting to be out of the conversation, but he was also curious about where Chess was.

"Damon said he sent you a text," Bijou also said.

Damon closed his eyes, wishing Bijou would just stop airing his business out like this, but when Chess pulled his phone out and looked at it, he just snorted and pocketed his phone again, pulling Damon's attention to him.

"Didn't see it until now. Sorry."

Bijou was slack-jawed at the apology, and Damon looked at Chess with a slight smile. He uncrossed his arms and stepped forward, his hands at his sides. They shook, wanting to reach up and slam down on Chess's shoulder so badly, but Damon kept his hands to his sides the best he could.

"Wanna train?" Damon asked.

"You're on," Chess replied, a grin on his face.

Bijou watched them walk off, a small smile on her face. Maybe there was hope for them after all.

CHAPTER TWENTY-FIVE

The Arena was devoid of any people by the time the team got to the venue. It had been shut down for the day besides custodians and maintenance workers for the USA team practice session. The rules were free reign, a free for all match for Farren to gauge each person's strengths and weaknesses. Armed with binoculars and her clipboard, she sat in the pilot house above the land in the Control Room. She would have access to the media drones flying around to the places she could not see.

"You gonna go easy on me this time?" Chess asked, pulling his black jacket over his shoulders. They were allowed casual clothes for this match.

"Not a chance," Damon responded, pulling fingerless gloves over his hands.

"Good."

Bijou looked between the men and smiled, pulling her own coat over her shoulders. She was going to go into this trying to have fun and treat it like pleasure, even if these boys and the rest of the players were treating it like hardcore training. She was here for them; she wasn't here for the competition.

"You guys seem to be in good spirits today. Something happen?" Bijou asked.

"No, I still hate him," Chess said, adjusting his shoulders and popping another crick in his neck.

"But?" Bijou goaded.

"But what? This is just competition. Another chance to get even," Chess said.

"It doesn't mean anything, though; this is only practice. You're really going to go all out for a scrimmage?" Damon asked.

Chess looked at Bijou for a split second and then back at Damon. He didn't want to say anything in front of her in case it upset Damon, but at this point, what he knew, Bijou should've known as well. They were all the same caliber of friends within their small group.

"What's going on with your dad—"

"Chess, don't," Damon warned, his smile dropping.

"You can't control it, so im not going to hate you for it. You're doing what you have to do to survive, and I can respect that," Chess finished.

Damon looked away, a scowl on his face. He didn't want to talk about this or even think about it. He wanted one match where he and Chess could just fuck around and have fun. It was looking like Chess wasn't going to take it as lighting as he thought he was going to, however. Chess was going to go all out again. On top of that, the problem of him and his dad aired out for them to know, it wasn't like it was a dirty secret or anything, but he would've rather kept it to himself.

"I'm... gonna go line up. See you guys there," Bijou said, walking off toward the exit toward the Respawn Pods.

Chess watched her go; now it was him and Damon in the waiting room, along with a couple of other stragglers. People on their phones or heads in their hands, getting into focus for the match. It wasn't supposed to be anything serious, but most people were treating this as if it were the most important match of their lives. Damon looked up to Chess as Chess turned his attention back to him.

"I wanted to say that I was sorry. For... all of it," Damon whispered.

Chess looked away and noticed a man in the corner watching them but sheepishly looking away when he caught Chess's attention. This wasn't the place for this, and Chess wasn't ready to hear it. He could understand why Damon had to do what he did now, but he still wasn't in the right heart space to accept any type of apology.

"Not now. Later," Chess said, holding a hand up.

Before Damon could get any other word out, Chess turned away and walked to the exit himself. Exiting the waiting room without Damon, he saw Bijou at the end of the hallway. She was talking with Levi. When she looked back over, she suddenly dismissed herself from him and ran over toward Chess, a small smile on her face.

"Ready to go?" Bijou asked.

"What was that? Did Levi want you for something?" Chess asked, walking alongside Bijou toward the Respawn Pods finally.

"Nothing important. We were just talking about how the World Royale was going and my headspace. I'm trying to stay on top of my game after all," Bijou responded.

"You're a terrible liar." Chess grinned.

"No, it's the truth! I'm telling the truth!" Bijou doubled down.

"Uh-huh. We'll find out when you're given a bump up in the tournament," Chess joked.

"I thought you didn't care about the World Royale?" Bijou asked, turning into the Respawn Room and getting in line.

There was already a line of people queuing up to get scanned for the game today. Chess picked the line that had fewer people in it, while Bijou was a couple of people behind. After a couple of seconds, Damon walked in and stood behind Bijou.

"I don't. It's just weird that you're so invested with the coaches as of late when you wanted to get out of this since day one," Chess accused.

"I didn't want to get *out* of it. I just needed to be able to work at the same time I was doing this too. Simple stuff."

"Uh huh," Chess responded, not buying it.

They each got scanned into the mainframe and came out on the other side, adjusting their clothes and thinking of their plans of attack. Chess was going to play this by ear, while he knew Damon was more than likely studying the map of the arena this morning at some point. Damon always had a plan. Bijou didn't know just yet what she was going to do, but she knew she couldn't rely on Chess this time. She would be on her own.

"This is just a practice, Royale. No eliminations. Have fun out there, and remember to keep on your toes. You're being evaluated on your performance. If you think you're being watched, you more than likely are. Make me proud, and may the best Runner win," Farren announced in the waiting room.

Everyone was a buzz with conversation, waiting for the trolly to take them up and above the stadium. It was a short drop, but as long as you hit your parachute at the right time, it didn't really matter. Plus, if you fell to your death, you would just respawn, which would be more embarrassing than anything else.

"When is later, by the way?" Damon asked.

Chess just looked at him with passive eyes and shrugged, moving his gaze to the window.

"Not sure. Not now, at least. Not sure when it will be." Chess looked back over to Damon. "Probably never."

Damon nodded and adverted his gaze away from Chess, pursing his lips in annoyance. Holding his hand, asking his questions, smiling, but not wanting to accept an apology. When was it truly going to be the right time to apologize to Chess for everything that happened between them?

"Look, I understand I was shitty to you when we were together." Damon grabbed Chess's arm before he walked away completely and thanked the stars when he didn't pull away. "But you have to believe me. I'm sorry."

Chess looked at Damon with buzzing eyes but then eventually looked away again. He softly pulled his arm out of Damon's grasp and adjusted his jacket.

"Later," Chess responded, and then he walked away.

"He's never going to accept it; I can tell you that now," Bijou said, coming up from behind Damon.

When Damon whipped around, he gave Bijou a spurred look. That wasn't really something Bijou would normally say; she always tried to lift the mood or mediate the situation. She was being strangely real at the moment, mostly because of the finality that Chess was showing in his response. There wasn't much left to pull comfort from it.

"What makes you say that?" Damon asked, his voice low.

"The Chess we knew back in the day is long gone. I haven't seen him in years. The way he treats you and talks to you is the way he talks to everybody." Bijou looked at Damon with clear eyes; Damon was scared of them because he knew. He just knew Bijou was telling the truth. "This Chess is the Chess I know. You don't know him yet. He's not going to accept your apology."

"You never know..." Damon popped his neck a couple of times and smiled his famous grin. If anything, he was convincing himself that he could do it. "I might break through this Chess and get back to my old one."

"*Your* old one? Okay." Bijou huffed a single laugh and shook her head.

"What's gotten into you people? Bijou, you're not normally like this either."

Bijou turned to Damon before she made her way to the trolly exit. Ahead of her, Chess could be seen making his way into the elevator, the doors shutting on him without so much as a look his way.

"Damon, it's always been like this. You're the one stuck in the past. Yeah, Chess is holding a grudge, but he's moved on with his life and become a new person. I have too. You have to meet us halfway a little bit and move on too. Maybe Chess doesn't want to hear an apology because it takes him back to a place he doesn't want to be."

Damon didn't think of it like that, but at the same time, he felt it was still important to apologize so that he could move on with his own life as well. He wanted to move on too, but he felt he really couldn't until this was done first. He wanted to hear it again. From Chess's lips. Hear him ask how he felt again, to see him like he did last night.

He knew that was Chess in there; he saw it in his eyes. He smiled and talked, walked with him. This Chess that wasn't hell-bent on a grudge last night was as close to the old Chess as he was going to get, and he had to be okay with that. What he got last night, he had to accept that this was Chess now.

So, he would work around this new Chess then.

THE TROLLY WAS THE SIZE OF A REGULAR SCHOOL BUS BUT A little bit wider and longer, not by much. Everyone was sitting in assigned seats waiting for the moment they were allowed to run and jump out of the designated doors on the sides of the trolly. Chess's fingers were itching to get ahold of a gun. He was going to take this as chill as he could, but it was still a match. To him, this still counted.

Whatever was happening with Damon and his dad, he couldn't change. He had no control over that. However, he had control on the battlefield if he knew how to take it. He cared, and he didn't care, more so he was indifferent to what Damon had going on. It wasn't like he couldn't sympathize, but his feelings came first in this situation. Until he could best Damon in a Royale, he could start putting the past fully behind him.

Right now was the present. And right now was the game. Chess could feel the wind on his scalp as the breeze rolled in. The scent of fresh rain and clouds in the air. It was a long way from the oil and gasoline he could smell on the C-130 flying over Santa Catalina. This smelled clean, whimsical. It didn't feel like Chess was about to drop down and shoot people; he felt like he was taking a hike somewhere magical.

With the bump of turbulence on the trolly, and the wind knocking the car back and forth, some people expressed worry but were promptly told that the trolly runs these cables every day without fail. It was a little scary, but so was jumping out of a plane.

"Welcome to the Kansas City Temporal Arena noon games; we will be defending in about thirty seconds; if you could double check the straps on your parachutes and do one more locker of your person before departing the trolly, that would be much appreciated. Again, this is the Kansas City Temporal Arena, Noon Game. Thank you, and good luck!"

The trolly conductor at the front put the radio speaker back and kept the trolly going at a calm pace. It was going to feel weird to fall out of a listing trolly that was going, at most, five miles an hour on ropes, but he would do it. Eventually, a buzzer sounded, the conductor's arm shot out and made a 'get off' motion egging the players to jump out, and people were jumping. One by one, people were pushing past others to get to the doors first and fall out of the wide-open trolly doors to the ground below. Chess was one of them.

When Damon noticed Chess was pushing to the front to fall out of the trolly, he pushed his way to the front, almost catching hands with an eager teammate who was hoping to be next. He watched as Chess fell out of the trolly to the ground below, let the teammate go first, and then he jumped out, doing a slow backflip to Earth. First order of business, take care of the guy that kept him from getting to Chess. Second, take care of Chess himself.

It was only practice. He was truly sorry. However, Blood Running was Blood Running. Practice or not, every game had to be perfect. Falling to earth, Damon swallowed, knowing what he would have to do, knowing that doing this might make his apology seem like nothing.

CHAPTER TWENTY-SIX

Chess hit the ground running. The second his feet hit solid ground, he shed the parachute for the storm to eat and made off toward a hamlet of houses in the distance. The normal strat he liked to take and would land him in hot water one of these days by an intuitive Blood Runner was a tried and true one. He wasn't the only one going after the houses, though; when he looked up into the sky as he ran, a flurry of parachutes was dropping on his position, and he had mere seconds to secure a firearm and bunker down. Either that or get out of the houses guns blazing.

He didn't know where Damon was, but by the way, he was trying to force himself out of the trolly at the same time he was; he couldn't be too far behind him. Maybe in the nearby trees or towers littered across the arena. He would be a fool to believe that Damon wasn't going to come for him. Bijou might come for Damon, too, as payback for shooting her head off in the Santa Catalina game. He never knew, but what he did know was that he was fifteen seconds at the most from a fight, and he had just climbed into the window of the first house.

Nothing on the first floor; he didn't bother to check the kitchen. Bounding up the stairs, he found a pump action shotgun and a knife.

Better than nothing. He loaded the weapon with bullets and searched the cabinets and drawers of the room. One more weapon, a revolver, was found, and he prioritized this weapon over the shotgun. It had limited ammo, so he had maybe six shots before he would have to move to the shotgun anyways. He hoped he wouldn't have to use it all.

Bounding down the stairs, he heard the tell-tale signs of footsteps in another room, running around and knocking things over. Someone was frantically looking for a weapon, and Chess didn't know if they had one already. As he turned the corner and raised his weapon, the assailant turned as well, brandishing a long hunter's rifle. He was too slow on the draw, and the bolt wasn't even pulled back yet. Chess fired, hitting him square in the center of the forehead, and he went down in a flurry of crystals.

He didn't have any time for a reprieve as another person came running through the door, and Chess naturally turned and fired twice. The first shot missing, but the second shot hitting its mark, downing the player. Now that the player was on his knees and crawling away to try and heal, Chess wasted no time coming up from behind and slamming the knife to the hilt into their back, killing them. He picked up the knife and a couple of crystals off the ground, popped them, and then ran out the door.

The neighborhood was a shitshow. There were people running in and out of houses, bullets flying everywhere, and people falling off roofs and turning into crystals. Chess could take action, but this was cutting it a little too close for his comfort. He knew he would catch a stray bullet or another player's attention if he stuck around. He bounced on his feet several times, made a break to the right toward some trees, and made his way deeper into the forest.

The gunfire was becoming muffled the longer he ran, but he wasn't alone. He could hear the fast footsteps of people running beside him, farther away in the trees, but they were there. When Chess stopped suddenly and took cover behind a thick tree, a bullet hit the tree in front of him, splintering the wood. Chess checked his ammo really fast. Three more bullets and he had to make them count as it would take time to pull the shotgun back out from his back, and he would hate to have to bring a knife to a gunfight.

"Come out, Chess! I know you're in there!" a player hollered.

Chess made it a point not to remember any of his teammates' names or faces since the Final Royale would be a free for all like this anyways. They were a cog in the machine just like him, faceless and nameless. Just another body, so Chess treated them as such. He would've expected the same from his teammate, but here one was, calling him out by name. He didn't think he was making waves the way he was this year, but people knew him and were looking for him.

Chess slammed the revolver back into place right before he heard the sounds of feet running up to his position. Chess backed up, letting the player round the tree, and he shot first. The round whizzed past the assailant but only by a hair. The player was holding a semi-automatic rifle, and this was likely to be the end if Chess didn't think quickly on his feet. Diving behind another tree and earning a bullet to the leg, Chess groaned and forced himself to stand, lucky that the bullet didn't hit bone, or he would've been downed. He could still walk, but he ditched the revolver; it wasn't going to help here.

Pulling the shotgun from behind his back, Chess quickly rounded the tree he was hiding from and readied it. The man that was hunting him had his back turned to Chess. A rookie move, but he's the one that shot first. Chess unloaded two shells into the man's back, not even able to watch him fall into a flurry of crystals before another person came out of the trees and advanced onto his position. They were carrying a rifle and running at max speed toward Chess, likely running toward the noise of a gun firing than Chess's position. Chess wasted no time turning and reloading his weapon as quickly as possible to unload it onto this person.

The player saw Chess and raised his gun to fire. It was looking like Chess wasn't going to reload in time, but when Chess noticed the shadow of a person right behind the paler running up to him, Chess stalled for a second too long. However, the assailant fired and missed as a knife was plunged into his back and stuck out the other side. While he couldn't feel pain, the surprise of the matter and the subsequent blood loss leading to his downfall pulled Chess's attention to the next player at hand. It was Damon.

"Howdy!" Damon greeted

"You already did that one." Chess gritted, raising his weapon.

He didn't wait. Pulling the trigger and letting the buckshot fly in Damon's direction, Damon barely escaped the bullets as he dove behind a tree. Chess reloaded and banked back behind his own tree and bit his lip. Damon could be anywhere, and he needed to keep his eyes on him at all times. Even taking his eyes off him for a few seconds could've been fatal.

Chess reloaded and broke off from the tree, running forward and deeper into the forest. He wanted to put as much distance between him and Damon as possible before he could formulate his own attack plan. Right now, it wasn't safe enough to just turn from the tree and fire blindly. Running as fast as he could, he weaved in and out of trees until some wood splintered by his head. Damon was on his trail and catching up fast.

Looking behind him, which was a rookie mistake, he was Damon running with the rifle pointed to the sky as he pumped his other arm to get to him. Once he saw that Chess looked back, he dropped the rifle into his hand and fired, missing every shot. Each shot was going wide, not hitting its mark, and Chess was able to get away and behind another tree.

They did this song and dance of circling the trunk, trading bullets and buckshot until Chess fully reloaded and Damon was on his last rounds. They met in the middle, aiming at one another but paused. Not one of them moved, and it was silent. What was once a battlefield, the sounds of gunfire and grenades filling the air was now as silent as the wind. Damon couldn't help but smile.

"No one can see us here. There's no drone," Damon started.

"Your point?" Chess bit back.

"You would be satisfied with killing me here? No one to see it?" Damon asked.

"Stupid question."

Damon shot first. Right as Chess made a move to raise his gun to his shoulder and aim precisely, Damon hip fired and hit Chess in the torso and legs, downing him. Chess grunted and started to crawl backward, a feeble attempt to get away, even though he knew he had lost again. Damon walked up to the crawling chess and climbed on top of him, straddling his torso, and Chess laid flat on his back, breathing heavily, trying to keep oxygen in his brain and not die. He didn't want to lose this early in the game. When Chess looked over at Damon's hand, he saw that he was holding a large hunting knife. This was it.

"No hard feelings, love. I want to see you win, but you have to earn it," Damon said sweetly.

"Fuck you!" Chess seethed from behind barred teeth.

Damon only emailed an almost pitiful smile before bringing the knife up, but then he stopped. There was a reason it was so quiet. Why everything had just stopped all of a sudden, as if people had all died out. They didn't die out. They moved on.

The sound of leaves and bark tearing from the ground started to roar in Damon's ears, and Chess looked over to see the clouds of purple and lighting crawling across it advance toward them.

"Oh, shit... oh shit!"

Damon got off of Chess and helped him to his feet. Dying by a bullet was one thing, but the feeling of being in the storm, of withering away and feeling like you can't breathe—like you're drowning—was one of the worst feelings the human body could go through. No, you couldn't feel pain, but the fear in your eyes, the constraint on your lungs. Damon wasn't just going just to leave Chess there to suffer through that.

Chess slung an arm around Damon, and they both booked it, running as fast as they could back toward the housing developments in the arena. There had to of been a car left behind. The storm was so close; a couple more minutes, and it would be right on top of them. They didn't have any more time to waste being petty about getting even. Damon was going to get Chess out of here.

"Not doing too hot." Chess grunted, feeling his blood seep out of his body. He was going to bleed out soon if he didn't get a hold of a medkit.

"Come on; we're almost there. We'll drive out of here," Damon said, pulling Chess more than running with him.

"And then what?" Chess grunted, dragging his heavy feet. "You're gonna throw me in a ditch and shoot me?"

"If we make it through this, I'll let you shoot me," Damon said, pulling their bodies past the first house and into the street.

"Promise?"

"Promise, love."

Luckily there was a car sitting on the street as if it were waiting for them. Shoving Chess in the passenger seat and giving him his rifle, Damon quickly got into the driver's seat and started the engine. It was a piece of shit four-door sedan, but it would get them from A to B. B, being out of the storm's range for more than a couple of minutes. They could continue whatever offhanded foreplay they were doing later once they were safe.

The engine was stalling, however. As if the rotor was spinning, but nothing was starting, Damon tried the key over and over again as the motor just spun and spun with no promise of ignition. Chess looked behind them to the rear windshield and saw the clouds like smoke crawling across the asphalt. The storm had come to collect.

"Damon..."

"I know!"

"The storm!"

"I know!!"

Eventually, the engine did flare to life, be it a miracle, and Damon slammed on the accelerator. The tires spun out and then gained traction, peeling out of the housing development as fast as they humanly could. Chess could feel the tendrils of the storm creeping up on his shoulders right before the car busted out of dodge and took a deep breath, knowing that they were steering clear of it.

"What's stopping me from blowing your head off right now?" Chess asked, his head lolling back on the passenger seat. He was bleeding out fast.

"Nothing, really. Except you'd be stuck in the storm," Damon said, looking over at Chess with a knowing eye. "You don't want to be stuck in the storm, though. I know you."

"You don't know shit." Chess coughed.

"Yeah? I know enough. And what I don't know, I want to know." Damon turned down a long street heading to the North section of the arena, more toward the middle. "This new Chess. I want to know him."

"New Chess?"

"The only Chess I knew is long gone. You're a new man now." Damon looked over at Chess, and Chess was just staring at him, his eyes half-lidded. "I want to know that man."

CHAPTER
TWENTY-SEVEN

The storm for the Temporal Arena was a quick one. A 30-minute game with no breaks. The storm was ever passing and did not stop for short periods. Damon was driving like a madman trying to get ahead of it, and was making good headway. Every so often, he would look in the rearview mirror to check the storm's position, the clouds getting farther and farther away every time. Looking river too, Chess, it was obvious he wasn't doing so hot. Breathing deeply and eyes half-lidded, he was getting blood all over the seat as his legs were splayed out and his back slouched on the passenger side.

"We're almost to the center," Damon said in a rushed voice.

"Leave me here, man."

Chess went to open the door, but Damon reached over, swerving the car a little bit to bat his hand away. Chess made little to no attempt to stop him. He was officially too weak to even fight back.

"We're getting to the center, and I'll find you a medkit. We'll do this again, fair and square," Damon announced authoritatively.

"It was already fair. You shot me, game over," Chess complained.

It was quiet in the car for a few moments before the telltale signs of a media drone flew over them. It was more than likely catching them in the car as they drove to their destination, and given their history, this was going to spark conversation. Chess turned a tired eye to it and then back to Damon. He knew he saw it too.

"Your dad's gonna be *pissed.*" Chess giggled, turning into a cough as his lungs were starting to fail him.

"My dad isn't watching a practice session. This has little to do with the World Royale, so he's not gonna give a shit."

"How can you be so sure?"

"I just am."

The car came to a stop in a clearing of grass just off the road, and ahead, Damon could see the bullet trail from a weapon shoot across the sky. There were people here, which meant supplies. If he played this smart, he would have Chess back up in no time.

"Stay here," Damon said, unbuckling from the car and getting out.

Armed with only his hunting knife now, he sprinted toward the first house on the hill and climbed into the window. The fighting was coming from way farther away, but if it was coming toward or away from him, he didn't know. Inside the house was a small pistol with some ammo and Temporal Shards. Someone was taken care of here, and the winner moved on. Damon took the weapon and loaded it up with ammo, a full clip, and then made his way upstairs.

He took the stair two at a time and busted his way into the first room. He was pretty sure he was alone in the house, so he didn't make any attempts to mask his footsteps. Sitting on the bed was a full health kit and a couple of sodas. He didn't need the food, but the medkit was appreciated. He took it and clipped it to his hip, making his way down to the first floor again. Just as he stopped at the top of the stairs, the door busted open from downstairs, and whoever had come in was coming in guns blazing. Damon stopped and watched as a girl player was standing at the open door, shooting out to the field at some other person in an attempt to suppress them away.

Damon made his way back upstairs in the middle of all the noise and hid behind a banister. If she made her way upstairs, he would blindside her with his own suppressing fire or as much as he could with a peashooter. Eventually, the firing stopped, and that was when Damon took a bad time to adjust his footing. The wood creaked under his feet, and the girl made a surprised sound. However, she never did come up to meet her as gunshots rang out and filled the bottom level with ammunition. The girl called out in surprise, then a couple of impact grunts, and then she fell silent. She was eliminated.

He wasted no time getting up from where he was hiding and making it to a window on the second floor. The person that got her was likely going to come and check her body for weapons and crystals, so he had to get out of there fast. Opening a window and climbing out was a fair drop, but with the help of a wind blast, he should be able to cushion the fall well enough. It would make noise, but he didn't have much of choice. He jumped.

The wind blast was loud, and he was ninety percent sure the winner had heard it, so he booked it laterally from the house and into the trees, looking to loop his way back to the car and help Chess out. No, he didn't know why he was doing this. He didn't want to leave Chess there to just die in the storm. They were hardened men, sure, but even the storm scared Damon. He didn't want to leave Chess in there too.

That, and if he were trying to get back on Chess's good side, to know this new Chess, as Bijou put it, he would have to stick his neck out for it. Nothing good came without sacrifice. He would have to sacrifice this win possibly to make sure he and Chess got a fair match without the threat of a storm eating them both. Self-preservation? Sure, but he wasn't going to leave Chess to suffer the same consequence.

Running back toward the car, Damon pulled his phone out while running and glanced at the number. Four left. Meaning him, Chess, the winner, and someone else. Whomever it was, Damon hoped the winner and the unknown player duked it out amongst themselves, and then Damon could pick up the scraps. As if his prayers were being answered, he heard a couple of shots ring out in the distance, meaning the winner and the unknown were fighting. He could see the car.

Pocketing the phone and pulling the medkit off his hip, he slowed to a stop outside the car as the unknown fighter had made themselves known. Standing over a pile of Temporal Crystals—both littering the grass and the passenger side seat—stood Bijou. She was holding a double barrel shotgun in her hands, and before Damon could realize it was truly her, she whipped around and fired.

Two buckshots ripped through Damon's torso, and he dropped the medkit. Before he succumbed to his damage, he remembered the look on Bijou's face. One completely devoid of emotion. Her eyes dead behind her corneas.

DAMON DIDN'T WASTE ANY TIME IN THE RESPAWN POD, halfway to ripping the doors open before he completely materialized to make it to the pilot house. As expected, he didn't see Chess anywhere in the Respawn Room; some people were even pointing to the exit doors for him to tell him where Chess went. He booked it to the Pilot House to see Chess, or at the very least, see Farren. He wanted to see what she was seeing with the media drones, not what was just shown on one feed in the Respawn Room. By the time he got to the room, he saw Farren and Levi both up off their chairs and watching intently, not giving Damon the time of day as they watched and waited for the ending to unfold.

"Sir, you can't be in here!" a maintenance worker hollered.

When Farren looked over to see who it was, she calmed the worker down and motioned for him to come over. Her eyes were then fixed on Bijou hiding behind the car he was driving a couple of minutes ago. Looking like a last stand as bullets whizzed by her and impacted the car. She would either be the winner or the loser, and Damon wanted to know how and why.

It wasn't like he didn't believe in Bijou, but suddenly, she played as professional Blood Runners do. He didn't want to believe it, but as he watched her take Chess's rifle out from the passenger seat and pop some of the crystals, he huffed a laugh. It was almost too funny to watch.

"I gotta say, didn't see this one coming," Farren said, her eyes transfixed on Bijou on the screen.

Levi didn't say anything, just opting to write sparse notes on his own clipboard and then cover them up with another piece of paper. Damon watched as who was once the winner came running up toward the car, a primed fire spell in his hand. He was going to blast her away, or at least attempt to. As if she was expecting it, Bijou primed a wind spell on her hand and shot it out the second the man rounded the car. The man and the fire spell both went flying in the air and landed unceremoniously in the grass not feet away from Bijou. She got up from where she was crouching and aimed the rifle, firing on the felled loser.

Bijou was The Winner.

"Where's Chess?" Damon asked, now that the confetti had been dropped and Bijou was being teleported back to the Respawn Room.

"I don't know, figured he'd be with you. He hasn't been in here," Farren said, collecting her things and getting ready to leave the pilot house. "I have congratulations to give; you should too. She played a pretty solid game."

"Yeah."

It was all Damon could say, but as he watched Levi and Farren leave, he had too many things pounding through his mind. Why Bijou killed Chess, how Bijou got so good, so fast. She had been spending all her time with her new friends in their rooms or shopping; he had called before and knew of it. At least, that's what Bijou was telling them. Something else was at play here.

Pulling his phone out, Damon noticed he had one text message from Chess and quickly opened it.

"She's going to kill us in Trios."

It was a simple text that sent a chill down his spine. No matter who he was going to be sacked up with, fig they didn't play perfectly and carefully, this new Bijou was going to hunt them like dogs. The look in her eyes as she gunned him down, he knew. He knew.

"Wanna team up for Trios then?" Damon texted back.

It took a couple of seconds, but the text bubbles were a sight to see from Chess at the bottom of his messages.

"Are you an idiot? If we group together, she has a better chance of mowing us down. I don't know what drugs she's on, but either she needs to chill, or I need some."

Damon snorted at the quip and texted back.

"So what do you propose?"

It was then that he left the pilot house and made his way down back to the Respawn Room. Wherever Chess was, he was long gone from the stadium. More than likely back at the hotel and cooling off after a piss poor game like that. Where more than half of it was spent dying in a car, the anger Damon felt not being able to save him and have a good old shootout for old time's sake without the prying eyes of his father was palpable. There was not going o be another chance like this. The next games were back to back like this one, only days apart. Then after that, the World Royale. Then it was all over. The phone buzzed in his hand. A text from Chess.

"We get Bijou first."

CHAPTER TWENTY-EIGHT

Bijou exited the Respawn Pod with a sigh and was immediately greeted by her teammates. Some were congratulating her, while others just looked on in wonder. She was good, wiped out more than half of them, and seemed to have the stamina to finish the game as she did. It came out of nowhere, it seemed, and they all wanted to know why.

"Bijou, that was some serious playing; you wanna team up for Trios?" a player asked.

One of the friends she made, Becca—whom she also shot dead—ran up to her and patted her on the shoulders with a wide smile on her face.

"Nah, if she's pairing up with someone, it's her girls! Right?"

Bijou could only give a weak smile and pat Becca on the arm as she pulled her hands away. What came over her during the game was something else. Something she really couldn't explain right away, and she would have to see Chess or Damon about it soon. It wasn't like she didn't know what she was doing; she very much knew she was on a rampage. It was the timing of it all. She shouldn't have shown this side of her so soon, but she couldn't stop herself.

What were Chess and Damon thinking about her now? More than likely angry or confused. They didn't expect little Bijou to turn the tables like that, and to be completely honest, Bijou didn't expect to do it. Her cover was blown, however, about how she could really play, and she was going to have to continue this until the end. Until it was done.

DAMON MADE HIS WAY BACK INTO THE RESPAWN ROOM, where Bijou was just exiting it. Trying to walk past him, Bijou found herself caught when Damon grabbed her by the shoulder and pushed her up against the wall outside of the doors. No one was around, but Bijou didn't feel in danger; she knew he was here for answers. Answers that she couldn't give. Not yet, anyway.

"What was that? And don't give me the 'what was what' runaround," Damon demanded.

"Maybe I've always been this way, and you guys just didn't know," Bijou said, looking away.

"One, you're a terrible liar; two, no, you're not. You were invited as a mediator and made it this far on good graces and luck. Damnit, Bijou, I love you, you know I do, but that wasn't like you out there. Are you getting special training?"

Bijou tensed up but kept looking away from Damon's line of sight.

"You are, aren't you?"

"No, I'm not."

"You're a terrible liar."

Damon let go of Bijou's shoulder and took a step back. Bijou still didn't meet his gaze; she felt ashamed almost, but for what? For playing the game? Maybe getting in the way of him and Chess. Something about their feud was sacred. In the arena, they fight on their own holy land. Stepping in between that somehow felt like sacrilege.

Maybe that's where the brunt of her guilt came from. She shouldn't feel guilty for playing well, but coming in between the two boys proverbially fighting to the death felt wrong. She sniffled and moved to get off the wall, still feeling like she was under scrutiny from Damon. With both of them not saying anything, Bijou moved to walk away, and Damon watched her go. Eventually, they would all be in the same room when the night would come, but he didn't even know that. He wasn't

Bijou's keeper, and he wasn't about to become that; wherever she went, that was her business.

The night had come, and after a couple of awkward looks between everyone, they had settled into bed not long after they had all arrived in the room. Having to take a supplement to get to sleep that night, Chess found himself having to get up in the middle of the night to go to the bathroom. He shuffled out of bed, not giving the rest of the room any time of day as he moved like a zombie toward the bathroom.

He used the toilet, washed his hands, and opened the door to move out of the room when he saw it. He didn't shit the light off, and the bathroom light poured into the room where Bijou's bed was sitting. The sheets were open, and the bed was empty.

Looking behind himself as if Bijou would be in the bathroom with him, Chess even checked the shower and didn't find her; he then shut the light off and walked to her bed. He lifted the sheets, and she wasn't there. She was gone. Quickly moving to Damon's side of the room, he silently shook the man awake until Damon stirred, slurring words in his thick accent.

"Wha—wuzzat... what's happening?" Damon whispered, slowly sitting up in his bed.

"Bijou's gone!" Chess hissed, looking over at Farren, trying not to wake her up.

"What?!"

"She's fucking gone! Look!"

Chess pointed to the empty bed, and before he could look back and tell Damon more, Damon was already putting a jacket on over his shoulders and getting out of bed, slipping his sneakers on.

"Let's go."

Chess looked back at Bijou's bed and then at Damon, incredulous.

"Go *where*? We don't even know where she is!" Chess whispered.

Albeit his confusion and protests, Chess followed close behind Damon, throwing his sneakers on, untied, as they ran to the elevators.

He bent down and tied his shoes when the elevator car opened and closed with them inside.

"So where are we going? You seem to have an idea," Chess said, standing back up.

Damon looked Chess up and down first before he answered. It was a quick look; he didn't even move his head, just his eyes, and then faced forward, pushing a hand through his hair. Chess was wearing only a white t-shirt and grey sweatpants that showed everything. It *took* everything within Damon not to blush. It had been a long time since he and Chess were any sort of intimate with each other, and seeing him wearing such loose-fitting clothes and pants wrapped around his form was making him flushed.

Chess was nonchalant, not even noticing that Damon gave him a once-over and crossed his arms over his chest, waiting for his answer. Damon sighed and leaned his back against the elevator car door.

"She's at the Arena."

"And you know this how?" Chess asked.

"Call it a hunch," Damon replied, tilting his head in Chess's direction and giving him a look. "She's been off for the past couple of weeks and always hanging out with her friends, but I asked her friends today if she's stopped by recently, and she hasn't."

"Look at you keeping tabs on her." Chess snorted.

"More like accountability. I want her to be truthful with us. That she doesn't have to hide anything from us; if we find her there, we can't get mad," Damon said.

"Who said anything about getting mad? I'll join her," Chess said.

Damon smiled at Chess's offer but then focused his eyes on the doors again, waiting for them to open. Once they did, both boys shot out of the elevator and made their way to the front entrance. The concierge watched them go with a confused look on his face, and that's when Chess doubled back and pointed at him.

"You. Blonde short girl come through here recently?"

"Miss Williams? Yes, she was walking out of here two hours ago," the man said.

"Two hours, holy shit. It's late as hell; what is she doing for three or more hours a night?" Chess asked.

"Not sleeping. Come on."

They decided to hoof it to the Arena; the building itself lit up like it was Christmas. The storm inside was likely raging for its midnight run-through, and if Bijou were in it, they would be able to catch her on a TV somewhere in the venue. The media drones never stopped, and neither did the TVs. Either way, they were going to try and find what or who they were looking for when they got there.

The run to the Arena didn't take too long, just a couple of minutes, and they were running through the door. It was pitch black again, and Chess tried not to think back to the other day when they sat together on the floor in front of the massive windows showing the storm roll by. He was conflicted about how Damon's father treated him, but that didn't mean that he forgave Damon for everything he had done to him. There was still retribution to be had for that, but on things Damon and Chess couldn't control, he felt for him. Maybe he shouldn't have come that day, giving Damon the wrong idea.

What happened already happened, however, and Damon and Chess ran down the halls toward the massive windows, trying to see if they could spot anything. As usual, the storm was raging in its midnight reset. If Bijou were in there, they wouldn't be able to see her.

"There's other training grounds around here with practice weapons. Come on," Damon said, breaking away from the window.

"The place with the Nerf guns?" Chess asked, running alongside Damon.

"They're beanbag guns, and they're for off-storm practice, so you don't kill anybody," Damon corrected.

"Nerf darts," Chess finished, looking away from Damon.

They had run down another hallway toward a couple of double doors that were locked from the outside. When Chess tried to pry the doors open, he couldn't even make a dent in them. That's when Damon looked up and then pointed.

"Chess, look."

Chess looked up as well to see a large TV screen above the door showing a media drone sitting still in midair, looking and focusing on nothing in particular. In the distance of the shot, however, was a small dot running for its life away from the oncoming storm. In their hands was a shotgun, and slung on their back was an automatic rifle. They were running for their lives, and the only informative piece of information that Chess and Damon could get from the running speck was the blonde hair attached to the head. It was Bijou.

"What is she doing?" Chess asked, stopping his attempt to open the double doors.

"I don't know, running. But from what?" Damon said.

Bijou reached the middle of the map where the storm was going to end, and she pulled out her phone. That's when the media drone decided to swoop down and get ahead of the storm about to engulf it. Getting close to bijou but not close enough that it was in her face, Chess and Damon got a good view of her tapping a couple of things on her phone and then fizzle out of the Arena as she more than likely went back to a Respawn Pod. Next to the boys, the doors unlocked and opened as if they were waiting for her to leave the field to operate.

"Must be on lockdown, so no one goes in to mess with the Respawn Pods," Damon muttered.

"Whatever, let's go."

Chess and Damon made their way down the hallways that led to multiple rooms and multiple Respawn Pods. Essentially, the whole lobby area beyond those doors was a big Respawn Lobby with a sitting room at the end of the hallway. Chess kept walking until the silhouette of a person caught his eye, making him stop in his tracks. Before Damon could say anything or make any more noise, Chess grabbed his arm by the wrist and kneeled. When Damon hissed, Chess brought a finger to his lips, telling Damon to be quiet. He pointed toward the Respawn Room and the man inside, and they both kneeled to look at him.

It was so dark in the room, all the lights were off, and the person was wearing a hoodie with the hood up to make matters worse. Chess couldn't figure out who it was, but they were waiting for Bijou to come in through the Respawn Pod; he could figure that much. Within seconds, the Respawn Pod glowed, whirred, and materialized Bijou inside itself. Now without weapons and wearing the team tracksuit, she walked out just in time for the Respawn Pod to stop glowing and the mysterious man to turn around. Chess cursed under his breath at not being able to get a clear view of the man's face, and Damon grimaced. In the darkness and behind soundproof glass and closed doors, Bijou spoke quietly with this man. They couldn't hear anything that was going on inside the room.

"What are they saying?" Damon whispered.

"Do I look like I know? What you can hear, I can hear, and I don't hear shit," Chess said.

When Bijou turned to come out of the room suddenly, Chess's blood ran cold, and he grabbed Damon's wrist again and pulled, making them run out of the hallway before either of them were spotted. The sounds of their sneakers hitting the linoleum flooring echoed through the walls, and they were forced to stop around the corner when Bijou finally made it out of the room.

"We got to get out of here," Damon hissed, and Chess nodded in agreement.

They ran out of the Arena's front doors, praying that the doors didn't slam on their way out, and hit behind a bush on the side of the venue's entrance. Bijou showed herself not a couple of minutes later, looking despondent and exhausted. Whatever she was training for, it was wearing her out, but she *was* training.

"We have to make it back to the room before she does or she's gonna know something's up," Damon said.

"How would she know we went to look for her?" Chess asked.

"I accused her of side training earlier today, and she would know that I would come to make sure I was right. Either way, if she sees us out of theorem, she's gonna be suspicious," Damon explained.

"Alright, how do we beat her there?" Chess looked over at Bijou again, and she was making her way to the street and the sidewalk back toward the hotel.

"Come on; we'll take the other way around these buildings."

Damon and Chess broke off into a sprint around the other buildings on the long way around back to the hotel. Sure, Bijou might've beat them if they had walked, but they were running as fast as they could back to the hotel, and by the time they made it to the doors, Bijou was on the horizon. Sweaty and winded, Chess and Damon slammed on the button to summon the elevator a couple of times before she came through the doors and saw them, caught red-handed. Eventually, the elevator did come, and just as it was closing around them, Bijou had made her way back into the hotel.

"Just get back in bed, and we'll ask her tomorrow," Damon said.

"More like you'll ask her. I want no part of it," Chess said.

"You're not even a little bit curious why she's taking this seriously now? Like at all?"

"I never said I wasn't curious, but I'm not here to win either." Chess looked at Damon again. "You know what I'm here for."

God, Damon wanted to kiss that look off of Chess's face so badly, but he withheld. Licking his bottom lip and biting it, Damon looked away, albeit a little annoyed that he didn't have the backup of Chess in this. He would be getting his answers one way or another.

CHAPTER TWENTY-NINE

The second game.

Flown halfway across the world to Japan in the Nara region, close to Kyoto, the Temporal Storm wasn't contained by any arena. Miles and miles wide with mountains and abandoned villages abundant, it would be a test of skill and teamwork if they wanted to get through this alive and win.

"You'll pair off into groups of three. The last 16 standing will move on; the last half will be eliminated. You're playing against Japan on their home turf; don't think it's going to be easy. Again, they could wipe you all out within minutes, and the last 15 to be left standing are the ones that continue forward. You'll be logged when you come into the Respawn Room. Best of luck, make me proud out there."

Farren addressed the 30 players in the room as they all listened to her speak. She explained the region, the Kii Mountains, and the various villages left to time since the storm rolled through. It was going to be tough, the terrain treacherous. There might even be bears and other dangerous animals in the way sometimes. Chess swallowed and sized up his options.

He could play it safe and ask Bijou to pair up with him and someone else. There was no way in hell he was going to pair up with Damon. Call him petty or a child; he was here to get even, not buddy up with him.

"Friendly Fire, again, is something you'll have to look out for. In these games, anyone is a target, and you can very well hurt or eliminate your own teammates if you're not thinking clearly enough or you're not acting right. Make sure you remember trigger discipline and the right way to aim your weapon.

"On top of that, the running and training you all have been doing this past year and up until now is going to show. A lot of you gained muscle out of it, and it's time put it to the test."

Everyone nodded along with Farren's words, people already linking up to pair together. Damon was in a group with two other girls that had been eyeing him up since the beginning of the tournaments. Damon smiled and made small talk, but Chess knew he was as gay as it got. Whatever these girls saw in him, they weren't going to get anything out of it. He watched them fawn over him, one of the girls rubbing a hand up and down his arm. Damon let it happen, giving the girl the warmest of smiles. He tucked a tendril of hair behind one of the girl's ears and winked at her; the girl looked away, blushing and laughing. It wasn't until Damon looked over at Chess that Chess realized he was staring at him.

Rolling his eyes, Chess looked away from the view and turned his attention to the person standing in front of him. It was one of the players that had barely made it to passing in the last game. He was kind of chubby, but some of it had turned into muscle, and Chess could see the look of determination on his face. He was going to ask him to join his team.

Looking over toward Bijou, Chess watched as two girls circled her and hugged her, talking about how they would win the game now that she was fighting with them. Chess sighed and then turned back to the player standing in front of him and offered a hand.

"Chess Harlow," Chess introduced himself.

"I know who you are; we've been training for a year straight together," the player said.

"Yeah, but I don't know your name," Chess shot back, his hand still extended.

The player took it with a smile and bounced his hand up and down several times.

"Gavin Hendrix. Nice to meet you. This is Charles." Gavin motioned to another man that came around the side of him and waved at Chess. Chess nodded his head toward him.

"Nice to finally *formally* meet you, Chess," Charles said.

"Likewise."

Chess didn't smile, but as he looked over to Damon, he also saw that his ex wasn't giving him the time of day either. Tucking hair behind girls' ears and whispering things they wanted to hear. It was enough to make Chess sick to even think about. His mind was a whirlwind of excuses he could make to go over and tell the girls that they don't even stand a chance. Not because Damon was his or anything like that.

"Chess?"

Chess snapped out of his second staring contest of that day and focused on the men standing in front of him, sizing them up. They weren't the worst on the team, mostly muscle and height. They looked like they could take an order and follow it, and from what he remembered from this past year of seeing them train with him, they could cover ground pretty fast. He would roll with them for Trios.

"Let's do this then," Chess said, standing up and shaking Charles's hand.

As Charles smiled, Chess looked into his eyes and found himself smiling as well. It wasn't like he was falling for Charles, just the genuine notion of his expression made Chess smile as well. When he looked back at Damon for one last time before turning away, he caught a glimpse of Damon boring holes into the back of his head. Not moving.

It was going to be a classic Royale of Trios. Getting into a plane and jumping at the height of 10,000 feet into the forested mountains below. Landing within the trees was going to be tricky, and keeping together as a team was going to be even harder. There were going to be moments when they would have to split up and look for supplies, not get bunched up and slaughtered in one go. This was going to be a test Chess wasn't about to admit he wasn't ready for.

Rocking together in the C-130 over Japanese airspace, Chess looked to the other side of the seats at the Japanese team that was going to jump at the same time as the American team. They were sizing each other up from across the walkway, and tension was high. Who was going to be the first to jump from the plane? Who had a plan, and who didn't? Chess caught the eye of a girl on the other side, smiling at him before he looked away with a scowl.

This World Royale was supposed to be the best of the best competing, and a lot of people treated it like the Olympics, where they could make friends with other players and network between countries. While some on the American team have taken up the same thought, Chess wasn't here to make friends. He didn't meet the girl's sight again, opting to look out of the lowering exit toward the back of the plane.

"Welcome! Yokoso!" the announcer said the same greeting in both languages. "This is the Kii Peninsula Trios Royale for the second game in the World Royale Games!"

The announcer said the same greeting and announcement in Japanese. Everyone had their hands on their seatbelts, ready to jump.

"Please be advised; this storm takes 24 hours to reset. You will have one day to finish on top! Good luck!"

After repeating himself in Japanese, the lights at the end of the plane buzzed and flashed yellow. It was almost time. Chess looked over to his teammates and motioned for them to look at him, having to yell over the wind so that they heard him.

"We're jumping early! Getting a head start on the outskirts for weapons!" Chess hollered.

Charles gave a thumbs-up while Gavin hollered back an affirmation.

"We're with you!" Gavin hollered back.

Chess nodded and smirked. It felt good to have teammates willing to listen to and work with him. How long that was going to last, though, he didn't know. It was going to be a full 24 hours of constant walking and team management. The stress was already high, but if he could keep his head together and his team collected, he should make it out of this unscathed.

Searching for Damon was going to be a challenge. All these trees and mountains were going to make it hard to find anyone that wasn't holed up in a town or village. He would still have to try. He wasn't here to make a name for himself; he was here to kill Damon Kennedy.

"Three... Two... One! Go!" The announcer hollered over the loudspeaker. Everyone knew what that meant, and many American and Japanese people were jumping out of the plane with great haste. Some of the teams held hands as they jumped tighter in an attempt to stay close when they popped their parachutes, but some went ahead of their group. There were going to be a couple of people that were going to treat this like solos, and to be fair, Chess thought about abandoning Gavin and Charles to get ahead in the game. With terrain like this, however, it would be easy to get lost, and he would need the help, so he decided to stick around.

Chess unbuckled quickly and looked to his teammates, who were also unbuckled and waiting for Chess. It was looking like he was the leader of their group. Good, he could manage that. Go here, shoot that. Easy enough. Chess nodded and sprinted toward the exit, Gavin and Charles quick in tow. They jumped together and soared through the air, listing toward a far corner of the map where the storm was beginning to form. They would hit a few villages and then move toward the center.

Chess fell, his arms at his sides as he plummeted toward the earth. He didn't look out to see if his teammate were with him; he would just have to trust that they would land near or at least close the where he was going to land. Regroup in no less than a couple of minutes. He moved his body toward a place on the map that no one was falling toward to give them a wide berth from other players for a while. He wanted to get loaded up with weapons and ammo and move on to the center, keeping his eyes out for his one and only goal: Damon.

Popping his parachute when he was getting close to the trees, Chess looked up into the sky to see Gavin had also popped his parachute, but Charles was still plummeting toward the ground. Chess hollered out, but it was no use against the wind and the speed Charles was falling at. Eventually, Charles did pop his chute, but he was much lower than Chess and Gavin. Chess was going to have to land wherever Charles was going to land, but that was risky. He was likely falling much faster than he thought toward the earth. They would have to hunt for him when they landed.

The trees came, branches and leaves scraping Chess's skin as he prayed that his parachute didn't get caught in the trees. Eventually, he hit solid ground and quickly shook his parachute off his shoulders. Gavin wasn't too far from him, just a few yards away in a small clearing.

"Charles!" Gavin hollered out, taking his parachute off and running toward Chess.

They were empty-handed and out in the open proverbially. Anyone could drop on them in a second, and people were still jumping from the plane in the sky. It was going to be a long game, and they all needed to be together.

"Charles!" Chess hollered out as well.

"Charles!" Gavin tried again, dragging out his name into the trees.

"Over here! Over.. argh! Over here!"

They heard Charles in the distance beckoning them over, and they both broke off into a run toward the noise. Above them, Charles was hanging from a dangerous height; his parachute stuck in a tree. He was actively trying to unshackle himself from the chute in an attempt to drop down to the ground.

"No! No, don't! We'll catch you! We'll—"

But Charles didn't listen to Gavin. He unbuckled the parachute from his body and plummeted much faster than he thought he would toward the ground. With a sickening snap of his leg, he choked on air and instantly felt lightheaded.

"Shit! Aw fuck!" Chess put his hands on his head in shock, and Gavin just stopped and stared at the display in front of them.

Charles's leg was completely snapped at the bone, bending at an unnatural angle. When Charles finally sat up and looked at the damage, he screamed.

CHAPTER **THIRTY**

"Aw fuck! Aw fuck!!"

Charles was freaking out, holding his broken leg while trying to drag his body up off the ground. Blood was everywhere, and not even Chess knew if a medkit would heal a wound like this. They could try wrapping it and setting it with gauze and see if it would heal on its own, but they would have to find a medkit first. They didn't even have guns, and their first person was down.

"You have to leave me!" Charles hollered.

"No! We're not leaving you! Right Chess?" Gavin asked.

Chess didn't answer, looking away from the whole mess in a mixture of disgust and internal calamity. He was going to leave him. They didn't have any weapons to take care of him right here and there, but what else could they do?

"Chess, come on! Help me get him up!" Gavin strained, hooking his arm under Charles's shoulder, and tried the haul him off the ground.

Charles hollered out in surprise as he felt his leg dangle on the skin as the bone was broken away at the shin. He hobbled a couple of times before stumbling and catching himself before falling back to the ground.

"Arrrgh! Just fucking shoot me!" Charles called out.

That's when Chess clicked his tongue and rolled his eyes, putting his arm under Charles's waist, supporting him. Together, all three trudged through the forest, hoping and trying to come across a village or a building. When Charles's broken and limp leg would bump into Chess, Chess had to suppress the urge to vomit. The pain would've been excruciating in the outside world, and he was grateful that Charles couldn't feel any pain in this pocket dimension. As long as the storm swirled around them, he was safe from pain.

"We just have to get to a building where he can sit. We can figure our shit out from there." Chess grunted, trudging along the grass and sticks as he and Gavin pushed along, Charles in their arms.

"Praying they have a medkit in there," Gavin said.

"Praying they have a gun in there. I'm starting to feel it, guys," Charles groaned, hobbling forward the best he could.

"You should've waited for us to catch you. What were you thinking?" Chess chastised.

"I was thinking that the drop wasn't that far. I thought I could make it. You know, all hero-like." Charles tried to laugh but ended with another groan as he felt his head go heavy.

"So what I'm hearing is that you weren't thinking," Chess said.

"No. I wasn't."

Charles groaned again as they lifted him up and over a log. Walking a little farther into the forest, there was an opening in the trees ahead, and they decided to stop in the middle. Just ahead was a small building in the middle of nowhere, a large gate standing in front of it.

"A Shrine?" Gavin asked mostly to himself.

"What makes you think that?" Chess asked, adjusting his grip on Charles.

"I did some research on the mountains before we got here, and the forests are littered with shrines just like this," Gavin answered.

"Let's go inside; there might be something we can use," Chess said, and all three of them continued to the building.

Sitting Charles on the step, it was easier to see the broken bone protruding from the skin and the blood seeping out onto the wood beneath him. He was going to bleed out and die if they didn't get a medkit and quick. Chess left Charles with Gavin and ran inside the shrine's main room, looking around. There wasn't much to see, a big mirror in the back of the building and lots of food scattered around. He decided to take something that looked like a rice ball and bring it back outside, handing it to Charles.

"Here, eat something," Chess said.

"Dude, you can't be taking from the gods; that's their food."

Chess handed Charles the rice ball and gave Gavin an incredulous look.

"Really, Gavin? At a time like this, you think I give a shit about who resides in the shrine? Food was there, so I took it. The storm is going to reset everything anyways," Chess bit back.

"I'll check the back," Gavin said and rose.

Watching Gavin run to the other side of the building, Chess knelt next to Charles and looked at the wound. It was bad, and blood wouldn't stop seeping from it. Charles was eating the rice ball, but Chess could tell every other second Charles's head would lull back, blood loss gripping him. He knew how he was feeling, but he didn't hope Bijou would appear out of nowhere and put an end to it as she did to him. When Gavin exclaimed from the other side of the building and came running back, Chess was happy to see a gun in his hand. It wasn't much, a Hunter's Rifle, but it was a weapon.

"We're in business. We can defend ourselves now," Gavin said, slinging the weapon to his back.

"Good, shoot me with it," Charles groaned.

"Charles, no. Not after all that shit you told me about your mom. You're winning this Royale, so get up," Gavin grunted, hooking Charles around his arms again. Chess also helped.

"Your mom?" Chess inquired.

Charles was quiet for a few moments as they limped and trudged through the forests again, looking for any other weapons or medical supplies. So far, all they found were sparse plants and sticks, and one rifle. Charles sniffled after a couple of minutes and then began talking.

"My mom, she's got cancer. The money I could earn winning the World Royale would pay her medical bills. All I ever wanted was to see her walk again and smile."

Chess looked down at Charles and didn't say a word. He knew this was heavy stuff. Chess never knew his mom, her abandoning him with his dad after he was born and never coming back. If she was alive or dead, he didn't know, but with his dad dead, he considered himself an orphan.

Money like this wouldn't go toward anything other than more Blood Running games in Santa Catalina. People like Charles were here for a real reason.

Thinking about that, Chess hoisted Charles up more on his arm and kept walking. He didn't look at Charles, but he could feel Charles's eyes on him for a moment, looking up at him.

"We'll get you fixed up, and you're going to make your mom better," Chess said.

Charles dropped his head and continued limping.

"Yeah."

THEY FINALLY MADE IT TO A VILLAGE AFTER AN HOUR OF walking in the forest. Using the app on their phones, they were able to hobble their way to the outskirts of one of the villages close to the storm's border. With the storm not yet expanding, they had a little bit of time to settle down and tend to Charles.

They picked a house at random and opened the door. The inside looked like a modern household with a TV and toys strewn about. They laid Charles on the couch, and then Gavin and Chess began ransacking the entire place for weapons and med kits, Chess being fruitful in his endeavors. He came back downstairs with a semi-auto pistol and a pocket of spare ammo, and when he saw what Gavin was holding, he almost broke out into a genuine smile.

He had found a medkit, holding it up in the air triumphantly.

"Come on, let's get you fixed up," Gavin said, opening it and taking out the gauze and splints.

It took no longer than a couple of minutes, but the leg was set in place and wrapped up tight with gauze. Because of some anomaly that Chess and Gavin didn't quite understand, Charles was healing and could stand on his leg within thirty minutes. Rapid healing and no pain.

This place would be a paradise if it weren't for the storm that eats everything. Without Respawn Pods, the storm would kill them and never reset them. They would simply be lost to time.

"You're up? Can you walk?" Chess asked.

"I'm a little wobbly, and it might be a bit until I can run, but I'm set. I can walk," Charles said.

"Good, here."

Chess tossed him another pistol he had found outside the building while Charles was healing up. It was a basic M9 Beretta. Now, all three, albeit with piss poor weapons, were armed and ready to defend themselves.

"It would be best to make our way to the middle now; we've been skirting on the edge for too long for my liking," Gavin said.

"I'm with Gavin, this was great getting me fixed up, but we gotta go."

Chess bit his lip and nodded his head, taking his phone out. There were 60 players at the start of the match, and now only 43 remained. The ratio was unknown to him at this time, but they had to keep going and defend themselves when necessary.

"Alright, let's get a move on," Chess said.

They made their way through the forgotten village, eaten over and over again by a storm that reset its time to when it was first engulfed. They didn't run into anyone, and before they really knew it, they were walking down a mountain road toward the middle. Chess didn't like it. Being on a major road, you might as well put a bullseye on your forehead and yell for people to shoot. People were going to be watching the roads for Blood Runners passing by and pick them off one by one. As soon as it was safe to get off of the road and continue through the trees, they would do so.

"Doing ok back there?" Chess asked.

"Yeah, but I—"

FWIIIP

A bullet landed right between Charles's legs, kicking up the dirt into his eyes, but his adrenaline started to also kick in. Someone saw them and was shooting at them.

"Disperse!" Chess ordered, and they all ran in different directions, hiding behind trees and waiting.

Chess peeked his foot out from where he was hiding, and a bullet rained down on it, barely connecting with his shoe. They were on the hunt once again, and he didn't know who it was this time. He watched as Gavin made his way up some rocks and tried to get to a good vantage point.

"Distract them; keep them on you!" Gavin harshly whispered.

Chess nodded and started to make himself out to be bait. Peeking his head out from the tree and sticking his arms out to be shot at. Every time, the shooter took the bait, and Chess even fired back a couple of times blindly into the forest.

Why weren't there three of them shooting at them? This was Trios. It could be that this person's team was wiped out, and they were on their own, or this was one of those Solo Only players that didn't play by the rules and ran off the second they hit the ground.

Gavin had reached his vantage point and looked down the scope. Chess looked up at him in hopes that he could see who it was and get a clear shot, and Gavin was taking his sweet time. Chess fired two more shots into the trees before he hissed back at Gavin.

"Hurry the fuck up!"

Gavin looked down at Chess with an impatient look and then back through the scope. A rustle in the leaves next to him pulled his attention, however, and before he knew it, a woman was bearing down on him, shoving a machete into his neck. Gavin turned into a flurry of crystals at the top of the rocks, and Chess could only watch.

It was a trio, and the third one could've been anywhere and anybody.

CHAPTER THIRTY-ONE

Chess tried to aim and shoot at the woman at the top of the rocks, who was now popping crystals into her hands from Gavin's body. He couldn't get a clear shot, and worse, she sent down a roaring wind spell his way to throw him off. Discombobulated, Chess tried to get up from the ground in time to save his own skin before the third Blood Runner came out of the trees and ambushed them.

When Charles started firing and yelling, Chess made a break for it from his safe spot, risking getting shot by the first sniper deeper in the forest. Sure enough, a bullet splintered the wood next to his head, and Chess kept running. He didn't stop.

Luckily, he could see the third woman in the forest advancing with her own handgun and firing sure and true at Charles. Chess decided to round around and flank her from the side. Taking her by surprise, Chess held up his gun before she could turn and fired twice. Once center mass and the second in her neck. She turned into crystals before she hit the ground.

Charles ran up and popped a couple of crystals while trying to stay behind the tree. In the distance, one of the girls yelled out a name in anguish. No doubt the girl they just killed and were now sitting on top of. If they didn't move soon, they would be found quickly.

"I'm good with magic. Let me clear us a path," Charles said, popping more and more crystals.

His mana must've been at max by now, but he kept taking the essence of the Temporal Crystals into himself as if he could break his limits. When he stood back up, Charles nodded toward Chess and moved to the other side of the tree, getting ready to run.

"Follow close to me, no matter what. Don't be afraid," Charles said.

"Can you even run?" Chess asked, his voice rising.

"We can get out of here; just follow me. Here we go."

What happened next, Chess figured, was a bad dream. It was magic like he had never seen in his entire career of Blood Running. From his hands, Charles began running laterally from the trees and bursting fire from his hands. The trees and grass ahead of them were engulfed in hellfire that reached the sky and did not stop as they kept running. It was like a massive fire shield between them and the girls hunting them. Chess ran as fast as he could, Charles keeping up and setting the trees ablaze ahead as they made their way through the forest. It would burn down the whole forest around them. They had to get out of the trees before the blaze spread and ate them alive.

Chess looked up toward the sky, seeing the leaves set ablaze and the ashes of leaves falling around him. The bark of the trees was red with fire, and the reeds of grass turned black, replaced with licks of fire. They ran. They ran until they could get to a clearing wide enough to collect themselves and move on. If Charles had to continue to raze the forest to get out of this situation, then he would do so. However, even as they were running, Chess could see that he was starting to slow down, his mana dwindling and his energy evaporating.

"Come on! We're almost out of here!" Chess yelled.

Charles stopped conjuring fire and focused on running out of the forest. Pumping his arms to catch up with Chess, he ran as fast as he could on his leg, hobbling several times as the bone had not yet set. When Chess looked back to Charles, avoiding fire and running ahead, he watched as Charles smiled at him, thinking they were going to get out of here. They were going to get the upper hand. Then a bullet sliced through his neck, dropping him to the ground.

"Charles!" Chess screamed.

The bullet came from the fire. They were following them through the blaze, and he was more than likely in the sights of the sniper right now. Did he go back for Charles, or did he run for it? He hid behind another tree that wasn't on fire as he weighed his options. Charles wasn't dead yet, but as Chess looked at his body, he knew it was coming. Charles was gurgling on the ground, his back arching and falling in pain he could not feel. He was choking on his own blood in a way he could not experience. The feeling of suffocating and not being able to feel it, Chess knew he must've been scared out of his mind. Chess couldn't save him.

Before he broke off from the tree to run, another bullet rained down on Charles, turning his body into crystals, a flurry of purple that Chess had never seen. Almost turning the ground into a geode. It was only him now in this trio. The rest were dead and likely watching him from the Respawn Room. It was all riding on him now.

He broke from the tree and ran forward, deeper into the forest, knowing that the assailants were going to have to go around the blaze that Charles conjured just to get to him. He could make a good dent between them and the forest before he could gather his foundations to attack back. Right now, he really had nothing to defend himself except for a pistol that could only do minor damage. Unless he got a lucky shot to the head, they would live through a bullet from his gun.

His teammates were gone. It was only him on the map that could carry it on now. With that, he had to get away from these two assailants as fast as possible and hope the fire would hinder them long enough to find another building. That's when it hit him; he could go back to the village.

Doubling back and running toward the village they sparsely explored, it took him five minutes of constant running to make it back to the outskirts. The first house he busted into yielded little. Ammo for his pistol and not much else. Looking down at his hands, he realized he had been burned, and he hoped that this wouldn't affect his aim later. He didn't know if they were following him or if they knew that he went back to the village, but he had to hurry nonetheless. The Storm was still threatening to engulf him if he didn't get out quickly.

Three houses and a couple of shops later, he finally found a DMR Sniper and ammo. He quickly slung it over his shoulder and bolted out of the village, grabbing an apple on the way out. He had to eat something before he continued. He wouldn't be taking the roads this time; he would brave the forests and make his way to the center of the map alone.

It was funny; he was so ready to go solo on these Trios, to ditch his teammates whose names he didn't care to learn. But now he was missing Gavin and Charles. He was missing the sounds of their voices. He thought it was funny. Missing people like that. He would have to catch up with them after this was over if they were not already eliminated from the World Royale. He hoped that they hadn't been, that it had been long enough now that they all would've been able to go forward with the games.

Chess made his way through the forest, getting back to the charred and blazing trees and grass and running through the ash. If the other people hunting him were still here, they weren't showing themselves. However, he didn't look a gift horse in the mouth and did not stop to look for them. He pulled out his phone and logged the distance he would have to run to get to the middle. He was down two teammates and on his own and didn't know how many other teams he would be coming across on his way to the middle. He would have to find a place to hunker down and do what was preyed upon him. Hunt.

There was nothing more than charred trees and soot on his way back through the forest, the black of the char sticking to his clothes and shoes. If there were any animals in the vicinity, they were surely gone by now, he remembered hearing about bears in the area, but even they wouldn't stick around through a fire like this.

He kept running, hoping he didn't run into them again, the clearings not showing themselves any time soon. It was nothing more than trees and shrubs, but the fire was starting to die down. No doubt there would be a massive black tube of smoke in the sky showing everyone where he was. He had to get out of this area.

Feeling safe enough behind a massive tree, he pulled out his phone to check the status. 15 people left. He was safe, but he didn't know if his teammates were safe as well. Knowing he was going to go forward didn't do much for him, but he could at least focus on getting even with whoever took Gavin and Charles away from him. Either that or find out where Damon and Bijou had gone to. The map was so big already; he didn't think he would even run into them. Getting even with the people that wronged him was harder than he thought it was going to be. It should've been easy to shoot Damon in the face; it should've been easy to get back at the girls that had cornered them in the trees and flanked them. They only got one of them, and there were two more to account for, and he was pretty sure they were from the Japanese team. People from both sides of the team were looking out for him, and he was looking out for them, great.

He was nowhere near the middle of the middle, and he would have to run for almost five hours straight if he wanted to make it. With the first two hours gone from the game already, he only had 22 hours to make any headway. He was going to run for an hour, then rest, and then run for another hour. Having his entire team wiped out so early wasn't a good feeling. He felt like a failure of a leader for it. Were they watching him now, wondering what was going to happen next? Yeah, him too. He didn't know what was going to happen to him now.

The thought of just giving himself to another team for elimination milled over in his mind, but then he wouldn't have given searching for who he was looking for a chance. Santa Catalina was big, but this was something else. Mountains and winding roads, villages, and shrines. It felt like eyes were on you everywhere; no matter when he moved, someone was watching him. He shook off the feeling, pocketed his phone, and started to run.

The first hour of running proved unfruitful. No clearings or villages, not even a shrine. Just more and more trees. Falling to his ass on the ground against a tree trunk, he breathed evenly, head up to the sky as he rested. He didn't have anything to do other than run. He had to keep going, but his back was slick with sweat, the humid heat of mid-Japan taking its toll on him. He wished he had brought a water bottle for a trek like this. He had to find a village after this. There was no other choice but to.

Another rustle in the leaves pulled his attention from his relaxation. Unlike the last time, this rustle was coming from far away, as if someone was moving leaves out of their way to walk. Chess got up from where he was sitting and walked over to a couple of bushes to hide his body. Using the scope of his DMR, the visage of brown hair with a part in the middle was hard to miss.

CHAPTER THIRTY-TWO

Shaking, his finger trembling on the trigger, he watched Damon and his group of girls walk unknowingly through a patch of grass. One of the girls seems to call out and say something to Damon, which causes him to stop. In his hand is an AK-47 and a knife on his hip. He was stocked to the nines, and he would only have this one shot to pull this off unless he would give away his position.

Did Damon and his posse of girls drop right when Chess did? He was an hour away from his last position, but this was still really close to where he and his group dropped off at. If anything, with gear like that, he was more than likely close to another town or village he could hit. That was if those three didn't clear it out first. Would he let them go and hit the village for better gear, or did he take care of business right here and now? He was conflicted only because Damon wasn't stupid. If this shot weren't perfect, Damon would be on him like white on rice within seconds.

Damon stopped and looked behind his shoulder, his classic grin on his face. Chess bit his lip. His finger moved to hug the trigger, and he sucked in some breath. That's when he decided to take note of the girls with him.

"DAMON, HOLD ON!"

Damon turned around and gave Ana his signature grin as she tried to keep up with him. Sure he moved fast, but they all have been training this year; they should've been keeping up. Nevertheless, he gave her some compassion and flashed her a smile.

"What's up?"

"I gotta pee. Can we take five real quick?" Ana asked, her tone high in need.

"Oh! Yeah, real quick. There's a group of bushes over there; we'll stand over here and cover down," Damon said, pointing toward the packet of bushes off in the distance.

Ana gave a thumbs up and moved to walk behind the grass and sticks while Damon and the other girl, Heidi, moved to the other side of the small clearing. As Damon kneeled and aimed off in the distance with his weapon, Heidi did the same, only for his six o'clock. How ever long Ana was going to take was on Ana; Damon was willing to wait as long as he needed to before the storm came down upon them. It was quiet for a long time, the only sounds in the background being the call of birdsong and the sway of the trees.

Damon breathed in and out, focusing on his gaze into the forest, looking for something, anything moving within his sights. He thought he saw a flash of something in the trees above them in the grass and rocks but didn't get a chance to check it out any further as the feeling of something bearing down on him from behind pulled him from his thoughts.

"Huh? Heidi?"

"Hey, Damon... I want to ask you something."

Damon turned around, giving a slight look back to the glint he thought he saw before giving his whole attention to Heidi.

"What is it? Wha—woah!"

Damon had been kneeling, but with Heidi's weight, he was pushed onto his back as Heidi crawled on top of him. Only to steady himself, he put a hand on Heidi's shoulder and gripped in surprise, to which Heidi put her hand over his on her body, the other hand in the grass beside

Damon's head. She was looking down at him, and he was looking up at her, her hair falling around her face and curtaining Damon's frame. Her knee was skirting up further and further up between Damon's legs, and she was breathing a little hard.

"Do you like me?"

Damon didn't say anything, but the grinning was gone. He looked at her with his cold, hard eyes and didn't move. He didn't want to do anything that would disrupt the group, hurt her in any way that could be taken horribly. She was already advancing on him in a way he didn't want, but he had to play this smart, or he would be in the wrong. He hoped that glint in the trees was someone about to put him out of his misery.

"Where'd you get that idea?" Damon asked, his tone deep and controlled.

"The way you touched me in the lobby. The smile on your face when you look at me."

Because I was using you to get at Chess.

"I could feel the connection we had then, the way you gave your attention to me."

Because I was using you to get at Chess.

"Don't you feel it too?" Heidi asked.

"No," Damon responded curt and tight.

Heidi's eyebrows furrowed, and she searched his face for any inkling of a lie in his eyes, but she couldn't find any. Moving at the right time, Damon looked up and over as Heidi lowered her face onto him, kissing his neck and cheek. Damon growled deep under his throat, and Heidi took that as an invitation to keep going. When Damon put his hand on her chest and pushed her up, Heidi finally sat up and looked at him with incredulous eyes.

"You're telling me I'm in the wrong here? You lead me along!" Heidi shrieked.

"I wasn't even hitting on you; I don't know where you even got that idea," Damon said, propping himself up on his arms to look at her.

She was straddling him now, looking down at him with a face of thunder. She felt scorned and betrayed. Her hands bunched up in his tracksuit, and tears welled in her eyes. She scooted forward, inadvertently rubbing themselves against each other, making Damon look away with a scowl on his face.

"You—"

There was a distant sound, and before Damon could realize what it was, Heidi's head separated from her body, her torso flying backward into the grass. Damon wasted no time, rolling over, picking ups his weapon, and aiming it toward the glint he saw before. He saw Chess.

They just stood there looking at each other. Chess had more than enough of a shot to kill Damon, but he didn't. He was saving him, sending a message. However, Chess took what he just saw; he would have to deal with it later. He probably thought that he liked girls now and was getting into it. He was going to have to clear the air later and wasn't looking forward to it.

They stared at each other. Damon watched through his scope as Chess looked up from his own scope toward him, more than likely unable to see him too clearly. He got up, put his DMR on his shoulder, and continued toward the center. He left Damon to the rest of his team. Something was telling Damon that he was waiting for him to fire, shoot Chess down despite what had happened or in retaliation of what had happened. For some reason, Damon did not fire. He just sat there; his finger wasn't even on the trigger. He was just watching Chess, and Chess was watching him, and he let him get away. Maybe in thanks, maybe for something else.

Chess made it to the middle in no less than six hours. He was exhausted, sweat dripping down his body, and hungry as all get out. In the center of the map was a massive town with stores, houses, and shrines littered everywhere. It looked like it was densely populated at one point, but the Storm had pushed out everyone who had lived here. This place belonged to Temporal Space now.

Pulling his phone out and checking the count and time, the storm wasn't due to eye at the center for another 12 hours. This would give him time to get something to eat and even sleep before he had a showdown with whoever would eventually show up. Whether Damon or someone from the Japanese team, he had to prepare for it.

He found an abandoned but stocked convenience store on a corner and walked inside. Grabbing a milk tea carton and a couple of rice balls stuffed with salmon, he stuffed his face with food while sitting behind the counter to hide from anyone who might've passed by. It took him only a few minutes to fill up his tank, but he used the bathroom in the backroom and moved on.

There was a massive soviet style apartment building on the other side of the street, and Chess figured that was the perfect spot to pick a house at random and get some rest. Hopefully, he would be able to lock the door behind him. He took the stairs to the fourth floor and picked at apartment 408. The door was unlocked, and once he was inside, he pulled the deadbolt and popped the second lock above the door. No one was coming in unless they took the balcony. Drawing the curtains until the apartment was pitch black, he moved to the rooms hoping to find a bed. The first room he walked into was a child's room. A crib was nestled in the back against the window. Chess stood and looked at it for a moment. The Temporal Storms had taken so much from humans, and he was using them for pleasure and sport. He wondered where this family was now. If they got out of the storm in time to live long lives. He hoped they did.

Moving to the next room, he found a large Queen bed with a duvet neatly made. He dumped his DMR on the right side and fell on the left side, pulling his phone out. With his back relaxing, he moved around to pop his bones from stress and checked the map. The storm was slowly moving inland, but he still had 12 hours to get serious. He busted his whole ass to get here first, and he was going to take advantage of it, getting sleep wherever he could.

There were seven people left. He, Damon, the other girl, and whoever or whatever team was left. It was going to be a shootout in the town come the time they all converged in the same place. He had to get his sleep in now so that he was ready.

He didn't bother taking his clothes off, just in case someone did come around and he could get up quickly and work, but he did kick off his shoes. He could easily slip them back on, still tied. The bottom of his socks was almost entirely black, sweat and dead skin collecting on the cotton. Chess grimaced and laid on his back, the pillow feeling like heaven.

Then he was alone with his own thoughts. Sleep didn't come fast enough; the thoughts came rolling in hard and fast. The images of the girl hovering over Damon. Kissing on Damon and moving like she was over him. Giving herself to him and Damon putting his hands on her. He bunched his eyes shut and furrowed his eyebrows at the thought of Damon... what? Moving on? Isn't that what he wanted? Whatever who whoever Damon did wasn't his business anymore.

So why did it hurt?

Why did it hurt to see that girl move on top of him like that, to see his hands move over her and flatten his palms on her body? Every move of his hands replayed in the back of his eyes; he couldn't get it out of his head. He shouldn't care. He should not care.

But he did. He did care. And it hurt.

With the image of that girl's head separating from her body and falling off Damon, Damon looking back up at him but not firing. He fell asleep with the flush of blood on Damon's face fresh on his mind.

CHAPTER THIRTY-THREE

The sounds of gunshots woke Chess from his sleep. How long had he been out? Pulling his phone from his pocket, he felt it was warm to the touch; he must've been sleeping on it on his side the whole time. Seven people were still left on the field, but the Storm had progressed much faster than Chess had predicted. It was practically on top of him now and would take another thirty minutes before he was caught in the middle of it.

He threw the DMR on his back and moved to the window, throwing the curtains open and moving to the balcony. He could've given himself away here, but he kept low and surveyed his options. There was a team of Japanese players at the bottom firing on the remains of Damon's team. Chess could see Damon hiding behind a bus, reloading his gun. It would've been so easy to line up the shot and take it, and Chess did just that.

The girl was one thing, but this was the end of the game. Bijou was nowhere to be found, more than likely taken out by another team before she could get to them. Nevertheless, Chess was seeing five people down there, and he made the sixth. Who was the seventh? More so, *where* was the seventh?

Chess wrapped his hand around the strap of the weapon and risked standing up, aiming at Damon. The girl with him seemed to be taking her time reloading her weapon, but she eventually stood up and started blindly firing in the direction of their aggressors. They didn't have a plan and were practically sitting ducks. Perfect for Chess. He aimed, squaring Damon's head in his sights, and fired.

The girl was one thing. She was another thing entirely. This was the end of the game. There was no more time to get into his feelings about it anymore. He didn't care to win, but he wasn't looking to lose either. As much as he despised the World Royale and what it's done to his friends, he wasn't looking to lose that easily.

The bullet flew through the air, and Chess breathed in after pulling the trigger. It felt like it was traveling in slow motion straight to its target. When it landed, even Chess sucked in a breath at how much it must've hurt or surprised Damon when it landed. Square in the shoulder downwards through the torso. Chess would've been surprised if he didn't hit his lungs or a main artery, but he didn't turn into crystal.

Being the smart Blood Runner he was, Damon figured out pretty quickly that the bullet didn't come from the Japanese team but from above. Chess dipped down out of sight before Damon could see him and crouch walked through the apartment. He was going to get out of the building and onto the street where the main action was. The thought of him still passing didn't flutter in his mind as much as winning did. He didn't have a problem getting into the heat of battle if it meant he knew he could get the upper hand. The problem was the seventh player, the one that hadn't shown their face yet.

Wherever they were hiding, they were looking to wait the maximum amount of time before showing themselves. They were more than likely waiting in the shadows, watching the fighting play out. He should've been doing the same thing and waited, but he had already put himself in the action by shooting Damon. The fact he didn't die left a hole in Chess's gut, and he was afraid he would miss the moment he turned into crystal. However, Damon's will to live was stronger than Chess anticipated.

As Chess made his way back to the street, the scent of gunpowder and dirt filled his nose. Many grenades had been used, turning around the dirt in the area. It smelled like mulch mixed with iron. A metallic kind of smell. He moved from car to car, keeping himself out of the line of sight of the other players as he moved closer to the action. Passing through another street, a bullet came out of nowhere and slammed into Chess's right leg, downing him. He crawled as fast as he could behind another bus, close to the action but still too far away for any other to land a shot like that on him. This was someone else.

He looked down the street he had just crossed and saw the visage of someone walking down the road as if this was just another normal day and she was going out shopping. Bijou was advancing on him, a sniper rifle in her hands, and she was aiming down her sights.

Chess's blood ran cold, and he moved to hobble to the other side of the street. If he was quick enough, he could get into the bushes, make his way down another street, and get away from her before reaching Damon and the others. He wanted to see Damon turn into crystal or just see the crystals at all. It was like a thirst, a hunger at this point. If he could just see that, then he would let Bijou kill him. He would let her have him all she wanted.

This new Bijou, he wanted to get ahead of her and take her out first before anything else. He was sure that he and Damon agreed on that, but here they were, back to their old ways, trying to kill each other. Some things just felt like they would never change, and Chess vowed he would kill Damon once before the World Royale finished. He swore it.

As he finally made it to the road that Damon was holed up in, he was despondent to see that Damon was patching himself up with a medkit he had. Holding his shoulder with one hand as if it were in pain. He had failed and was too weak to aim his weapon again to get another clear shot. At this point, he had to get as close as possible and terminate him at the source. This was going to be next to impossible. However, Damon was patched up, and he was fast. Chess didn't even have a knife on him, and Damon did. It was a suicide mission, and he knew that, but except for sitting like a duck and letting Bijou catch up to him and kill him, he might as well go out trying to get back at Damon.

The hate he felt, the rage. It was all pooling at the bottom of his stomach as if it was the only fuel he needed to keep going. As he crawled closer and closer to Damon, the man in his sights but Damon hadn't noticed him yet; he could feel the blood seeping out of him. The tell-tale signs of lightheadedness and fatigue were starting to wash over his body. The feeling of rage within him was starting to subside. He could see Damon now. Just a little further.

The girl that Damon was with had gotten herself shot. As he was pulling himself toward Damon. The bullets kept flying, and he was getting closer and closer, eventually dropping to his belly on the street, dragging himself toward him.

Damon saw him but didn't shoot. He sat and waited, breathing heavily and waiting to heal. He was in a bad way and unable to even pull up his rifle to protect himself. Before he knew it, Chess was on top of him, straddling his body and pulling the hunter's knife from his own pocket. The bullets stopped for a moment, and Chess raised the knife above his head and stopped. He just stopped.

Both of them were breathing heavily, Damon keeping one hand on his shoulder while the other was spayed on the ground weakly. It was the opposite of what had happened a couple of games ago, only this time, Chess won. He won. All he had to do was push the knife down and watch Damon explode into a mountain of crystals. That was all he had to do.

"Do it..." Damon gurgled.

Chess was shaking, and the whirring of a media drone above them pulled his attention from Damon. He was going to be watching. Watching his son lose to the son of an old rival. At the very least, he was watching his son lay on his back, a knife to his own throat. It wasn't going to end nicely. It was going to get nasty no matter what happened now.

"Do it!!" Damon screamed with the rest of his strength.

Chess screamed with him and slammed the knife down, the blade landing on the side of Damon's head. Chess was breathing heavily, breathing down the neck of Damon, who was wide-eyed and staring up at the sky. Around them, the storm was closing in, and the sounds of people yelling and running could be heard around them. People were going to move in on them, shoot and kill them, but at this moment, all Chess and Damon could focus on was each other.

Chess's hand was trembling on the hilt of the knife, and his nails dug into the rock and rubble of the street next to Damon's head.

Damon raised a hand, still staring at the sky, and placed it on Chess's chest.

"Chess..." Damon breathed.

Life stilled around them in slow motion. The Japanese team that took out Damon's other teammate rounded the bus he was hiding behind and flanked them. Bijou came around the corner with a pistol in her hand and sniper rifle in the other, opening fire. Damon watched, looking from the sky to Chess as their eyes met. It was dark, but Chess's eyes glittered, glistening with tears as Damon couldn't help but cry as well. So many things were wrong, so many things were going to go wrong. Damon's life was retrospectively over; his father's hellfire would rain down upon him. Chess didn't know what he was feeling. The rage he felt before. The anger. It was for something else.

It wasn't for Damon.

Damon watched as Chess was shot twice in the back and erupted into crystal in front of his eyes. Shards of purple and clear glass fell into his eyes, and the hand resting on Chess's chest shot up into the sky, no longer hindered by a body. The pressure of what would've been pain wrought through his arm as it was shot through a couple of times. He felt the strike of bullets on his torso. A cheap kill, but he wasn't fighting back. The world went black, and the blinding white light of the Respawn Pods collecting their atoms flared to the back of his eyeballs. He was nothing more than crystals on the battlefield now.

After a couple of seconds, his eyesight was once of a storm-filled sky; now, it was of the egg-white innards of a Respawn Pod. Damon just stood there, not moving. Breathing in a couple of times, trying to center himself. So many things were going through his mind. How his father was going to take this, what Chess was going to say, dealing with Bijou, and the stress of the final game before World Royale.

There was one game left, and he made the cut. He was almost killed at the hands of his ex, but he was spared. He wanted to know why. Hopefully, during the final game, he could get the answers he was looking for.

Walking out of the Respawn Pod, Damon looked to his right and saw Chess sitting on a bench outside his own pod, his head in his hands. He was rubbing his buzzed head over and over slowly as if he were in agony. He then looked up and looked at Damon, and Damon looked at him. They held eyesight for a while before Chess got up from the bench and walked away. That's when the buzzing in Damon's pocket started, telling him he was getting a call. He already knew who it was going to be.

CHAPTER
THIRTY-FOUR

"I don't know what you two have got going on. You're off again and on again on the weirdest shit, but it has to stop."

Farren stood over Chess and Damon as they sat in chairs in front of her. They had passed to the final game of the World Royale, but the display they showed in getting there was less than stellar. Millions at home watching the games were not pleased with the cop-out of letting them die like dogs in the streets as if they were nothing. Chess and Damon were two of the most sought-after and voter fan favorites this season, and that last game tarnished all of it.

The whole gimmick that the World Royale committee was trying to spin was to rivals after the same brown, but after this, it seemed like Damon and Chess were trying to get on amicable levels of understanding. Bad for business, worse for field execution. Farren rubbed the bridge of her nose and ran a hand through her afro, fixing the strands and then letting her hands rest at her sides.

"So what is it then?" Levi asked from the corner, his arms crossed and looking rather pissed off at something. "Are you two rivals or lovers?"

"Neither," Damon said. "I don't see him as a rival."

"I thought I did," Chess said, letting his head hang at his shoulders and shoulders hunched. "I don't know anymore. This whole thing is pointless."

"No, what was pointless was your dad's death!" Levi shouted.

Chess slowly looked up and over at Levi; his face fit to be killed.

"What the fuck does my dad have to do with any of this?" Chess seethed.

"The son of the man that killed your dad is sitting right next to you, and you feel nothing?" Levi said, outing himself.

"My dad didn't kill Rhett Harlow! That is a lie!" Damon roared.

"He did, and I can prove it! The night he took his life, he only got one phone, and it was from Kennedy telling him to take his life. He tried to call you while you were at academy, but you never answered," Levi said to Chess's face.

Chess sat back in his seat and grimaced. "If he wanted to get ahold of me, he would have. It wasn't like him to give up so easily. What's really going on?" Chess asked.

"What's really going on is your dad died while his rival and son lapped up the rest of the money and fame that your dad couldn't obtain." Levi looked to Damon, hate in his eye. "You're doing nothing but living off the back of someone that killed another for it. I don't see how you can forgive him," Levi finished the last sentence to Damon.

"Because he didn't do that," Chess said.

It was quiet in the room for a long time, and Chess sat higher in his seat, adjusting his footing and looking long and hard at Levi. The old man was trembling with rage, but Chess didn't let it get to him.

"Damon didn't kill my dad. I believe him when he says his dad didn't kill my dad. Damon is a piece of shit, but he's never been a liar," Chess said.

Damon rolled his eyes at the pass but shook his head and smiled at it. This was Chess, the new Chess. Old Chess was still gone. Slowly, he was getting used to this new Chess, but it seemed that the new Chess still remembered a lot of the old Damon.

"I believe him when he says his dad didn't do anything. I don't understand why you're so adamant about getting us to fight each other," Chess said.

"Because it's good for ratings, let's be honest here, love." Damon snickered, sitting back in his own seat and crossing his arms.

Chess snickered in kind and shook his head. "This is fucking ridiculous."

"Levi, I get it's great for TV and all, but do you have to bring up dead relatives, especially dads?" Farren asked, crossing her arms.

Levi looked at Farren and then at the boys. When they weren't breaking in the way of emotion or listening to him anymore, he turned and stormed into the hallway away from the three. Farren sighed.

"Look, I think it's great if you guys are making up finally; just stop throwing the game away in the middle of figuring your shit out. The game is the game; you guys can always talk after it. Promise?" Farren said, pointing to the two boys.

Chess held up his hands in mock surrender, and Damon nodded, glancing at Chess from the side of his eye. The situation was felt with, and now was the even stranger situation of dealing with Levi. The grudge he had against the Kennedys rivaled Miller's. Chess had to remember what Miller told him at the beginning of the games as well when he was delivering money.

That it was all Kennedy's fault. That they killed Rhett. Chess didn't want to believe it; worse, he had already gotten over his dad's death. Why bring it up now? Their revenge missions weren't his to bear.

He looked over to Damon, who was looking at him. Not with a smile or anything like that, but with a careful look in his eye. He knew this was a touchy subject for both of them and wanted to see how he was doing.

"I'm okay," Chess said, sighing. "Just don't know what the fuck his deal was in all of this. He really has it out for you."

"Maybe he's betting on the side for you to win so he can get that payout," Damon thought out loud.

"No, it seems deeper than that. I don't know. Just the look in his eye," Chess said, looking back down to the ground.

It was quiet again in the room, and Farren had since left. Having ignored the phone call from his dad, he knew Damon knew he would have to pay later for it. Either when he got home or sooner, he knew he would pay. Chess was more critical anyways. He would wait for doomsday for Chess.

As Farren was walking down the hallway toward the main atrium getting ready for interviews and tabloids, she saw Levi walking the opposite way from her down a corridor that led back to the Respawn Room. She stood there and, against her better judgment, ran off to meet with him wherever he was going. She was stealthy about it, not letting herself be seen or heard as she tailed Levi back to the Respawn Chambers. Everyone was either in a locker room or the main atrium of the building they were all staying in. On top of that, they all had to stay together so that they could make it back to the hotel in one piece.

So what was Levi doing breaking away from everybody?

Farren let him go down the hallway a little farther before she decided to pick up the pace and meet him halfway. He still didn't see her, which was good, but she quickly lost sight of him. It wasn't until she passed the double doors leading to the Respawn Rooms did she see his silhouette in the glass farther away. Someone else was in the room, and she could hear them talking through the glass. Well, the other person was talking in a low tone, words unable to be made out between Farren's ear and the glass, but then Levi would speak and yell. He was not happy, whatever was going through his mind right now. After what he tried to pull with Chess and Damon, he was more than likely trying to pull the same thing on whoever was in this room.

She shouldn't have chanced looking, but Farren couldn't help but try and see who was in the room with Levi. Peeking her head up over the glass, she prayed they weren't close and weren't facing her. The first thing she saw was Levi's back toward her and Bijou standing in front of him, her hands at her sides. He was still yelling, but Farren couldn't make out the words. They were all muffled in the space around them. When Farren locked eyes with Bijou, her blood ran cold, and she gasped, but before Levi could whip around and spot her, Farren ran away.

She ran down the hallway toward the atrium and tried to get to

Chess and Damon before Bijou could. Whatever he was saying to Bijou, her sudden change in demeanor in Blood Running, and her progress as of late. It all had to have come from Levi. The late nights training and disappearing in the middle of the night. It all made sense that it had to have been him. It had to have been him.

Farren made it to the atrium of the building before she saw the group of USA team members walking out of the lobby toward the busses back to the hotel. Farren was about to call out when something sharp was sticking into her back. It didn't push inwards, but it was clearly a knife. Something sharp that could hurt her. She didn't say a word, but she felt shaky as she knew who was standing behind her.

"Not a word now... Not. One. Word," Levi's voice came.

The object was pulled away, and when Farren looked behind her after it was withdrawn, she saw it was only a pen. She felt stupid, but at the same time, the boys and other members of the group were already on their way to the hotel. Farren still had things to say to the press, and she couldn't leave yet; neither could Levi or Bijou, who won the game.

"What is this? This sick joke?" Farren asked, motioning toward Bijou.

"You want a spectacle; I'll give a spectacle. The Harlows are not going to forgive the Kennedys that easily. Not on my watch. I'll give the people at home a World Royale they won't forget, what they've been waiting for. She's helping me," Levi said, nodding toward Bijou.

Farren looked at Bijou with sad eyes. "I wanted you on because you were such good friends with both of them. What happened?"

Bijou looked away, but it was obvious that she was pained behind her eyes. She wanted to say something but couldn't. Biting her lip, she simply shook her head and looked back at Farren.

"It doesn't matter anymore. This Royale is going to destroy them whether they know it or not, anyways. I'm just here to... further it along."

Farren could tell she was lying through her teeth, but for some reason, she couldn't speak her mind. Something that Levi had over her, perhaps? It wasn't safe to ask her in front of him now; no telling what he could do to her career or her in general.

"You don't mean that," Farren whispered.

Bijou looked away from her, and Levi pushed her along to walk down the stairs toward the venue doors. They would return to the hotel they were staying at, and the cycle would go on. The next game would come, and Bijou would be on a hunt for the boys again. For what purpose, she didn't know, but she would find out.

She first had to find the boys and tell them that Bijou was working with Levi. How they would take it, she didn't know, but they had the right to know.

CHAPTER THIRTY-FIVE

Despite Levi threatening her, Farren knew she had two options. Get to the boys and let them know what was going on, or isolate Bijou and squeeze the information from her. They were thousands of miles away from the hotel they were living in and wouldn't be able to be alone for a long time, and Bijou was always seen hooked to Levi's hip, which was creepy. He had to have something on her or something.

The final game was going to be played in the Tundra of Serbia for a week straight, and she only had a limited amount of time to get Bijou alone to ask her her own questions because once bijou was freed into the game, that was it. She could hunt down the boys and kill them, ending their game prematurely. She knew that the boys had what it took to make it to the Final Royale, but whatever Levi was scheming, whether it was truly for television or not, was going to hinder that.

It didn't make sense that Levi was only obsessed with the TV show ratings and the subsequent interviews and press that would come from it. If that were the truth, he would just let the boys act as they have been and let it all play out. It was like he wanted them to have this unhealthy rivalry that would kill them one of these days. Maybe that's what Levi was going for. She didn't know. She felt like she didn't know anything.

What she did know was that she had to get the final 16 members ready for the Tundra. There was going to be a short week of training and preparation that she might not even have the time or chance to single out the boys or Bijou even if she wanted to. So much was riding on them to make it to this Final Royale that she didn't have time for individual care. At the very end of it all, this was just a feud between two families she had no bearing on. What was it to her to butt in?

Sitting at the front of the second bus heading back to the hotel, Farren tried her best to shake the whole thing. The Final Royale would come and go, and everyone would go home. Whatever happened to them after that wasn't important to her.

But it did feel important.

CHESS RETURNED TO HIS HOTEL ROOM IN TIME FOR DINNER later that night, with soba noodles and rice with chicken. He opted to eat alone in the back corner of the cafeteria and get his food out of the way before going back to his room and passing out. Today's Royale took everything out of him, and he still didn't want to admit that he made major headway with Damon today.

Like, he did, but he didn't want to. The rage and hate he was feeling for so long were for something that was dying out slowly, and he just wasn't realizing it. The effort wasn't worth it. Bijou was also becoming a problem that he wasn't expecting. How she was quickly becoming one of the strongest Blood Runners he had ever seen in such a short period. He felt like he couldn't talk to her anymore, like she was hunting him mercilessly with no sign of backing down. He was missing his best friend already.

Everyone was staying in their own separate rooms, and Chess wouldn't have the time to hunt down Bijou or Damon until the next day. Sitting alone in the cafeteria, he thought to himself about what was going to happen now. The final Royale Game and the Duos. Who would he be paired up with? Would he fail them too? He chewed slowly as his eyesight focused on his food. He didn't hear the sound of someone walking up to him and pulling up a chair, sitting across from him.

Looking up, Chess saw Gavin sitting across from him, Gavin giving Chess a meek smile and looking away. He was wearing normal clothes and had a tray of food in front of him. If anything, he looked a little guilty, but he was trying not to let it show.

"Hey," Gavin started, his voice low.

"Hmm," Chess hummed in Gavin's direction.

It was awkward for a couple of moments as they sat there in silence, eating their food. It was painfully obvious that Gavin wanted to say something to Chess but didn't know how to lead into it. Chess looked up a couple of times, not moving his head to look at Gavin and then back down to his own food, trying to let him take the lead, but it was becoming more and more obvious that Gavin wasn't going to say anything, despite wanting to.

"Tough fight today," Chess started.

Gavin only nodded, Chess not seeing it as he was focused on chewing and looking at the food on his tray. They were two completely different people on either side of the spectrum. Gavin being upbeat and inviting, and Chess is cold and standoffish. Chess wouldn't give someone like Gavin the time of day if it weren't for the fact that he had gotten him killed in Trios. At least, that's how he felt.

"I wanted to say thank you," Gavin said.

Chess stopped chewing and looked up at Gavin, his eyes searching for any hint as to why he was saying thank you. He had told him to get on those rocks and scout out for the other assailants. He was the one that got him slaughtered as he did on top of those rocks. What in the world could he be thanking him for?

"You could've killed us off and gone solo like that girl did, but you didn't. Charles and I were almost certain you were going to do that," Gavin said.

"Why would I kill you off myself? That doesn't really help in Trios. I don't normally play Duos or Trios, but I'm also not stupid," Chess said, putting a thick sauce over his chicken.

"Well, in any case, I just want to say I am blessed to have fought with you, no matter how short it was. Charles thinks the same way," Gavin said.

"Where is Charles?" Chess asked.

"He hitched a bus to Narita Airport early; we both are disqualified."

Chess looked at Gavin for a couple more seconds before looking back down to his tray, almost out of pity. He felt horrible; this was all his fault that they didn't go ahead, and now Charles's mom...

"I'm sorry," Chess said.

"Don't be. Charles is gonna win a ton of Royales back home and raise the money." Gavin dropped his head too. "I know he will."

"Yeah."

They ate in silence, and when the quiet became too much to bear, another person showed up to sit with them. Damon. Chess looked up at him, not with contempt or anger, but with a look of passive awareness. He perceived Damon and then went back to his meal. On the other hand, Damon watched Chess as he took his seat across from him and next to Gavin. He only had a glass of tea and was sipping it languidly. Gavin cleared his throat at the obvious awkward situation of it all and put his chopsticks back on his tray.

"Well, anyways, I just wanted to say thank you for the experience. Even if I were eliminated, I'd still look back fondly about this."

Gavin stuck out his hand for Chess to shake, and Damon looked at his hand and then at Chess, who was looking at the hand for a couple of seconds. Slowly, Chess raised his hand and gripped Gavin's hand tight, shaking it.

"Thank you too," Chess said with a rare smile.

Gavin got up and took his tray to the trash bin. This was more than likely going to be the last time Chess ever saw Gavin again, and Charles was already gone. Two people he feels like he failed, coming to say thank you to him. It didn't feel right; he felt like he had cheated them out of a win. Especially Charles. It should be Charles sitting in his seat getting ready for the Final Royale, not him. This feeling of finality washed over him as Gavin put his tray away and walked out of the room from the left. When he was completely gone, Chess started to breathe again, not realizing he was holding n his breath.

"Intense," Damon said, putting his arms on the table.

"Hmm," Chess hummed and continued to eat. "I got them killed, and he wants to say thank you to me?" Chess asked with his mouth full.

"It's rude to talk with your mouth full," Damon said with a smirk.

He started laughing when Chess began chewing in earnest, his eyes low and sporting a middle finger in his direction.

"Maybe it wasn't the fact that you got them killed; it was more for the fact that they had a good time Running with you," Damon said.

"But I *did* get them killed," Chess argued.

"Did you, though?"

Chess chewed more on his noodles and looked Damon square in the eyes for a few moments. After he swallowed, he dropped his chopsticks and sat back in his own seat, crossing his arms. Damon sat forward, trying to drive his next points home to him.

"The way I see it, it wasn't about who was getting who killed to them. Yeah, maybe something was on the line for some of them, but in the end, the only thing that mattered to them, in the long run, was the game itself. You're not an easy man to please nowadays. They probably saw it as an honor," Damon said.

"What do you know about me nowadays?" Chess countered.

Damon shook his head and sipped his tea. "Not much."

It was quiet for a long time between them, the sounds of the clock ticking in the background filling their ears. In the distance, the late-night cafeteria workers were washing dishes and chatting quietly, killing the silence they were trying to bask themselves into.

"But, I'd like to get to know you. This... you. What you are today," Damon said, motioning his hands around Chess's frame.

Chess took another bite of chicken and looked away from Damon. He chewed roughly and kept his gaze off of him. It was obvious that a million things were going through his mind all at once, the things he wanted to say, hated to retort with. He had been filled with hate and contempt for so long, but the ice was finally melting; Damon could feel it.

"I'm not ready yet. Still, some things I need to get over," Chess said quietly, almost in a whisper.

Luckily the cafeteria was so quiet that Damon heard every word and nodded to his response. The ice was melting, but the guard was still up.

It hadn't cracked yet, and he was going to have to prove himself that he, too, had changed since Academy to get to know this new Chess. He so very badly wanted to know this new Chess.

"Well. The next game is in Serbia. A week-long Run. You up for it?" Damon asked.

As if rejuvenated, Chess looked back over to Damon with a snide smirk on his face. He swallowed his food and took a quick sip before answering.

"More like, are *you* up or it. You haven't been Blood Running outside the UK since I last saw you haven't you?" Chess accused.

"Nope, not true; I've done Blood Runs in Africa and Australia since we last saw each other," Damon said.

"So you're up for running long distances and spending a week in the storm?" Chess asked.

"You gonna be up for dealing with your partner for Duos?" Damon asked back.

"I won't get them killed this time. I'll do my best to make sure we both make it out alive and win," Chess promised.

"Well, good." Damon got up from his seat and grabbed his tea. He looked at Damon with a sharp eye and his famous grin. Chess swallowed.

"Because I'm your partner."

CHAPTER
THIRTY-SIX

Japan had come and gone. The last 16 left in the USA team were traveling by train to the venue locale in Russia. This would be a true test of determination, power, skill, and will. The week-long Blood Run in Serbia.

This was the largest Temporal Storm in the world, covering hundreds of miles of snowy land, and on top of that, it was one of the slowest moving storms out of all the Temporal Storms in the world, taking a week and a day to completely reset the whole area. It was a place devoid of many buildings, many structures, and one's best bet of finding shelter was making their own.

Chess sat in his train seat in front of Damon and Farren as he looked out the window. In his hands was the new backpack he bought alongside a two-person tent big enough for duos. He knew he was going to be paired up with Damon, the powers that be setting this up on purpose; he was convinced. Nevertheless, he still had to get ready for the game as if he was playing this by himself. The cold weather of Serbia and the vastness of its plains were going to be a stretch to cross. They could cut out the middleman and land in the middle, but then again, almost everyone was going to land in the middle anyways. For a week straight, the town of Zhigansk was going to be a war zone with people fighting for the high ground and safe spots. If they were smart about it, they would at least drop a couple of days out from the town and let the other players cull each other out. This would also give them the time to search for better weapons, ammo, and gear in sparse forests and towns on the way.

It was going to be hard. Camping in sub-zero temperatures and taking through forests and snow. Chess could feel his resolve being tested already, and he wasn't even on the plane yet. On top of that, they were playing the Russian Blood Running team, this time on top of hunting their own team members. Chess and Damon had to play this smart and safe. Yeah, it was a lot of open space where it should've been hard to run into another person, but it can also be very dangerous if they didn't have anything to hide behind if they did run into someone.

Damon was sitting next to the window of the train as well. Damon and Chess's legs were splayed out, almost intertwined with each other but not touching. While Chess was trying to get on his social media despite the horrible Wi-Fi service on the train, Damon was thinking up his strategy. It wasn't like Chess was going to leave all of the planning to Damon, but he was too nervous about the space to think about it right now. Plus, Chess was more of a boots-on-the-ground type of planner, his tactics and plans usually coming up right after he landed.

"How long until we get off the train do we get on the plane?" Damon asked, his gaze still staring out the window.

"Immediately. You won't have time to do anything else but change into your uniforms," Farren said, writing something in a notebook.

"It's going to be a week-long Blood Run; where are you going to be staying?" Chess asked, looking at Farren.

"In the pilot house. I'll sleep in the chairs and on the floor if I have to, but I'm not leaving those monitors. The Serbian Pilot House is one of the most technologically advanced buildings for Blood Running, and they offer rooms for me to stay in, but I can't risk missing something, and..."

She trailed off, looking toward the hallway of the train. They weren't in separate rooms or cars; it was an open train with everyone sitting at tables, food and drink strewn about. It was obvious that she was hesitant to say something out loud, so she sat forward so that she could whisper to Chess.

"I don't really trust Levi to make good calls right now. Something is off about him," Farren finished.

Chess nodded and sat back in his seat after he let Farren whisper to him. He looked out the window, watching towns and trees pass by, rivers and lakes strewn about the terrain. It was warm on the train ride there, Chess not even having to wear his jacket in this cold climate, but he knew he was about to get the shock of his life when they landed on the snow and grass of Serbia. They were required to wear the tracksuit uniform but were granted extra clothing to survive in the climate. The Storm might reset everything, but the weather was still the same. It was going to be cold, and the tents and jackets they were awarded for the Run were well appreciated.

"After what he tried pinning on my dad and me, I wouldn't trust him to breathe the same air as me," Damon said, his hand on his chin.

"He's just looking to bump ratings, isn't he? We can just pretend to hate each other the whole time to give him what he wants," Chess joked.

"Yeah, but then there's Bijou," Damon countered.

He looked behind himself to the other rows of train seats to see if Bijou was close or around before he continued to speak. The train tracks were loud, but talking still carried sound throughout the train. It wouldn't be hard to eavesdrop on them.

"She's going to be hunting us. She's been hunting us the last couple of games and avoiding us. I hate it," Damon finished.

"You and me both. I wish she would just talk to us," Chess said.

Farren didn't say anything. She knew that Levi had something on Bijou or was holding something over her to make her act this way. Whatever it was, it had to have been something important. Information or something else that Farren didn't know about. She couldn't get close enough to Bijou without Levi being close behind. She couldn't get anything out of her.

"We're just going to have to bath when she jumps, and if she waits for us to jump, we have to veer wide away from her. I have a bad feeling she's going to follow us," Chess said.

Damon looked away from the window and at Chess. After a couple of seconds, a smile emerged on his lips, and his eyes were filled with glee. Chess raised an eyebrow at him.

"What?" Chess asked.

"Us. Back together again on the field," Damon said, sitting back in his seat and crossing his arms.

Chess rolled his eyes and blew out the air in his lungs in response, looking out the window himself. Another small town rolled by. He put his hand to his mouth and elbow on the window with his eyebrows bunched up in frustration. If anything, he was more so fighting with himself.

"Don't get too excited. We're not going to do anything other than running for our lives," Chess explained.

"Right, right. Of course," Damon said, a smile on his face the entire time.

Chess looked over at him and then rolled his eyes a second time, opting to give his attention to the world outside the window. Nothing more than snow and trees as far as the eyes Ould see. It wouldn't be long now until they made it to the airport and pilot house. The thoughts of Media Drones flying around for days and not seeing anybody made Chess want to laugh, but there was also a good bet they wouldn't be found out there. Either way, live or die, they would come back to the Respawn Chambers. The thought of being lost in that tundra didn't scare Chess as much as it should have.

Looking back over at Damon, he was also looking out the window, watching the world pass him by. Chess was staring at this point, just taking in his features. His perfectly parted hair shook at the bangs with the movement of the train and the freckles on his face glittered in the sunlight beaming through the train window. When Damon looked back over at Chess and smiled, Chess realized he was staring and tried to look away in time.

"See something you like?" Damon asked.

"Shut up."

———

BIJOU GOT OFF THE TRAIN AND WALKED INTO THE AIRPORT and pilot house to be scanned into the Respawn Pods. The rest of the 15 members left of the USA team surrounded her as if she was nothing special, just another player in the machine. She walked, her bags in her arms, as she entered the building and was escorted to the right, toward the USA team's locker room and base of operations. The game was going to start first thing in the morning, and they would be staying in the rooms provided by the Russian government.

It was warm. As bijou walked into her given room and put her bags down, she made a small inventory of everything she had and would need for the game. Her partner—who would not be joining her the second they landed—wasn't of grave importance. She was just going to kill him when she landed. There was no penalty against it; yes, it was frowned upon, but she had to do this. She had to do this, or else she would lose everything. She didn't want to lose Chess and Damon. She just wanted to run her shop and be a businesswoman. Now, she was hunting two of the most dangerous Blood Runners in the world and catching up to them.

All she had to do was eliminate them. Find them and eliminate them from the game. That's all she had to do. Finding them was the hard part. She landed close to them, jumped when they jumped, and still, it was like she was miles away from them every time. She couldn't close in fast enough, and by the time she finally found them, they were already past the point of safety. It wouldn't matter if she killed them or not.

However, this was going to be the gauntlet. Only five people from each team would continue onwards to the Final Royale in Point Nemo, and she had to make sure those boys were not part of the roster. This was her final chance, or else she forfeited everything.

Why did Levi have to tell her those things? The things that he did, the lengths that he went to? None of it made sense, but at the same time, she was entwined in the story now. Whatever happened years ago had now come back in full force from the resurgence of the Harlows and the Kennedys. Levi wanted to quell old demons and would go to great lengths to do so. Lengths that split friend from friend just to make sure he got the last laugh. It was evil, but Bijou didn't have any chance to run now. If she told anyone or failed this mission, he was going to sabotage the Respawn Pods, and no one would come home. She didn't want anyone to die, so she would play the game, get through the World Royale and go home. After the runaround with her friends who think she hates them, making them think she wants nothing to do with them. It couldn't be farther from the truth. She wanted to tell them so very badly, but she didn't want them to die either.

She would do this final game, and she would do it right this time. No more screw-ups, no more blunders, no more lies. After this game, win or lose, she would tell them.

And then she would never Blood Run again.

CHAPTER
THIRTY-SEVEN

The plane rattled, and the faces of the Russian team sitting across from the USA team were less than inviting. A lot of glares and a couple of smiles. They had all been through a lot, knowing that this was the final hurdle between them and the chance at the trophy at the end of the road. The Final Royale was upon them, and they just had to get through Duos to get it.

Chess sat next to Damon; both dressed to the nines in cover-down gear meant to keep them warm in the cold climate. Chess was wearing his backpack on the front of his person while the parachute was hooked to his back. Inside were a couple of water bottles he hoped wouldn't freeze over and some hand warmers and stick-on warmers. When they landed and were clear of insurgents, Chess would apply these before they moved on. On top of that, there was a two-person tent and two whole boxes of food supplement bars. Enough to keep them going for more than a couple of weeks, let alone one week and a day.

Chess had stocked up, and it was looking like Damon was just going to let him do all the prepping as he only brought a small pack with him. What was inside, Chess didn't know yet, but he hoped that it was something beneficial to the Run. The sound of the back pit opening up for the jump pulled Chess from his thoughts about Damon's gear. It was time. The final Run before the World Royale Finale. Chess was conflicted about how he felt about it. On the one hand, he didn't really care too much about the World Royale and what it stood for; he was here for one mission and one mission only.

Then again, that mission had clouded his mind and made him a hateful, spiteful person. He didn't bother to think about how Damon was taking everything, what he had gone through during those years without each other. Chess turned to Damon and tapped him a couple of times on the hand, getting his attention.

"Hey," Chess hollered over the air rushing out of the plane. "How do you feel?"

Damon looked at chess through his goggles and his mouth agape. Before he answered, he turned away and pulled his balaclava over his mouth to shield him from the cold. Chess couldn't hear his answer and gave him a cocked eyebrow look. It was the one question Damon wanted to hear, and now he was getting flustered by it.

Looking like he wasn't going to get a clear answer, not yet anyway, Chess moved his attention to the people getting ready to jump from the plane. Plenty of people were already unbuckling and leaning forward, ready to run and jump.

"Hello, and welcome to the Final Royale Duos in Serbia! The aircraft will take roughly five hours to cover the entirety of the playing field, and we will advise you when it's the last call to jump. The Storm is projected to move inwards to the center of the map, where the town of Zhigansk awaits. The storm's eye will hover for one day and then close, resetting the field. May luck be on your side, and happy Blood Running!"

The same message was repeated in Russian, and Chess sat back more in his seat when he heard the flight time. Five hours was a long time, this was a huge storm, and they were expected to run through most of it. Again, it wasn't smart to jump at the middle of the map and bypass the whole game because that's what everyone else was going to be doing as well. Chess knew that the majority of people were going to jump to Zhigansk. He didn't want to fight that many people at once. He'd rather suit up, arm up, and be ready than scramble for his life in the cold. Chess looked around at the people that were going to die in the process of trying to take the town for themselves at the very start of the game.

The time came and went, and after about two hours, the announcer spoke over the speakerphone. They were over the town, and people started to unbuckle again. Before then, some people had already jumped and started their games. It was most likely cold wherever they were, and they were running like hell.

People were starting to run out of the cabin now. They jumped to the snowy tundra in pairs of two, hoping to hit the town below them. Chess watched them go in droves, and soon only a couple of people were left in the plane. Looking over, Chess saw Bijou and her partner—a girl around Bijou's age—sitting at the back end of the USA team's side of the plane. When he looked over, Bijou sat back, implying that she was watching them as well. She was going to jump when they did; he just knew it. It was going to be a hunt exclusively for them, and he still didn't know why.

"We're going to jump in about an hour," Chess said to Damon, leaning in so he didn't have to shout as loud.

"What about Bijou?" Damon hollered back.

"We'll deal with it when we get there, but we have to jump at some point, and I don't want to be running for a week straight in the snow," Chess said.

"Fair enough."

The hour had come, and Chess unbuckled from his seat, Damon following suit. Looking over to Bijou, she was still sitting securely in her seat, not looking over at them. This was their chance to run for it and flank to a wide position in the sky, landing farther away from the plane than they had hoped. If they could catch a wind current and strafe away from Bijou far enough, they could save precious time. At the very least, get the sticker warmers on and hydrate before getting hunted down.

They made a run for it. Chess did a backflip off the tarmac and plummeted to the world below, seeing nothing but brown and white in his wake. Next to him, falling just as fast, his arms to his sides, was Damon. He was focused on the world below him and not looking at Chess. Chess focused on dropping, banking a little bit away from

Damon so he could pop his parachute safely away from him when he saw it. Above him. Bijou was dropping.

Chess wasted no time; he banked his whole body to the left and took hold of Damon's hand, gliding them away from the fall path. They were going to land wide, somewhere far off from the plane's flight path, but it was for their own good. Bijou was going to land right on top of them.

Damon struggled in Chess's grip, and Chess eventually wrapped his whole body around Damon and hard-banked left, coasting in the air toward a different destination. In the distance, approaching fast was what looked like a small settlement or train station up ahead. Chess finally let go right before they had to pop parachutes and tried his best to separate from him in the air. Finally, they both pulled their chutes and safely landed on the snowy ground below them. Chess knew he was in for an earful, but he shed his parachute and goggles, leaving them in the snow before getting the very angry face of Damon Kennedy approaching him. His parachute was still connected to his back, the sail collecting snow, and his goggles were lopsided on his face. He looked like hell, but Chess looked up to the sky, only to find no bodies in the air. Either Bijou had already landed, or she was farther away than he thought.

"What the hell was that?!" Damon hollered, his voice echoing across vast lands.

There were trees and sparse bushes around, and a couple of paces to their left was what looked like a train station. The railroad tracks covered up by snow and had not had a train on its rails in years. They would start there.

"Bijou is hunting us. I saw her falling with us, and I fixed our course accordingly. She's either miles away or on our ass, and I'd rather get ready before she's on our ass," Chess said.

"Agreed. Fine. Where to?" Damon asked, raising his arms and then letting them fall to his sides.

Damon listened to Chess as he shed his parachute and goggles.

"We'll hole up in this train station for a couple of minutes. Scour it for weapons and get ready for the cold." Chess pulled out the sticker warmers and showed them to Damon. "We'll apply these to wherever thick veins are, and they should keep us warm in this cold as we move. Or so I hope."

"Or so you hope?" Damon asked, already moving to walk to the train station.

"I read it in a magazine that that's how it worked. At the very least, it's help out of the cold. Should help us move better too. Not so stiff," Chess said.

"Okay. We'll get fixed up and get ready to set out. Eat something, too, and check our phones. We should still have signal through satellite here, but it's not going to be the best," Damon said.

The stairs to the train station were rickety and creaking. It was a wide but small building with doors that were rusted at the hinges. Years of cold weather and snow have not been nice to the buildings here. They walked inside anyways, and it was just as cold inside as it was outside.

"Storm's not even popped up yet, and the planes still in the air for another couple of hours. Let's get warm and plan our trek," Damon said, moving quickly to a room on the side of the building.

Chess took the other side and came out lucky. A Grach MP-443 sidearm with some ammo on the side. He loaded up the handgun with ammo and moved to see what Damon had found. When he came out with a compound bow and a couple of arrows, Chess almost wanted to laugh.

"The weapon choices here are... a choice," Chess said, trying not to snicker.

"It's all I could find," Damon grumbled. "Come on, let's switch."

"No way, I'm a better shot than you."

"That's not fucking true, and you know it!" Damon countered.

Chess holstered the weapon on his hip without another word and moved to the middle of the station room. It was cold because the building was split in half, open air so a train could easily come in and out of it. There would be no trains passing today, so Chess took a wooden chair that was forgotten by time and slammed it against the wall, shattering it. Damon jumped at the sound, trying to cover his head, and slowly looked up in surprise at Chess as he slammed another chair against the wall.

"What the fuck are you doing?!" Damon hollered.

Chess bent down to pick up the dry pieces of wood, and when he had an armful, he moved to the middle of the abandoned tracks and started piling them up. Within his pack, he pulled out a couple of matches and stuck them on the paper, lighting them. Within seconds, they had a bonfire to sit around, slowly melting the snow around them. Chess pulled out the stick-on warmers and turned to Damon.

"You're going to have to take your clothes off for this."

Damon raised an eyebrow at Chess and grinned.

"Oh ho ho?"

"Shut the hell up and get over here so I can sticker you up. We won't be here for very long."

CHAPTER THIRTY-EIGHT

Damon sat with his side to the fire as Chess lifted the back of his shirt. The tracksuit uniforms were on the station platform as they sat in their pants and undershirts. Chess was applying a sticker heater to the base of Damon's neck and the middle of his back. They were silent as they applied the stickers, and the fire was warm. In the back of Damon's mind, he was wondering where Bijou landed and if she was going to be close by. If so, she was going to get one hell of a jump on them, seeing as they were practically unarmed.

They left their weapons on the platform; it would take time to climb up and re-arm to defend themselves. Damon's eyes looked left and right as Chess smoothed out the heating packs on his skin and slapped it a few times. Damon immediately felt the warmth spread through his body, and after he put his tracksuit and down coat back on, he was extremely toasty.

"Okay, your turn," Damon said, holding a sticker.

"Do you know where to put it?" Chess asked, pulling his shirt completely off and throwing it on the platform. Damon took one look at his formed muscles and paused.

"I... uh. Yeah, I know." Damon hesitated, his eyes betraying him by looking at his abs.

Chess wasn't phased. He stood there, looking at Damon, and waited for him to hand him a sticker for the middle of his belly. Sticking his hand out, Damon gave him the peeled sticker, and then Chess turned around, showing Damon his back. He didn't bother to hide it this time. Looking at Chess's shoulder blades and defined back, Damon was almost gawking at the sight of him. Chess had changed a ton since he had known him at the Academy. The lithe boy turned into this rock of a man. Blood Running had done Chess's body some good.

Damon was the same way, toned in all the places he needed to be to perform his best but seeing Chess like this felt almost too intimate for what they were trying to accomplish together. What he was still trying to accomplish was getting to know this new Chess. He felt like he couldn't look at him like this yet, that he didn't deserve it.

"You gonna patch me up or what?" Chess called behind him.

Damon actually jumped and peeled the sticker film off of another patch silently. Two patches were placed at the base of his neck and the base of Chess's back. Damon hummed in satisfaction and backed away from Chess. As fast as the shirt had come off, it was back on Chess's body within the second Damon had placed the sticker. Damon watched as Chess dressed in his tracksuit and down coat, pulling his beanie over his buzzed head. His blue eyes looked like ice under his skin as he looked into Damon's eyes.

"We head west. The storm doesn't emerge for another half a day, and we're already a couple of days ahead of it. If we're lucky, we'll hit a house or shack along the way," Chess said.

"And if we don't?" Damon asked, kicking the snow over the fire, snuffing it out.

"Then we keep running until we hit the middle town of that Russian name I forgot," Chess said, hoisting himself up on the platform again.

"Zhigansk," Damon answered.

"Yeah, that one."

Chess and Damon took hold of their weapons and exited the station. It was nothing more than show and grass as far as their eyes could see, and they were going to have to walk it. Knowing that Bijou was somewhere behind them and more than likely catching up on their trail didn't conjure good feelings either. They were both wanted men, and they had to keep moving.

THE FIRST COUPLE OF HOURS WAS NOTHING MORE THAN following the compass Chess had brought with him and harboring the cold. The wind had picked up and was blowing rubble and snow into their faces every chance it got, almost as if the weather had it out for them. They put up with it, however, because night was soon falling, and they were going to have to find somewhere to hole up. Chess knew he could set the tent up, but they also needed to make a fire, and they would need wood and a clearing for that, and there wasn't a lot of wood around.

As if the answer to their prayers, far off in the distance, a deep forest could be seen. If they were lucky, they could get rocks and dry wood from the trees and post up camp. The sun was already dipping out of the sky and setting by the time they even reached the forest border. They had to act fast.

"I'll set up the tent, and you get some wood. Nothing remotely wet or with snow on it," Chess informed.

"A little hard to find something without snow on it," Damon grumbled and dropped his own pack at camp.

Chess wasted no time pulling the tent out from his pack and setting it up. The land was flat enough for them to be able to lay out without a tarp, but it was going to be a bit bumpy with the rocks and grass under the tent. All in all, it took close to ten minutes to set the whole thing up, and it was much roomier on the inside than Chess realized. The sleeping bags he had bought were on the pricey side, but they would be good enough to sleep in a cold climate like this. He took them out and laid them down inside the tent, one beside the other.

When he exited the tent, Damon was coming out of the thicket, an armful of wood in his hands. It looked dry enough, and he had good enough sense not to just drop it on the wet snow once he got back to camp. His face was flush red from exertion, and he was panting. It must've taken him a lot of work to get these branches for the fire.

"What do we have to eat?" Damon asked.

"Nothing more than a couple of protein bars and some water. That's all I have anyways," Chess said, lining up rocks in a wide circle. "Is there anything in the forest we can eat?"

"I'm not a professional on berries and foliage, and I don't think there's an animal alive out here except for us. We're just..." Damon looked at his pack and then back to Chess, giving up. "Just going to have to eat what you have."

"Yeah, sorry, it's not steak and potatoes," Chess humored.

"As long as it's food."

Damon started to stack the wood, the smaller sticks in the middle and the larger ones on top. Chess took out some paper from a notebook he brought with him and stuffed it in between the sticks. Lighting them up, it took less than a couple of seconds for the sticks to ignite. The sun had gone down, and their campfire was the only bastion of light within the tundra's plains.

"This won't make us a target, will it?" Chess asked, sitting on the snow. There was nowhere else to sit, no logs to rest on.

"If anyone were smart around here, they would be setting up camp too. It gets dark, real dark out here in the middle of nowhere. That said, this light would be seen for miles, so we should snuff it out right before we hit the hay," Damon said.

"Hmm."

They sat and ate granola protein bars until the sun left the sky, and the sight of the universe opened up to them. The arm of the Milky Way Galaxy surrounded by a vast amount of stars could be seen in its entirety, faraway lands that could have had Temporal anomalies like they were having. Chess didn't know.

He sat there, gloves in the snow, looking up to the sky as each star twinkled into existence. He didn't notice or see it, but Damon was staring at him. Looking at Chess as if he were the only man in the world. Every star in the sky couldn't compare to him, and he wasn't looking back the same way. Damon had a feeling he never would.

They sat by the fire and talked about a lot of nothing, a lot of everything, and their plans for the next day. If they were lucky, they would find a house, get better gear, and stay leagues ahead of Bijou. Houses and outposts would be their saving graces; if they could get their hands on better weapons, then Zhigansk wouldn't be much of a problem. Damon figured that plenty of the people who landed in the town were already gone. Fighting and claiming territory. Either way, they had to get ready by the time they set foot in there, at least make it to the last five players. Then they could continue together. They might never get back together, but they would be together in the game. They always had the Royale.

DAMON WOKE FIRST.

The fire had since shouldered out in the middle of the night, opting to leave it be for the extra warmth. They would have to reapply the patches as they ran out of heat in the middle of the night. Luckily the sleeping bags were made with down feathers and retained their body heat throughout the night. Damon woke up grateful for that, but he was also sweating; he was wrapped up so tightly. He must've thought that he would freeze to death in the middle of the night, so he tucked himself into the bag deeper than he should've.

The light was coming up over the horizon, and the warmth of the day was starting to set in. Damon could feel the heat of the sun on his cheeks despite the climate. He stood outside with a protein bar, chewing slowly on his breakfast as he waited for Chess to wake up. It was looking like he was going to be a late sleeper. Damon finished his bar and then turned back to the tent. Chess was only a face wrapped up in a sleeping blanket in the middle of the tent.

"Chess... Chess! Chess, wake up," Damon commanded.

Chess wriggled around like a worm and opened his eyes. He looked pissed off, and after a couple of seconds of being awake, he milked a yawn and then sat up, pushing his arms out of the sleeping bag and immediately regretting it. It was cold, really cold.

"Where are those patches? I need em," Chess said between clacking teeth.

"Never seen you like this; you look like a drowned rat," Damon joked, trying not to laugh.

"Fuck you."

With new patches applied and the camp broken down, they moved on. It was another long day of walking across a no man's land to whatever they could come across. Mostly a lot of ponds, lakes, and shallow rivers. Crossing the rivers was a pain, and walking around lakes and pods were even worse. Having to find their way back West after taking the long detour was demoralizing, to say the least. However, they couldn't see the purple of the storm creeping up on them, so they had to count their blessings somewhere.

The walking continued well into the day until something else on the horizon came up. A small, small town consisting of nothing more than ten houses maximum by the river. It would be enough to search for weapons and food while walking to Zhigansk. They still had a couple of days ahead of them to get there.

"Better than nothing. We can bunk there in real beds tonight," Chess said.

"Eat a real meal, too," Damon said, patting his pack.

Chess eyed it with a curious gaze but then looked forward at the town again. It was better than nothing, so they decided to stop.

CHAPTER
THIRTY-NINE

He first couple of houses didn't yield anything. Empty cupboards and homes. Not even beds. Most of the 'homes' were shacks filled with tools and sparse handheld weapons. Nothing usable, that was for sure. The final couple of houses were proper housing with beds and kitchens. If the gas worked, it wasn't apparent. The sun was going down again, and they would have the shack up somewhere. The final house they searched had not only a fireplace with an open chimney, but also had a full kitchen and a couple of beds. They decided to settle down there for the night.

"I'm trusting you to give this back to me when I ask for it," Chess said, handing Damon his handgun. "You're on the watch."

"And what are you going to do?" Damon asked, taking the handgun and checking the ammo inside. A full clip.

"I'm gonna break down some furniture and start a fire in the fireplace and then lay our shit out for the night. Unless you wanna do all the hard work," Chess said.

"No, I'd rather leave it to tall, dark, and handsome to do it for me."

"Wouldn't want to ruin those pretty hands of yours, pretty boy," Chess snapped back.

"Pretty boy, huh?" Damon mused as he moved to the window. He pushed the curtains out of the way and took overwatch.

Behind him, the sounds of furniture being broken down and piled up in the fireplace filled the air. Another night of eating protein bars and water, it was going to be murder on his gut later. Not seeing anything on the horizon, Damon turned to look at the full kitchen that had been sitting there for years, unused. At the very least, they could use the fireplace for cooking fire if he needed to. He had a better idea other than bars and water.

"How long until you think you'll have a fire going?" Damon asked.

"About a couple minutes. Why?" Chess replied.

"No reason. Wanted to cook something," Damon said.

"With what? There's no food in the cupboards, and there's nothing to eat but snow out there." Chess complained, snapping another stick with his knee and chucking it into the fireplace. In no time, the hearth was roaring with flame.

"Just... give me a second."

Damon moved from the window to the kitchen, where a deep oven was in place. The kind you put coals in to heat it for cooking and place a hot plate on top.

"It's been so cold, I was able to keep all of this fresh for this long, but I knew I was running out of time. I was hoping to hit a house by yesterday, but it didn't happen," Damon said, pulling his pack out from the floor.

"What about the train station? Couldn't cook there?" Chess asked.

Damon pulled out a plastic-wrapped medley of meat, vegetables, and what looked like cooked rice. Something that could be placed in a bowl and eaten pretty quickly. A stir fry of sorts. Chess looked at the package with hungry eyes.

"No pot back there. I can make it here, though. Are there bowls and spoons?" Damon asked.

"Look in the cupboards. I think I saw some when I was searching for weapons," Chess said.

Setting the meat on the counter, Damon moved to the fireplace and picked out some smoldering sticks. Quickly moving back to the stove, he shoved them into the coal pile and let them burn down, taking a few more stray pieces of wood to feed the fire. Once it was hot enough, Damon put the cooking pan over it. It was getting hot and fast.

The cooking pan looked seasoned enough, but the layer of dust on top was a little concerning. Using water, he wiped down the top only to hear it sizzle and steam rise from the cooking pan. He did the same, wiping down a couple of cooking utensils that hadn't seen the light of day in a long, long time. Unwrapping the food, Damon poured it all onto the clean cooking pan and heard it start to sizzle. Soon an aroma of vegetables, spices, and meat filled the house. It felt like a proper home at this point. They were going to eat a hot meal and sit by the fire. The next day, they would move on and head into Zhigansk or get as close to it as possible.

Once the fireplace was properly taken care of and the sleeping bags were placed on the beds in the other room, Chess came back to the kitchen to see how the food was coming along.

"You really skydived with a whole starry in your pack?" Chess mused.

"I wasn't about to eat sticks and berries for a week straight. Plus, I have other meals in that pack that will last us as long as we keep finding houses," Damon said.

"This isn't glamping. There's no promise that we're gonna keep finding houses like this. We got lucky," Chess explained.

"And we should continue to get lucky. As long as I'm with you," Damon said.

"What the fuck is that supposed to mean? Also, give me my gun back if you're cooking. I'll keep watch," Chess demanded.

"No, I'm going to go back to watch after I get this cooked up."

"That's going to take forever, and someone could come now on us at any time. Give me my gun back," Chess demanded.

"Come and take it," Damon goaded.

"See, I knew you weren't going to give it the fuck back; I just knew it."

"Then why did you give it to me in the first place?"

"Because... I thought I could trust you."

Damon looked into Chess's eyes and then looked away. The food was sizzling on the hot plate and threatening to stick to the metal. He would have to flip it soon. Looking down and then at his hip where the gun was, he pulled it out and handed it to Chess. No fuss and no rebuttal. Just handed it back over.

"I'll keep watch. Just bring the food over when it's done," Chess said. "And thank you."

"Yeah," Damon said.

It was quiet for a good couple of minutes as Damon continued cooking, and Chess was looking out of the various windows in the house, moving throughout the house to keep watch of the whole perimeter. Even going outside to walk around the town just in case they missed something, and by the time he came back in, Damon was plating the food.

"There's no one out there. Let's eat," Damon said.

"If they get the jump on up while we're eating, I'm blaming you."

"Fair." Damon smiled.

He handed Chess a plate of food, stir fry rice and meat with vegetables. Something simple and more than welcome in a cold climate like this. They sat in front of the fireplace with their wooden bowls and cutlery. Within moments the food was gone, hints of thyme and rosemary cooked into the mixture. Chess figured this was the best meal he's had in a long time, even though it had only just been days out in the tundra. Chess was grateful for the meal.

They sat in silence, eating and not looking at one another. The bow and arrows and handgun were laid out on a table. The food was eaten as fast as possible, and soon enough, they were laid out on the floor in front of the fireplace. There was no TV, and also no sounds of media drones anywhere either. It was peacefully quiet in the tundra. Chess lay on his back while Damon was sitting cross-legged on the floor. He picked at the rug on the floor idly as time passed. The sun was going down out of the sky, and they were going to have to get to bed soon.

"Some Duos so far, huh?" Chess asked from the ground. His arm was laid over his eyes as if he was trying to get some sleep.

"Haven't seen one soul out here yet, but we're getting closer and closer to the city with each passing day. We're bound to see someone soon," Damon said.

"You don't know that."

Damon looked at Chess, who still had an arm over his eyes and breathing normally. He spoke softly as if he was out of breath and rested. They both had been pushing it really hard these past couple of days, and they were going to have to push it even harder the next couple more. As for tonight and right now, Damon didn't know what they were going to do. The smoke billowing from the chimney could be a marker for anyone close enough to see where they stayed up for the night, but the land was so vast that he had a hard time thinking anyone would be out there watching them or hunting them.

"Better take care of these bowls then," Damon said, giving himself something to do.

He picked up the bowls and moved to the deep pot sink filled with water now that the snow had melted inside it. They weren't going to wash well, but this was better than sitting on his ass doing nothing. After a couple of seconds, Chess had come up from behind him and put the cutlery in the dish bowl as well. Damon froze for a bit, not turning toward him but feeling his presence in the meantime. Chess was so warm, and he didn't even have to touch him. He could feel the warmth radiating off of him.

"Hey," Chess started.

Damon dropped the bowls and turned to Chess, leaning back against the sink. "Hmm?"

"Remember that time in Academy right before graduation when we hosed all the buses on campus down with fire extinguisher foam because we didn't want to go back to school?"

Damon huffed a laugh.

"I specifically remember a couple of kids that got pinned for it besides us, the ones who *did* it. How'd you pull that off?" Damon asked.

"Easy. Wrote a letter in this kid's name and stuck it somewhere where people would find it. Yeah, they got kicked out, but we didn't have school for another week while they were cleaning out the buses," Chess said, trying to hold back a laugh.

Damon was the same way, biting his lip and stifling a giggle.

"We're horrible people," Damon said.

"We were dumb kids, not demons," Chess responded.

"Well, I still feel like a bad person. Leaving you out to dry like that as I did all those years ago," Damon said.

Chess rolled his eyes and leaned against the table. "You have to bring that up?"

"I wanted to say I'm sorry."

It was quiet again. Chess looked out the window at nothing and didn't want to look at Damon. All those years of despair and the apology comes now when he couldn't get away from it. He was stuck in the middle of nowhere with him, and he would have to confront it now. Chess huffed a sigh and then turned to Damon.

"You know..."

Damon looked at Chess after Chess addressed him. His brown eyes linked with Chess's blues.

"Back then... I would've done anything for you. *Anything*. And now..."

Damon waited for Chess to finish his thought before he butted in. He didn't want to say the wrong thing and risk pissing Chess off anymore. He didn't want to see Chess mad anymore.

"Now, I still... I still feel the same way. I just never thought you felt that way about me," Chess said, looking away from Damon. "After everything that happened, I was convinced you didn't love me like I loved you."

"That's not true!"

Damon broke away from the sink and took a couple of broad steps toward Chess, his hands going into his tracksuit. The coats had since been hung up by the door since the house was properly warm now. With handfuls of tracksuit and Chess's eyes on him again, Damon spoke.

"I always loved you. What I did was shitty; I know that. I *know* that. I'm sorry, I'm so so sorry for what I did to you, how I used you. I never, in my life, stopped loving you."

Chess's hands went to Damon's elbows, and they just held each other there for a little while. Looking into each other's eyes and breathing real hard. The tension was building, and the cord was about to snap. And then it did.

Chess picked Damon up by the waist and turned him around until he was sitting on the table Chess was once resting on. Standing between Damon's legs, he surged forward, claiming Damon's mouth with his own. He remembered him like home, their lips moving together in perfect tandem, tongues intertwining as they tasted each other. Damon still tasted the same as he did all those years ago, the same musky scent of sandalwood and blackberry.

Damon's hands and arms wrapped around Chess's neck as he pulled him in closer and closer to him, eventually tumbling off the table and rolling around on the floor until they ended up in front of the fireplace. Chess was straddling him, and he sat up long enough the quickly shed his tracksuit from his upper body, and Damon did the same. In the middle of nowhere, they were going to do this. It had been too long, too damn long, that they both wanted each other like this, and now, it could finally happen. They could put it all past themselves and love again.

The sleeping bags went forgotten in the other room, the two lovers opting to spend their time by the fire entwined in each other's bodies until the sun came up.

CHAPTER FORTY

Chess woke first.

They were both stark naked in the middle of the rug, the fireplace nothing more than embers at this point. The chill was starting to seep in and take over the house they had worked so hard to keep warm. He looked down at a sleeping Damon and then looked around. Realizing he was naked, he picked up his boxers and slipped them on quickly, opting to put Damon's tracksuit over Damon's body until he woke up.

He grabbed a protein bar from his pack and chewed lightly. They had done that; they had sex in the middle of the Temporal Storm, doing Duos, and hunting other players. Not only could he scratch that off his bucket list to get laid during a Blood Run, but for it to be with Damon again, of all people. He huffed a laugh at the absurdity of it all and moved to wake Damon up.

He still loved him.

He had always loved him, but the hate he had repressed for so long had clouded his mind to that realization. He accepted Damon's apology. Chess could tell that he truly meant it.

As he walked by the window on his way back to the fireplace to wake Damon up, he saw it. A small blip on the horizon. Someone was moving toward them and fast. The blonde hair under a baseball cap was hard to ignore, and Chess was sure there was still smoke billowing from the chimney. She found them.

"Damon! Damon, wake up!" Chess hissed, shaking Damon a couple of times.

After snorting away and shaking his head, Damon quickly noticed he was naked and grabbed his boxers, slipping them on.

"It's Bijou. She's just outside!" Chess hissed again, taking his phone out. There were still 16 people left in the game., If they were killed now, it would be game over for them; they would have to go home.

In a way, it felt almost comforting to lose and be done with the World Royale, but on the other hand, Chess knew that Bijou was hiding something; he wanted to get it out of her before he was forced to go home. Who knew if he would ever see her again after this game was over. If she would terminate their conversations and go dark on him. He wouldn't get his answers, just lying back and taking the death.

"Bijou is here? Where?" Damon asked, taking the bow and arrow off the table after putting his tracksuit back on.

After Chess was dressed as well, he pulled the down coat on and made for the back door, opening it.

"I'm going to flank to the right. You keep a lookout on the front window. She's coming in from the front, and she's coming fast," Chess said, exiting the house.

"Chess, wait!"

But Chess was already on his way out of the house and on his way to the side of the house. Hoping and praying that Bijou didn't move to take the backdoor and run into Chess, Damon locked the front door and backed away from the knob. She would likely slam her whole body into the door, trying to open it. This would buy Chess some time.

He wanted answers just like Chess did. Incapacitate her and take her weapons to get the answers he wanted. They were in the middle of nowhere, and she should be able to speak freely. That's when Damon saw it out of the window, a Media Drone following Bijou very, very closely. It more than likely paid off by Levi to keep a close eye on her, and given her track record, she more than likely killed off her teammate to run long distances by herself. She was cold-blooded, and that scared

Damon more than anything, how she was suddenly so cold. He wanted the old Bijou back. The new old Bijou, not this new cold Bijou.

From the side window, Damon could see Chess making his way around. He stopped just on the side of the house and waited. Bijou was practically at the front door by now, and just as Damon predicted, she slammed into the front door, trying to break it down but to no avail. She grunted and backed up quickly, aiming her weapon at the door knob. Damon knocked an arrow and gasped, knowing what was coming next, but the sound of a gunshot, not from a rifle, freed him from the fear. Bijou hollered out and fell to the ground, quickly trying to scurry away and get to the other side of the house for cover. She had been shot in the leg and was trying her best not to pass out from blood loss. She had to keep going; she couldn't lose now. If she could find a medkit, she would be back in the game.

Damon sprinted to the backdoor and took the other way around the house to where Bijou was trying to crawl and pulled the string, priming his shot. Eventually, he saw the blonde ponytail trying to wrench away from Chess, and Chess wasn't far behind her. Damon stopped when Chess raised a hand and turned to the media drone. He shot it a couple of times, and the hunk of useless machinery plummeted to the ground, sparks flying out of its chassis. Bijou looked on in horror at it. Without eyes and ears on her, she was technically free to speak her truth, but the threat of the Respawn Pod sabotage was high now. She didn't know if she would even be able to come back.

"Kill me!" Bijou hollered. "Quick!"

"Why are you acting this way?! Why are you hunting us?" Chess hollered. His eyes were full of hurt, just wanted to understand.

Bijou looked to the broken media drone and then back to Chess and Damon. She was breathing erratically, and before any of the boys could realize what she was doing, she pulled out a handgun she had hidden in her pants and blew her own head off. She was disqualified.

"Fuck! Goddamnit!" Chess hollered, watching Bijou's body turn to crystal and fall apart.

"She's hiding something, or she would've never done that. Bijou has always been scared of Blood Running; she's desperate," Damon said, out of breath.

"Should we follow her?" Chess asked, looking at his own pistol.

"No! Chess, no. We can't give up the World Royale either," Damon said, holding a hand out to stop Chess.

"Look, I know your dad is watching and expects a lot from you, but Bijou is hiding something. She just got disqualified too; she could be halfway to the airport by now," Chess argued.

Damon gave him a hard look and then shook his head. "I'm staying in. If you want to chase Bijou, be my guest, but I would rather finish the World Royale with you. I'm not going to let Bijou run away from what happened. We'll track her down after the game. I promise," Damon said.

Chess looked at Damon for a long while and then nodded his head. Holstering his weapon, he bent down to pick up the second handgun Bijou had dropped while Damon ditched the bow and arrow for the semi-automatic rifle. It was now or never. They had to make it to the city and fight their way to either victory or defeat. Either way, they were going to meet with Bijou once all this was done.

The town of Zhigansk was like a ghost. Not one sliver of life was found in its streets and buildings. Finding first aid and alcohol to drink in some of the buildings, Chess figured the fighting and holing up was happening further inside the town. They were only on the outskirts of it for now.

"We have to go deeper in. Maybe split up," Damon offered, looking down the main road into the belly of the city.

"Split up? That's a death sentence," Chess said.

"Maybe. But we can keep in touch over the phone. Call me if you see anything," Damon said.

With that, Damon broke off from Chess and ran East into the town. Chess was not too on board with this plan but headed West into the buildings as well, finding a high-rise to hole himself up in. If he could get to a high vantage point, he could see if any patrols or people were walking around trying to scavenge. It had already been a couple of days, and they had to have been looking for food. It only made sense to look out toward the market district of the town.

He didn't have any rifle to scope with, so he squinted and laid low between balcony bars to try and see anyone passing by. After five minutes, his phone buzzed, and he answered.

"See anything?" Damon asked.

"Nothing yet. I'm looking down the shopping district thinking people would scavenge for food, but I've seen nobody yet," Chess whispered. He didn't know if there were people on top of him or close by at all, so he kept it down.

"I'm going further into the town; if you see me, don't shoot," Damon said.

"Don't worry; I remembered what you're wearing."

"Chess, wait."

Chess was close to hanging up before he heard Damon call out one last time. He brought the phone back to his ear and hummed in question.

"I love you."

Chess swallowed and looked out toward the district again. He saw someone.

"I love you too. Bye."

Chess hung up and got up on one knee. He only had handguns, but the right shot could incapacitate them. It wasn't Damon; the jacket was dark, and he wore different boots. This was a completely different person. Pulling out his phone, Chess zoomed in on the camera, snapped a shot of the patrolling man, and sent it to Damon.

"Shopping District. West."

Chess waited a few moments for Damon to respond and watched the man. He wasn't with anyone and looked like a lone stranger in the middle of nowhere. In his hands was a pump-action shotgun. He meant business as he was a burly-looking guy. He wasn't going to be put down so easily. They would have to take a distance shot.

"Okay, omw."

Chess made his way down the building, knowing it would take Damon some time to get to the West side of the town. Once he was on the bottom floor, he peeked out to make sure the guy was still there and then went back inside the building. He took a breath and then crouched down to crouch-walk across the road, using broken-down cars as cover. The guy was still there, but someone ran up from the road to meet him this time. So he did have a buddy for Duos. That made this whole thing a little more hard.

They were speaking in Russian, and as Chess was getting closer to the two, he couldn't understand what they were saying. When the bigger guy started pointing toward another section of the town and saying something urgently to his teammate, he understood it was an order. They were patrolling and scouting for people or something else. Either way, they would have to take them down before they spotted them.

Getting closer to the large man, Chess knew he was going to chance the other man coming back if he were to fire right now, the sound of his firearm ringing out amongst the buildings announcing where he was. Everyone in the town was going to fall on him within minutes, and he wouldn't have time to protect himself. Looking on the ground, he saw multiple shards of broken glass and picked up a shard. It was thick and sharp and would do the job if he were to get close enough.

Holstering his guns, he took the shard of glass in his hand and crouch-walked toward the man slowly and quietly. Step by step, carefully, and by the numbers. When Chess's boot landed on an unfortunate pile of glass that made noise, he decided to lunge before the man could realize that he was already on him.

Chess tackled the man to the ground and fought with him, the Russian pushing his gun up to make a barrier between him and Chess. With a grunt from the bottom of his gut and a swing of his arm, Chess brought the shard down on the man's neck, dug it in, and twisted it. The Russian man started shooting blindly in surprise, knowing he was dying and hollered something in Russian. Chess pulled the shard out and slammed it back into the man's jugular over and over until he stopped moving. Chess was covered in blood, and the man turned into crystals, bursting into nothingness.

Before the other guy could come and realize that he had killed his teammate, Chess slunk back under the dilapidated cars and waited, smelling like nickel and dirt. Sure enough, his teammate came running back, hollering to the pile of crystals that used to be his friend. Wasting no time, Chess stood up and aimed both handguns at the man's head. Scared out of his mind, the poor Russian man dropped his weapon and put his hands up in surrender, mumbling multiple English words such as "sorry" and "please don't shoot" toward Chess.

Chess didn't get the chance to shoot. A long-range bullet slammed into the side of the Russian's head, the man downing him immediately. He turned into crystal before he hit the ground. Chess put his guns away, moving to meet Damon in the middle of the street, but what he saw was not Damon but another USA teammate, and he was still aiming down the sights.

CHAPTER FORTY-ONE

Chess dived out of the way just in time for another bullet to slam into the building behind where he was once standing. He landed on glass and crawled frantically toward more cars to find cover, pulling his handguns out and breathing erratically. His phone buzzed in his pocket as he felt the slug of another bullet hit the car next to him. He answered, propping the phone up in his ear so he could hold both guns.

"Where are you?! I'm taking fire!" Chess hollered.

"Still in East Sector! I'm hoping to get there in a couple of minutes. People are coming out of the goddamn walls now. I'm trying to take it slow," Damon hissed.

"Well, hurry the fuck up!" Chess hollered and peeked out from the car, aiming his weapons center mass and firing. He missed and then went back to hiding behind the cars.

"On my way. Hold on."

Damon hung up, and Chess just dropped the phone from his shoulder onto the ground. He would pick it up in a second, but he had to focus on the guy hunting him down. Another bullet hit the side of the building that Chess was hiding next to, and Chess ducked out of the way, standing up to shoot a couple of times in the man's direction before crouching back down again. It was a rock, paper, scissors game of who would get hit first, and if Chess didn't play this smartly, he would be the one cornered. He picked up his phone and pocketed it, reloaded his guns, and moved to hit the neighboring road that the American was shooting down from.

Just as he stopped behind a tree to get cover, another person, who wasn't Damon, was running across the road toward the man hunting Chess. Rapid fire rang out, and the tell-tale sounds of crystals hitting the pavement hit Chess's ears. He moved to the other side of the building and peeked around it, seeing a Russian girl collect crystals and pop them in her hands. Chess had no mana to speak of and didn't gather any crystals from his first kill as he didn't have time. Seeing as the girl was preoccupied, Chess turned from the building and aimed down the sights of both guns, firing rapidly. Three bullets hit their mark, and the girl was down but not out. She suffered, trying to summon a weak ball of fire before going out; she hurled it toward Chess, who dodged it easily. He aimed, fired, and she was out.

Fourteen left.

He had hurried up this game so he could meet up with Bijou. He didn't know if she was in trouble if Levi was doing something to her, saying something to her, or threatening her. He didn't want to leave Bijou out to dry like that; he had to save her. So he did something drastic.

"Over here, assholes!!" Chess hollered out, waving his hands in the air. "Come and get me!!"

Damon had just gotten to the West sector of the town when he heard Chess's voice ring out around the town. He stopped in his tracks, his blood running cold. That was definitely Chess's voice.

"What the hell is he doing?" Damon hissed to himself.

He had to hurry and get into the West sector before Chess got his head blown off by another player. He hurried down an empty street and kept to the shadows as he grew closer to the noise of Chess hollering. Eventually, gunshots started to pair with the yelling. He had to hurry.

"That's right, you sons of bitches! I'm right here!"

The gunfire continued as Damon closed in on Chess's position. He could see him. He was now crouching behind a bus and shooting out of it every other second. He slid on the asphalt, landing next to Chess, and pulled out a couple of ammo clips for him, handing them over. Chess took them and reloaded.

Thirteen left. Twelve.

Two more had to go for Chess and Damon to be in the clear, and it couldn't be one of them. Once Chess was in the clear, he would give himself up. He had to get to Bijou as fast as possible, but he didn't want to disappoint Damon either by just throwing the World Royale away like this. Chess took a deep breath and focused. At least he stopped yelling.

"What the hell are you trying to do?! Get yourself killed?!" Damon hollered over the gunfire.

"Yeah, actually!" Chess hollered back. "I have to see Bijou!"

"Can't you do that after you win?!"

Another couple of shots landed next to their feet, and Damon primed his gun to fire. Peeking out from his side of the bus, he saw a couple of girls heading in their direction. Targets number one and two.

"We need to kill two more, or two more people have to drip for me to give it up completely!" Chess yelled and started firing.

"Bullshit!" Damon countered back.

"Huh? Woah?!"

Damon pulled Chess by the collar and slammed him up against the bus. For the time being, it looked like the one group, and the other person on the other side of the map saw each other and were duking it out. Better for Damon and Chess that they cull themselves before they get to them. However, Damon wasn't worried about the other players. He was worried about Chess, and it was evident on his face. The barred teeth and anger behind his eyes. Chess watched him, mouth slightly agape and breathing heavily.

"You can't just play the game? Wait until you've already won. I want to see Bijou too, but getting yourself killed on purpose isn't sending the right message to her. She's going to think you're hunting *her* down now!"

"I wasn't thinking of it like that!" Chess said, pushing Damon off of him.

The sounds of footsteps quickly approaching broke them from each other, and they primed, ready to fight whoever was going to come out of the sides of the bus. Chess crouched down and thumbed back the hammer on his weapons, waiting for the faces to show up. Damon started shooting before Chess did, a girl going down in seconds as Damon took the time to reload.

"We see Bijou after we win this!" Damon hollered, slamming the hammer back on his gun. "And we will win!"

"How can you be so sure? Big ass town with people coming out the walls every second, we're gonna get surrounded," Chess pointed out.

"No, we won't; look!"

A balcony above them was open for the high ground if they could figure out a way to get up there without getting shot. The bus was pretty close to the entrance; all they would have to do was run and make it up the stairs. At least three other people out in the open knew of their position, and if they moved now, they would be risking getting shot and eliminated. They had come too far to blow it now.

"There had to be at least one more elimination for us to be in the clear. I think," Chess said, scooting back closer to Damon. "We'll never make it up there without proper cover."

Damon looked around, worrying his lip, overthinking the situation when he saw a blown-off car door on the ground. Bingo.

"Come on," Damon said, running o the car door. He picked it up while grunting, his gun slung on his back.

"What the fuck, Damon?"

"Come on, you shoot, and we'll run! It's better than nothing!" Damon convinced Chess.

Chess wasn't completely convinced but ran to Damon anyways, his gun turned down and running low. They both got behind the car door, and on the count of three, they ran from the bus to the entrance of the building. Gunfire was heard almost immediately, bullet holes entering the car door and barely missing the two men wobbling their way to the building entrance. Chess did his best to cover down. Popping out every other shot to return fire and crouching when he needed to. They were so close to the building when the assailants figured out to aim for the feet, grazing Damon in the process.

Luckily, they were close enough to the entrance that when Damon dropped the car door out of surprise, Chess was able to quickly drag his body inside the building and shut and lock the door. It wouldn't hold them off for long, so they had to get upstairs fast.

"Come on, can you walk?" Chess asked, propping Damon back up on his feet.

He was limping but able to make good strides and keep up with Chess as they moved to the stairs.

"Can't take the elevator, huh?" Damon grunted as they climbed the stairs.

"Don't think it would even be working even if we tried it. These buildings haven't been serviced in years thanks to the Storm," Chess said, putting an arm under Damon to support him.

Damon tucked his head into the crick of Chess's neck as they climbed the stairs, the sounds of gunshots and yelling heard in the background, muffled by the walls. They were getting higher and higher from their assailants; if they were lucky, some med items could be found in some of these rooms. They would have to be quick, though, because once they were done with each other out there, they would be coming for them.

Stopping on the fourth floor and kicking open a door to an apartment, the first thing Chess saw was bandages sitting on the coffee table. He quickly got Damon to sit down on the couch and started wrapping his foot—shoe and all—with the bandages, hoping they would heal quickly. Especially if they needed to make a quick getaway.

A couple more shots rang out, and then, silence. It was quiet for a good couple of minutes, and Chess was starting to worry if they were silently coming for them or not. He decided to shut the apartment door before going to the window to assess the situation, but what he saw stopped him in his tracks.

A man was laying in the snow. Blood and brain matter was pooling around his head, spreading to the white powder around him. However, he wasn't de-crystalizing. He wasn't going back to the Respawn Pods. He was dead.

"Oh, what the fuck... What the fuck!" Chess started hollering out.

Before Damon could ask any questions, Chess bolted from the

room and onto the balcony they were going to shoot from. He put his guns in his holsters and held his hands up in surrender.

"Hey! Don't shoot! Is he dead?!" Chess hollered out.

One of the players from the Russian team looked up at him and shook her head.

"Ya, it looks that way!" she replied in perfect English. "What do we do?!"

"We shouldn't shoot each other anymore; that's what we should be doing! Meet me at the door. I'll let you in!"

Chess went back inside, tossed his weapons on the coffee table, and turned to Damon. His face was grim, and Damon heard the whole thing too. He wasn't looking any better, either.

"What's happening?" Damon asked.

"Whatever it is, it's happening outside the storm. I'm letting them in so we can figure this out before moving on."

"Is there really a dead guy out there? He's not crystal?" Damon asked.

Chess looked out of the window, and the man was still lying there, the blood spreading further and further into the snow. It was a horrible sight. One of the players took a tarp hanging in the wind and put it over the man's body as a sign of respect; then, he made his way to the door.

"We'll figure everything out before the storm comes. Right now, we all have to have a talk," Chess said.

With that, he bolted down the stairs to unlock the doors.

CHAPTER FORTY-TWO

Bijou ripped her way out of the Respawn Pod the second she was corporeal and lucid. The gunshot she administered to herself was seen by no one, the only media drone in the vicinity having been shot out of the sky by Chess. His first mistake. She knew she had to get out of the game as fast as possible, or she might not have made it back. When she did get back, however, what greeted her was absolute pandemonium.

None of the media drones were working; the screens were offline for most of the Pilot House crew. Bijou ran in and saw Farren biting her manicured nails and looking from one security camera to another. Nothing was showing up, no one was anywhere, and the drones weren't coming back online. Levi was nowhere to be seen.

"How much time left until the storm gets them?" Bijou hollered out, trying to get someone's attention.

A maintenance worker stepped up and answered her, "Three days. Give or take."

"Farren, Levi is sabotaging the game. I got out right before he could do it. He's more than likely still in the Respawn Room maintenance," Bijou said.

"What do you know? Levi has been down your throat since day one! Tell us!" Farren demanded.

Bijou grabbed Farren's hand and pulled her along as they ran down the hall. Farren was following close behind her but had a careful eye about her. Bijou had been so secretive this whole time up until now, and now she wants to spill everything. She didn't trust it, but she had nothing else to go off of. The cameras were down, and none of the drones were working; she could very well be telling the truth that he may be down there.

"Bijou! Bijou!!"

Farren ripped her hand away, and Bijou stopped in her tracks, looking back at her coach, pale as a ghost. She was bouncing in one spot, eager to move down to the maintenance area of the Respawn Room. Whatever Levi was doing, it had to be bad, and she wanted to stop it before it became serious.

"Farren, we don't have a lot of time. People are going to die—"

"Then what was his angle then? Why Levi?" Farren snapped back.

"He's after the families. Not just the boys; it was never about the ratings! He wants revenge!"

"Revenge for what?!"

Bijou stalled for a moment, and then a massive tremor shook the building. Something was blowing up under their feet, which wasn't far from where they were standing. Bijou wobbled a little bit and then righted herself. If she wasn't already pale as a sheet, she was even paler now.

"He's really gonna do it. He's gonna do it," Bijou said with horror in her voice.

"He's going to do what?" Farren asked, her voice shaky.

Another boom rocked the space; this time, Bijou and Farren fell to their knees. Farren could feel the ground shaking under her fingers, and her eyes were locked to the floor. Something was going on underground, underneath them.

"We have to get to the maintenance area! He's going to destroy the Respawn Pods!" Bijou hollered, getting back up on her feet. "If he can't eliminate the boys, he's just going to kill them!"

Farren didn't say anything else; she started running along with Bijou down to the stairwells, followed by maintenance workers that also felt the rumbling. The majority of them worked on a multitude of machines within the pilot house and knew something was going on with them. They had to act fast, or else something serious was going to happen.

By the time they finally made it to the stairwell, they were forced to climb down the twenty floors as the rumbling locked the elevators from working. While Bijou was in boots, Farren was able to keep up right behind her despite being in heels. The stairs were steep, made of metal, and resounded with every step of their shoes. Anyone down there was going to know they were coming, so they had to make it quick.

By the time they made it to the maintenance room, the door was half off its hinges, and whoever was there was long gone. The servers and machines that kept the upkeep of the Respawn Pods were destroyed. There were still over twelve people still stuck in the game. Looking at all the damage, busted consoles, and live wires everywhere, Bijou slowly turned back to Farren and the maintenance workers with horror washed over her face.

"I don't know where he is," Bijou mumbled. "I don't know..."

"We have to find him. Team, clean this mess up and get it somewhat functional! There's people that are going to die out there if we don't do something!" Farren instructed.

The foreman of the Pilot House and the maintenance crew sprung into action, doing what they could about the wires and damage. It looked like a small bomb had gone off in the room; judging by the residue left behind, it might as well have been. Something strong with a blasting agent, at least. Where did Levi get something like that?

"We have to find a way to warn the people in the game that they can't be shooting people! They won't be able to come back!" Bijou said.

Farren nodded and looked to the foreman, getting a nod from him as well. They made their way back upstairs and ran to the Respawn Pods. As expected, they were all offline and not showing any lights or signs of life. This was bad. If someone got shot and eliminated right now, they wouldn't come back and would grow cold in the Storm. If these Respawn Pods weren't up and running before the Storm reset them, they would be lost to time. Those who are eaten by the storm never come back.

"This place doesn't have backup generators for the Respawn Pods or anything like that?" Farren asked the Foreman.

"Only in dire circumstances have we used them, but it's going to take a day for them to get back online. They haven't been activated for years," the Foreman said.

"They have three days until the Storm engulfs them; I think getting started on getting the generators up and running is a good start," Farren said.

The Foreman agreed with her and ran back down the hallway to give more orders. Farren called out for him, and he stopped, turning around to look at her. They all wore Hell on their faces.

"Keep that room locked tight with security! Round the clock! We don't want a repeat of what happened to the main generators," Farren commanded.

"Right. We'll get on it!"

With that, the Foreman disappeared down the hallway and down another stairwell. Soon, within the day, hopefully, they could have the Respawn Pods back up and running for Chess and the others to come home. With the media drones down and the cameras showing empty streets with no action, it was hard to say what was going on. The only option they had was to wait.

"What do we do?" Bijou asked.

Her eyes were on the empty streets of the cameras, but Farren was looking at Bijou with sharp eyes. They were working on getting the generators up and running; all they had now was time. Time to find Levi, time to guard what was left of the Respawn Pods, time to wait for the Storm to engulf everything around the players. However, Bijou also had time to talk, and Farren was going to get everything out of her that she could.

"It started simple enough. He spun me this sob story about how no one ever liked him, that he had to make his own luck to get by. I ate it up, tears and all. I felt bad for him; like, he deserved to reclaim the recognition he deserved," Bijou started.

"Did he promise you money?" Farren asked.

Bijou nodded, a guilty look on her face.

"Yes. For my business. I wasn't going to tell you or the boys, but I'm hurting. Badly. I needed money like this. If I didn't win the World Royale, then at least this was something I could fall back on. The price was high, the elimination of the Kennedy and Harlow boys," Bijou explained.

"Why does he want the boys out of the game so badly? What did they do to him?" Farren asked.

"It's not about what the boys did to him; it was about what the namesakes of those boys did to him. Rhett and Lucas Kennedy. He was once friends with them."

Farren sat back in her seat and took a deep breath through her nose. Things were starting to add up. Why Levi wanted the boys to continue to hate each other so badly, to eliminate one another. To get them out of the game and enact his revenge.

"He didn't want a Kennedy or Harlow winning the World Royale ever again, and when I figured out what his real angle was, it was too late. He had blackmail on me to give to the World Royale Committee. Bribery and fraud. I wouldn't just be kicked out of the games; I'd be arrested," Bijou explained.

Farren scooted forward and rubbed Bijou, now softly crying, on the shoulder. It wasn't her fault, none of this was her fault, and Farren felt for her.

"You're not to blame. Levi is, and we'll find him."

"I don't even know where he could be. That makes me scared, that he might come for me," Bijou said between sobs.

"He's not going to get you. You're going to stay in this room until the game is over—until those Respawn Pods are back up and running. There's safety in numbers, and you'll be safe here."

Farren was referencing the Pilot House and the control room. People were always coming in and out, and there was always someone present so she would be safe from an attack from Levi. He could've killed someone with a blast like that; she didn't want to know what else he was capable of.

CHAPTER FORTY-THREE

One by one, people marched into the apartment where Damon was resting and set their weapons on the floor or the tables. There were eleven of them in total, six Americans and five Russians. Only one Russian within the group could speak English, and she offered to be the back-and-forth translator with the group.

"What the hell was going on out there?" Chess asked, sitting next to Damon.

"We were playing the game like normal, and then someone on the Russian team went down." One of the USA players, Fredrick, said. "We all stopped once we saw he wasn't crystalizing."

The woman on the Russian team listened to one of her teammates speak something in Russian, a long-winded sentence about something, and nodded along with him. After he was done, she turned to Chess.

"We were on the leeward side of the city, coming to close in. One of your team members shot Androv's Duo's partner, and now he's dead. We can't keep playing, Androv said," the woman said, motioning over to the man that was speaking innately, Androv.

"And what's your name?" Damon asked the Russian woman.

"Leia."

"Ok, Leia. Tell your team that we are having a ceasefire. No one is to fire any weapons; no one is to kill anyone else. We're going to stay in this building until..." Chess started but stopped when he realized what the end game truly was.

"Until the Storm eats us," Leia finished.

Chess nodded, his eyes hard on hers, and she nodded. She was afraid but holding herself rather well. She turned to the other Russian players and started speaking. While she relayed what Chess had said, Damon tapped him on the shoulder to get his attention.

"Do we have enough food to go around for everyone? We still have three days until the storm hits," Damon said.

It was a fair observation. Getting up from his seat and looking into his pack that he had thrown to the side, he saw he only had about fifteen protein bars left. Enough if he split them in half and they rationed, but more than likely not feasible. They were going to have to turn the whole town over to scour for food. There had to be something lying around.

Chess turned back to Damon and shook his head no. Damon responded by belting out a sigh and letting his head roll back to hit the back of the sofa. It was a stressful time, people were dying, and now they might starve before the Storm even gets to them, or at least they'll be too weak to do anything about it.

"We're going to have to look for food. I have protein bars, and if anyone else has stuff, now would be a good time to pool our resources," Chess said, bringing the protein bars over to the coffee table.

The guns and ammo were moved out of the way as Chess laid the food out; he took one for himself and unwrapped it, taking a massive bite. Call it nerves or what have you; he was on edge about this whole thing. There was a dead man outside, only twenty feet from him, and the rest of them could be next if someone got trigger-happy. At the very least, the Storm would roll through and get them all in the end, so there was that to look forward to.

One by one, people started taking out the food they had brought. Noodles, meat, snacks, and even candy were pooled in the middle. Still not enough to live off of for three days, but they would be able to manage.

"It's going to be a long three days in here, but we can do it," Chess said. "We have to."

"And what about the Storm? There's no running away from that!" another USA team member belted out.

"We'll think of something! Blood Running didn't get this far to just fail us like this. We'll think of something," Chess hollered.

The teammate looked at Chess was hard eyes and then threw his hands up in the air, scoffing. He was frustrated, Chess was frustrated. Pretty much everyone in the room was fed up with the whole situation already and sick of waiting to die.

OVER 12 HOURS HAD PASSED, AND NO ONE HAD MOVED FOR their spots. Damon was still propped up on the coffee table, resting his injured foot, and Chess wasn't leaving his side. A couple of hours ago, one of the USA team members announced they were going to scour the town for more food and hadn't come back yet. The sun was starting to go down, and a hint of purple could be seen on the horizon. Only two days left until the end.

They ate silently and picked their spots on the floor to sleep on. It wasn't five star, but it was a roof and four walls all the same. Chess destroyed another chair to put into the fireplace so that there was at least some heat throughout the house. It wasn't a roaring fire, but it was enough.

Come the morning, the purple haze in the distance looked a little more purple, and the swirling of the clouds could be seen. They only had hours left despite one more night to go. Who knows when the storm would decide to close in on them. They knew they had at least one more day before the end.

The teammate still hadn't come back from looking for food yet, and Chess was starting to get worried. The teams were pretty broken off, the Russians on one side of the apartment and the USA members on the other, but everyone noticed that this guy had not returned yet.

"We should go out and look for him," Damon said, getting to his feet.

He was still kind of limping, but he was healing. He would be able to walk if he really wanted to go out and look for the lost teammate.

"It could be obvious that he got lost; we are in a random building in the middle of the city," one of the USA team members said.

"We're going to go get him," Chess said, grabbing a gun and holstering it.

He caught the eye of a couple of people watching him holster up weapons to look for someone on his side, but he didn't know what was going to meet him out there. If this guy was truly lost or sane at all. They knew they were going to die, lost in the storm. If anything, this guy could've gone AWOL and made his way to the Storm to end it altogether. It would've been one hell of a walk, but Chess could see it happening.

"I'm going with you," Damon said, getting up and slinging a rifle over his back.

Chess looked at him and then down to his foot, making Damon scoff and sigh.

"I'm fine. I can run and walk; I'll keep up," Damon argued.

"Are you sure? I'll be right back," Chess said.

"You're not going out there alone. Who knows what kind of mindset this guy is in? I know you're not taking the gun for nothing," Damon said.

Damon was right; Chess was worried about how this guy was thinking and acting. What state was he going to be in when they found him again? If they found him, that is. He hoped that he wasn't going to the Storm. Whatever was happening outside the game, maybe it could be fixed before they were all killed by the oblivion. Hopefully, that would be the case.

"We'll be back before sundown with or without him. Wherever he is, we're gonna find him," Chess said to the rest of the group.

Everyone nodded and sat around, waiting. Waiting for something, waiting to die. Some of them were staring out of the window at the oncoming purple haze that was the Storm closing in around them. It would form into the eye of the Storm and hover there for a day before engulfing them all. The thought was harrowing. Would be enough to make anyone go mad, but to run off into nothingness, not even coming back and lying about it. If he were really going out to look for food, he would've been back by now.

"Stay here and don't do anything stupid. We're all going to get out of here," Chess said.

"They should send for a helicopter at least, right?" one of the USA members asked.

Someone on the Russian team spoke, and Leia listened in, nodding along.

"A plane or helicopter wouldn't be able to reach us in time, and a plane definitely wouldn't be able to take off and reach the height it needs to clear the Storm. It's useless," Leia said.

She repeated what she said in Russian to her teammates, who all shook their heads and moaned. They knew it was true, but no one wanted to believe it. They wanted to believe there was a way out of here without dying. The worry and agitation were starting to set in.

With a last look at the people inside the apartment, Chess moved his way out of the room. It was going to be a long walk, and the only things he had to lead him along were his cell phone and his wit. Pulling out his phone as he descended the stairs, he shot a group-wide text to everyone left on the USA team.

"If you're out there, we're coming to get you. Let us know where you are."

A couple of moments went by after he sent the message, and more messages came in from the other USA team members wishing Chess good luck and thumbs up emojis. However, a message from the missing teammate never came in. They were on their own.

CHAPTER
FORTY-FOUR

Bijou woke up on the floor of the Pilot House main console room. Someone had placed a coat over her overnight as she tried folding in when she sat up and placed her back on the nearest console box. She sighed, feeling the crick in her back and the soreness in her joints. The sounds of machines whirring around her and the TV still showing empty streets filled the room.

Bijou sat in silence, not really thinking much about anything. A day had come and gone, and they were getting closer and closer to the end. The Storm was going to come and consume her friends, and there was really nothing they could do about it except to try and get the Respawn Pods back up and running—if they were able to do so. They had to; they had no other choice.

She wished she knew more about how they worked so she wasn't just sitting here doing nothing but waiting. However, she ran the risk of running into Levi if she went out there alone. There was an area-wide search for him, but he had yet to be found. This only worried Bijou more. He could be anywhere, waiting for her, and he had to have known that she talked. Of course, she talked. She had wanted to tell someone since the beginning, but the bribes and the money were all too much.

She stretched and felt her joints pop from tension. Getting up from the floor, however, she was aghast to see there was no one in the Pilot House with her. No maintenance crew or staff was present. She shuddered a little bit and looked around. No one behind her either. The whole room was vacant.

Bijou couldn't help but think of what would happen if Levi were to show his face right now. To take her hostage and threaten her for even speaking a word about his plans and aspirations, no matter how horrible they were. Perhaps everyone was home for the night or working down in the generators. Not even Darren was around, and she knew that she had fallen asleep with her in the room last night. When they stayed up past the point of exhaustion and couldn't keep their eyes open anymore. They talked all night, Bijou telling Farren everything she knew, but in the end, she really didn't know too much. She only knew what Levi told her, which wasn't a lot. Just sob stories and revenge, that's what Bijou got out of it.

Why did she feel so stupid? To take money dangled in front of her face like a thick, juicy steak to a dog just because her business was failing. She couldn't help it and, for that, felt like a failure for stooping so low as to train to knock out the boys from the competition. She owed them an apology the next time she saw them. If she were to ever see them again. She had to; there was no other choice.

She didn't know anything about the generators, but she figured she would go and check on the Respawn Pods. Surely someone would've woken her up to tell her everything was back online, but she wanted to see with her own eyes if they were still offline or not. If they were working, then great. Problem solved. She didn't have a plan for it they weren't. Go back to the Pilot House and wait everything out. It was going to be a long day and an even longer next morning when the storm would shut itself around the rest of the players. They had to get things up and running before then. She couldn't handle the thought of them dying like that, lost forever within the storm. She wouldn't accept it as reality.

Moving out of the Pilot House, despite her best judgment, she walked down the carpeted hallway toward the Respawn Room and peeked inside. She didn't go inside, but the glow of a Respawn Pod was hard to miss. Sadly, they weren't glowing. They were still as dead as they were yesterday. The urge to go down and look in the maintenance sector was too great to see if anyone was still working on getting them home or if people were taking the day off. With a situation as dire as this, she was spurred to find literally no one around. As she made her way to the stairwell exit to walk down to the maintenance area, Farren came around the corner holding coffee and food. They spotted each other, Bijou's hand still on the door.

"They're still working on it. They stayed up all night trying to reconnect the backup generators," Farren said, handing her a coffee and motioning back toward the Pilot House.

They walked back and inside the control room, where they picked random seats and sat down. Bijou idly sipped on her coffee, it had a cinnamon flavor to it that was pleasant, but she wasn't hungry enough to eat the apple fritter that came with it. She stomach could barely keep the coffee down.

"Where is everyone? The maintenance room, then?" Bijou asked.

Farren nodded and sipped her coffee. "Some are talking to press outside, and others are getting spare parts from warehouses to help with the generators. Either way, you look at it, it's a massive shitshow, and the whole world knows what happened now. If Levi ever gets caught, he's going to jail for a long, long time."

"Why would he do such a thing if he knew he was going to be arrested for it? Surely he knew that this was not going to end in his favor?" Bijou asked.

Farren shrugged and adjusted in her seat, setting her coffee down and pulling out her phone.

"He has a lot of money and resources that I'm not privy to. If he really wanted to, he could change his whole identity and live somewhere else for the rest of his life. Not saying that he's going to do that, but he has the assets for it. Wait a minute..."

Farren checked her phone to see the text Chess sent in a player-wide blast. Bijou pulled out her phone to see the text as well from the Blood Runner app. Chess was calling out to someone and pinged his location. He was in the middle of the city heading North toward somewhere or someone. Getting up and out of her seat, nearly spilling her coffee, Bijou went to the center console where the cameras were recording. It was easy to figure out how to rewind and look back at footage she might have missed.

Farren was standing next to her as Bijou held down the rewind button, trying to find anything, any clue of Chess walking in front of the cameras and where they could be. Eventually, she found it. Pausing right as they crossed the camera facing the middle of the city and down a main street, Chess and Damon were walking together, loaded up with weapons, toward the North. Chess was composing the text right as she paused. This was earlier in the morning; Bijou was still asleep.

"They could be anywhere right now," Farren said.

Pulling her phone back out, Bijou quickly made a text also open to the whole USA team. Since she wasn't in a group anymore, she wouldn't be able to text Chess on his own. Everyone should've seen her messages anyways; it was important information.

"The Respawn Pods are broken. Levi has sabotaged them, trying to get Chess and Damon kicked from the game. We're trying to fix them and bring them back online. Hold on!"

She sent the message and waited. No response for a little bit, but then the replies were pouring in. Mostly from the rest of the USA team members.

"Bijou! Where were you?"

"Chess and Damon just left to go find Chris! He bailed."

"We're pretty sure Chris is dead, but we don't know. Chess and Damon just left to find him."

The replies came one after the other, and while she could sit there all day and talk with them, she had no information other than what she had just relayed. She had to wait just like they had to wait. Wait for them to die or wait for them to live. It was agonizing. She couldn't imagine how the rest of the team was feeling, knowing that in a couple of hours, their fates were going to be decided for them. The Storm did not discriminate against who or what it ate up. Everything was reset or removed in time.

Damn the Temporal Anomaly. Bijou felt her hands clench over her phone, squeezing it until it might crack. None of this was fair. The fact that something like this could happen and take all of her friends away from her, something so simple as a Respawn Pod down, and that was game over. She would never see Chess and Damon again.

She hunted them, yes, but she was so happy to see them working together. To not fight anymore. They had grown closer and, as far as she could see, were working together to find Chris, their teammate. It was like a dream come true. They could all be a friend group again, just like in Academy. Then this had to happen. The Respawn Pods had to go down, and Levi had to destroy everything. It was as if he couldn't play God anymore, and everyone had to die because he said so. It wasn't fucking fair.

CHAPTER FORTY-FIVE

Chess and Damon made their way through the city heading North. Bijou had since texted everyone in the USA team about what had happened. Levi sabotaged the game, killing them off because of God knows what. He wanted to ask more, but in an open channel like this, that kind of business was best for when they got back. If they got back. The Storm on the horizon was looking more and more purple by the minute as if it was about to fall right on them. They still had a day.

Spending it out looking for their teammate, Chris, wasn't how he would want to be spending it, but it was better than just sitting around waiting to die in an apartment room. Chess barely ate; his stomach was rumbling, and he was running on fumes. He hadn't drunk any water in the past 12 hours and was exhausted. Damon was feeling the same way. If he had known that Chess needed a drink of water, he would've saved up and shared with him. Nevertheless, they were without water and only had bare bones for food, looking for a man that seemingly didn't want to be found.

So far, there hadn't been any response from Chris on where he was or where he was going. No response at all about his whereabouts. It was starting to look fruitless, but they still had a whole day to go and search for him. When the Storm was hovering over the city, they would turn back.

"He said he left to go find food, but that was twenty-four hours ago," Damon said, walking calmly next to Chess.

"Which means he has a twenty-four-hour head start from us and could be anywhere," Chess replied.

"Well, he has to be somewhere within the Storm. He can't just be anywhere," Damon said.

"Who's to say he didn't walk into the Storm?"

Damon looked at Chess, who was looking at him as they walked. They didn't want to think about something like that, that someone would just walk into the Storm and kill themselves to get out of dealing with it all. Chris could've had a panic attack and ran off, lying about foraging for food. It could've been anything, and they weren't going to get any answers until they found him.

Walking to the northern side of the city, the buildings had mixed into a medley of apartments and businesses. The border of the city was obvious as it petered out into vast landscapes of snow and trees with nothing more on the horizon other than the Storm. However, there were no bodies in the distance, no one walking aimlessly or back toward the city. It was just empty land as far as they could see.

"Doesn't give us much to go off of," Damon said.

"Come on, let's look this way."

They both ended up splitting up and venturing into random buildings until the sun started to go down. They didn't hear back from Bijou, and there was no news about fixing the Respawn Pods. The only thing they could go off was that Levi was behind it, and it was because of the boys. For whatever reason, Levi wanted the boys out of the competition. If that was all, why didn't he just ask? Even Chess had to admit that he would've stayed out of spite. He didn't take kindly to doing things just because people told him to do it. He knew Damon was the same way.

Chess found himself in an apartment building, trying all the doors until he found some unlocked ones. Searching these didn't prove fruitful as they were devoid of any people or food. Entering one apartment, found an open window to which Chess walked to it. The curtains were flowing peacefully in the breeze as if this were just another normal day in Russia. A calm, peaceful day. There were flowers on the windowsill and bread on the table. It looked fresh, or as fresh as it could be after sitting out for a couple of days. He didn't touch it.

Looking out to the road below him, he saw the silhouette of Damon walking down the north alley to another building. He decided to follow him, hurrying out of the building he was in and going in through the back of the building Damon entered into. The sun was starting to go down, and off in the distance, the rumbling of the Storm could be heard. It was going to fall upon them in the morning; they would be caught in the eye of the storm for the last day and then nothing. It would all end for them right then and there.

Taking out his phone and composing a quick text to the rest of the members back at the apartment, Chess didn't get to finish as he was thrown up against the wall and a gun held to his head. Chess dropped his phone and immediately pulled out his handgun, aiming it at Damon's head.

"Ahhh, man! I thought... I thought you were..." Damon breathed out, lowering his rifle.

Chess lowered his handgun just as slowly and bent down to pick up his phone. The text was still on the screen unsent when Damon fisted two handfuls of Chess's jacket into his hands and pushed him up against the wall. It was cold in the air, but Damon's breath on his lips made him feel like he was standing in the middle of summer. Tight breaths and clicks of lips together filled the building's hallway. It wasn't until Chess pulled away, his own hands in Damon's jacket, that he opened his eyes and looked into Damon's dark-colored irises.

"Almost blew my head off." Chess breathed into Damon's mouth. "You almost blew my head off."

"You almost killed me too." Damon's tongue licked quickly over his bottom lip. Chess watched it happen and then looked back into Damon's eyes.

Chess let go of Damon's jacket in lieu of holding his face and pulling him in quickly to kiss him again. Ever since that night in the house, it had been nothing but a whirlwind of problems and action, both unable to bask in their newfound and rekindled companionship. Damon wanted so badly to wrap his arms around Chess and never let him go again. Chess was feeling the same way. The feeling of love and borderline obsession Chess felt when he was with Damon those first few months; those feelings were all coming back now.

"Sun's going down," Chess said in between kisses. "Wanna hole up here?"

"Yeah, I do."

Chess managed to break away from Damon long enough to send the text that they would be staying in an apartment on the other side of town and coming back in the morning, still looking for Chris. Chess quickly pocketed his phone, and they made their way up to the roof, opting to get an overwatch of the town and try to find Chris walking around somewhere. It was worth a shot. That lasted all of two hours, and then they were back in a warm apartment room, the fire going, clothes shed, and limbs tangled into one another on the rug. No one to stop them, no one to watch them, no one to tell them no.

THE STORM WAS RIGHT OUTSIDE THE CITY WHEN THEY WOKE up the next day. Still in boxers and not much else, Chess sat up, groggy and out of it, only snapping to attention when he saw the haze of purple outside the window. This was it, the final part of the Storm, and then it was going to be lights out.

Chess looked at Damon for a moment. He was still sleeping. At the very least, Chess can say that he truly got what he wanted and made up for it before he died. He got to make up with and be with Damon at least one more time before the end. Somehow, thinking of it like that, it didn't seem so bad anymore, but he still wanted to live. He wanted to live the rest of his days with Damon by his side. He didn't want to stare at walls anymore or squander his money anymore. He wanted to live and live with Damon.

Pulling his phone out from his pants, he checked the text messages from the Blood Runner app, only to be met with dead silence. The last text sent was the text that Chess had typed last night before they went up for the night. Before they even did the overwatch on the roof for Chris. Just silence, no responses. That was strange.

At the very least, one person should've responded to what he typed; he would've taken an 'ok' by any of them. However, this radio silence was not sitting well with him. He composed another text and sent it, hoping for a response this time, but nothing came. At this point, Chess started to shake Damon awake.

"Hey, hey! We gotta go," Chess commanded, pulling his clothes on.

Damon shot up, but the tiredness in his eyes was still evident. Nevertheless, he started pulling his clothes back on himself as well.

"What's going on?"

"We have to go back to the apartments. No one's responding to the text messages," Chess said, clicking his jacket back onto his body.

"That is weird. Maybe they're all still asleep?" Damon wondered.

"No, I sent that text last night before we even went on the roof. They had more than enough time to get back to us, and they didn't. Something else is happening, and I don't like it."

Chess holstered his weapon, and Damon slung the rifle over his shoulder, tired but ready.

"I'm ready to go." Damon yawned.

Together, they both ran down the streets of the city until they made it back to the South side of the town. There was silence everywhere, almost an oppressive type of droning. On the ground at their feet in front of the apartment building, almost as a macabre waypoint to let them know where they were, the body of the Russian player was still lying. The blood had dried, and the tarp draped over the person out of respect. Chess grimaced at the sight of the pooled blood leaking from the top of the tarp. This man was dead; he was never going to see his family again, never get to Blood Run again, never get to smile again. It was all over for him. Chess felt for him, but he didn't want to end up the same way. He wanted to live, get out of the game and live.

"Come on, let's get inside," Damon said, pulling Chess's arm.

Chess hadn't realized it, but he was staring at the body left on the ground. It wasn't like they could move him; everyone was in shock. Now it feels too late as if this man is a statue on the street. Dead cold in the middle of winter. Being pulled by Damon, Chess snapped back into reality and where he was. Looking up into the sky, he realized it was snowing softly. The last precipitation they were likely to see before the

Storm took their lives. For now, however, they had to make it up to the apartment room.

They climbed the stairs one by one, taking a couple of minutes to reach the top where they had holed up. Chess checked his phone several times on the way up, making sure no one responded before he went up there and ripped them all new assholes for the radio silence. They could be out looking for Chris, but they were babysitting the rest of his teammates. When Damon stopped at the top of the stairwell and just stared, Chess bumped into him. When Damon didn't respond to the bump, Chess looked ahead to what Damon was looking at.

The door to the apartment building was wide open, and blood was spilling out of the threshold.

"No... oh hell no!"

Chess pocketed his phone quickly and ran into the apartment room, Damon close behind him. He almost slipped and fell on his ass from the blood splattered all over the walls and the floor, and when he saw his team members' brains and blood all over the room, he turned and threw up behind the couch.

"Someone did this to them. They didn't kill themselves, look," Damon said, pointing to a couple of people by the far wall.

Wiping his mouth, Chess looked up and noticed that Damon was right; they were all lined up facing the wall, almost as if they were instructed to do so. There weren't any random bullet holes in the walls or the floor. They were executed.

Before Chess and Damon could discover more horrific findings about what happened to the USA and Russian teams, a loud gunshot rang through the air, then another. Chess went to the window to see who it was, and sure enough, Chris was standing in the street, just having put two more bullets into the head of the already dead Russian player covered by a tarp. He looked up to the window, saw Chess, aimed, and fired.

CHAPTER FORTY-SIX

"We're cutting it close, but the generators should be up and running within the next twelve hours," the Foreman said, walking back into the Pilot House. He was surrounded by maintenance members that quickly ran to their stations, ready to do their jobs.

"Twelve hours *is* cutting it close; that's not enough time to get them out of there!" Farren exclaimed.

"It will be more than enough time to get them out of there if they all stay in the middle of the Storm," the Foreman said.

"Who's to say they all around running around right now, in different places on the map?" Bijou asked.

"Something tells me that they won't be doing anything like that. These are the finalists for the World Royale; I don't see them making impulsive decisions like that," Farren chimed in.

"Wait, what's that? Look."

A maintenance worker had spoken up from the back of the room, but he was pointing at the screens on the Pilot House monitors. Most of them were still offline, the media drones having fallen out of the sky days ago, but the stationary cameras around the city were still operational. On one of the smaller cam feeds, a figure could be seen. It was of a stockier person, wearing nothing more than a tracksuit as if they weren't freezing in the snow falling around them. They were just standing there, watching something or someone with their air extended. After a couple of moments, the sound of a gun firing came through the speakers. Bijou's blood ran cold.

"Oh my god, they're still playing the game," Bijou whispered.

"How can that be possible? They were all in an understanding that the Respawn Pods were down," Farren said, rounding a chair to get a better look at the screen.

"Some of them decided they didn't want to listen?" the foreman proposed, looking around at both Bijou and Farren.

"They were listening; someone is just going rogue," Bijou said, putting her hands to her mouth in shock. "What do we do?"

"There's nothing we can do. There's no one that can go in there and get them out, let alone get in. If They can't protect themselves from this one person..."

Farren couldn't finish her statement. She knew what this meant and what would happen if this gunman got his way with the rest of the players. It wasn't going to be good either way. The gunman was going to kill people, or the gunman himself was going to be killed; either way, someone was going to die.

"We have to do something! There's nothing we can control from here?" Bijou asked, looking around.

"We can control the speakers to the streets and the cameras, and that's about it. Other than that, the rest of the intervention is going to have to be done on the phone, through the app," a maintenance worker said from the back of the room.

"Better than nothing, but what do we even say?" Farren asked. "Anything we say could set this guy off even more than he already is. He seems isolated right now."

"Could be worth a shot to see what he might do. He might calm down; you never know," Bijou said, moving toward the console that controlled the speakers to the streets.

Before Bijou could press the button and make her announcement, Farren cut her off at the pass and covered the button with her hand, giving Bijou a look of concern.

"Why is my gut telling me that he's not going to calm down? That it's not going to get any better than it already is, and it's pretty bad right now."

"I don't know, but we have to try," Bijou said, putting her hand back on the microphone and waiting for Farren to move her hand from the button. "If we don't say anything, they're going to truly think we left them. We—"

The sounds of gunfire had come back over the console. In one of the cameras looking off toward the side of the main street, the visage of Chess and Damon could be seen hiding behind one of the buses that had been toppled over in a previous explosion. They had since come out of the building they were holed up in and taking fire. Now or never, either way, this was going to end badly.

"Farren, get on the phone with them somehow, text them that we're watching and trying to figure all this out. Get someone else on the line if you can!" Bijou called out, moving the microphone into position, getting ready to speak out of it.

With a press of the button, Bijou leaned into the microphone, letting the speakers on the other end whine to life as if they hadn't been activated in years. The gunman, Chris, stopped, and Chess and Damon couldn't be seen from behind the bus. Bijou hoped that they were okay as she began to speak.

"Please stop shooting! No one has to die! We're still working hard to get you all out!" Bijou yelled as loud as she could into the microphone.

Chris turned to a random point in the road where he thought a camera was and opened his arms out as if he was trying to challenge Bijou. His face was covered with a handkerchief, and he was wearing sunglasses in the dim light. The clouds of the Storm were starting to eat the sunlight around them.

"What's the point in stopping? There's nothing you can do!" Chris yelled out. "There's nothing you could possibly do anymore!"

Chris then turned on his heel away from where he thought the cameras were and aimed his weapon back at the bus where Chess and Damon were holed up at. He advanced further, walking closer to the bus hoping to cut them off at a choke point. He knew that if they fired, they would kill him, or he would kill them. Either way, someone was going to die tonight before the Storm consumed all of them. He already took care of the rest of the players. There wouldn't be anyone else to oppose him or anyone else. The games would end, and this would be the last of it. Whoever would fight in the World Royale, it wouldn't be them. This was a sign that they had to suffer the Storm. He would make sure that they did. That they were eaten by the clouds.

"There's nothing anyone can do anymore!" Chris shot several times toward the bus, trying to scare whoever was back there. "Nothing!"

Chris rounded the bus only to find no one was back there. He was sure that he saw Chess and Damon run behind it. When he looked up and down, his gun honed center mass in front of him; nothing was there. Then, all of a sudden, his vision went black. Something had thumped him on the back of the head, hard. What Chris couldn't see was the body of Chess standing right behind him, holding his pistol in a hard-gripped hand.

"Why'd you have to kill them, Chris?!" Chess hollered loud enough for everyone in the maintenance room to hear. Bijou stood back with her hands on her mouth.

"You killed them, and for what? For what?! What was the point in any of that?!" Chess continued to yell. 'They're gone, and they won't come back; why did you do that?!"

The Storm continued to swell around them. This was their final moment on the ground; the Storm would come for them in no time. The bodies of the people still in the apartment would be swept away, lost to time, and there was nothing they could do about it.

Chess just looked down at the body of Chris, who had killed all those people inside of the apartment; with no way to defend themselves as they had put their weapons away, it was all over. All of it was over; there was nothing else to do but to wait.

He wanted to kick him. Chess wanted to put pain onto Chris's body the same way he put pain onto the bodies of the Russian and American team members before him. It wasn't fair that they didn't get to see tomorrow and wouldn't be saved. There was only a finite amount of time left in the day, and it would all be over. Was this some sort of sick mercy? So they didn't have to feel their bodies ripped to shreds by the purple Storm coming for them? That a bullet was better than that? Chess didn't want to believe it. He couldn't.

"Chess! We're still working on getting you out! We're almost there!" Bijou's voice came over the intercom around the town again, and Chess and Damon looked around.

They couldn't hone in on any of the cameras hidden around the town, and the Media Drones were still offline. He just had to talk to the wind if he wanted to get his message across.

"They're dead! They're all dead inside! What do we do?! Will they come back if you get it fixed?!" Chess hollered out.

There was a long pause as Chess and Damon stood there waiting for an answer. He hoped it wasn't going to be a solemn one, one they didn't want to hear. Looking up to the clouds hovering above them, there were only hours left in their lives before it all came crumbling down. Waiting for an answer didn't seem like it was the most effective thing to be waiting on; their deaths were right at their doors. This was it; this was the end.

"We have twelve hours until we get things up and running! Can you hold out that long?!" Bijou's voice came over the intercom again.

"That's really close!" Damon hollered out, looking around at the Storm that was circling them.

"Yeah, tell me about it," Bijou murmured, not over the intercom.

"We have about that much time left anyways; if you don't get it up and running in that time, that's it. We can try and hold out here, but the rest of the team members are dead. Chris killed them," Chess said solemnly.

"We're hoping that the Respawn pods will be able to pick them up before the storm does. Here's hoping. We're working on it!"

With that, Bijou's voice went away, and Chess and Damon were left standing in the middle of the city with nothing more than themselves and the Storm to accompany them. Chris was still there, but Chess decided to tie his hands and ankles with a rope that was lying around so that he couldn't run away and try to hurt anyone else. It was a miracle that they could get him incapacitated the way they did in the first place. Now, all there was left to do for them was to wait. Wait for oblivion. Wait for the end.

HOURS PASSED BY, AND EVENTUALLY, CHRIS WOKE BACK UP. He shook his head and looked left and right, finally noticing that his hands were tied behind his back and his legs were strapped. He wasn't able to move from his spot. He wiggled a couple of inches and grunted but stopped when Chess came around and kneeled in front of him. They just stared into each other's eyes for a moment, Chess's face one of complete thunder. Enough to rival the Storm that was roaring behind them.

They could now hear the storm, the howling of wind, and electricity crackling through the clouds. It wouldn't be long now, a little less than an hour until the clouds ate them up. As Chess looked into Chris's eyes, Chris quickly looked at Damon, who was looking up at the sky. The eye of the Storm was above them, and it was in its final hours. This was the end for all of them.

"Why'd you do it?" Chess demanded.

Chris looked back at Chess and then down to Chess's hands. He was holding a knife, a long one. Somehow, he didn't think it was to cut him free of his bonds anytime soon. For what he did, he was sure that Chess would kill him.

"Better than the Storm eating them. Better than what's waiting for them outside of this hellhole of a game." Chris spat.

Chess, losing his temper, reared back and smacked Chris across the face with the back of his hand. Chris spat out some spit and shook his head, groaning in pain as he tried to hold himself up and look Chess dead on in the eyes, his thunderous visage rivaling the other Blood Runner. They were both sure of themselves. Chess wanted them to live, but Chris liberated them from pain. It wasn't his token to take; it wasn't his burden to bear. Chris had to have known that, but somehow, he just didn't care.

"You think what you did was the right thing? Not letting them get a fighting chance? You're going to be arrested if we get out of here for what you've done!" Chess hollered.

"We're never. Getting. Out!" Chris hollered back, punctuating every word as a sentence. "Don't you get it?! We're never getting out of here!"

"You don't know that! They're working on it!" Chess said.

This earned a throwback of Chris's head, followed by him laughing his ass off. A huge belly laugh stopped Chess and Damon in their tracks, looking at him as if he were more insane than he was already showing. After a couple of moments, he finally allowed himself to calm down and look to the side, not really looking at anything other than rocks on the ground.

"Blood Running. Royales. All of it. What's the point? All to win some money? Killing each other just to come out the other side like nothing happened? Is that what it all is to you? Just nothing?" Chris lamented. "Life is nothing more than to get shot at and die, just to do it all over again the next day? You all just want to die! This is what you wanted!"

Chess and Damon just looked on at Chris with pity. No, this is not what they wanted, far from it. The hours were ticking down, the twelfth hour upon them, and now they were being told that this was what they had wanted all along. The final liberation of death in a sport of blood. The clouds swirled around them, and as Chris picked up his laughter again, the sounds of buildings being broken down echoed in the background. The roots of trees being uprooted and thrown into the air following the buildings came after.

Chris was going to get what he wanted, death for everyone. Liberation from the game. This is not want they wanted, but now they had no other choice. It was either take the bullet or take the Storm. As Chess got up from his crouching position and walked over to Damon, he took his hand and looked him in the eye. The Storm was starting to close. It was the end of the road, and this was their final moment together. Either they came out the other end, or they died.

"At least I got to see the real you again," Damon said, smiling.

Chess grinned and looked to the ground. He then looked up and around at the Storm closing in around them. He was trying to stamp out the hollering and laughter of Chris behind them. Soon it would all stop. All of it would stop.

"Never thought I would even see you again, to be honest," Chess said.

"Was it everything you hoped for?" Damon joked, his hair whipping in the wind.

"No." Chess laughed. He tried to brush off the fact that a stop sign flew past him and into the Storm. "It was better. It was honestly better than I hoped for."

"I love you."

Damon said it under his breath, but Chess heard every word. If people were watching, he didn't care anymore. If there were even any cameras left showing them in the middle of the town, he didn't care if they were on them. He leaned in and claimed Damon's mouth in his, giving him a soft kiss on the lips.

Chris's laughter slowly died out. The roar of the wind was upon them. They didn't separate from each other, and the Storm finally closed around them, engulfing their bodies in darkness.

CHAPTER
FORTY-SEVEN

There was a bright white light.

Chess felt his body floating above the clouds that had engulfed him. As if he was being carried up toward the heavens only to be brought back down again. He had been caught in the Storm plenty of times. Every time he fought his way out or perished within the clouds themselves, he instantly found his way back to the Respawn Pods. This time was different. This time, he was flying.

Almost like he was having an out-of-body experience, he felt his mind go up into the clouds, flying around as if he were nothing more than a fleeting thought in the wind. He couldn't feel his body, but he could feel his eyes. He could feel his face, he could see, but he couldn't feel his body. He was nothing and everything all at once. No one loses, and no one could ever win.

He didn't see anyone else around him. It was only him and the clouds as he went up and up into the sky. He didn't know how high the Storm was going to take him, but he just laid back in the air and let it pull him along. There wasn't much else he could do anyways. It wasn't like he could run from the Storm, swim, or fly out of it, and he couldn't control it. It was an anomaly that the human race was still trying to figure out, and he was stuck in the middle.

This reminded him of people that came back from near-death experiences. People who have seen God or the kingdom of Heaven or perhaps Hell and the Devil himself and lived to tell the tale. Others talked about the void they saw, the empty nothing of space they were stuck in as if it were their personal purgatory. There was everything and nothing all at once, and they were stuck there until their heart started beating again.

All these people had come back to tell other people what they saw. The adventures their minds went on before the oxygen was snuffed out. They all came back. He wasn't going to be able to come back from this and tell his tale. Talk about how he flew above clouds and saw outside his own eyes. The electric tendrils of lightning coursed through his body as he climbed up and up into the sky. How painful it was, but he did not yell out. This felt like his own personal Hell, but as he flew above the Storm and saw the vast circumference of the Earth as he was lifted out into space, it felt like Heaven.

He couldn't breathe. Was Damon feeling the same way? Was he somewhere in the sky next to him, listing along the clouds, suffocating without oxygen like he was? He couldn't breathe, but he wasn't calling out in pain. He wasn't choking on his own spit. He was just watching. Almost waiting to see what was going to happen next.

Then he dropped. Almost like a stone in water, he dropped and plummeted to the Earth. He could see from his own eyes again; his full body could be felt whipping around in his loose clothes as he tumbled in the air without any parachute or protective gear, and he finally started to scream. He hollered as loud as he could, the sound of his screams being eaten by the clouds surrounding him as he fell back into the Temporal Storm. This was the end for him. He wouldn't be able to tell his story to anyone. He was going to join his father in death; this was it.

Chess closed his eyes and let the wind whip across his face, flutter into his clothes and through his skin. From the back of his eyes, he could see a white light, the feeling of falling turned back to floating; then, nothing. Like a retro TV blinking out of power, the bring light came and went, and then there was nothing. It was quiet. No sounds of roaring winds and rumbling of thunder. If anything, there were the sounds of beeping and compressed air whirring from a pipe. Something more industrial other than an otherworldly meteorological event.

Chess opened his eyes. He was surrounded by white. A glossy white surrounded by frosted glass, and the air was cold. Chess blinked a couple of times and inhaled a slow breath of compressed, sterile air. He could see the breath coming out of his mouth. It was cold. He was freezing. Was he dead?

He could feel his feet set flat on the ground, the idle push of air on his skin from a pump on the side of the vestibule he was stuck in. This wasn't death; it was a Respawn Pod. He was sitting inside of a Respawn Pod. Chess looked up and saw the checkerboard ceiling the Pilot House was known for. He huffed a bit of a laugh and spread his mouth into a full-blown smile. He had made it; he was alive. He made it out of the Tundra.

Scrambling to his feet, his legs felt wobbly. Perhaps a side effect of falling through the air and inhaling Storm clouds like he did before he was zapped back to the outside of the Storm. He had to find Damon and Bijou and make sure that they were okay. He pressed his hands to the glass of the pod and looked around, waiting for the doors to open to let him out. They weren't opening. Pushing, he tried to force the doors open so that he could go and look for his friends, but it wasn't budging.

"Hey! Hello?!" Chess called out, his throat sounding a little blown out. "Anyone out there?!"

He looked over to the other Respawn Pods next to him and couldn't see anyone inside them. Perhaps Damon was in one of them, but he hadn't woken up yet; he hadn't realized he had been saved. Chess stood and waited for a couple moments, hoping that Damon would pop his head over the frosted glass and look at him, but it never happened. When Chess turned his head back forward to call out again, Levi Jones was aiming a gun at him.

"You just couldn't stay out of it. You just had to be the best, didn't you?" Levi snarled.

Chess looked around and backed away from the doors, not really knowing what to do. He could crouch, but the bullet would find him either way; he was trapped.

"Levi! Calm down; we can talk about this!" Chess hollered out.

"What's there to talk about?! How your fathers humiliated me?! Left me for dry while they went and had their own rivalry while I wasted away in the background?! I was nothing to them, and now their sons are finishing what *they* started!"

Levi bent down and pulled something up, muttering to himself and the person the whole time.

"Get up, get UP."

Damon was now standing in front of the pod, his hands bound in front of him with zip ties. He had a nasty red mark on the side of his face, the signs of a pistol whip to get him to comply. Wherever they were, they were far away from where Bijou and Farren thought they were. A different area of the Pilot House or even in another building entirely. Chess didn't know where they were and was trapped in the Pod, weaponless. He could only watch and listen.

"We have nothing to do with what our fathers did to you," Damon grunted, his eyes fixed on Chess.

The click of the hammer cocking back and aiming at Damon's head filled the room. Chess bit his lip and looked around for anything he could get his hands on, and Damon tried not to flinch. Chess looked back to Damon, and their eyes met, not knowing what to do.

"Why are you doing this?" Chess called out.

"It's fair. It's only fair that I end the bloodline here and end this whole tirade. Then you both had to go and *make up* like you did out there. What you think we weren't watching?!"

Damon and Chess sported a harsh blush but didn't look away from each other. Damon adjusted on his feet, and he could feel the barrel of the gun following his head. How Levi got his hands on a gun outside of Royale Space was beyond the both of them. Guns and weapons had been heavily regulated after the Temporal Spaces arrived, so getting a gun was almost virtually impossible. It was possible to get your hands on one, but it was next to impossible to keep a hold on it. Crackdowns were tough, and it wasn't easy to keep your hands on a gun no matter where you were in the world.

"It ends with you both. It ends tonight," Levi said.

"And what about you? You're not going to get away with murder.

All those people that died in the city, that's all on you," Damon said, stopping when the barrel pressed harder into the back of his head.

"Shut up!"

Levi put his hand on Damon's shoulder and moved him over and away from Chess's pod, telling him to walk. He pulled out a chair and forced him to sit, aiming the gun at his face the whole time. Damon was doing a good job not showing any fear on his face, his eyes forward or looking toward Chess. Chess, on the other hand, the second that Levi turned his back on him, attempted to force the doors open on the Respawn Pod as hard as he could before his attention was back on him. With a fist to the glass, he stood, heaving air into his lungs as he was forced to watch Levi point a gun at his lover. He had to find a way out of there and fast. What he would do when he got out, he didn't know, but he had to get out first.

"Don't do anything stupid, or you're a dead man," Levi said to Damon.

Damon just gave him a dirty look and then looked back to Chess. Levi walked back to the Respawn Pod with another zip tie in his hand, the gun in the other. Chess watched him press a couple of buttons on the Respawn Pod and glance up at him every so often. He was about to open it only to bind his hands; he just knew it.

"You try anything. You're getting shot along with your boyfriend. So don't try me. Come out with your hands up," Levi said, raising the gun.

Slowly, the Respawn Pod opened up, and Chess could smell the sweat in the air now that the compressed, recycled air was gone from his senses. It smelled like gunpowder and sweat mixed with hurried breaths. The scent of exhilaration. Chess slowly put his hands together and presented them, a scowl on his face the entire time. Levi put the gun down for just a few seconds, but that was all he needed to place the zip ties on his wrist and pull him out by the arm. The gun was back on him as he was led toward Damon and sat on a chair next to him. On the one hand, he was happy to be back next to him; on the other, he was pretty sure they were about to die like dogs in some backstage Respawn Pod room, where no one was going to find their bodies for a long, long time. Chess gave Damon a look before sitting down and looking forward, not at Levi but toward him. Almost through him. He didn't want to give him the time of day.

"So our fathers were your friend at some point. Shit went down, and now you want revenge." Damon started. "What does that have to do with us?"

"You both live in the lap of luxury," Levi started.

Chess snorted and huffed a laugh but stopped when the gun was trained on him. He rolled his eyes and looked away.

"You both reap to rewards of what those fuck faces did to me. Winning Royale after Royale until they became filthy rich beyond their wildest dreams. And where was I? Left at the bottom. Couldn't keep up, so I was left behind. It's not fair. I'm going to make it fair," Levi swore.

"And by killing us and then hopefully yourself, you're going to even the score of being left behind to make your own wealth? What, were you just bad at Blood Running?" Chess goaded.

"Shut. Up. Stop talking. None of you little shit stains knew what it was like to be around them. Having to listen to them bicker day and night, fight over every little thing. Have me part of their group until I was no longer of use. It was humiliating. Then they go off and have kids, and the cycle continued. You bickered and fought, and I was sure you would take each other out, but no."

"Sorry to disappoint you," Damon said sarcastically.

"No disappointment. Not anymore," Levi said.

He thumbed back the hammer on the gun and trained it on Damon. Chess's breathing was increasing, and he didn't know what he was going to do, but he couldn't let Damon get shot. He watched as Levi's hand shook, this finger moving to the trigger, and then Chess acted. He launched from his chair and slammed into Levi's chest, knocking him over. The gun went off, but the bullet hit the wall behind Damon, who dodged it with a holler.

Chess wasted no time trying to get the gun away from Levi's hands, stomping on his wrist and kicking his arm with as much force as possible until Levi eventually let go. Chess kicked the weapon all the way to the other side of the room, and Damon launched from his chair toward it. Levi swept his leg under Chess, knocking him down, and

Chess didn't have enough time to get up and save face. Levi was already on his feet, rushing toward the gun that Damon was trying to capture.

However, he was too late, and Damon picked up the weapon, aiming it at Levi, who stopped, huffing air into his lungs. His wrists were still tied together, but his hands were steady, if not shaking just a little. This wasn't like Royale, he was going to kill a man for good if he pulled the trigger, but it was in self-defense. Still, he would be ending a life. He didn't want to do that if he could help it, but Levi wasn't leaving him with any other choices.

"Shoot, you're only going to kill a man," Levi quoted. "Not like the game, you put me down; that blood is on your hands forever."

It was quiet, Chess standing by right behind Lei, ready to pounce on him but not moving because Damon had the gun. Everyone was stopped, but Levi took a test step forward. Damon took a step back and aimed the gun harder toward him.

"Stop, last warning!" Damon hollered.

"What are you going to do? Become a killer for real? Like your dad? Go ahead, continue the legacy, kid. It's in your blood," Levi snarled.

Chess looked from the back of Levi's head to Damon's eyes. He knew what Levi was talking about. The death of his own father. None of that was Damon's fault. None of it was, but the pain still remained. The facts still readied of what happened. It was within the family, but it wasn't in his blood.

Damon looked to Chess for a split second; that was all Levi needed. A second of distraction and he pounced. Before Chess could catch up and pull him off, both Levi and Damon were wrestling for the gun, Damon's grip iron tight on the handle while Levi had a grip on the barrel. This was a dangerous game of tug and pull, and there was only going to be one winner. The pit in the bottom of Damon's stomach grew as he reared back, shoved his finger in the trigger chamber, and squeezed. The sound of a bullet ringing out stopped everyone, and Levi stopped in his tracks.

He took a few steps backward, his hands no longer on the gun but on his gut. As he turned away from Damon and toward Chess, blood spilling out from the wound in his abdomen, the doors to the end of the room flew open, and a flurry of people ran inside. More than likely following the sound of the gunshots. Bijou, Farren, and the rest of the Maintenance Crew stumbled in to find Levi falling to his knees, clutching his gut and breathing a couple of words, a string of nonsense, before falling to the ground.

Farren quickly ran to his side and put two fingers on his neck, waiting. After thirty seconds, she looked up at Damon, still holding the gun, his eyes buzzing and breathing wrecked.

"He's dead," Farren whispered. "He's dead."

CHAPTER FORTY-EIGHT

It was going to be a long process of trials and court dates to determine that what happened was self-defense, but before any of that could be ruled, there was one last game to be played. The Final Royale at Point Nemo.

The people that died in the Serbian Royale had eulogies, ceremonies, and funerals. It was a long, long month of burials and tears that neither Chess, Damon, nor Bijou was ready for. Bijou was finally free from Levi's clutches, and while she was disqualified from the Final Royale, she was allowed to stay on to watch Chess and Damon compete in the final game. After what had happened in Russia, the security detail for the Respawn Pods was ramped up to an eleven, and no one was going to mess with the Temporal Storms. There wouldn't be any more deaths on the committee's watch. It was already a media nightmare with what happened to the rest of the team members.

With more funerals, court dates, and media hovering over them, it was hard for Chess and Damon to get into the right headspace to play the final game. Point Nemo was once a point in the ocean that was the farthest away you could be from land in any direction. There was nowhere to go, no one to save you, and it had been hit by one of the quickest Temporal Storms seen on Earth. A whopping three hours, and that was it. You either killed or were killed by the Storm. After what Damon and Chess went through in Serbia, they were sure they could be up for anything. After braving the Storm itself, there wasn't much else that could phase them.

However, it was only them. The rest of the USA team was dead, and Chris, the murderer, was arrested and held in prison for what he did. The whole world saw his reaction and reasoning for doing what he did. There was no way out for him. So it was now Damon and Chess and the World Royale. A couple of players from other countries were going to join in, but all in all, the final count was only 25 players. It was going to be a close game, and this was a free-for-all battle. It didn't matter how much he and Damon made up in the end; they would be hunting each other like dogs when they landed at Point Nemo.

It was a barren wasteland of ocean water. The only thing in the middle was a massive cruise ship repurposed as the battleground for the World Royale. Even from the TVs Chess was watching the listing ship on, it was covered port to starboard with media drones. You couldn't even blink without them catching it; every move they made was going to be documented. The whole world would be watching. Winner takes all.

"I wasn't supposed to be here, you know," Chess said.

Damon looked up from his hands to Chess and cocked an eyebrow. "How so?"

"I was going to quit the World Royale after I got you one time. Just once," Chess said, holding up one finger.

"Instead of killing you, you just had sex with me. I don't know if that counts," Damon said with a smile.

Chess also tried to smile but looked away from Damon, worrying his fingers over one another. It was clear as day that he was nervous about what was about to happen next. The final fight and he might not even make it the first couple of moments. They would all be landing on the ship all at once; no matter how big it was, they were all in close proximity to one another. It could end as quickly as it began, he didn't know.

With that in mind, he thought of everything that had happened since he had gotten there. Swore revenge, failed revenge, got back with Damon, killed a man, saved Bijou, and the list went on. Now he was going to make good on the revenge he didn't want anymore. He was going to kill Damon Kennedy.

"You still have a chance," Damon said, sitting back in his seat, rubbing his sweaty palms on his tracksuit pants. "Still a chance to strike me down for good."

"Not sure if I can anymore," Chess said, not able to meet Damon's gaze.

"If you don't even try, I'm dumping you. For good."

Chess didn't look at Damon, but he could feel the scowl. This wasn't joking, jovial Damon. This was serious, scary Damon. The kind of Damon that Chess didn't like to see. He was serious about hunting him down and finishing the job, and he didn't want to look at the look on his face. More so, he didn't want to face the reality of reaping what he had sown. He wanted it so badly, to kill him on the battlefield so badly that he all but spoke it into existence. Revenge is a dish best served cold, but this was overkill. He didn't want to shoot down the man he loved anymore, but now he didn't have any choice.

"Okay... Okay. Last battle," Chess said, finally looking over to Damon.

"Last battle."

They linked hands, and in the quiet of the locker room, with no one else to walk in on them or bother them, they leaned forward and brushed their lips together, ending with a click of a kiss. Chess closed his eyes and leaned in, wanting more and Damon obliged, their kiss blossoming into something deeper. When they separated, Chess looked into Damon's eyes with hard eyes of his own.

"I mean it. After this battle, I'm down with Blood Running," Chess said.

"Win or lose?" Damon asked.

"Win or lose," Chess answered.

They still had their hands intertwined, but Chess could feel Damon squeezing a little bit in response to Chess's ultimatum. It was hell or high water now for them.

THE PLAN WAS ONE OF THOSE SMALL BIPLANES USED FOR hobby skydiving. There were only 25 of them, and the load wasn't that heavy. People from all over the world were stationed on the aircraft, and once it took off, there was no going back.

Chess sat across from Damon, goggles on his face and a parachute on his back. This was it, his final Blood Run. Win or lose, succeed or fail, this was his final Run. He looked into Damon's eyes and found that Damon was looking right into his as well. He was going to give it his all; Damon was. He loved Damon, and he was sure that Damon loved him too, after all of this time, after everything that had happened. Even so, that wouldn't stop Damon from playing the game. There was a trophy to win, and Damon wasn't going to let their relationship get in the way.

Chess knew him all too well. How he handled himself on the battlefield. As if nothing else mattered to him, all relationships, friendships, and enemies were out the door. There was just you, him, and the game. If you got in his way, he would cut you down; that was just how Damon worked. Chess steeled himself and hardened his eyes. Now wasn't the time to get sentimental. He knew that Damon was well past the point of preparing for the fight.

He went back to what he was used to. Breathing in and out in a rhythmic pattern. Calming his mind and getting into the right headspace for the fight ahead. There was no Damon; there was no attachment. For the next three hours, it was only his boots on the ground and the gun in his hand. He would stamp out all other obstacles. There was only the game.

Looking out the window beyond Damon, Chess could see the Media Drones flying alongside the plane. The show had already begun, and it wouldn't be long until they would be dropping onto the ship. It was going to be a close shave of a drop, but it would be manageable. The problem was getting to cover right after landing and finding a weapon. It was going to be a chaotic game.

"Welcome to the World Royale Finale here at Point Nemo! The rules are simple. A Free-For-All match here in the middle of nowhere! Everyone back home will be watching to see who will be crowned the World's Best Blood Runner! Are you ready?!"

The intercom sounded cheap, but the pilot was in high spirits. No doubt, a media team and voice-over panelists were letting everyone watching back home know that the match was about to begin. The stats and profiles of every player left on the field and the loss of life that occurred in Siberia. The game was going to be tight, with no room for error.

Chess tried not to think about the people at home, hoping for his demise. The thought of having fans was even more asinine. Not even he would root for himself; he wasn't even supposed to be here. Looking back to Damon, he tried to think of the people hoping for him to win. A part of him wanted him to win as well, but he couldn't let him. If Damon wanted a fight, he would give him one hell of a fight. One for the ages.

Turbulence rocked the ship, and Chess looked behind him outside of his window. It had been a while since he was this high up. Ever since flying through space from the Storm, he never thought he would find himself back in the clouds again. For this one final time, he would do it for Damon. Do it for himself. From the waves, he could see the image of the ship below. It was massive, something along the lines of a cruise liner and an aircraft carrier. There would be plenty of places to hide and plenty of places to fight as well. It was going to be a bloodbath, but this time, he would be able to come back from it.

People were tightening the straps on their parachutes, getting ready to jump from the plane. It would be a long drop, and even though the ship was huge, there were only a few places to land. If Chess were smart, he would try to land on top of a gun and book it for cover the second he got a chance. His luck was good but not that good. He was going to have to try his best, but even if his best weren't good enough, he would have to play to the best of his ability.

It wasn't just Damon; the rest of the people on the plane were some of the best on the planet in Blood Running, and Chess knew that. His chances at survival were slim, but he had to remember he wasn't some pushover either. He fought to get to this position, too; he was one of the best of the best as well. Taking a deep breath and sitting back in his seat, he remembered that and smirked. Damon caught it and matched it with a smirk of his own.

Did he know that Chess was going to go all out like he promised he would, wipe the floor with everybody and come out on top as the victor? Or was it going to be the other way around? The score had not yet been settled. They may be lovers again, but there was a clear score to settle at the end of all of this. Like Damon had said many games ago, he wasn't going to make it easy for him.

A long buzzer snapped everyone out of their stupors everyone got into position. The back hatch of the plane opened, and one by one, the contestants started dropping out of the plane into the open air. The Storm was already forming and closing in, and they didn't have much time to land and get right before the bullets started flying.

Chess and Damon swapped a look and then bolted from their chairs. Following tradition, Chess hit a slow and long backflip off the tarmac and into the air before plummeting down toward the ship. He and Damon were falling close to one another, but after a few seconds and a sure-fire look from both of them, they broke off into the sky, aiming to land on different parts of the ship. They would meet up eventually at the showdown.

CHAPTER FORTY-NINE

The ship was dead in Chess's sights. The wind whipped past his cheeks, the safety goggles protecting his tear ducts from the salty sea air. He would do his normal procedure and get as close as he could to the ship before popping his parachute, having the best chance of landing first. Not to say that someone else had the same idea, and he knew that Damon was going to do the same thing as him. He didn't have the luxury of waiting to see what the other contestants and Damon would do. He just had to act.

The ship was coming up. He could smell the salt coming off the waves; it was overpowering. A far cry from the snow and ice that he had just come out of. The fire and wood swapped for surf and splendor. This was a far cry away from hiding in a shack or torn down, weathered old train station. There was going to be glitz and glamour on this ship. Chess would never know how it was maintained, but as he plummeted toward the deck, he didn't care. He just had to play this game, and he had to win.

He pulled the pin on the parachute just shy of the deck and lowered. He saw a gun out in the open tie for the taking, but a glance up garnered him the view of someone else falling right on top of him. He wasn't going to be able to land on this gun and fight his way out of this without a scrape himself, but he had to try.

He landed, rolled once, and didn't even take the parachute off before grabbing the carbine off the deck. Whipping around and aiming, the parachute flew into the air, catching a draft as Chess aimed and fired twice. The bullets ripped through the man's body center mass and in the neck, and he fell to the deck in a pool of blood before dissipating into a flurry of purple crystals. He had never been so happy to see someone die in his life, to see the Temporal Crystals float into the air like that and leave behind their residue. He could continue the game with ease. One down, twenty-three more to go.

Unclipping the parachute from his body, Chess held his new rifle and turned, making his way into the main foyer of the ship. It was massive, with a double staircase and a hanging chandelier made of crystal and diamonds swaying with the ship. On top of that, it was quiet, with the faraway sounds of gunshots breaking through the walls. This was close combat, and he couldn't stay in the same area for long unless he wanted to get gunned down soon as well.

Before he moved on, he unzipped the track jacket from his body and dropped it to the floor, only wearing his track pants and a tank top. He didn't want anything to hinder his movement in a tight space like this; anything that could slow him down had to go. On top of that, the gun he had was a bit cumbersome, and if he found a handgun, he would be quick to swap it out for one. The rifle had massive stopping power, it was true, but for maneuverability, he would need a handgun.

Chess took the left staircase and climbed. Taking the stairs two at a time, he swayed the rifle from side to side as he struggled to keep up his pace. He needed a handgun; this was slowing him down. He was faced with a long, long hallway filled with shops and delicacies. Toys and clothes were displayed in a wide atrium that could hide several guns and people. While it was quiet on the floor he was on, he couldn't take any chances. People were landed on the decks and could be anywhere on the ship by now, and he had three hours to snuff them all out.

Walking into a souvenir shop, Chess turned the turnstiles over and looked behind counters. Where the register was, under it in a cubby, a Beretta was sitting next to some 9-millimeter ammo. Chess wasted no time ditching the rifle under the counter and taking the handgun, testing the weight in his hands and holstering it on his hip. That was one problem squared away. Next, he had to force himself to go toward the source of the gunshots he heard in the background. It could've been poolside or somewhere near the back of the ship. Perhaps where the shows took place, the theater. He would try there first.

Not taking the time to search the other shops around him, Chess bolted from the hallway toward the theater venues. It was a long run, but he was certain he would run into someone when he got there. Past the kitchen and into an access hallway for workers and toward the back parts of the ship, Chess quickly made his way to the entertainment area. When he finally saw the massive stage with a grand piano on top of it surrounded by a massive velvet curtain, he looked around for any signs of life.

It was quiet as it could possibly be. The sounds of gunfire even stopped. Chess pulled his phone out to check the count and was surprised that only 19 people were left in the game. However, he didn't have time to dwell on the number as the tell-tale sounds of a Media Drone buzzing nearby pulled him from his thoughts. He looked up at it, and its camera lens was focused on him, hovering a couple of feet away from his head. He was on display, more than likely being broadcasted to millions of homes around the world of him picking around on his phone and not shooting anyone. That was all about to change. If he just camped this spot, someone was bound to come around.

Pulling the Beretta from his holster and holding it defensively, he made his way down the carpeted walkway between the chairs and tables, his footfalls and the buzzing of the Media Drone filling the air. The cameras were following him, which could only mean one of two things. Either people were waiting for him to die, or someone was coming. Media Drones always followed packs of two people at a time, never missing the action. Chess had a feeling that the action was going to be falling into his lap soon enough.

He stopped. Because he heard a noise above him. It wasn't like the shuffling and whirring of the Drone; it was footfalls. Heavy ones. Chess whipped around and aimed his gun up to the sky but backed away when he saw a mass of purple crystals falling toward him. Someone was shot out of the sky and landed on the carpet next to him, hitting the Drone on the way down, making it spin comically before it righted itself.

Chess couldn't stop to loot the body; the killer—the winner—was still up top and was more than likely going to be looking over the edge soon enough. He was going to see Chess, and the battle would ensue. Chess managed to pick up a couple of crystals and pop them in his hands, sucking up the mana, and then backed away from the refuse. Eighteen people left.

Chess saw the shadows of someone running past the balcony up top, but they never looked over to spot him. Chess aimed his weapon but didn't fire, knowing that if he could get away with being undetected for as long as he could, it would give him a fighting chance. All he could gather from the assailant was dark hair and a large rifle, the same kind that Chess ditched. Could this person have been right behind him the entire time? Couldn't have been; there had to have been other rifles on the ship.

The first hour had already passed, and the death count had risen. Fifteen people left and no hide or hair of Damon. Chess wasn't stupid enough to think that Damon was part of the death count. He was out there somewhere, killing people and making a name for himself.

Running in front of a massive flat-screen monitor, the game was shown on the LCD screen. Chess stopped for a moment to watch, if not just to know the locations of some of the people on the ship. There were people from all over the world competing, and they were all over the ship. In the kitchens, on the bridge of the ship, there was a shootout happening in the bedrooms and lodgings—and there would only be one winner. He was somewhere on the east side of the ship, near lifeboats and a minibar. He was close to the pools and surfing attractions.

Checking his phone one more time, the counter was at ten. Ten people left. He had to hurry if he wanted to win. He already had a kill under his belt, and he had to get at least one more if he wanted to settle his score with Damon. It was like a hunger now almost. Damon knew what he was put on this ship to do, not to be here for the World Royale. Chess couldn't give a shit about that right now. He was hunting Damon. No matter how it ended, it was Damon he was after. As if he could taste him in the air.

Taking the stairs, Chess rose to the top of the ship. The ship was listing in the water, and the wind had picked up. He could taste the salt on his lips and smell the overpowering stench of the ocean in his nostrils. Sea salt crusted the waterline of his eyes, and he squinted in the sunlight. It was hard to see, and he was just standing out in the middle of nowhere, letting anyone get a sneak attack on him. The Media Drone whizzed up to meet with him and hovered nearby, snapping Chess out of his thoughts. Crouching down, he crouch-walked toward another bar and looked around for any signs of life. Anyone could be anywhere, and his best bet wasn't to look for the people but the Drones. Drones were going to be following people everywhere, and even though there was an abundance of them in the sky, some were still hovering nearby. There were people around. The problem was getting close enough to land a shot.

Soon enough, he got his wish. The whizzing of another Media Drone came out over a far-off bar, and the top of someone's head could be seen running off to the east part of the ship. More than likely hoping to get underside and down to the shops to wait it all out. Camping until the Storm hit wasn't wise; they were all going to die at the same time, and it was going to be the one with the largest body count to take the gold. Again, Chess really didn't care, but this person could've been Damon, so he followed.

Coming back the way he came, Chess followed closely behind but not too close that the assailant could hear his footsteps as they went back down toward the theater and through the bar. The restaurant was a barren wasteland with the napkins and silverware still perfectly pristine on the table tops. Blood Runners haven't fought in her yet, but that was soon about the change. The long hair, albeit dark, was reminiscent of Damon, but it was a girl running away. In her hands was a shotgun that would've done better damage at point-blank range. Chess stopped and aimed, his shoes squeaking on the marble floor. The girl heard it.

As she turned around, bringing her weapon up to aim as she did, Chess shot first and slammed a bullet square into her shoulder. She stammered back, dropping a hand from her shotgun before righting herself and getting a shot off quickly, to which Chess dove out of the way. The perfectly placed napkins and dishes flew as buckshot after buckshot went flying over the tables. She was wounded, but she wasn't out of the game yet.

When the shots stopped long enough to let Chess know that she was reloading, he popped out over the table he was hiding behind and aimed down the sights. He fired twice, missing both times, but she stopped nonetheless. She was across the room, and Chess couldn't see what had happened too well, but the glint of red through her torso was a dead giveaway. She had been stabbed from behind.

The knife was pulled away, and as the girl withered away into crystal, all that was left was Damon. Standing there covered in blood and holding a machete. On his shoulder was the rifle he had seen earlier. It was him from before; now he was here.

"Damon..." Chess whispered.

Chess quickly dropped the half-spent clip and chambered in a new one, reloading as fast as he could, but before he could aim down the sights, Damon bolted out of the door he had come in from. Chess wasted no time giving chase, knowing this would be the end-all-be-all fight for them. This chase was going to end with one of them dead by the other's hand.

CHAPTER FIFTY

There were six people left. Chess didn't have to check his phone to know; the massive TV in the foyer was showing the number proud and clear for all to see. Chess didn't know where they were, and he didn't care. He was hot on the heels in pursuit of his lover, his rival. Damon Kennedy was right ahead of him, yet he didn't turn around and shoot back. Almost as if he was leading him toward somewhere to fight rather than just duking it out right here and now.

Chess wasn't going to question it. He knew that Damon was leading him somewhere, so for that fact, he didn't shoot either. He just followed closely and quickly. He didn't let the man out of his sight. They traveled up staircases and down long hallways until they were back on top of the deck toward the bow of the cruise liner. It was a ghost town. No one was around, and then Damon finally stopped.

Chess also stopped, heaving air into his lungs as he didn't slow down at all, giving his chase of Damon. His hands were shaky, gripping the Beretta with both hands as he slowly rose it to aim at him. And yet, he didn't fire. He just stood there and waited for Damon to say something, anything. He knew it was coming, so he didn't shoot. He wanted to hear it. His last words as a Blood Runner before either one was gunned down.

Damon turned around, breathing just as hard, and dropped the machete. Chess didn't watch it clang away across the deck. His eyes were trained hard on Damon. His hands were starting to stop shaking, and eventually, his breathing was evening out. Damon was becoming the same way, pulling the rifle from his back and slanging it onto his hip. They were aiming at one another but wouldn't shoot. Not yet.

"Do you remember the second month of Academy when I finally walked up to you and asked for a pen?" Damon called out.

Chess took one step forward. Damon matched it, taking a step himself.

"How could I forget?" Chess called back.

"That look in your eye was the first time I thought I saw heaven," Damon said, taking another step forward.

"If I was so precious to you..." Chess started.

"Don't," Damon warned.

"I just want to know." Chess took another step forward. "I just always wanted to know why. Your father..."

Damon flinched and made the mistake of looking up at a Media Drone. Chess knew he shouldn't have said anything, but he had to hear it from Damon's lips. He had to hear the reality from the man that did all of that to him. There shouldn't be any secrets and lies, uncertainty, or animosity between them anymore. He just wanted to know why.

"I know he expects a lot from you, but why me? Why use me like you did?"

"Because it was easy. Because you put yourself in my way," Damon admitted, pain in his voice. "I don't ever want to do something like that again, but... Chess, you were in my way."

They both stopped walking. They were mere feet in front of each other now, still aiming down the sights. The shakes had come back, and it was the end, the waiting of who was going to pull first. There was still so much more they wanted to say to one another. It wasn't like they weren't going to see each other outside of this battle, but as Blood Runners, there was so much more to say.

"Getting that license was the worst thing to happen to me," Chess said, half laughing.

"How so?" Damon asked.

"Because I met you."

Damon winced, not really knowing where Chess was going with this. He watched as Chess stopped, stood at a regular height, and dropped his hands. He didn't drop the gun, but he looked at Damon with clearer eyes

"If I had never met you, I probably wouldn't be as obsessed with Blood Running as I am. I wouldn't have strived to become the best Blood Runner in the West, wasting away all my money on games and paying people back that don't give two shits about me. Staring at my walls and waiting for the next game, thinking of the day I would get you back. If I had never met you, I would've been a completely different person."

Damon didn't say anything. He just stood there, watching Chess and lowering his own gun.

"For years, I sat in one spot in my house, thinking of the day that might come when I would get even with you, where I would get the chance to see you again. To ask why. Just to ask that one question."

A tear slipped from Chess's eye as he looked toward Damon. Both of them had completely lowered their defenses. Chess shrugged and looked away before biting his lip and stifling a laugh.

"All I wanted to know was why. Now I know."

A breath of a second passed before Chess raised his hand again, the one holding the gun. Damon didn't retaliate and didn't lift his gun to fight back. He just stood there, and Chess didn't fire. The sounds of the waves hitting the side of the ship filled the air, and more Media Drones flew in to get every available shot. There wasn't an angle that they weren't captured at.

"Raise your weapon Damon," Chess whispered.

"No."

"Raise your weapon!"

Damon took a couple of steps back, and Chess did the same. He looked behind him for a split second to see if there were any places to hide behind and move in between before this showdown happened. Damon took his weapon in both of his hands and kept backing away.

"I'm sorry, Chess. I won't make it easy, even though I should," Damon said.

"Wouldn't want you to," Chess said back.

After that, Damon fired, and Chess fired back.

BIJOU WAS SITTING IN THE CONTROL TOWER OF THE Aircraft carrier outside of the Storm, watching the fight ensue. Her hands were to her mouth, and she couldn't help but cry at the display. They were finally here, fighting each other for the end. This was going to be the finale of all of it. They weren't fighting for the cup, money, or fame. They were fighting for themselves.

Farren watched with feverish anticipation. The last two players on her team were facing each other down in the middle of the ocean at the front of the ship. While she would have rather them go after the other nine contestants, she couldn't argue with the personal aspect of it all. She knew why they were here, why they had fought this hard tighter to be here, where they were at this very moment. They were born to face each other on this battlefield.

"Do you think Damon knew?" Farren asked.

Bijou looked over at Farren with a confused look, but Farren's sight was looked on the monitors. She couldn't look away from the boys as if it were a train wreck. She had a finger to her chin in thought as she watched the fighting ensue.

"Do you think he knew Chess wanted this the whole time? Why did he come to America then?" Farren asked, finally looking over to Bijou.

"To see Chess again."

Bijou and Farren looked at each other for a couple of seconds before looking back to the cameras. Chess was hiding behind a dry bar reloading his weapon, looking toward where Damon could be. Bullets were still flying every which way, and after a couple of seconds, Chess bolted from the bar and ran toward the adjacent tables and chairs firing. None of their shots hit their marks, but Damon had taken the time to move from his spot to a better vantage point. No one else was around, and it was a shootout only for these two.

"The whole reason he came back was to see Chess again. Even going so far as to be in with Levi at one point just to get into the competition. It was Levi that got him into the USA bracket. He told me," Bijou said.

"All of that just to see Chess again?" Farren asked.

Bijou nodded and looked back from the monitors back to Farren. "Levi tried to get his hands into me after Damon stopped working with I'm midway through the application process. Damon was just using Levi to get closer to Chess. When Levi figured out that Damon wasn't going to work for him anymore, he tried to go after me. It worked, but... I guess it doesn't matter anymore. He's dead."

"All of that just for revenge on them. Crazy. I'm sorry for not stepping in sooner," Farren said.

"It's not your fault; you didn't even know. I think what's important is what's happening now. Levi is dead and gone; he can't hurt anyone anymore."

"Hmm."

Farren agreed but the reality of her once friend being dead and gone was still a shock to her. What was done was already done; now, she would have to witness the next death of a Blood Runner's career. This was the finale for at least one of them.

Chess reloaded, his ammo becoming low as he hid behind an overturned table. Behind him, the fountains for the pools lit up, spraying water into the sky and hitting a couple of Media Drones, sending them spinning out of control. A couple of droplets landed on Chess as he rounded the table and ran from his hiding place, a Media Drone hot on his heels. The image of him running at top speeds toward Damon's hiding place and firing off bullets filled the screen, making Bijou and Farren hold their breaths.

Damon popped out from his hiding place and aimed his weapon, firing in quick succession. Chess dove down just in time to miss the flurry of bullets aimed at him and fired off a couple of shots of his own. One of the bullets hit Damon in the arm, and Damon stumbled for only a couple of moments before righting himself and aiming again. The look of pure murder was on the man's face as he aimed his weapon at Chess and fired again.

Chess fell back on his ass before pivoting and trying to get away as Damon righted himself and fired again. A couple of bullets trailed on the ground, snaking their way toward Chess before a couple of shells hit his foot and ankle, downing Chess for a small moment. Luckily, he was able to crawl behind another table to reload his gun. His ammo was becoming low, and he would have to make his next shots count, or else it was going to be game over for him.

"Come on, Chess!" Damon hollered out. A couple more bullets flew in the air, mostly to mock him or goad him out. "Storm's almost here! Come out and fight me!"

"They're gonna kill each other at the same time," Farren whispered to herself. "I can just see it now. They're going to shoot each other in the head at the same time."

"I don't think either of them will win. The Storm is gonna get them before they get each other. Look," Bijou said, pointing to an adjacent monitor on the other side of the wall.

The Storm was fast approaching, and it wasn't going to be long until it engulfed the entire ship. Piece by piece, it was going to be destroyed only to be rebuilt and reset in the middle of the ocean forevermore. They would come out on the other side with unresolved tension and broken promises unless they settled it here and now.

Chess holed out to the other side of the toppled table and crunched his hand on some broken glass. He groaned at the sight of it, the pain not being an issue, and brushed the pieces off his pants. Blood was covering the fabric, and his sock was flooded with plasma. He was bleeding out and put on a timer on when he would be able to finish this fight. He had to hurry.

It was quiet again. The sounds of the jets spraying water had died down, and the only sounds now were Damon's footsteps skulking around outside the arena. Broken glass and china plates were crunching under his feet, and Chess could hear him coming closer and closer with every step he took. It was now or never. The end of the road.

Chess stood up. Damon turned. They both aimed at each other and fired.

CHAPTER FIFTY-ONE

"The World Royale Winner! Number one Blood Runner in the world! Damon Kennedy!"

Damon stood on the podium, dead eyes and blazé as a bouquet of roses was thrust into his hands, and a crown was placed on top of his head.

The battle had come to a standstill, and the remaining players on the ship didn't have the body count close to Damon by the time the Storm came and ate them all up. Chess went down like a box of rocks, the stopping power of the rifle being no match for the Beretta it was up against. Damon took a couple of bullets, but he was still standing. When Chess exploded into purple crystals, he couldn't help but feel a little disappointed.

Revenge was something universally frowned upon. Something that was a waste of time than anything else in the world. However, standing there in front of thousands as they clapped for him, the streamers and confetti flying through the air, Damon couldn't help but feel like taking revenge on himself. He didn't want to make it easy for Chess; he couldn't just give his life for him like that. He knew it wouldn't be worth anything if he just laid down his gun and walked into the knife. Chess wouldn't have accepted it.

Now he stood there. The Winner. Chess was nowhere to be seen in the procession. He was somewhere on the ship, the Respawn Pods having brought him back at some point before Damon returned. However, the people running the ship and the rest of the contestants standing there clapping for him, not one of them was Chess. He just wasn't there.

Was he mad? Jealous? Maybe disgusted with himself for not being able to finish what he started? All of these presumptions that Damon didn't have any answers to but wanted to find out. He had to get out of here. He had to find Chess.

"Good job, Damon!"

"Congratulations, Damon!"

The praise was pouring in, but Damon wasn't really listening. His eyes kept scanning the crowd for any hint of Chess, but he just knew he wasn't there.

"Damon Kennedy! What are you going to do after your coronation into the Hall of Fame?" someone called out from the crowd holding a microphone. Of course, the news media was here.

Damon focused on the man talking and looked into the camera that accompanied him. This was more than likely being broadcasted all over the world as he breathed, and all he was doing was looking into the lens. He didn't want to say anything; he didn't want to do anything. He wanted to go home with Chess.

Tearing off the crown and throwing the roses on the floor, Damon shocked everyone in attendance on the ship as he made his way past the reporter and other media crews, quickly snapping pictures of him as he made his way to the p-way of the ship. Chess had to be in one of the rooms, more than likely the room they were both staying in as they sailed to Point Nemo.

Throwing the door open to the room, sure enough, Chess was sitting on the bunk with his head in his hands and face toward the floor. Damon just stood there for a moment, not moving. After a couple of minutes of silence, Bijou had also made her way to the stateroom, stopping just shy of Damon and looking in. Chess had raised his head, but he wasn't looking at either of them. An unreadable expression was spread across Chess's face that Damon couldn't follow. Eventually, Chess did look up, and he didn't scowl. He was smiling.

"That was a game," was all he said.

Damon exhaled, letting loose a breath he didn't know he was holding and walked into the stateroom, Bijou in tow. They all sat down, closing the door behind them as they just enjoyed each other's company.

"I didn't see you out there," Damon said.

"Was tired. Took a lot of bullets." Chess lied, leaning back on the bunk and looking away.

"You never were a light loser, Chess." Bijou giggled, and Chess matched her grin.

"I guess no matter how much shit changes, some things stay the same. I'm still the same old me," Chess said, stretching.

"Are you, though?" Damon prodded. "Or are you another Chess now?"

"What do you mean?" Chess asked.

Damon adjusted in his seat before continuing to speak. "I mean, you've gone through so many iterations of Chess now; maybe this is a new one."

Chess looked at the stateroom ceiling for a moment before sighing through his nose and falling back onto the bed. A thick blanket surrounded his head, and he was wearing his regular clothes again. He felt like Chess, the old Chess. The new Chess. Something in-between what he was and what he used to be. He was Chess.

"Nah. This is still the same me. I just fucking hate losing," Chess said.

Damon could hear the smile in his voice as he spoke and turned away, smiling himself.

"So what now?" Bijou asked.

It was quiet again for a while, and Damon breathing hard out of his nose wasn't helping the silence any. Chess didn't have any answers, and neither did Damon.

"You go back to your job, right?" Chess asked from the bed.

"I meant about you two. What happens now?"

"I already got what I wanted," Chess said nonchalantly.

Damon and Bijou looked over to Chess with curious gazes, but Chess wasn't giving up more than he had already said.

"And what did you get?" Bijou asked.

"I got back. Got back at Damon."

Damon and Bijou gave Chess a bewildered look before Chess sat back up in the bunk and looked Damon dead in the eyes. Bijou looked between them a couple of times, pure bewilderment on her face.

"You did?" Damon said, trying not to laugh.

"Yeah. I did. I vowed I would get back at you no matter what. And I did. I killed the old you and killed the old me and got back with you," Chess said.

Bijou couldn't handle it anymore and dropped her head by the neck, trying to stifle a laugh. "That was the lamest thing I have ever heard, don't ever speak again."

"While Bijou is right, I think you're right in what you said, Chess. You did kill off the old me. I was so obsessed with finding the old Chess and the old Bijou in coming back here. Doing whatever I could to get you guys back, but I neglected to realize that you both had grown up. You changed, and I had to change too. In that sense, Chess; you won."

Chess and Damon looked at each other for a couple of minutes, and Bijou smiled, watching them take each other in.

"I'm gonna let everyone know where you guys went."

With that, Bijou left the stateroom, and only Damon and Chess were left inside. It was quiet, the swirl of dust in the room and the sounds of pipes pumping air and water throughout the ship filling the space. The boys were just looking at one another, not knowing what to do or say next. It was over; it was all over.

"So, what do you plan to do now?" Damon asked.

"I don't know. Might ask Bijou if she's hiring," Chess joked.

"Might have to apply with you then," Damon said, stretching his back out.

"What? You're giving up Blood Running too?" Chess asked.

"It's not that I'm giving it up so much as I'm growing up along with you. We've both been stuck for too long, and it's time for us to move on. If you'll have me."

Chess took Damon's hand in his, and they leaned forward, sharing a kiss. It was warm, long, and sincere. They separated and looked into each other's eyes, seeing each other as new men for the first time.

This was the start of their new lives. Together. The Blood Running had come to a close for both of them. Now was the time for a change, something new.

THEY HAD MADE IT BACK TO LOS ANGELES, AND AFTER weeks of news reports, ceremonies, and fights with his father, Damon finally sold everything he owned and separated from his father's estate. Miller had forgiven all of Chess's misgivings and debt that he had occurred, and now it was just him and Damon living in the Harlow manor.

Blood Running had become a thing of the past for them, having now acquired work-from-home jobs that paid rather well, and being the World Blood Running Champion had its perks with sponsorships and interviews. They weren't hurting for money and happily figuring out what their next adventure would be.

Temporal Spaces weren't going away anytime soon, and they had all the time in the world if they wanted to go back and play just a couple more rounds in the future, but a well-needed break was in order for the both of them. Chess had not stopped Blood Running for years, and this would be the first time in a long time he could just sit back and not worry about it. To be a man and live his own life.

There were days that passed when Chess thought he would like to go for a Royale, but then he remembered: he wasn't staring at the walls anymore. He was buying cars again and things for himself. He was smiling more and laughing. He wasn't angry all the time.

Being with Damon like this, getting back with him was the best thing he could've done for himself and his health. He was truly in a better place and wouldn't trade it for the world. Sitting in their house, holding hands and watching the sunset, Chess looked over to Damon and smiled, loving how good he had it. How good he finally had it.

And it was good.

ABOUT THE AUTHOR

Shaine Smith is a mother of two children and wife of a US Navy Officer. Together they travel the world and play copious amounts of video games. Shaine started writing in 2016.

CPSIA information can be obtained
at www.ICGtesting.com
Printed in the USA
BVHW041201090123
655885BV00011B/35/J

9 780578 271842